RESISTANCE

by

FENEK SOLÈRE

Skylore Books

2021

For PB

"Now is the time for a dissident generation to rise."

—Guillaume Faye

CONTENTS

Part I

Part II

Part III

PART I

The United Nations, in New York, reports under the title "Immigration Replacement: A solution to a declining and aging population": "Europe will need 159,000,000 migrants by 2025."

LOWLANDS

"We live in the age of deception."—Horst Mahler

The Janssen family gathered in a tight circle around the television to watch a documentary about asylum seekers and refugees. They saw heartrending footage of a child's inert body rolling back and forth amid the looping waves on a shingle shore, trailing brown arms and curly black hair, the now-famous cotton red T-shirt smeared with chalky sand. A police officer lifts the dead and empty human shell from the ebbtide, head lolling like a jellyfish, his eyes staring accusingly through the flat screen.

"This is little Aylan," the newsreader explained. "Yet another poignant example of how closed borders, like closed minds, bring death and destruction to the innocent."

"Shocking," Peter's mother Ninette said with a tremolo of indignation, a hardback copy of Robin DiAngelo's *White Fragility* dropping from her bitten fingernails, a matriarchal arm instinctively hugging her youngest, Nina, to her fleshy hip.

The CEO of Save the Children came on camera. "This tragic image of a little boy who's lost his life fleeing war is a shocking reminder of the dangers children and families are taking in search of a better life. This child's plight should concentrate minds. The EU must come together now and agree on a plan to tackle the migrant crisis."

Then the programme segued into footage of the latest offensive by Israeli-backed Turkish forces strafing Egyptian and Emirati military convoys supplying renegade

General Khalifa Haftar's rebel army in the Great Sand Sea, rockets laden with sarin poison exploding in the Syrian town of Khan Sheikhoun in Idlib province, quickly followed by a montage of still photography of the Ghouta suburb of Damascus and the chemical attack on Douma, with yet more pictures of blue-faced children stretched out on the scorched tiles of a paediatric hospital. "These are the same surface-to-air rockets the Assad regime used previously in attacks on civilians in Ein Tarma, Moadamiyah, and Zamalka," the newsreader stated. "At what point will the international community intervene?"

"Mankind doesn't seem to learn from the past," said Bram, Peter's rather sullen and earnest father, his head shaking indefatigably. "With walls, travel bans and national populists like Tom Van Grieken and Theo Francken's New Flemish Alliance, you'd never guess it was the 21st century." His hands squeezed his son's bone-china thin shoulders, as he winked benevolently at his wife.

"We can do better than this," Ninette responded. "We are all part of the human race, and civilized people like us should do more to help. Just look at Jugend Rettet and Pia Klemp, who saved all those migrants on her boat, the *Luventa*. Other Western leaders should follow the example our own King Philippe—who wrote that letter of apology for all the cruel things we did in the past in Africa to President Tshisekedi of the Democratic Republic of the Congo—and Angela Merkel in Germany and Pedro Sanchez in Spain, not that fascist Orbán or that Salvini monster who refused to allow those poor migrants to land in Italy. Macron was right when he said that this populist trend is like a leprosy breaking out all across Europe. We should do what they did in America. The Californian Democrats ring-fenced $213 billion in medical support for irregular migrants and threatened to secede from the United States rather than accept the immoral laws that crazy Trump started with his ICE roundups. Anna Lind-Guzik was right when she called those places on the border concentration camps. Those Right-wing Republican

Christian types were trying to do everything they could to roll back Roe v. Wade, oppose the HR5 Bill, Equality Acts and oppress the LGBT community. The dignified way the Black Lives Matter people like Demetria Hester behaved in Portland showed us all how to respond to that type of racist victimization."

"But their methods," Bram shrugged, "mass civil disobedience, looting and ransacking cities like Minneapolis, tearing down statues, declaring autonomy in places like Seattle, taking up arms against the state and assassinating their own President?"

"He was in bed with those Russian gangsters and used Federal paramilitaries to attack innocent protestors. Trump was this far from becoming a tyrant!" Ninette brought her thumb and forefinger together. "George Soros was right when he said in Davos that the Trump administration was a danger to the world. Then there were all those stupid racist accusations about the Chinese virus, trade wars with Beijing and taking away money from the World Health Organisation just when those poor South Africans, after suffering for years under apartheid, had just registered over a million cases of Covid-19. He deserved every bullet they pumped into his ego-bloated body. Remember how his border Nazis locked up those little Hispanic babies in wire cages far away from their mothers? Shame, shame, shame!"

Ninette was spitting invective. "Everyone knows he only fired those cruise missiles at Syria to divert attention from his own domestic policy disasters, like the way he handled the migrant caravan crises. It was just the same as when he moved the American Embassy to Jerusalem because Jeffrey Epstein probably had him on film with those under-age girls, dirty old man. And anyway, what would you have normal everyday Americans do, wait for the police to come for them one by one?" she countered. "Many, like that Domingo guy who tried to set off nail bombs to kill those white nationalists in Los Angeles, felt justified after the New Zealand mosque shooting and the Poway

Synagogue attack, especially given the alternative, a return to racial discrimination and the deportation of millions back to places like Honduras, Guatemala and El Salvador. No Trump, No KKK, No Fascist USA!" A similar scene was being played out in millions of living rooms all across Europe, North America, Canada and Australia, while in the background, adverts on the television, social media and the radio were asking for donations to sponsor an African child for as little as five euros a month, hundreds of thousands were shaking their heads and muttering, "Something must be done, we have a duty to mankind." The sense of urgency ratcheting up as reports that the Russians had developed hypersonic Sarmat cruise missiles and had intervened yet again in Syria, sending Backfire, Bear and Blackjack bombers to the region, their battleship *Admiral Kuznetsov* skirting the NATO fleet in the Black Sea. "The Russian President is embarking on yet another dangerous foreign adventure," claimed one former President of the EU. "He is forcing us into a new Cold War." Clandestine excerpts of the ZAPAD 2 military exercises in Belarus filled the news channels. Leaked photos of Sukhoi Su-35s being put on combat alert, motor rifle, artillery, missile and anti-aircraft brigades undergoing snap checks and camouflaged tanks wheeling about on the Lithuanian border were sent to all the media outlets.

Ninette shook with rage.

❖ The US uses a squadron of Reaper drones to oversee Russian troop movements in Eastern Ukraine.
❖ Russia joins with Syria's President Bashar Assad and Iran's Hassan Rohani in establishing a missile defence shield to safeguard against further Tomahawk cruise missile attacks like that on the Sharyat airbase.
❖ NATO spy satellites reveal the presence of the Russian Super Submarine *Knyaz Vladimir* off the Turkish coast at Mersin.

- The *Admiral Grigorovich* frigate, armed with Kalibr missiles, moves to counter the USS *Porter* and USS *Ross*, part of the American 6th Fleet.
- US and NATO Special Forces link up with anti-Assad groups, like the fanatical White Helmets in Manbij, in order to bolster support for pro-democratic regime change.
- Democratic Chairperson Abba Chodosh and the son-in-law of the former president work with the CIA to appoint Leib Dahan Head of a new foreign intelligence bureau to counter Iranian influence in the Middle East after protestors on the streets of Tehran begin chanting nostalgically for Mohammad Mossadegh.
- Many former Israeli Unit 8200 operatives, responsible for communications espionage, are recruited into senior executive jobs in the Silicon Valley's Big Tech industry.
- *New York Times* journalist Michael Levenson writes that it is imperative that the US army bases currently named after Confederate officers are re-branded to celebrate the black Union troopers who won the Congressional Medal of Honor for their gallantry during the American Civil War.
- The US PSD-11 Task Force meets with Israeli Mossad commanders in order to better coordinate in relation to the Muslim Brotherhood, Al Qaeda and the resurgent Ikhwan terror complex.
- NATO expresses concerns that Russia is meddling in the politics of Burkina Faso, Niger, Chad, Mali and Mauritania.
- In a rerun of the black ops attack on the USS Liberty in 1967, Mossad agents attack UAE oil tankers in the Persian Gulf in an attempt to implicate Iranian naval forces.
- ISIS fanatics repeat their destruction of the ancient Roman city of Palmyra by setting charges among the archaeological remains of the 5000-year-old

city of Mohenjo Daro in Sindh, Pakistan

Simultaneously, Reuters was quoting Indian and Israeli delegates at the UN Security Council clamouring for more sanctions. "The Russians are conducting joint exercises with Egypt and Pakistan. This represents a direct threat to global security." The memes multiplying daily. "Just look at the invasion of Crimea!" "Reactionaries rule the Kremlin!" "Remember the last time they got involved in Afghanistan?" Then there were the constant reminders of the simmering rows with the Zelensky government in Kyiv, the ongoing ground war in Donetsk and how the Ria Novosti and Tass news agencies had confirmed the Russian army was incorporating South Ossetian militia units into its forces on the border with Georgia. Claims that Putin had even staged the metro bombings on his own citizens in St. Petersburg went viral. "Everyone knows that poor Kyrgyz guy, Akbarzhan Jalilov, was set up. Moscow is a pariah on the world stage!"

Similar anti-Russian sentiments were also being expressed by Major General Berel Feldner of the Israeli Defence Force who went on record with his insistence that Tel Aviv would support ISIS against the Kremlin-backed Assad Regime in Syria. His government confirming that they were responsible for the devastating explosion in Beirut's port and the air attack on thousands of supporters of Hezbollah and Hamas gathered in Martyr's Square.

Then came a timely announcement from the steps of the White House:

> I want to reassure our allies that the United States will not allow this aggression to go unchecked. My government will, of course, endeavour to seek all peaceful means at dispute resolution, but there comes a point when words and good intentions need to be supported by firm resolve. I am hereby putting the Kremlin on notice. Come to the table and enter into meaningful dialogue or there will be

severe consequences."
—Statement by President Rahm Emanuel

The television crews crowding the White House lawn filming ecstatic journalists eagerly pushing microphones into the faces of the joint Vice Presidents, Maxine Waters and Kamala Harris, Secretary of Defence, Susan Rice, Head of the Justice Department, Alexandria Ocasio-Cortez, and the Director of Homeland Security, Susan Rosenberg. All were crowded into the Rose Garden to welcome the announcement that the new administration would enforce Obama-era regulations to push low-income housing into more affluent neighbourhoods to encourage racial diversity and to celebrate the unveiling of the black marble busts of George Floyd and Civil Rights veteran John Lewis by Barack and Michelle Obama. Obama's long-time pastor Jeremiah Wright and the Duchess of Sussex, Meghan Markle, offering up a heartfelt eulogy in memory of the two martyrs while the hawk-beaked Madeleine Albright looked on approvingly from a window in the Oval Office.

Every time Bram or Ninette watched TV, the talking-heads on 24/7 news channels were predicting that as a result of the Covid-19 pandemic, environmental catastrophe and Russia's unilateral military actions, ever greater numbers of destitute and displaced people from the southern hemisphere would need aid and support.

- ❖ Xinjiang, a province in northwest China, is the epicentre of a fresh wave of Covid-19 infections.
- ❖ The UN Office on Drugs and Crime reports there are 650,000 migrants currently in Libya making ready to cross the Mediterranean to enter Europe.
- ❖ The EU Commission, responding to calls from the Bill and Melinda Gates Foundation, confirms it will introduce mandatory vaccinations in all its member states in response to the ongoing pandemic.

- The EU President, joining the Pope on the balcony overlooking St. Peter's in Rome and wearing a face mask, repeats her commitment to the 2030 Agenda by allocating additional expenditure to combat inequality within and between nations, addressing systemic racism and issues of gender inequality including reproductive rights and continuing to transfer technology, research, wealth-generating IP and production facilities to developing nations in an attempt to re-balance wealth distribution around the globe;
- Scientists like Bjorn Lomborg and Michael Shellenberger are derided as "lukewarmers" by David Nabarro, the World Health Organisation's special envoy on Covid-19 and former advisor to the EU on climate change. Their books *False Alarm: How Climate Change Panic Costs Us Trillions, Hurts the Poor and Fails to Fix the Planet* and *Apocalypse Never: Why Environmental Alarmism Hurts Us All* are branded as false science and banned from distribution.
- When reports of Covid-related deaths reach 3 million in Africa and 4.5 million in India, an emergency summit is held in the Fontainebleau Palace to sign a multilateral agreement to quadruple medical aid to the worst affected zones.
- The extensive use of wind farms in Germany is suspected of being responsible for a 35% decrease in the native insect population.
- Following talks in Strasbourg with a delegation from China the introduction of the 5G network is described as a strategic imperative by the EU Committee on Communication.
- The second volume of Greta Thunberg's long-awaited autobiography *No One is Too Small to Make a Difference* is released to media applause while her nemesis, the child prodigy Naomi Seibt's counterarguments, are removed from so-

cial media.

❖ Under 15s across the EU are encouraged to be "Goalkeepers" for "Global Goals"

"We must do something for these poor people by supporting pro-refugee groups like VluchtelingenWerk in Holland and not those haters that came to protest against the UN Global Compact in our capital city," Ninette would say to acquaintances whenever the issue came up in conversation. "Covid is killing them like flies! The polar ice caps are melting so their countries are drowning! Even our own immigration minister Theo Francken suggested that some of these people should be turned back. Thank God we let in 62,000 of those poor people last year and those ISIS brides and children before such things were said. I read somewhere that people are saying that 73% of these refugee children are really adults, what nonsense! Just look at the facts, three billion people live on less than $2.50 per day and over 80% of the world's population lives on less than $10.00 a day. We must be realistic. The combined populations of India, China, Pakistan and Bangladesh are set to reach nearly four billion in the next twenty years; that is forty percent of the world's total population. Where are all these people going to live? Did you know only 14% of China's landmass is arable? We all need to share our resources. There is plenty of room in Europe for all of us."

And she was not alone. The same moral imperative informed the opinion of many other Americans, Europeans and Australasians who cheered on rescue boats like the *Aita Mari* from Spain and the work of the German NGO Sea Eye. She was just one of hundreds of thousands who recognised that the threat of crime and terrorism was providing the Right-wing extremists with ammunition. Female harbingers of doom like Marie Le Pen, who had already revealed she had inherited her father's infamous anti-Semitism when she questioned dual Israeli-French citizenship and denied the French people's collective responsibility for the Vel' d'Hiv round-up of Jews in 1942. Unforgivable acts that were compounded by Holland's Geert Wilders's inflammatory speeches, Denmark's Pernille Vermund of the Nye Borgerlige Party and in Germany by Alexander Gauland and Alice Weidel of the Alternative for Germany, along with their retinue of Holocaust deniers, demanding the repatriation of 200,000 asylum seekers per year. Each had, in their own way, harnessed all the ignorance and hatred that had been so long locked up in the dark heart of Europe. The very enmity and vulgarity that mainstream politicians like Angela Merkel, Mark Rutte and Sophie Wilmes had in Ninette and Bram's opinion fought so hard to suppress.

"And what is worse," Ninette would curse while standing shoulder to shoulder with Turkish protestors in Rotterdam, "is that very many of them are women. Le Pen with her violent tweets about DAESH and those awful German women marching in Berlin against immigrant rape with their "We Are Not Fair Game" placards, it's disgusting. I'm really glad they banned their 120 Dezibel video about so-called immigrant violence on YouTube."

Closer to home, Peter recalled her signing up for the Kick Out Black Pete group, fighting the age-old tradition because it was a racist manifestation of blackface, and sending money to the Helden van Nooit group who were attacking statues to seafarers like Joannes van Heutsz because he was once the governor of the West Indies. As well as venting against the Dutch government's Nazi-style banning of President Erdogan's Foreign Minister, Meulut Cavusoglu and Family Minister, Fatma Betul Sayan Kaya from entering Holland to make speeches to immigrant communities. This apparent act against free speech, firing her up to join with others, traveling over the border to symbolically stab oranges with knives in the street. Where she also vocally supported the initiative of the Gulzar e Madina Mosque in Zwolle to host prayers to Mohammed for Dutch children and turned out against Geert Wilders when he led an anti-Islamic march through Rotterdam.

Then later, with her recently shorn and streaked hair bristling with righteous indignation, counter-protesting the Alternative for Germany in Budingen, alongside Anti-Pedophobe Aktion, leading celebrations of anti-fascists in the streets of Bruges, after Wilders' PVV was defeated by Mark Rutte's People's Party for Freedom and Democracy in the Dutch elections and cheering as King Leopold's statue was torn down in Antwerp.

EU Leaders welcoming the result of the Dutch elections with jubilant applause:

- ❖ Outgoing French President, Francois Hollande, said, "It is a clear victory against extremism."
- ❖ Angela Merkel described the result as a "Good day for democracy."
- ❖ The German Chancellor's Chief of Staff, Peter Altmaier tweeted: "The Netherlands, O, the Netherlands, you are a champion. Congratulations on this great result."
- ❖ Jean-Claude Juncker, President of the European Commission said, "This is a vote for an integrated Europe."
- ❖ The European Union declares that Black Lives Matter and denounces white supremacism.
- ❖ President Recep Tayyip Erdogan of Turkey, speaking from the reclaimed Hagia Sophia mosque, reminds his fellow countrymen of one of his previous speeches, "From here I say to my citizens, I say to my brothers and sisters in Europe . . . educate your children at better schools, make sure your family live in better areas, drive in the best cars, live in the best houses. Have five children, not three. You are Europe's future!"
- ❖ Following the warm welcome in the media of the Irish Government's 2040 strategy, the Dublin legislature agrees to the Taoiseach's joint proposal to lower the age of consent for homosexual relationships and the further extension of its demographic

vision to 2050, in order to more rapidly increase expenditure on the development of its infrastructure to accommodate a further one million additional immigrants.

❖ United Nations Secretary-General Antonio Guterres outlines his plans for increasing rates of Third World migration in his thesis "Migration Can Benefit the World."

❖ Following Salvini's immigration restrictions in Italy, US border agents notice a dramatic rise in the numbers of African migrants being detained on the US-Mexican border.

❖ Migrants assault security guards at a charitable establishment in Hortaleza, a district of the Spanish capital Madrid.

❖ Marion Maréchal, the queen in waiting of the French Right, is told by the Dean of the College of Cardinals in no uncertain terms that her brand of Catholic traditionalism as espoused in the journal *L'Incorrect* and her private school, the Institute de Sciences Sociales, Economiques et Politiques in Lyon is a stain on the Faith.

❖ The leaders of the Portland Autonomous Zone are invited to the White House.

❖ Two Afro-American troopers are accused of raping girls in Vilnius, the capital of Lithuania.

❖ The US ambassador to Estonia complains about the way the people of Tallinn interact with black conscripts in the camp established on the city's Toompea Hill.

❖ Latvia's ambassador to the UK repeats his assertion that "the Soviets killed, deported, exiled and imprisoned hundreds of thousands of his fellow citizens after Russia's illegal occupation in 1940 and ruined three generations, while the EU has brought prosperity, equality and respect."

❖ The US political activist SumOfus group warns of the risk of fuelling Right-wing sentiments unless racist and Holocaust-denying advocates are totally expunged from platforms like Facebook, Google, Twitter, Patreon and PayPal.

❖ New York's first African-American woman Mayor, Letitia James, confirms that former Trump supporter Rudy Giuliani has been arrested for defaming the Black Lives Matter movement by calling them a "domestic terror group."

❖ The former US Ambassador to Germany, Douglas Macgregor, is retrospectively indicted for criticizing Chancellor Angela Merkel's prioritization of "unwanted Muslims," claiming the "EU's goal is to eventually turn Europe into an Islamic State" and saying "These people are not coming to assimilate or become Europeans, quite the opposite. They're coming to take over whatever they can get. That's a bad thing for the West. It's a bad thing for Europeans."

❖ The new American President promises to end the trade war with China and repeals all import tariffs on Chinese goods entering the United States on terms dictated by Beijing.

"At least that awful Norbert Hofer's not going to get another chance to repeat the performance of a certain gentleman from Braunau-am-Inn," Ninette joked at the time of the Austrian Presidential election to fellow members of the women's support group she attended twice a week. "But now," she had to admit, only a few months later, "We have Sebastian Kurz and Karl-Heinze Strache to deal with!"

Then, sipping a coffee, "Can you imagine that Nazi Interior Minister Herbert Kickl actually sent Black Hawk helicopters to Spielfeld in Austria to train his armed forces to protect the country's borders against some desperately scared and tired migrants coming through the border with Slovenia? I mean to say, it is like the Luftwaffe bombing Guernica. Thank God Tal Silberstein worked with *Der*

Spiegel and *Suddeutsche Zeitung* to prove they were taking money from those Russian nationalists!" Her fingers curled around the warm cup. "Then there are those awful Identitarians claiming to be defending the Alps against invasion," she laughed. "Personally, I agree with Martin Schulz, when he said, 'What the refugees bring us is more precious than gold!' And we all know Macron was right when he spoke about there being no such thing as French culture. There is culture in France, and it is diverse. I mean, just look at the French World Cup team. How much more diverse can you get?" Then, chuckling, she continued, "After all, the founder of the Islam party, Redouane Ahrouch, predicted that Brussels will be majority Muslim by 2030, and all they want is to create a fairer country. And 92% of our Muslim and African brothers voted in the last election in order to get it!"

And people like her and her long-suffering partner Bram were as good as their word. Taking their lead from Mirjam de Bruijn, an anthropologist at Leiden University who said, "There's an inherent racism and acceptance of inequality, racism is inside all of us," 50,000 Took the Knee out of respect for Black Lives Matter across the Lowlands and despite the ongoing economic recession following the pandemic millions upon millions of dollars, pounds sterling and Euros were set aside to assist the cause of reparations and equality for centuries of racism.

❖ Objective 17 of the UN Global Compact saying "We commit to eliminate all forms of discrimination, condemn and counter expressions, acts and manifestations of racism, racial discrimination, violence, xenophobia and related intolerance against all migrants in conformity with international human rights law" is universally endorsed.
❖ The World Bank reported foreign aid rising to an all-time high of $750 billion, with the donations of the highest European contributors representing 2%, 5% and 6% of the domestic economies of the

UK, France and Germany respectively.

❖ The EU confirms that following discussions with the European representatives of the Black Lives Matter movement it will set up a Truth and Reconciliation Commission as per the South African model in order to overcome the endemic political, economic and systemic institutional Apartheid that is embedded so deeply in European culture.

❖ The *Aquarius*, a boat operated by the German NGO Mission Lifeline, having previously been turned away from Italian and Maltese ports, is greeted in Spain by an army of volunteers including doctors and translators.

❖ Demographic experts postulate that by 2070 the majority of the world's population growth will be of African descent, representing a 16% increase in overall world population by 2015, a 25% increase by 2050 and a 39% increase by 2100.

❖ Population analyst Stephen Smith, who predicts a further 150 to 200 million Africans will attempt to migrate from Africa to Europe, says in an interview with *Le Figaro* that Europe should welcome these people and create a Eurafrica, a multicultural Europe that "should fully accept being a mixed-race land of immigration and interbreeding." President Macron taking the opportunity to declare "Africa and Europe share the same destiny!"

❖ The Pope calls for more understanding of migrants from his balcony in The Vatican.

❖ Thousands of members of Italy's USB union protest in Rome for greater rights for migrant workers after one of their members, Soumayla Sacko from Mali, is killed.

❖ The EU's Guy Verhofstadt says EU countries should be punished for being illiberal, citing Poland considering a Pol-Exit, as per the British Isles, Hungary deporting abortion activist specialists Francis and Anne Furezi, the Danish Conservative

Party leader Soren Pape Poulsen unveiling radical
new laws that mean doubling the penalties for
crimes in immigrant ghettos and Herbert Kickl of
the Austrian Freedom Party promising to toughen
up issues relating to asylum.

❖ Avigdor Shine, the owner of Trans-World Airways
introduces visa inclusive direct flights from Jinnah
airport in Karachi, Allama Iqbal airport in Lahore
and Bacha Khan airport in Peshawar at the cost of
ten euros a seat for flights into Gatwick in the UK.
Ezer Joseph, the speaker in the House of Commons, made famous for hilarious tirades against
Right-wingers and his blocking of moves to im-
plement Brexit, responding to Shine's decision by
saying "This is ground-breaking and should be
implemented across Europe."

Thousands of charities flew emergency response teams
loaded with medical supplies into the transit centres being
built alongside the routes the hungry columns of migrants
were tramping on their long march to the West. C17
Globemaster III transport planes began taking off from all
over Europe, dropping food supplies in Albania, Serbia,
Greece and Lesbos. Ships were dispatched from ports like
Puerto Portals in Majorca to intercept the ramshackle vessels from North Africa sinking in the Mediterranean,
providing fresh water and woollen blankets to the needy.
Returning with their decks laden with Tunisians, Libyans,
Moroccans, Sudanese, Mauritanians, Senegalese, Algerians, Chadians, Nigerians and Pakistanis who had joined
with the multitudes queuing five-deep in the Plaza Alta in
the Spanish port city of Algeciras.

At the same time, the military was erecting reception
centres in places like Lesbos and Chios to greet the newcomers as they struggled up the beaches. With the Chief
Operating Officer of Amnesty International commenting
"The fear and desperation are palpable."

Listening to a radio announcer speaking about even

more lives being lost at sea when an overloaded rescue boat sank off the craggy Cretan coastline, Ninette decided it was time for direct action. Throwing down her copy of Chandra Talpade Mohanty's *Feminism Without Borders*, she shouted, "Peter, choose what clothes and games you want to give," as she and Bram hurriedly volunteered to serve at the soup kitchens when the trains carrying refugees began to arrive in Bruges. She scoured Peter and Nina's bedrooms, happily donating her children's favourite toys to the cause. Holding up a French-language edition of *The Diary of Anne Frank* for Peter to see and saying, "We'll give this for the children." Then, jumping into the back of a fully loaded car, Peter and Nina were given a tour of the city and shown the makeshift camps that had sprung up at the rail and bus terminals.

"It is not right. We should have been better prepared," Ninette insisted. The children watched wide-eyed as their mother threw herself headlong into the cause, organising a meeting in the town hall.

Two days later, the local mayor called the gathering to order. His potbelly slumped on the desk atop the podium.

"We all know why we are here today," he said. "We simply cannot turn our faces away from our brothers and sisters who come bereft to our municipality."

The audience roared support. A single voice cried out from the back. "But these are strangers. We have all heard of the troubles in France, Germany, Sweden and Great Britain." There was a scuffle and catcalls of fascist and PEGIDA as the protester was shouted down.

"That is Dutch PVV talk!" the mayor answered, "We, like our neighbours in Holland, decided upon the path of safety and stability, and that is why reactionaries like them got wiped out in the last European elections. Wilders called my friends in the D66 suckers and said they cried crocodile tears over Islamic honour killings and look what happened. He got banned from Twitter for violating their rules on hateful conduct. And yes, we know it will be difficult. Of course, there will be challenges, but with

God's help, we will overcome them!" he continued somewhat bombastically.

Queues formed to give money to the volunteers ambling around with collection buckets. Women began
gathering woollens, gloves and hats. "They will be cold
here," the assumption went. "We need practical items."

At the back of the hall, a venerable older woman observed the meeting with great interest. She moved slowly
forward through the swell of bodies, compelled by an inner need to speak. The mayor, recognising Madame
Aaldenberg, the former headmistress of the Sint-Leo
Hemelsdaele School, greeted her with a warm hand of
friendship as she mounted the platform.

"You wish to say something?" he asked. She nodded.
His fleshy fingers extended the microphone.

People turned towards her. "I am an old woman now,"
she wheezed, "and many of you will know me and know
what I am like, I think?" For a second she was distracted
by the wasp-like whisper of conversation below her. Then,
refocusing her thoughts, she continued. "I say now, I fear
for the future. What passes for kindness today may come
back to haunt the generations yet to be born."

The mayor raised his arm, snatching back the microphone. "Thank you," he rushed to say, "But this is a moral
imperative, and we all know Belgium was among the first
to recognise Islam as one of our state's religions back in
1974. The hand of brother and sisterhood we extend today
will be more than repaid in the years to come, I'm sure."

Madam Aaldenberg's eyes scanned the enthusiastic
crowd one last time. She knew it was time to make her
exit. Her presence was unwelcome. The audience parted
before her as she passed down the aisle between the hard
wooden chairs, former friends and colleagues muttering
"She's one of them," as she approached the outer doors,
bending on her stick down the stone steps and out into
the damp dark.

Later, Ninette led the community group down to the
main refugee centre on the banks of the Minnewater Lake

to hand out blankets, bedsheets and tinned food. There was already a sizeable crowd of well-wishers clapping the arrival of the "new Europeans," as the press had labelled them, stepping off the NMBS Class 18 trains coming into Brugge Centraal. Many local girls, faces painted with bright smiles, held up signs welcoming the newcomers all along the *stationsplein*.

"Mamma," Peter remembered asking, as he watched the young men talking excitedly in a babel of languages he could not understand, "where are the children who can play with me?"

"They will come later," Ninette assured him, "When the family unification requests are processed."

❖ Following his warning that European nationalism is on the rise in an article in Project Syndicate, philanthropist George Soros announces his intention to triple funding for his No Borders Campaign Group and double his donations to Black Lives Matter groups worldwide.

❖ Yigal Unna, Head of Israel's National Cyber Defense Executive, says "A cyber winter is coming and coming sooner than I thought" and calls for national governments to engage with the Black Cube portal designed at the Bar-Ilan University in Ramat Gan.

❖ *La Demiere Heure* publish footage of FC Brugge football fans chanting anti-Semitic catcalls during a match with Anderlecht.

❖ The EU Commission confirms the former Luigi Di Maio and Matteo Salvini government in Italy was indeed in breach of its fiscal rules and seeks a judicial mandate to pursue private prosecutions against both men.

❖ The American Justice system sentences twelve Russian nationals living in the US to between ten and fifteen years in prison for hacking the US Presidential election in order to assist the Trump campaign.

❖ German and British secret service operatives refuse to share intelligence with their counterparts
in Budapest, Vienna and Rome.

❖ A Papal decree exonerates the Pharisees of any responsibility for the crucifixion and emphasises the
culpability of the imperialistic Roman Empire for
the death of Christ. Rabbi Rosen of the Jewish interfaith group God Speaks Through Us welcomed
the announcement by saying "This clear apology
opens up the opportunity for reparations given the
centuries-old libel of our people and the way it has
been used to fuel anti-Semitism around the
world."

❖ The Belgian Red Cross remove crucifixes from all
staff and office buildings.

❖ In Graested, Denmark, the Gribskolen School cancels Christmas because it says it is now multicultural in character.

❖ The Swedish Minister for Justice instigates a judicial debate to consider if the wearing of runes or
Thor's Hammer symbols constitutes a hate crime.

❖ Aleksandr Bortnikov, Chief of the Russian FSB,
says migrant ghettos are hotbeds of terrorism.

❖ The new US Ambassador to Russia, Meira Axelrod,
shares a platform in Vienna with Issur Babel, leader of the anti-Putin Coalition for Renewal, stating:
"The human tragedy unfolding in the East requires
bold leadership. The current President only offers
us a return to ancient ethnic and religious rivalries
and pointless confrontations like those in Chechnya."

❖ The No Mas Muertes Foundation raise a statue to
Scott Daniel Warren in Ajo, Arizona, where he
helped thousands of refugees enter the United
States for decades.

❖ Doctors working in the Del Rio sector of the US-
Mexican border report a 200% increase in cases of

Ebola infection.
❖ Pro-LGBT protestors in Kyiv are attacked by nationalists with smoke bombs and pepper-spray.
❖ Ukrainian patriots attack Covid-infected evacuees from Wuhan in the spa at Novi Sanzharya in central Poltava.
❖ French Interior Minister for Security, Said Ben Hassi, speaking in his familiar charismatic manner, after an emergency summit in Budapest on what was now being described as the Caspian Crisis, saying: "I do not recall the British sea Captain James Cook being denied entry into Australia or the South Sea Islands. Likwise, was Samuel Champlain's visa checked by the Algonquins in Canada or Hernan Cortes deported for committing crimes against the Aztecs? If they were exempt, why not Abdul from Pakistan, Olabisi from Nigeria and Anisah from Morocco? The world is on the move and we must make room for all. We cannot hide forever behind chain fencing and visa quotas. This is a new era of mass mobility and opportunity. A new millennium of hope for those who were once denied all hope. Who are we to stand in the way of history?"

When Peter looked in the mirror he was confronted by the clash between his freckle-splashed complexion and those of his heroes gazing out from the poster of the French Les Bleus and the Belgium football team hanging on his bedroom wall. Superstars like Kylian Mbappe, Samuel Umtiti, Karim Benzema, Paul Pogba, Adil Rami and Hatem Ben Arfa staring down on his *Rogue One* duvet cover. So what if a few high-spirited youths rioted in the Champs after the World Cup win and half the cities in France were looted? Just like all the other kids in his district, he went with his father to the Jan Breydel stadium to watch Club Brugge on match days. Singing "We Love You Belgium" and screaming how he loved Christian Kabalese,

Dedryk Boyata, Mousa Dembele and Romelu Lukaku at the top of his voice. He walked home, almost hoarse, draped in his blue and white team scarf under the graphite glare of the leading high street brands like the United Colours of Benetton, Ralph Lauren and Nicole Farhi.

His eyes lingering longingly on the airbrushed faces of Natalie Portman, Heidi Klum and Carla Bruni. Miley Cyrus and Tiger Woods were *de rigueur*. Lady Gaga's songs were ace:

> No matter gay, straight or bi
> Lesbian, transgendered life
> I'm on the right track, baby
> I was born to survive
> No matter black, white or beige
> Chola or orient made
> I'm on the right track, baby
> I was born to be brave

"I hate Saint-Donaas High School," he told everyone as he grew into his early teens. The only advantage he could see was the opportunity it afforded him to indulge his growing interest in the opposite sex, which delivered some degree of success with the loss of his virginity at fifteen.

Queuing outside HMV in the high street, after watching the double-header Freddie Mercury and Elton John biopics *Bohemian Rhapsody* and *Rocketman*, he felt the collective pulse of excitement buying the new release by Drake.

"When will the tickets for Azealia Banks go on sale?" he asked.

The woman in the box-office replied mechanically, "She'll announce dates after Usher plays Paris."

"Great!"

Discussing *X-Factor*, Eurovision and iconic people like Conchita Wurst amused him. He supported Black Lives Matter attacking King Leopold's statue in Antwerp, the new Congolese exhibitions in the palatial Royal Museum, the campaign to rebuild Notre Dame as a multicultural centre of many faiths, Gay Pride Worldwide, the imposition of rainbow road crossings in Paris and the erection of statues to people like Bayard Rustin, who, with his partner Walter Nagle, stood shoulder-to-shoulder with Martin Luther King in the States, Mark Ashton the co-founder of the London Gay Pride group, Hans Scholl, who fought back against the Third Reich and the hundreds of trans bloggers and YouTubers. "They are great because they challenge boundaries and accept no limits," he would argue with his more reserved and conservative friends, while blasting Camila Cabello's "Havana-na-na-na" into their faces. "Some of my crew in Por Que No are already transitioning. They are getting estrogen, androgens and GnRH analogues free from the health centre. Haven't you seen Chloe Grace Moretz in *The Miseducation of Cameron Post*? It's the new *One Flew over the Cuckoo's Nest!*" Then singing Conchita's lyrics:

Walking in the rubble
Walking over glass
Neighbours say we're trouble
Well that time has passed

Rise like a phoenix
Out of the ashes
Seeking rather than vengeance
Retribution

You were warned
Once I'm transformed
Once I'm reborn
You will rise like a phoenix
But you're my flame

Then, waving his new credit card like a swashbuckling cavalier from a Dumas novel, he would cover the Starbucks bill. "Facebook's Libra currency is offering twelve months interest-free and reward points," he gloated.

Later, while at home, trying to avoid Ninette's constant nagging about the sexist image on his Gangsta Rap hoodie, Peter lay on his bed, headphones wrapped around his baseball cap, and switched on the radio, the Berlin punk band Die Artze blasting "Schrei Nach Liebe":

Because you're scared of a cuddle, you're a fascist
Your violence is just a silent cry for love, oh, oh arsehole

and Nick Conrad's "Doux Pays":

Cock in France's mouth, I cum like a pig
This country has never been sweet
I fuck France, I burn France
until she reaches her agony

"Stop playing with that iPhone!" Ninette would demand at the dinner table. But Peter knew better. Quotes from Michael Ziff of the European Maccabi Foundation and Jay Z filled the little screen in his hand. The new 21st-century archetypes, a kaleidoscope of commercial Titans owning the global village, displacing what his teacher in philosophy class called Jung's original psychological hierarchy. He admired this new breed, like Sean "Diddy" Combs and Beyonce singing apeshit in the Louvre that embodied the independent multicultural mode of the moment.

In school, Peter learned that the freedom he currently enjoyed had taken a long time to win and meant shedding many old prejudices from the past. The catechisms he had been taught since kindergarten had certainly played a part.

"Everyone shares the same origins," Ms. Smet, the recently appointed sociology tutor explained. "The most obvious differences between people are merely skin deep.

Our genetics prove that. Professor Bryan Sykes from Oxford says we are all black. Also, in his book *Adam's Curse*, his research indicates men are becoming steadily redundant, with falling sperm counts and girls outperforming boys in school assessments at almost every stage of the curriculum."

That brought a high-pitched titter from the female contingent. Pushing her auburn hair to one side, fingers playing with her glitter venus earings, Ms. Smet looked about the room for feedback.

"How does that make you feel, Peter?"

"I don't want my masculinity to oppress the potential of my feminine attributes," he said firmly.

"Good," Ms. Smet clapped. "I can see there is hope for some of you, at least!"

By the age of nine, Peter's favourite book was Elie Wiesel's *Night*, and he had become so sufficiently skilled in engaging sensitively with diverse cultures that he was more familiar with certain Surahs from the Koran than the Lord's Prayer and did not even know that the liberal Pope Francis had changed its words in the Messale Romano.

Once, at his friend Jahid's tenth birthday party, he remembered being cajoled by a circle of Muslim boys to stammer out a Christian prayer. Reluctantly, he complied against a mounting crescendo of laughter and slaps. By fifteen, he had celebrated more Eid al Fitr feasts than Harvest Festivals and felt a natural disquiet when told of the attitudes and behaviour of his ancestors towards Arabs, Africans, and South East Asians. "Everything and everyone are more open now," he heard people say. His teachers would lecture that "The past was prehistoric, frozen in time. The former ignorance and intolerance of day-to-day life in the Low Countries was abhorrent." There was a new moral consensus and codified laws to protect minorities. Announcements that Belgium's anti-discrimination law of 2007, which forbade discrimination on the basis of religious convictions, was to be further strengthened was greatly reassuring. As was the news that Article 444 of the

Belgian Penal Code was to be reviewed in the light of the rise of anti-Muslim agitation.

After all, the gates to the Death Camps had been thrown wide for everyone to see inside. There could be no excuses. Europe's evil had a face, a flag, an army. It had marched through the streets, gathered under torchlight in cities, fought to the bitter end against what is good and right.

And Peter knew such ideas were still an ever-present danger and that people had to be on guard against them, to prevent such forces from ever rising again.

In that regard, at least, his education had proved supremely beneficial. In Citizenship class, his teacher would lecture them that after the last Great War of 39–45, the European Parliament, now abbreviated as Europarl or EP, had followed a policy of European integration in order to combat the rise of nationalism and mitigate the dangers posed by tribal antagonisms. The EU, he learned, through the books he was given, had gone through many gestations over the previous half-century. From its origins as the Common Assembly of the European Coal and Steel Community, to the European Economic Community or Common Market, before emerging in 1979, under the visionary Holocaust survivor Simone Veil, as the European Parliament. It was now, he understood, one of the most powerful legislatures in the world, with strategic command over the greatest knowledge-generating continent on the planet. Even the new French President eschewed La Marseillaise on public occasions, preferring to use EU's anthem *Ode to Joy*. Peter, like the majority of his contemporaries, felt like they were lucky to live under such a progressive organisation. They could travel freely across borders, meeting people like themselves from Gdansk to Granada and from Pisa to Pori.

He could fully understand the anger of the British youth who felt they might be cheated of these benefits. Why should all the older selfish people deny the next generation their chance to be happy? After all, Europe must be open to the world, and the world had now come to Europe.

When the school held mock-elections as part of their political studies programme, he found himself debating against a nominee representing the Eurosceptic faction. "We know who you are," he asserted, "So what if Frank Franz of the NPD is good looking, he's still an ugly Nazi! People like you may have cast off your armbands, but Tom Van Grieken's Vlaams Belang are finished. We turned away from Flemish racism a long time ago!" When his opponent countered with "The EU is big, costly and inefficient. It is run by unelected mandarins who are out of touch with the people," Peter's rebuff was "Better one government than twenty or more with their own bureaucracies, all arguing with each other."

"And you don't foresee a threat to individual cultural identities from the European Parliament?"

"No, not at all. Forging a European identity is one step towards establishing a Global Identity. And that is a good thing! The EU organises Euroweek which allows our citizens to be goalkeepers for global goals. They fund student exchange programmes like ERASMUS so that people from different countries can study together and provides vocational training like Leonardo Da Vinci so we can get jobs anywhere we want."

"And borders?"

"How predictable! You are playing on people's fears. I don't doubt you supported Szekesfehervar in Hungary to be the European City of Culture rather than multicultural Malmö because it is nice and white and Christian. Or perhaps you're going to quote that racist Janos Lazar, who was Orbán's right-hand man, walking through the Favoriten district of Vienna, saying things like the streets here are visibly dirtier, the surroundings are much poorer, and criminality is much higher. The white, Christian Austrians have moved away from here and the immigrants have taken over this district. Yet, twenty years ago there wasn't a single migrant here. Maybe, you are going to quote crime statistics next? You see, it is very simple, in order to ensure the EU's global competitiveness it is essential that we all understand and appreciate that our future well-being can only be sustained by continued economic growth. That can only be achieved through a free-market system with easy access to a mobile labour pool. The Schengen Agreement must be extended, not removed. It is imperative, as economist Michael Clemens says, that borders are opened. If this happens experts believe world-wide growth can increase by as much as 67–147%. That means the median GDP of nearly every country currently operating inside the European Free Trade Agreement (EFTA) would thereby double. Can you imagine that?"

"It is not all about money. What about quality of life and security?" His opponent insisted.

"Why do you want to focus on things like the riots in Paris and Malmö, the terrorist attacks in Manchester, London, Nice and Berlin, and the unfortunate New Year's Eve events in Cologne? Citizens should be reassured that the standard of living they presently enjoy is guaranteed, not jeopardised by the newcomers who bring new skills and new thinking to aid economic growth."

The debate was really flowing.

"Migration is costing Germany thirty-seven billion Euros a year. It takes thirty or so German taxpayers to fund an average-sized migrant family on welfare. How many, exactly, of the three million new migrants have jobs and are contributing to the economic growth you speak about?"

"The case for open borders, so humanely articulated by German Chancellor Angela Merkel way back at the start of the first Syrian crisis, must continue," Peter sighed. "In fact, it should be made even more forcibly and relentlessly and laws to prevent discriminatory behaviour passed so that opportunities for migrants can be maximized for the benefit of us all."

Peter's final remarks were rewarded with resounding cheers and his selection to represent the Bruge Schools Foundation in an Open Society sponsored debate on how the EU should continue the long-drawn-out negotiations with the British government following the triggering of Article 50.

"I still don't understand why Britain wants to leave; none of our generation do," he emphasised during his opening oration to a seminar of the Youth Parliament in Brussels. "People of our age in the UK think of themselves as Citizens of the World. They don't share the same prejudices as their parents. They already know immigrants work harder than whites, and they now have a bi-racial prince. Even half their soccer team is black with people like Jadon Sancho, Marcus Rashford, Raheem Sterling and Dele Alli wearing the Three Lions emblem on their shirt. Britain has always been a nation of immigrants. The refugees crossing the Channel are heroes. England should take even more of them. We all know the truth that the ten-thousand-year-old Cheddar Man was black. So the racist reactionaries in the Brexit Party and that awful fast-talking jailbird who the fascist English Defense League call a prisoner of conscience will eventually lose out, because polygamous marriages in the UK will mean that the Muslim population will increase ten times quicker than the aging white demographic and that fact allied with the growing numbers of young progressives in Momentum and Extinction Rebellion makes it inevitable that we can reverse Brexit!"

Then returning to the main theme, "We should support Tony Blair's Institute fighting populism not only in the UK but anywhere in Europe!"

"Let the English go!" some in the audience replied, "and the others too. They will all come crawling back with their begging bowls when we apply the sanctions."

"They owe us billions! They must pay their share to install the French broadband infrastructure, their portion of the German social benefits for the refugees, building the Polish road network and new business start-ups in the Czech Republic."

"And their part of the eighty-six billion Euro Common Defence Policy," Peter cut in, "And trust me, they will, especially now that José Manuel Barroso is with Goldman Sachs, and the pandemic means their economy will need to be bailed out by trillions in loans."

"An end to Farage insulting our authority!" shouted another. "Let him and people like Zanni in Italy, Kotleba, the Tiso acolyte in Slovenia and that Franco-worshipping Abascal go the same way as Trump!"

"Bang, Bang Bang!" went the cry.

Then the discussion widened, identifying other dissenting voices like those of Viktor Orbán in Hungary who had pardoned terrorists like György Budaházy and made inflammatory speeches about defending the European heartland from invasion; Milos Zeman, President of the Czech Republic, who had gone on public record to say the main tenets of the Muslim faith were incompatible with European civilization and called for economic migrants to be deported; and the Shipka National Movement who were committing acts of violence against refugees on the Bulgarian frontier.

"No!" Peter said, "This House supports the views expressed by Bert Koenders of the Dutch Labour Party, that closing the borders is not only immoral but would be ineffective in the fight against terrorism. It is the populists' divide and rule gambit. It would mean the foreign-born or those whose ancestry did not originate here but are already living within our society would no longer have any rights. Do you know the most popular name for boys being born in Antwerp is Mohamed? Isn't our neighbour human and entitled to rights just like us?" The participants rose to their feet in support. "And I ask you, would sending people home increase our security? I would suggest not! It would instead tear groups apart when our task should be to build sustainable and inclusive communities. What are fifteen to twenty million additional people to a population of five hundred million? We will not abandon our hope for a better world than that which we inherited. We will strive and endure to ensure all peoples, all cultures and all religions are respected wherever they may take root on European soil."

Wrapping up the session, Peter reiterated the general mood in the small auditorium. "So the consensus is that this meeting believes that individuals and groups using lawfare to distract and bankrupt anti-egalitarian parties is not sufficient and that we demand that advocates of European separatism should no longer be eligible to receive EU funds and the legal status of said organisations should be challenged on the grounds of their anti-humanitarian fascist views?"

A fellow student council member then stood up and proposed a motion of support for feminist Babro Sörman's comments about Swedish men's guilt being greater when committing rape than that of migrants because "despite ongoing gender equality they were making an active choice." The favourable response this statement received encouraged a particularly militant girl named Afra Ben-Zvi to insist the Youth Parliament nominate German Green Stefanie Von Berg as their Honorary Women's President following her statement: "I hold in twenty or thirty years there will no longer be German majorities in our cities. And I want to make it clear, especially towards those right-wingers, this is a good thing!" Both motions were moved by majority decision and greeted by gratifying applause. This was, as Peter knew all too well, a generation that could not only recite slogans like "Make Racists Afraid Again!" and "Better a Rapist than a Fascist!" but live and act them out. Their peers in FEMEN shaking their bare breasts in the faces of Catholic prelates and urinating on church steps all over the continent truly inspired them to fight on.

After the meeting had come to a close, Afra confided to Peter: "It is really important we confront people like those crazy skinheads in Sacramento in their homes, on the street and everywhere. Just like we shut down Milo Yiannopoulos at Berkeley and Richard Spencer at Charlottesville. I was with the Black Bloc when they attacked that dentist guy who stood for election for the Alternative for Germany. A friend of mine put his eye out," she laughed. "We gave money to Black Lives Matter and Reparations Now and By Any Means Necessary in the US, and we are starting to campaign here, too." Nodding conspiratorially, she whispered, "Our people were with the Muslims who stopped the Tommy Robinson rally in Oldham in the UK and equipped the black militias like The Not Fucking Around Coalition who marched on Stone Mountain in Georgia and through the heart of Brixton in London."

"The ones who held up banners saying, 'You're lucky we're just demanding reparations and not revenge' on Afrikan Emancipation Day?'"

"Precisely!"

Such sentiments made Peter think hard about his own life and the direction it was taking. He lay awake that night, at first fantasizing about ripping Afra's beret off her head, releasing her long dark hair to flow like a raging brown Niagra over her Che Guevara T-shirt. Kissing her lips till they were bruised and bled like mashed beetroot. Then he became conflicted, thinking about what he had been taught in his classes on Gender Theory, while listening to Little Mix:

> Ladies all across the world
> Listen up, we're looking for recruits
> If you're with me let me see your hands
> Stand up, salute!
> Get your killer heels, sneakers, pumps and lace up your boots
> Representing all women
> Salute!
> It's who we are
> We don't need no camouflage
> It's the female federal
> And we're taking off!
> You think we're just pretty things
> You couldn't be more wrong

We're standing strong. We carry on
Knock us but we keep moving on, can't stop a hurricane
Ladies, it is time to awake

He could still remember his first kindergarten friends like Lukas, Mathias, Robbe, and Daan. The fair-haired girls like Fleur, Lina, Eva, and Marthe. They would play kiss chase and doctors and nurses together in the Astrid Park in Minderbroedersstraat. The summer holidays were happier then. The winters seemed colder and to bring more snow. Now everything was different. Like the people, the seasons seemed to be altering before his very eyes.

❖ Climate change experts cite statistical evidence garnered from strategically located weather-stations, buoys and ships using the latest meteorological instrumentation, that the earth's surface is warming by 2 degrees Fahrenheit every 50 years.

❖ It is estimated that 47% of the 976 species surveyed in 2016 had been negatively impacted by weather gain causing "local extinction" on the warm edge of their habitat range.

❖ The use of neonicotinoid insecticides is proven to impact human brain cells and can lead to paralysis and death.

❖ A variant of the fungal Ug99 black stem rust infection decimates wheat crops in Uganda, Kenya and Ethiopia and spreads to the Asian wheat bowl of Pakistan and India.

❖ Climate change campaigners warn that 20% of global species could become extinct by 2100 if the earth continues to warm at the present rate.

❖ Inspired by Greta Thunberg's campaigns, school children like the 10,000 or more teen marchers in Brussels launch yet another wave of strikes across Europe, Australasia and the USA.

❖ Melting land ice is said to be causing sea levels to

rise by five metres per decade, literally displacing hundreds of thousands of people living in small island communities.

❖ Heatwaves like the one that killed 70,000 people in Europe in 2003 are predicted to occur with greater frequency.

❖ A genetically modified fungus wipes out malaria-carrying mosquitoes in the West-African Mosquito-Sphere which saves up to 400,000 lives.

❖ Canada's Mogadishu-born Minister of Immigration, Refugees and Citizenship, Ahmed Hussen, announces substantial increases in the immigration thresholds from 340,000 to 500,000 per annum while simultaneously the parliament in Ottawa outlaws the Federation des Quebecois de Souche and bans publication of their journal *Harfang*.

❖ China's ever-increasing need for raw materials results in resource depletion across the whole African continent, with exclusive extraction rights for mineral fuel and lubricants being agreed with Angola, Chad, Sudan and Equatorial Guinea.

❖ The Chinese naval fleet enter the energy-rich u-shaped nine-dash line in the South China Sea and its trawlers continue to over-fish the East China Sea jeopardizing the livelihood and food security of millions of people.

For these and many other reasons, like war and discrimination, boys like Ahmad, Abbas, Ali and Aman had joined Peter in the upper school. Then, of course, there were the Gambian boys Buba and Kebba, the Nigerian lads Abaeze, Abeo and Adejola, and the rowdy Somalians Aar, Abtidoon and Aweys who took seats close to Eva and Marthe in the compulsory Common Purpose classes that included studying the Quran.

There was a new frisson in the air. During break, the boys would hide in the toilets and smoke cigarettes. Aar and Aweys would talk about the girls.

"Do you think she would?" they would say about Marthe, laughing, making hand gestures in imitation of masturbation.

"I would love to fuck her," Ahmad confessed.

That would make them all giggle before they scurried off to citizenship studies where they would discuss white privilege and the value systems of the various creeds that made up the country's population. Peter trying to catch the attention of A'idah, who along with her best friend Amna, was one of the few Muslim girls allowed to attend a mixed school. He remembered wondering how her face looked under the batoul, and if those alluring roast almond eyes could ever look favourably upon on a boy from his background.

Peter's hormones were racing. By fourteen, he had French kissed his first real girlfriend, who turned out to be long term friend Eva, under the shadow of the tower of Our Lady. He remembered it clearly because it was the same day that Angela Merkel received her Nobel prize for the humanitarian work she had done to ease the Syrian refugee crisis. Peter could still recall the people coming out on the street shouting "Mama Merkel, Peace Be Upon You!" In France, it was much the same, with President Emmanuel Macron strutting like a tomcat on TF1 next to the Grand Rabbi of France, Haim Korsia, defending his decision to order the police to use live ammunition against the Gilets Jaune protesters on the Champs, while Rachida Dati, Najat Vallaud-Belkacem, Christiane Taubira and Anne Hidalgo were being carried aloft through the Marche Barbes. "You see," Le Kid President prophesied, "It is just as I predicted at my inauguration, the divisions and fractures in our society are being overcome!"

Walking back along the rubbish strewn Markt one day, Eva and Peter were confronted by Aar and Aweys, who were showing off to a new gang of cousins recently arrived from Boosaaso.

"Is he your boyfriend now?" they guffawed, stopping

their spray-painting and pointing at Peter. Eva smiled back embarrassedly.

"Sort of?"

"Is it because he's white?" Aweys sneered.

"No," the girl shot back.

"Then why not Aar or one of us?" Eva shrugged nonchalantly. Lifting a charcoal finger, Aar interrupted.

"Take a look around you, girl," his smudged digit pointing towards the people walking about the statue of Pieter de Coninck now covered by graffiti and topped by a Moroccan flag. "We're the new masters here!" Peter watched as Eva's eyes surveyed the scene. He could read her thoughts. The Somalian's point became obvious. Nearly half the young couples were bi-racial, just like all the couples on the television. The vast majority made up of a black male and a white companion. Eva's choice of partner was clearly at odds with the trend.

Just for a moment, Peter felt threatened, but then he overcame such base feelings. "And why not," he told himself. People should be free to choose who they want to be with. Social media like Facebook made sure everyone was aware and took advantage of such dating opportunities.

"After all, this is the way it is, right? Apartheid was beaten a long time ago," Peter would hear his friends say over coffee in Starbucks where they would listen to rappers like Joey Bada$$, Fetty Wap, Rich Homie Quan and Gwen Stefani.

Indeed, he bore witness every day to the psychedelic genetics that filled the towns and cities like Ostend, Sluis and Zedelgem. The port city's Dahlialaan district was now filled with Halal shops, and young cosmopolitan people just like him took every opportunity to celebrate this diversity, attending public events where other people from every corner of the globe, and with any sort of link to Bruges, Belgium, or indeed wider Europe, were represented on the platform.

Annual Gay pride parades and the Muslim calls to prayer, wafting along the Boterbekeweg, were to be encouraged. "They were clear signs of tolerance and cultural enrichment," as the saying goes. He agreed with everyone he met at the Reggae-Geel and Couleur Café Festival in Laeken, where he listened to acts like Princess Nokia, Kabaka Pyramid and Damian Marley sing:

In this world of calamity, dirty looks and grudges and jealously
And police weh abuse dem authority
Badges screamin' at young black children stop or I'll shoot
We sparkin' an iron march to Zion

Tagging along with his friends, Peter went to the fairground, mixing with the Roma and Turkish gangs, sharing bottles of Ruwet cider in the fluorescent glow of pulsing lights and the syrupy vapours of toffee apples. Then later he would steal off home under the watchful eye of the yellow box-like surveillance cameras. Fumbling with the remote to flick past the news channels playing re-runs of the German ARD TV show *Break-Out to the Unknown*, he came across a documentary of the Black Lives Matter Movement in the USA blocking highways and shooting down police officers in Dallas, Des Moines and Baton Rouge. Anti-Trump protests in San Francisco, Portland and Chicago. Armed Antifa militia groups marching in Phoenix. Then a video by Al Furqan of a man with a grey and red beard wrapped in a black robe with an AK47 propped next to him swearing revenge for the battle of Baghouz. Before his attention was finally caught by Yusa Khogali standing on top of a car amid hundreds of marchers in Toronto, Canada. "We have to rise up and fight back . . . We are the people . . .We have the power . . . We have the numbers . . ."

She was followed by a mocha-skinned man who gave a very powerful oration: "So, I say to you, become the enemy, become the enemy they have nightmares about. Gather in the hundreds, the thousands, the tens of thousands and hundreds of thousands to form organisations and movements. Movements that will take power and re-shape our society. We must re-write history. We must wrest the guns from those who wish us dead. We must break down the borders that keep out immigrants and refugees. We must tear down the prisons and detention centres. We must seize the farms and the factories. We must become the enemies, so that everyone in this city can live with food and shelter and dignity. We must be-come the enemies that sow terror in their hearts, so that laws like C15 shrivel away. We must celebrate our ways of life, our cultural practises, which they say are barbaric, in the street and in our houses until their way of life dissi-pates under our feet. Let us become enemies. Let us or-ganise. We cannot wait. Freedom is calling . . ."

Peter, like all his friends, had caught the soundbite news stories about the allegations of mass sex assaults at New Year's Eve celebrations in Cologne, Helsinki and Salzburg. Then there was the well-documented assertion by Kann Terzioglou, CEO of Turkcell, that migrants ask for WiFi before food and shelter. Like others, he saw the way the Right-wing media were twisting stories like the child grooming in Rotherham, England. Despite such neg-ativity Peter felt there was a genuine feel-good factor of community solidarity against discrimination and division as he moved through the crowds marching about police ID checks, his rainbow pennant in hand, breathing in a concoction of rasasi scent and bubble hash, stopping to listen to a street performer singing Bob Marley's "Get Up, Stand Up" on the corner of Kelks and Burg. He witnessed people everywhere demanding justice for victims of police violence like Anis Amri, the man suspected of the Berlin truck attack gunned down by police in Milan, Yassar Ya-qub, shot by police on the M62 in northern England and Rafik Yousef, who was killed in Spandau, Germany. "We know how Black Lives Matter responded in the USA to the murder of Michael Brown, Freddie Gray and George Floyd" went the cry from a man with a loudspeaker standing on top of a bus stop strung with a banner reading "Islam is a Religion of Peace." "How do you expect us to respond when your police anally rape young black men with truncheons in Paris!" "Faced with police impunity, let's be uncontrollable!" Peter read excitedly from a picture posted on the internet. Then below, the claim that the French police had murdered Ziyed Ben Belgacem at Orly Airport. While in Germany the authorities had been brutalising immigrants in the St Georg district of Hamburg.

Everyone in his circle were transfixed by Elisabeth Moss in the TV show *The Handmaid's Tale* and Gerard McMurray's movie *The First Purge* and thought it was perfectly acceptable to punch people who had roared "Hail Trump!" They circulated messages and images of white people taking the knee on their sleek personal communication devices, using social media platforms promulgated by Apple and media conglomerates like Google, Facebook, Newscorps, Paramount, Walt Disney, Sony, CBS, MGM and NBC.

"Of course, I supported Facebook's Hate Meme Challenge, the collaboration between Angela Merkel and Mark Zuckerberg to stop the haters using Twitter," Jonathan Greenblatt of the Anti-Defamation League, advising Susan Wojcicki of YouTube to tamper with their algorithm recommendation system and ban neo-Nazi sites who spread vile poison, said when replying to a journalist who interviewed him during one particularly controversial street protest in Brussels. "Look at the abuse the Dutch TV presenter Sylvana Simons took just because she is dark-skinned! The billionaire Koch brothers are right to pour money into supporting the After Charlottesville Project along with Comcast, NBC Universal, the Kresge Foundation and the Soros Fund Charitable Foundation. The German Justice Minister Heiko Maas is also right to push laws to punish Facebook, Twitter, Google and YouTube for failing to delete politically incorrect opinions from their platforms. The financial consequences should be huge, these people should be demonetized and Fashwave artists like Xurious and hate speech agitators like Morrissey should get no air-play," Peter insisted. "Just like Jeff Bezos and Amazon stopped selling books by Right-wingers and people that are sceptical about the Holocaust. They should take a lead from Pierre Omidyar, the guy who founded E-bay, giving a hundred million dollars to fight Fake News and Hate Speech. After all, where do we as a civilized and free society draw the line?"

He applauded Beyonce's "Black is King" project on Instagram and respected Sergey Brin and Larry Page, Ezra Klein, Peter Chernin, Brad Grey, Robert Iger, Michael Lynton, Barry Meyer, Harry Sloan and Jeff Zuckerberg for volunteering to act as gatekeepers on media platforms. When he read Article 13 of the Universal Declaration of Human Rights, Peter felt there was a perfect logic in the entertainment industry integrating with the educational curricula to reinforce the principles his eyes were scanning over: "Everyone has the right to freedom of movement and residence within the borders of each state; Everyone has the right to leave any location including his own . . ."

This all made perfect sense to him. When he sat in his School Learning Centre he was surrounded by textbooks and digital files that focussed on the negative impact of colonialism which had caused Third World Poverty in the first place and all the inter-tribal wars in failed states. Flicking through pamphlets explaining the deficits which would be caused by the increasingly aging population of Europe and the economic benefits of mass immigration, his head nodded in acceptance of the case that was being put forward. Social Studies teachers recommended reading works like Madeleine Albright's *Fascism—A Warning*, Philippe Legrain's *Immigrants—Your Country Needs Them*, Caren's *Aliens and Citizens: The Case for Open Borders,* and Caplan's *My Path to Open Borders.*

In an essay Peter wrote, "For Europeans of our generation it is clear cut, it is simply our moral duty to help those less fortunate than ourselves. The EU's plan to re-settle the victims of the warring parties from around the world, in the suburbs of cities like Amsterdam, Copenhagen, Stockholm and South London, and then provide them with jobs, homes and cars, so that they can become productive members of our society is a positive and progressive strategy that should be commended for its political pragmatism and its far-sighted investment in creating a truly multicultural community. Everyone gains from this exchange, and most importantly we all come together in an intimate and shared setting, devoid of walls and perimeter fences, passports and visas in order to begin to forge a joint new identity has one entity, namely mankind."

While visting an exhibition entitled Intolerance by Luc Tuymans in the Royaux des Beaux-Arts, his mind was opened to the wider possibilities art offered to shape the future. He saw how the Northern Renaissance masterpieces of the Brueghel dynasty, the Baroque sensuality of Peter Paul Rubens and the 16th-century sculptures of Jacques du Broeucq needed to make way for more socially aware works. Gallery staff spent time explaining to him the significance of Tuyman's figurative painting and the meanings of his pieces such as *Gas Chamber*, depicting the Dachau Concentration Camp, The Heritage Collection reflecting the mood of America after the Oklahoma militia bombing by white supremacists in 1995 and Heimat, a series mocking the Flemish Nationalist movement.

Having enjoyed the experience, he entered his name on the Museum's membership list and two months later got an e-invite to a specially commissioned art show displaying Tinga-Tinga paintings from Tanzania. After the lecture he joined a mêlée of young Belgians crowding around a small group hammering out the Bongo Flavour beat of the Zaramo people, playing marimbas and singing in their native tongue. Their exuberance was inspiring, and he happily joined in, dancing with the performers, dressing in their national costumes, trying to learn some of their words, as part of cross-cultural communications.

Peter remembered returning home after that particular exposition, feeling very ashamed despite the joyous atmosphere, flicking his father's cigarette lighter and burning all his Tintin comics, after being told Hergé's depictions of the Congolese was cruel and prejudiced, believing the dark whispers that Georges Remi had supported the German occupation by contributing articles to the *Le Soir* newspaper.

Thanks to the student Good Citizen Study Guide, he found a roadmap into the past, discovering whole episodes of history like the horrors of the Holocaust, the tragedy of the Atlantic Slave Trade, and the need for developing post-colonial study programmes that gave voice to those who had been denied the right to speak.

Sitting at home most evenings, fighting with Nina over the remote control, he would reluctantly join his family as they watched syndicated TV history programmes. Between episodes of *De Grote Sprong* he caught a newsflash which captured his attention:

"Today in Geneva a group of sponsors of Love for All, led by Ati Labkin, the media businessman who cut the Vision-Media and Networld deal and billionaire Grigory Abramov who owns six hundred thousand hectares of Russia's black earth agricultural district, demanded Russia be brought to heel, either by military or economic means," the newscaster read off the teleprompter. Then going live to the scene, Abramov, fresh from speaking at the latest wave of Frauenstreiks in Lausanne, was filmed against the backdrop of the Jet d'Eau Fountain saying "Putin is the Emperor of a rogue state. It is essential we recognise him for what he is and stop his murderous interventions in Syria and the wider Arab world. They are, after all, the rash acts of a criminal cartel, of which Putin himself is a key member, determined to protect his own greedy private interests in the oil and gas sector."

❖ After months of detailed consideration, a second wave of proceedings are launched against Matteo

Salvini by the EU following his attempt to introduce a Mini-BOTs parallel currency which would
have further undermined the stability of the Euro.

❖ Within days of the announcement that the Barca
Nostra, Our Boat, display at the Venice Biennale
celebrating migration will be replicated in all major Italian urban centres, thousands of migrants
form up in long winding columns along the Molo
Santa Lucia and the and the Via Domenico Scina
in the Borgo Vecchio district of Palermo.

❖ The Italian CGIL Labour Union praises the way
the new government in Rome reverses Salvini's
policies on migrant care by creating an additional
20,000 jobs in what it describes as "this growing
sector of the Italian economy."

❖ "We have every right not just to want sharia in
Belgium but to impose it in any way we want,"
says the leader of the Islam Party, continuing,
"Why can't mosques and Islamic culture attract
tourists and investment to Brussels, just like Christian holidays?"

❖ A coalition of southern European countries bor-
dering the Mediterranean launch a new regional
Refugee and Migrant Response Plan to cater for
the projected 3.5 million people who are anticipated to be displaced and forced to flee to Europe as a
consequence of the Covid-19 pandemic, political
persecution, armed conflict and poverty in the
coming twelve months.

❖ UNICEF's newly appointed Crisis Coordinator
Humayan Khan warns "There has been an increase
in the threats and distress refugee and migrant
children endure."

❖ An update from the 100 Resilient Cities Co-
Chairman Brian Mullins predicts a further 250 million people will seek to come to the USA, Canada,
Britain, Australia and Europe saying, "The phe-
nomenon of mass migration is not passing but get-

ting stronger. This is not a problem but a glorious
opportunity and like my predecessors have said,
rather than oppose that reality we need to em-
brace it."

❖ State-sponsored immunologists pontificate about
the advantages of the microbial diversity being introduced into Europe from Africa.

❖ 50% of Tunisians indicate their desire to move to
Europe.

❖ The UNHCR estimate that 230,000 risked their
lives to reach Europe by sea in the last three
months.

❖ Analysis of the ten million known mobile migrants
indicates that 22% come from the Syrian and Middle Eastern diaspora, 32% are from North Africa
and 17% from Sub-Saharan Africa. The next largest
percentage, some 12% or so, come from Pakistan.

❖ The Swedish parliament introduces laws to make
family reunification for refugees easier and cuts
the budgets to municipalities like Bengtsfors in
order to service the needs of state-dependent migrants.

Every weekend Peter would visit the red brick faced De
Striep CV bookshop on Katelijnestraat and take advice
from the proprietor on what to buy, the shelves in his bed-
room already creaking under the weight of tomes like
Frantz Fanon's *The Wretched of the Earth*, Joanne Ramos's
The Farm, Maya Angelou's *I Know Why the Caged Bird
Sings* and Nadine Gordimer's *July's People*.

Returning home one day with a copy of Chimamanda
Ngozi Adichie's *We Should All Be Feminists* under his arm,
he became incensed at a live debate on VTM Nieuws
when an anti-immigrant panel member quoted Albert
Camus to support his argument. "People are now planting
bombs on the tramways of Algiers. My mother might be
on one of those tramways. If that is justice, then I prefer
my mother," the man said, comparing the indiscriminate

bombings of the Algerian Fellagha in the 50s and 60s to the current actions of the Daesh fanatics. "Camus is one of us!" Peter bellowed at the flat screen, his copy of Adiche's book flying across the room. "What about your precious Jean-Marie and his paratroopers torturing innocent freedom fighters in Oran?"

He was soon part of a social group that celebrated holidays like Rosh Hashanah alongside Christmas as the prime holiday season in the West. His friends invited him to music festivals like "Victory over Hate" at the Grande-Synthe refugee camp near Calais. Then, there were the various dates throughout the year when German cities celebrated Chanukkah, the Festival of Light, by holding torchlit parades to thank Bomber Harris for their liberation. While the Dutch lit bonfires and threw scarecrows with Pim Fortuyn masks into the flames on Pesach or Passover.

Peter began to travel, hitch-hiking across the continent to take part in marches organized by the One World Alliance for Free Speech Against Hate Speech, in response to the growing strength of groups like Vlaams Belang in his native Belgium, Casa Pound in Italy, Falange Autentica and Vox in Spain and the Identitäre Bewegung in Vienna. He protested against the head of the Nationalistische Studentenvereniging student group at the University of Antwerp, spokespeople like Caroline Sommerfeld-Lethen, and the ongoing campaign of the German women against migrant rape attacks. He claimed in a moment of braggadocio to know one of the group that had ambushed the leader of the Austrian Identitarians at the Vienna U-Bahn and mixing with the gang responsible for disrupting Björn Höcke's promotion of his book *Living with Leftists* at the Frankfurt Book Fair.

After seeing re-runs of the French anti-Le Pen movies *Chez Nous* and *Hate* at the crenelated Lumière cinema on Sint-Jakobstraat, Peter willingly turned out with the anarchists to counter-demonstrate the Schild & Vrienden and Voorpost nationalists marching under their banner "Stop the Genocide Against the Boers." Excited by the experience, he travelled to the centre of Namur in support of students from the Université de Namur and the Haute Ecole d'Enseign opposing a coalition of young Identitarians and Walloon nationalists fresh from the Verdur Rock festival as they gathered on the Rue de L'Ange singing songs by the Swedish band Sabaton and songwriters like Darkest Sky. After the usual chanting, pushing and shoving, the police line broke and Peter found himself running freely with masked Antifa activists along cobbled streets, high on adrenalin, using fists and boots on their outnumbered opponents, driving them to take sanctuary in the Eglise Saint-Loup, where he stood proudly in the rain next to the Student Union President under the Gay Rainbow banner condemning the Catholic Church for protecting Neo-Nazis.

Fingering through the local newspaper the following day, hoping to find a photo of himself at the rally, Peter was disappointed to see a report that some black students had taken the opportunity to break into the lockers of their fellows who had been fighting on their behalf. But despite such abhorrent behaviour, thankfully the media enthusiastically featured extended coverage of the Community Harmony rave parties that were held to suppress anger against alleged African migrant crime in places like Rosarno in Italy and the No Return for Fascist Franco parades that brought social justice champions out *en masse* in Tarrasa, northeastern Spain.

❖ VRT's Radio One features an interview with Ebana, a Syrian woman, now living in Brussels, who says in a faltering voice: "I can live again. I thought we would be drowned in the sea." Then, after a tearful pause, she continued "I am so grateful to all the people who have helped me here. But now I miss my sons and daughters, my mother and father who I left behind."

❖ A sociologist writing an op-ed in the Flemish language news magazine *Knack* insists Belgium is an apartheid state and should allow all foreigners to vote in its election regardless of how long they have lived there in order to safeguard democracy and increase diversity.

❖ French language news weekly *L'Express* confirms that 53.2% of the residents of Antwerp are of immigrant origin.

❖ The Russian government denies claims made by the BBC that its secretive Wagner units are committing atrocities in Syria and that Yevgeny Prigozhin's agents are attempting to influence the governments of up to 13 countries across the African continent to fight back against Al Qaeda-spinoff terrorist groups.

❖ UNICEF re-launches their "Do Something Amazing Today—Help Build a Better Life for Every Child Suffering Discrimination and Disadvantage Everywhere in the World."

❖ Reports of a Dutch girl being raped after being picked up at Nijmegen-Lent station by a refugee are promulgated by reactionary groups on social media.

❖ The European Network Against Racism (ENAR) carries out research on racism and discrimination against migrants across all twenty-six EU countries and finds the media was continuing to conflate the Muslim community with issues of security and terrorism. A perfect example being the case of Gokmen Tanis who was convicted of a shooting incident on a tram in Utrecht. ENAR spokesperson Georgia Siklossy said "It is unacceptable that refugees are pushed in the media as a problem and not a solution to our problem."

❖ Geneticists promulgating the fact that DNA taken from a 37,000-year-old skeleton which proves that the fundamental constituents of the Caucasoid genome, still prevalant today, have been present and consistent for millennia are denounced as being racists.

❖ The Italian Constitutional Court bans wearing the cross in schools while simultaneously completing a 5,000 square meter Holocaust museum next to the Villa Torlonia, the former residence of Benito Mussolini, in Rome.

❖ Schools in Catalonia ban *Sleeping Beauty* and *Little Red Riding Hood* because they perpetuate sexist stereotypes.

❖ The EU award the Anne Frank Museum and the Institute of War, Holocaust and Genocide Studies 4 million Euro to conduct a study on the causes of endemic racism in white communities.

❖ A female Danish journalist is attacked on the street for continuing to make pro-Christian statements.

❖ The European Court of Human Rights demands the Polish government prevents any art by Stanisław Szukalski being displayed in his homeland due to his support for Polish ethnonationalism prior to World War Two.

❖ The conservative orientated *De Telegraaf* newspaper is truck bombed by persons unknown.

❖ The pro-ISIS website 5Pillarz defines Jihad as Muslim expansionism.

❖ An Islamist attacker kills two policewomen near the Café des Augustins in Liege.

❖ Bishop Agidius Zsikovics of Eisenstadt is given a humanitarian prize for refusing to have a wall built across church land that would have prevented migrants from entering Austria.

Sitting comfortably on the sofa back home in Bruges, Peter watched as hundreds of thousands of Muslims clutching sajjada mats surrounded the Colosseum in Rome and crowded into St Peters for prayer. This was followed by coverage of London's Muslim Mayor speaking at massive Eid celebrations in Trafalgar Square. Some of the biggest Open Society-sponsored rallies in support of refugees were being held in Hungary, Poland and the Czech Republic, where the Strasbourg-based officials sensed the strongest challenges to their ideas for a New Europe persisted and the European Court of Justice had ruled yet again that their governments were acting illegally by refusing to take in refugees. He had read that the Riksdag had introduced a new authority to identify, analyse and censor harmful news emanating from the country's media and that the racist Sweden Democrats had already been bankrupted by persistent legal actions throughout the previous three years. Victor Orbán's sudden death in a tragic accident, reminiscent of Jörg Haider's demise in Austria some years before, fed fears of populist risings in Budapest. This concern increased since the establishment of a new populist party, Mi Hazánk, My Homeland, by an activist who had cleared migrants out of his hometown of Ásotthalom and other dissident groups that supported the erection of a statue of Horthy Miklós in the capital's main park. Such an affront to human dignity had brought out hundreds of concerned citizens, many waving copies of the Quran in the air, gathering in the Hazatérés Temploma, demanding answers about growing Islamophobia. Mi Hazánk's glamorous frontwoman came under siege when she appeared at a rally amid a fanfare of flags and patriotic songs.

"Another bad sister!" Ninette moaned at the television, "We should all join Hillary Clinton's Onward Together Movement."

Even more stringent measures were reserved for Golden Dawn in Greece where the party leader Nikolaos Michaloliakos, who had already been arrested once before, along with thirty other organisers, allegedly on conspiracy charges related to the death of anti-fascist rapper and martyr Pavlos Fyssas, was taken into custody once again.

Peter nodded fervent agreement when he heard language experts argue that it was important to re-formulate the Swedish accent so that it was more welcoming to foreigners. Nils Muiznieks of The European Human Rights Commission, speaking passionately on television, reinforcing what he had stated in May 2013: "Europe must combat racist extremism and uphold human rights."

Eva rang asking if he was free to go to the movies. "There's some great stuff showing," she enthused. "They've got that new *Black Panther* movie playing all day, as well as *Queen of Katwi* based on the life of the Ugandan chess prodigy, Phiona Mutsi. Then there's *Where Hands Touch*, starring Amandla Stenberg as a bi-racial girl in Nazi Germany, *The Woman King* with Lupita Nyong'o about the people of Benin fighting back against the French slavers at three o'clock and that older controversial one, *Birth of Nation* with Nate Parker at seven o'clock."

"Isn't that Parker one really just *Django Unchained* with muskets rather than six guns?"

"It's got great reviews," Eva replied "And Marthe said it was better than *Twelve Years a Slave!*" Peter went silent for a moment tapping a question into his iPhone.

"*Denial* is showing at the Kinepolis. I'd rather see that!"

"That's because you like Rachel Weisz," Eva teased, adding, "By the way, can I borrow that Primo Levi book for my literature project?"

"*If Not Now, When?*"

"I think so?"

"*If This is a Man* is better.

"Will it help my grades?"

"Maybe? I've got Goldhagen's *Hitler's Willing Executioners*. When I used that I got top marks."

"So, we'll go to Kinepolis?"

"Yeah, sure!" Before dressing to go out, he listened to an old Snoop Dogg download from iTunes:

Bitches ain't shit but hoes and tricks
Lick on these nuts and suck the dick

After the movie and some private time fondling Eva up against the ramparts of the Gentpoort, Peter made his way home, avoiding the groups of young men hovering around the bus station with mobiles pressed to their ears and blunts rolled in cigar papers bulging in their pockets. He had to watch where he was treading, because the streets were strewn with Styrofoam fast-food packaging and half-chewed KFC chicken bones. Cats mewled outside kebab shops where young girls stood talking to greasy Turks slicing lamb from revolving rotisseries.

A forest of For Sale signs greeted him as he advanced through the St Kruis neighbourhood. He wondered if this was in any way linked to the fact that in similar districts, like Korendragersstraat, houses around the Blydhove No-no Kinderopvang nursery and Vrije Basisschool De Komme pre-school were now over-crowded by multiple-generation family groups. Children in headscarves skipped in the playground of what locals called concentration schools. Lines of dark smiling faces queued for free school lunches.

Arriving safely home, he navigated the predictable "Where have you been all this time?" conversation with Bram and Ninette, climbing the stairs to escape their fretting. His bedroom floor was covered in texts, everything from imperialist genocides in Africa, mainly focusing on King Leopold's debaucheries in the Congo, the German actions against the Herero people in South West Namibia and the French Conquest of Algeria in 1830.

Crazy photos of his gang, taken on a school trip sponsored by the Avi Chai Foundation to Auschwitz, sat above his desk. Copies of his essay submissions for prizes and scholarships awarded by philanthropist organisations like The Haas Fund and The Soros Fund Charitable Foundation, to educate European youth to better appreciate democratic governance, human rights, and economic and social reform, littered the tabletop.

Throwing open the window, Peter could see a hoarding that read *Oneness*, while below the chitter-chatter of

Ta'arouf and the calls of "Salam" filled his ears. A car passed with Contactorgaan Moslems Overheid blasting out of the radio.

Squinting into the distance he could see the extent of the districts where the new citizens lived, smell the spices and attar oil in the air. He could literally touch, taste and feel the cultural enrichment.

Of course, he understood everyone needed time to make adjustments. There were going to be misunderstandings. If cultural expectations and values were going to be challenged it required wider understanding of marginalised groups. The old monolithic and homogenous society that his parents and grandparents had been born into was fast disappearing.

The US-based Pew Research Centre reported:

* ❖ According to current demographic trends, Islam will replace Christianity as the world's largest faith by 2070.
* ❖ Indonesia, the country with the highest concentration of Muslims per head of population in the world in 2010, will be overtaken by Muslim population growth in India by 2050.
* ❖ The Christian population of Europe will fall to below 50% by 2050.
* ❖ The Lier district of Antwerp becomes a no-go zone for whites.
* ❖ A North African man predates female students at the Universite Libre de Bruxelles.
* ❖ The wife of convicted Jihadist Hakim Benladghem is found in possession of AR-15 rifles and MP5 submachine guns.
* ❖ Belgian Prime Minister Sophie Wilmes states she is very proud of her Jewish heritage and agrees with the Israeli ambassador to Belgium who goes on record to accuse the organisers of the annual festival in Aalst of anti-Semitism.
* ❖ Archbishop Carlo Maria Vigano is forced to con-

tinue to live in hiding after he criticises Pope Francis for condoning the sexual assaults on young boys, suggesting the Pope should step down "if he refuses to admit his mistakes."

❖ Muslim birth rates outstrip all other faith groups in European countries except Poland.

❖ Vox repeats its claim it is the party of "extreme necessity" after it increases its representation in Andalusia from 12 to 20 delegates.

❖ Eurostat analyses indicate that fertility rates among indigenous European populations have been consistently falling below replacement levels for five decades.

❖ The Catholic University of Louvain upholds a complaint by a feminist group called Synergie Wallonie against Professor Stephane Mercier for speaking out against abortion.

❖ The EU threatens to reduce financial allocations to Poland after 6 Polish towns declare themselves LGBT–Free Zones.

❖ A Finnish patriot is arrested for insisting that Finland owes Muslim migrants nothing and that her country will never become a Muslim State.

❖ Professor Valerie Hudson at Texas A&M University expresses concerns for the future of European society when she investigates the gender imbalances caused by the massive influx of male asylum seekers. "I looked specifically at the figures that Sweden provided on its immigrants, at least 71% of which were male, and in the 16 to 70-year-old category over 90% were male."

❖ 4 out of 10 Christians will be of Sub-Saharan African origin by 2050.

❖ By 2030 the African mega-cities of Lagos, Cairo and Kinshasa will be joined by Dar es Salaam, Johannesburg and Luanda.

❖ The Muslim population of the United States will rise sharply by 2050.

❖ *"Belgium will become Arab."*—Fawzi Zouari, writing for *Jeune Afrique*

In school, fights between rival gangs were a daily occurrence. He observed that due to their damaged backgrounds some of the new Middle Eastern, Somalian and Afghani pupils seemed to care very little for human life. Peter was shocked when he witnessed the Head Teacher being stabbed as he tried to prevent a small group from Chad from chewing khat.

Then over coffee in the canteen, one day both Marthe and Eva began crying as they watched live streamed footage from Fleur's phone.

At first they could only discern blurred images of three people moving to the soundtrack of a Michael Jackson song:

See, it's not about races
Just places
Faces
Where your blood comes from
Is where your space is . . .
I said if you're thinking about my baby
It don't matter if you're black or white

Then slowly, as the camera began to focus, panning the scene for the reluctant audience, they made out Fleur's pale distraught face. She was bleeding heavily from the nose. Her distinct auburn hair, matted and bunched tight in a black fist. Then the sound of cotton ripping and panty elastic snapping as it uncoiled when her knees were forced apart.

"We gonna beat Fouad's number," the voice said, "Two hundred and thirty chicken-skins ain't enough. We want Cologne every day!"

When the perpetrators were caught, Peter accompanied the girls as they attended the hearing at the Justitiehuis. They were led into an upper gallery where the families of the accused screamed "Racist justice system!" and "Your daughter is a lying whore" in the direction of Fleur's mother and father below.

When the African boys were brought in, waving to the spectators, they said in their defense: "She nuttin'," in their specious Jamaican patois, "She should have been down with the brothers. You all gotta to be good to us, no?"

Peter held his head in his hands. He could see how this was going to harm social cohesion. There was already gossip about ethnic taxi drivers making illicit advances on drunken girls, Muslims running the heroin trade and gangs of Moroccans and Algerians invading night clubs over the border in Germany, groping people's wives, sisters and daughters. He knew diversity counsellors were reading tracts by Mahatma Gandhi and Mother Teresa at school assemblies across the country. At Saint-Donaas he stood watching as the counsellors lined up three-deep under framed pictures of former UN Secretary Generals Ban ki-Moon and Kofie Annan. The lead counsellor, stepping forward to speak into the crackling microphone, emphasising one particular saying of the Matriarch of Calcutta: "If you judge people, you have no time to love them."

Which is exactly why on Sports Days socially inclusive Belgians such as himself, just like their British, German, Dutch, French, Scandinavian and Mediterranean counterparts, were happy to encourage the dark-skinned athletes regardless of the team colours they wore. After all, national soccer stars like Christian Benteke, Marouane Fellaini, and Vincent Kompany supported Black Lives Matter and the campaign to Kick Racism out of Soccer. Peter himself had seen the TV interview when Kompany, the team captain, said: "I'm not half-Belgian and half-Congolese, I'm 100% Belgian and 100% Congolese. It's a wealth I have!"

Fond of history and with an emerging interest in the world around him, Peter was all too familiar with the newsreels that showed Hitler and Mussolini, those maniacal clowns of yesteryear, strutting to and fro like proud peacocks on a sunny day. That such charlatans as these and Leon Degrelle's Rexist Party could have caused such rapture in sophisticated and civilized nations like Germany, Italy, and his own native Belgium intrigued him. How could his ancestors have been so gullible and so stupid? He was almost ashamed to be who he was. The son of men who had fought on the Eastern Front and turned the other way when the Zyklon B was used in Krakow and the gunshots echoed amid the tree-lined ridges of Babi Yar. Wherever he went, whatever he read, the chant "Nazis Out" resonated through all channels. Things began to change, however, after the coordinated terrorist attacks in Paris, Frankfurt, Brussels, London and Malmö, with automatic fire raking train carriages, planes being flown into power stations and suicide bombers exploding in school playgrounds. Victims now began talking openly about the backgrounds of the perpetrators. He had to admit to himself that the fact there had been a systemic problem with integration and that unemployment was especially high among the incoming groups did not help. Urban dilapidation and welfare dependency spread like a rash across immigrant conurbations. Peter had walked those streets and read graffiti like "He who kills police will go to paradise" scrawled over chipped brickwork.

Such daily realities presented real challenges to state governments and media commentators, who argued that this only served to incubate hatred and foster the rise of a noxious populism. Informed people like his mother knew there was a real danger that inherent racist pathologies that were so toxic that they had led to the worst crimes against humanity could be unleashed once more.

Television screens were reporting how the Interior Ministries of various EU states were forced to suppress anti-immigrant protests, with coverage of the resuscitated PEGIDA in Dresden being sprayed with water cannons, tear gas and a fusillade of rubber bullets. Strasbourg stressed the need for further sanctions against the continuing Kurt Waldheim clique in Austria, and reactionary parties that had made substantial electoral gains in the EU elections were being declared illegal all over Western Europe, with key figures among such groups being taken into custody from Athens to Aarhus.

Peter nodded as he listened to politicians say nothing should be allowed to interfere with the progress made since 1945. He agreed with Donald Tusk that EU member states should take in even more immigrants. He knew it was slightly different in Poland, Hungary and the Czech Republic where xenophobia was deeply embedded in their psychology. He reasoned they had barely been liberated from Communism and not yet had the chance to experience the benefits of multiculturalism. So, in order to contain the problem and prevent fascist contamination, he supported the travel bans that were imposed on known provocateurs in Poland who advocated for a form of Zadruga pagan nationalism, and firebrand female speakers from Silesia who represented Obóz Narodowo-Radykalny, the National Radical Camp, and who he had seen on YouTube speaking in Wrocław declaring "Islamic Imam, this is our land. You will not introduce your Islamic rules here. This is Poland. This is our land. Our country, our rules and our values!"

Various EU social and community funds were now being withheld from Eastern states that refused to fall in behind the Community mandate to welcome refugees. He favoured the proposition to expel countries like Poland and Hungary if they did not accept their share of migrants. Matters were coming to a head after a flying visit to European Heads of State by a former US ambassador to France. His trip, funded by the Bill and Melinda Gates Foundation, aimed to promote the full integration of Turkey into the European Free Trade Area.

"Prosperity for one and all!" he insisted at a press conference held at the Palace of Versailles. "We will have no more little boys like Aylan washed up on beaches because we closed our doors to the poor and needy!"

President Erdogan speaking from the Hagia Sophia about European visas for Turks and more financial support for the refugee camps in Killis, Oncupinar, Nizip and Karkamis, set off even longer convoys of refugees from the South and East. Normal people like Peter's family were shocked to see barbed wire draped with baby clothes in Slovenia, tearful faces staring through TV screens. "A Human Tragedy," ran the headlines across the internet. The beaches of Kos were overrun yet again by Iraqis and Libyans. Greek fishing boats landing their sun-baked human cargo on the harbour side, Frontex admitting they were being overwhelmed.

"The boats keep coming," a spokesman for the Frontier authority told news reporters, "We estimate 30,000 are putting to sea this week." Peter looked on as one man whose accent called to mind Baluchistan in southwestern Pakistan explained that he and his family were "Syrian refugees from Aleppo." Then staring into the camera, "My family were imprisoned by the bad man Bashar Assad!" No one had time to question credentials. This was a humanitarian catastrophe with people suffering and dying on a massive scale. Border and immigration staff were simply too busy stamping visas and finding shelter. Within a few days the US delegate's laws were being rushed through to commandeer empty rooms in people's homes in order to meet the demand for permanent settlement. There was no time for redress. When local people objected, they were scorned by officials as selfish and uncaring. "A precedent was set in Germany," the EU Legal Council concluded. "We must all abide by the same rules."

Those who refused or attempted to resist by blockading their residences were subject to draconian fines. If the authorities encountered physical resistance, they were empowered to use overwhelming force and even eviction. Thousands of native Europeans were charged before the courts within the first forty-eight hours of the bill being passed into law.

"This crisis must not be allowed to challenge our humanitarian instincts," added John Ngurugwe, the coordinator for refugee resettlement, as he welcomed hundreds of young Senegalese men disembarking from the Italian cargo vessel *Tichy* at Trapani in Sicily. "We must help. It is not a question of charity. It is our responsibility to these people!"

Meanwhile, in school, Peter found himself subject to daily hassles from Aweys and his followers. "You not better than us. We better than you, cos we is Wakandans!" was a constant refrain. "We better at football and better at sex." Everyone now knew how the American Empire had been built off the back of slaves taken by force from Africa and that the wealth of Europe resulted from the colonial rape of India and most of Asia. Any sense of Western superiority was easily countered by reference to Islamic mathematicians and scientists and the numerous inventions now being rightfully attributed to the Negro entreprenuers that developed them. There was no sense of supremacism in Peter's DNA. "We are all out of Africa, anyway?" he found himself saying to his tormentors in the hope that showing support for black power would off-set trouble.

Boys like Peter were in the minority now, and when rumours that his childhood friend Daan had begun secretly meeting Amna, a Muslim girl who dared convention by refusing to cover her face, reached her family, she was quickly withdrawn from school and an arranged marriage hastily concluded with a much older man from a respectable family. A few weeks later Peter was with Amna's erstwhile boyfriend when he was jabbed with a screwdriver.

"You're lucky I don't kill you," Amna's brother told Daan. "If you dishonour my family again, I will put acid in your mother's eyes."

Soon after Eva stopped seeing Peter. When he asked why she wanted to end their relationship, she could only repeat again and again that her friends did not like him.

"Which friends?" he asked. She would not say, but within a couple of weeks he noticed her hanging around

with Celeste, a leggy half-cast girl who wore short skirts
and flirted with the cannabis crowd. Slowly but surely the familiar smiling faces from his
youth began to dwindle. Locals like the Vermeulen and
Coppens families were selling up and moving out of the
district where he was born. The Charliers and the De Rid-
dlers had already moved away. He walked home past
boarded shop fronts and business premises that had traded successfully for decades. Over time the smell of cumin,
chili and rancid vegetable oil permeated the dereliction
along with the trails of rat urine. The scent of curry became almost claustrophobic. There were arguments at
home with Bram telling Ninette that the house was losing
value.

"What are you saying?" she demanded, "that we must
move because our neighbours don't want to live near
Muslims?" His father's head would shake.

"Of course I'm not giving in to that sort of bigotry, but
our house is our biggest investment."

"Our biggest investment," she emphasised "and I'm not
leaving just because ignorant people whisper words like
Taliban about Fatima and Saad!"

School debates about the merits of books like *Visions
for 2050*, predicting that in the future all Europeans would
have a family member from a migrant background, began
to lead to heated arguments.

"You should be glad!" argued Aslan, a Turkish boy from
Antalya who had started to grow a beard in recognition of
the prophet. "We have brought you corba, baklava, and
mezes. But what have you given us?"

"Yes," cut in Amira, "You eat dirty pork. It disgusts me!"

When discussion broadened out beyond name-calling
and insults, it became increasingly obvious that few students had real friendships that crossed racial boundaries.
Peter witnessed the distance widening between communities. Yawning fissures opening over time, emphasised by
the proportion of new citizens arriving compared to the

birth rate amongst families like his own.

He felt troubled. This was not the future he had been led to believe in. He had heard all about how two police officers had been savagely beaten by migrants in Saint-Gilles, the race riots in Anderlecht and that the spread of Covid-19 across nine out of the ten provinces of the country and Flanders was the result of Muslims disobeying the lockdown. Peter threw himself even further into his volunteering and encouraged Nina to come with him, signing up for increased hours helping at the asylum residences.

In the weeks and months that followed the Charlie Hebdo and Bataclan massacres in Paris, Ninette had sought to reassure Bram, constructing rational arguments for the anger they both felt rising all around them. They tried to ignore the car horns sounding off after news of the truck attacks in Nice and Breitscheidplatz square in Berlin broke. Driving home from work, they shook their heads at the spread of graffiti supporting the "Martyrs of Molenbeek" and people like Oussama Atar, Ibrahim el-Bakraoui, Mohamed Abrini, Najim Laachraoui, and Osama Krayem, names closely associated with the bombings at Zaventem airport and the Maalbeek Metro. When swastikas appeared in response, they were the first out onto the road to cleanse such signs of hatred from the area. Ninette, shaking her head in disdain, "What must Fatima and Saad think?"

They invited them around for dinner to make amends, Ninette spending the whole week before researching Bengali food and visiting the numerous Southeast Asian shops that had sprung up along the Goezeputstraat.

"So nice of you to come over," Bram said when he opened the door all eight members of the Banerjee family.

"We thought it would be nice to spend time together," Ninette assured them, while serving chingri malai curry, ladling creamy coconut milk over the spicy prawns. "Please do make yourselves at home."

Everyone made small talk over the table. Each of the

children were asked about school and what they wanted to be when they grew up. "A dentist," "a doctor," "an accountant," came the confident replies.

"Marvellous," Ninette beamed, looking to Bram with a nod of encouragement.

"Model citizens," Peter's father confirmed, "And our two, Nina and Peter, are doing a lot of community work."

"That is good," Saad nodded, "Our children are our future. We must do all we can to give them the best start in life. And there is so much misunderstanding about our religion. So many hatreds and troubles." Fatima smiled benevolently, sitting in her crimson Jamdani sari, saying very little, allowing Saad to continue, "You have four bedrooms like us, am I right?"

Weeks passed but no reciprocal invitation came from the Banerjees. One day Ninette literally bumped into Fatima in the corner shop while she was speaking in Bangla to the owner.

"Good day!" she said enthusiastically, only to be ignored as Fatima left hurriedly.

"Was it something I said?" she asked. The owner shrugged in a noncommittal way. Ninette tried to make light of it but after purchasing a few items summoned up the courage to ask more seriously if she had given offense. "If I have, please re-assure Fatima that I did not do so intentionally."

But she walked out of the shop having received no clear response from the woman behind the smoky veil who disinterestedly tossed back some loose change.

❖ A church in Malmö replaces statuettes of Adam and Eve with the image of a same sex couple;

❖ The migrants who raped and mutilated Desiree Mariottini in Via dei Lucani in San Lorenzo, Italy are freed.

❖ People who burned a copy of the Quran in Norway are sentenced to 15 years in prison.

❖ Ex-Swedish Prime Minister, Stefan Lofven, insists "There is no link between the rising problem of gang violence and migrant communities."

❖ A 55-year-old man from Xilingol in China is diagnosed with bubonic plague at a hospital in the city of Huade.

❖ Sweden's Board of Health and Welfare argues it needs to prioritize refugees and migrants over indigenous citizens during the latest outbreak of Covid-19.

❖ The Bjurback school in Emmaboda adds Islamic prayer to its curriculum.

❖ The JD Sports outlet in Liege is looted by Arabs shouting "Gwers," an anti-white slogan, and youngsters brandish blades and threaten a pregnant woman in Otterstraat.

❖ Scientists who re-created the face of a female viking warrior from a skull in Solor are told to remove their representation from Oslo's museum of cultural history because it fails to represent the new Norway.

❖ Israel's ambassador to Spain objects to images used during the Campo de Criptana carnival saying they are mocking the victims of the Holocaust.

❖ "I've said it a thousand times, the worst thing we can do is make an enemy of Islam. That is the worst thing we can do."—Jan Jambon, Belgian Minister for the Interior

A few weeks later Peter looked out his bedroom window and saw Saad trowelling excrement on their doorstep. When he told his parents, they looked woefully at one another and asked him not to speak about it. Within days, their windows were being smashed by roving gangs in the middle of the night and their car tyres slashed. Revving engines and loud music played all the time. When Bram went out to confront them, he was punched and kicked to the ground. Ninette reluctantly called the police but refused to tell them the identity of the assailants.

"I'm worried about police violence, look how Adil was killed at the police checkpoint," she whispered to Peter, "migrants are thirty times more likely to be imprisoned here and I have heard how they treat some of these refugee kids!"

Meanwhile Bram was taken to accident and emergency for a fracture to his right orbital socket and cuts and bruises. Upon their return from the Sint Jan clinic, they found their garden was being used as an open-air toilet. The smell lingering throughout the house as if it was a sewer.

Then around Christmas time Saad knocked on the door.

"Perhaps you are not happy living here," he hinted through a serpentine smile, "Would you like to sell your place?" Both Bram and Ninette were taken aback. "My sister and her husband have sold their business and are coming soon from Kolkata, you see," Saad added by way of explanation. "Fatima would like all the families to be close together." When the Janssens politely declined Saad's offer the campaign against them grew even more intense. Saad's extended family and other members of his community would spit at them and shout "Crusaders Out!" Ninette would sometimes catch Fatima's face looking covetously at their property from behind the bedroom curtain.

Over time, Peter saw the deterioration in his father's health. He was losing weight and needed medication to help him sleep. His shoulders drooped. Shadows grew around his eyes as worry like a vigorous cancer chiselled deep into his features. It looked like all sense of life was being sucked out of him. Ninette would berate Bram, telling him to "get hold of himself," but then one day he returned from the office in a state of nervous exhaustion, admitting "They have let me go." That was the first time Peter ever saw his mother cry.

"How will we manage without a salary?" she mumbled

through fingers, rubbed red to the bone after scrubbing the words Dar al-Harb off the front door.

Peter listened intently to the volunteer briefings provided by staff at the refugee centre. The Head Counsellor raised a copy of *One Child, Many Worlds* by Eve Gregory in the air, making it absolutely clear, "This is our Bible. Leave your prejudices and your own cultural values at the door. This is a safe space for our guests. They have enough to deal with out there beyond our walls. In here, we respect everyone equally and in all ways." Answering questions from the floor he advised, "Do not speak to journalists or the police unless one of our staff are present. Everything is confidential in here. We are trying to preserve the dignity of the people in our care."

Peter and Nina worked shifts both in the evenings and at weekends, serving food in the cafeteria and issuing cigarettes and mobile phone credits to the young men eager to speak to their families back home. When they talked to Peter in broken English, they would ask him for money and complain that they had no privacy to bring back their new girlfriends. "Watch this," they would cackle, thrusting forward a download of blondes bathing topless on a beach somewhere in France.

Occasionally Peter would find himself in the middle of a fight between the various nationalities and religious sects comprising the newly formed community. He had helped a security firm install metal detectors to stop guns and knives being smuggled in and out, watching as the charity's spokesperson explained to the press that the measures were necessary because of the increasing hostility the migrants were facing from local residents.

Finishing their shifts both Peter and Nina would be approached by bulky men in leather jackets. "Can you get us Jack Daniels," they asked furtively.

"It's against the rules," Nina spent time explaining, "your Muslim brothers might take offense, and there would be trouble!"

"But we are Muslim too," they would argue back. "Do all Christians do what Jesus says?" Peter had to agree but repeated the mantra.

"If we are caught, we will lose our jobs!" Then the men would laugh.

"What jobs? You do women's work. You serve us and wash our bed sheets after we jerk off. There is no honour for you. Clever people would take the chance to make some money! A dark hand full of small notes was proffered again. "Take it or else!" they insisted.

During a break in their community outreach class at the Centre, Nina confided to her brother as they sat hunched over a copy of James Banks' *Cultural Diversity and Education*: "They watch me and whisper together." Peter could see how agitated she was, as her fingernails, still discoloured by the excrement she had scraped off the shower room floors, danced across her chattering teeth.

"You've got to understand how traumatised they are," he said, "War, poverty and disease have scarred them," he pleaded, as much to convince himself as his sister. "You simply must keep coming back with me to help. You will never forgive yourself if you don't." So Nina reluctantly returned time and time again, because it was expected, and she felt that she needed to continue to match her mother's and her brother's commitment to the cause.

Entering the main office one morning to collect their work assignments for the weekend they saw a middle-aged lady being confronted by her co-workers through an open door to a private meeting room.

"Do you know what you have done?" went the refrain, "You have been utterly irresponsible. By giving the government evidence of multiple identity fraud you have jeopardised the lives of hundreds of refugees. They are at risk of being deported back to the war zones from which they fled in the first place."

"The crime is so large I could not live with myself," the woman spluttered in her defence. Cold faces stared back in amazement.

"Yet, you can live with the deaths of hundreds of children on your conscience?"

"But there are very few children here. This place is full of grown men!"

Then one afternoon Peter noticed Nina struggling to take off her nylon work coat.

"What's up?" he asked. With tears in her eyes she showed him finger shaped bruises on her arms and torn bra straps.

"Who did this?" She shook her head in refusal. Peter glanced into the dark corridor towards the dormitories. Nina's face followed his lead.

"We must not let mother know," he whispered conspiratorially, "She would feel so let down." Then, walking home in silence, Peter soon realised he was discovering feelings of anger and frustration that made him ashamed. Something primordial was bubbling up inside. He did his best to fight it, realising that he needed to contain his own demons, and not just those that manifested themselves in the blood-soaked banners of the past.

Fulfilling his penitence by continuing to work at the centre exorcised the worst of the dark spirits that occasionally welled up inside. But his inner battle continued to rage. There were moments when his knuckles tightened into hard skeletal knots and he wanted to strike back.

Like the time he sat alone in the school canteen chewing strips of dry lasagne. He sensed the threat behind him, hairs rising on the back of his neck, even before the blade scratched at his throat.

"Give me your money or I'll cut," a familiar voice threatened to a peel of jeering laughter. Then his head was wrenched backwards to meet Aweys' mocking grin. Just for a second, Peter saw something beyond mere robbery in the face confronting him. In that moment of recognition, which Aweys took for resistance, but was in fact the germination of a long-suppressed anxiety in Peter's version of reality, the metal bit, and a thin line of blood discoloured his shirt collar. Suddenly foreign hands were all over him, rifling through pockets, relieving him of his brown leather wallet and Bancocontact credit card.

"Is that all you got?" Aweys scoffed, emptying fifteen Euro onto the floor. "Your government gives me more!" Pulling on Peter's hair and turning to his friends, "He should rob us, cos we have all the money now!" After sending a fountain of phlegm in Peter's direction, the marauding horde went running off down the corridor in search of their next victim.

Still shaking, Peter vomited uncontrollably. Wiping himself down and staunching the slash on his neck with a paper towel from the toilet, he slowly began to regain some composure. Cold sweat mouldering into a sense of bitter humiliation. He felt the burning desire for revenge build up once again and tried to fight back such negative emotions, but they were getting stronger and stronger. His will to do good was being eroded hour by hour.

Then their house was burgled while they visited Ninette's sister in Aarschot. The Janssens returning home from a birthday party to find their valuables stolen and sentimental items like family photographs slashed and scattered in the road.

"Why?" Ninette cried into Bram's shoulder, while Peter and Nina scooped up their remaining belongings into black plastic bin bags.

"We'll have to install security cameras," he said between short rasping breaths, but God knows how we'll find the money." Then they retreated inside and threw the bolt on the door, all the while under Fatima's owl-like supervision from the neighbouring window.

Over the following weeks they increasingly felt under siege. Bram could not sell the house because no one would buy at the price they needed to break even, and Saad's offer reduced every week.

❖ Sociologist Felice Dassetto's book *The Iris and Crescent* predicts Brussels will be majority Muslim by 2030.

❖ Belgian secret service agents round up 47 members of Combat 18 Flanders.

❖ Flemish nationalists like Filip Dewinter are banned from speaking in public.

❖ Primary school children in Belgium are instructed to pray to Allah on a daily basis.

❖ Palestinian-Belgian jihad expert and adviser to the Belgian secret service, Montasser AlDe'emeh, issues a stark warning in *de Telegraaf*, saying Europe is importing a civil war by admitting refugees. Asserting in his book *Dubbel Leven*, that many immigrant "children live here physically, but mentally they mostly live in the Middle Ages."

❖ Brussels North Station is inundated with migrant squatters.

❖ Concerns that a new outbreak of the Covid-19 pandemic is sweeping Europe leads to claims that as many as 20,000,000 people are infected and up to 3,000,000 fatalities could be anticipated.

❖ A Viennese university professor, Ednan Aslan, who is herself of Turkish descent, authors a report indicating that nearly 10,000 infants attending Islamic Kindergartens are being introduced to what she terms a parallel society in Austria.

❖ Businesses desert districts like Molenbeek, with one American Advertising Agency citing 150 assaults on its staff by local youths.

❖ An Islamist city council member demands "Islamic rules for Anderlecht!"

❖ A man speaking a foreign language fires a Kalashnikov-style weapon through a restaurant window on the Avenue Louise in Brussels.

❖ The Mayor of Molenbeek refuses to pass the names of suspected terrorists to the police.

❖ Gang rapes in Belgium rise to epidemic proportions, with over 157 being reported each week.

❖ The Belgium 7 Sur7 network reveals a second attempt by the Belgian delegation to the UN to support Saudi Arabia's election to the UN Women's Rights Council.

❖ Speaking in Antalya, the Turkish Foreign Minister predicts religious wars will break out in Europe, suggesting he would unleash an even greater flood of migrants towards the West if Europe would not agree to further funding for his country for hosting refugees.

❖ Sweden's leading political scientist and Chief Prosecutor agree with the Director General of Sweden's Sapo security services when he says, "terrorism is the new normal" and that Stockholm is becoming a war zone.

❖ A woman who campaigned to stop asylum seekers being deported from Sweden is raped by an Afghan migrant while his friend masturbates at the scene of the attack.

❖ An underage girl is raped by refugees in a cemetery in Ostervala in the Heby district of Uppsala.

❖ The Archbishop of Pompei is ritually slaughtered for opposing Islamization.

By pure chance, while walking through Astrid Park one afternoon, his mind reminiscing about how he had played with his childhood friends all those summers ago, Peter saw Lina, one of his gang from way back when, sitting on a park bench under an umbrella.

As Peter approached, he could see how Lina trembled as she recognised the lean young man striding towards her under the trees. His eyes discerned the rabbit-like urge to bolt as he reached out. Then he realised why as she reluctantly turned to face him, revealing the deep purple tracks of volcanic skin lesions after the sulfuric acid had dissolved her beautiful green eye and shrivelled her ear to a dry sinewy husk.

For a moment he could not speak. His mouth hung open in shock and disbelief. Lina raised her hand to signal reassurance.

"I'm used to frightening people now," she said. Then pointing to the Somali children running around in their koofis, "They call me a monster."

Peter took a seat beside her. They remained silent for a long time, only responding to the teasing of the children who ran up to ask if Peter was the boyfriend of the monster?

"How?" he eventually asked.

"Last year after Kemi asked me to marry him."

"But why?"

"Because I refused."

"So this was revenge for hurt feelings?"

Lina shook her head.

"I dishonoured him. This is how such things are done where Kemi's family comes from in Pakistan."

"You had no idea this is how he would react?"

"Kemi's lived here almost all his life. He's one of us. I thought . . ." her voice crackled like burning autumn leaves, "But I was wrong."

"I think we all are," Peter nodded. "You must have been terrified!"

"I felt the skin sliding off my face like layers of wrapping paper."

"And the doctors?"

"I have another six months of grafts, after that there is no more they can do."

"But the grafts are good," he tried to sound upbeat.

"I read on the internet seven women have been attacked the same way in Berlin. Some crazy Muslim guy riding around on a bicycle spraying acid on women he thinks should cover up."

Peter's hands were locked in angst. Lina continued.

"He attacked one girl on the Freidrichshain in broad daylight."

❖ Two elected leaders of the Belgian Islamic Party, representing the municipalities of Molenbeek-

Saint-Jean and Anderlecht respectively, insist on the introduction of Sharia Law, stating "We believe Islam is a universal religion."

❖ An Islamic Party leader from Bruxelles Ville demands halal meals are served in school cafeterias.

❖ Muslim religious holidays are recognised by the Belgian government and laws are introduced to make women wear headscarves in public spaces.

❖ The spokesman for the Salafist group Sharia4Belgium says, "May Allah disperse the Belgians and their country!"

❖ An Ethiopian translator with ten years' experience working with refugees provides examples of anti-European attitudes among the migrants and quotes one saying: "We will multiply our numbers. We must have more children than the Christians because it is the only way to destroy them here."

❖ The 40 Point programme of the Salafists demand: re-designing the Belgian judiciary to comply with Islamic Law prohibiting alcohol and cigarettes, promoting teenage marriage, segregating males and females in the public realm, and establishing an official Islamic alms fund.

❖ A historian at the Free University of Brussels predicts that a Civil War in Europe is only a few short years away.

Meanwhile, despite the overwhelming evidence of mounting concern about the direction the European Union was taking in France, the Czech Republic, Hungary, Denmark, Poland and Austria, the steely determination of the grey-faced EU President, bolstered by public support from the President of the United States, remained undiminished. Sharing a platform in Graz with his long-time friend and colleague, Axel Mobwitz, he proudly announced "Events like Brexit will not stop us. Working with our allies in the American administration, we will advance our plans for an integrated Europe in the face of the Russian military build-up." Then, ripping up a map of European nation-states, he proudly repeated what others had said years before: "The future of Europe will not be held hostage by elections, party politics or the cries of foul-play by those playing to their domestic audiences. The European Union is more than a free-trade area. Europe is more than markets and good money. There are those who would wish to reduce the role of the Commission to only administer and manage a single market. I am strictly against that. Especially now, when we face hostility once again on our Eastern borders. I want to integrate pensions, welfare and defense."

Turning towards the press corps throwing out questions from behind flashing bulbs, "Yes, I also believe borders are the worst invention ever. I am calling for all European borders to be opened to all comers. We still have to fight against nationalism wherever it raises its repugnant face and honour our commitments to humanity as a whole. Otherwise, as the United Nations and my friend the American President, has indicated, economic and trade sanctions will be brought to bear on those who default."

❖ President Rahm Emanuel, working in unison with both the Senate and Congress, secures a $36 billion budget to increase NATO military capacity in Central Europe.

❖ American's senior foreign policy adviser tells President Putin to "Back down or get shut down!" in a speech in Opoli, Latvia, only a short distance from his family's ancestral home in Belarus.

❖ The American Air Force drops several GBU-43 Massive Ordnance Blast bombs in Syria and Afghanistan.

❖ The Russians respond by arming their ground forces in the battlezone with thermobaric weaponry four times more powerful than the 21,600 pound bombs used by the USA.

❖ America sends a squadron F35A Stealth fighter to RAF Lakenheath in the UK.

❖ Vast quantities of American military ordnance disembark from cargo ships named *Resolve*, *Freedom* and *Endurance* at Rotterdam in Holland and Bremerhaven in Germany.

❖ Sword Two military exercises begin in the Baltic, Scandinavia and Western Europe.

❖ The American President's chief military adviser, comments "We continue to advance our objectives in regard to multicultural states. The best way to maintain this momentum is to show some muscle, not just in Europe but the Middle East and anywhere our interests are threatened."

❖ Left wing M.E.P. Otlod Smets welcomes a law to ban the wearing of chivalric Christian regalia associated with political movements or processions in public spaces.

❖ The Vesna Human Rights Group who support Belarussian opposition leader Svetlana Tikhanovskaya spark riots against President Lukashenko's regime.

❖ Anti-Putin protests become violent in Pushkin Square, Moscow.

❖ Thousands of people march in Khabarovsk, a city in the Russian Far East, in support of nationalist governor Sergei Furgal.

❖ The First Estonian Infrantry are moved into tents near Lasna to make way for the British 5th Battalion the Rifles Battle Group "to confront threats to global security."

❖ A hawkish former advisor to past George W. Bush, asserts Russia is conducting a cyber-war against the West at a *Times*-sponsored "Global Economic Summit."

❖ General De Jong, the Dutch Chief of Defense, confirms that storage facilities across the Lowlands hold sufficient material to support 38,000 ground troops.

❖ Columns of German Leopard 2A6 tanks take to the roads around Siauliai in Lithuania, pointing their Rheinmetall 120 mm smoothbore guns towards Minsk.

❖ The newly appointed Polish Defense Minister, Mayim Bialik welcomes NATO's deployment of 97,000 troops in and around the small town of Zagan on the banks of the Bobr river as part of the Anaconda 2 exercises.

Then, one day, Nina did not come home after working late at the refugee hostel. They waited, counting the minutes as they ticked by on the cracked enamel face of the Hubert Bequet clock staring blankly back at them across the silent room.

Ninette began phoning her girlfriends, hoping she was visting Agneta, Emmeline or Juliette. No one had heard anything, so they put on their coats and searched everywhere.

"No sight of her," Peter said as dawn broke over the Onze Live Vrouwkerk. "We'll have to inform missing persons." The colour draining from Bram's face later that morning when the police found footage on a security camera of Nina walking alone on the tree-lined Groenerei Canal.

A few sleepless nights and days passed and then Ninette ran crying down the middle of the street when stories spread that her daughter had been taken to Schilderswijk in Holland, known colloquially as the Sharia triangle. "They are trying to politicize our personal tragedy," she told her husband and son.

Peter locked himself in his bedroom, hoping the rumours were untrue but fearing the worst. He cursed himself, bitterly regretting persuading her to work with him at the Centre. Scanning the internet, he came across reports about grooming gangs in Holland forcing girls to inject heroin under their toenails before selling them for sex. Then he followed a link to where there were stories posted about immigrant gangs molesting Swedish girls at the Bravalla music festival. The website of *Il Giornale* in Italy covered the case of Nigerian drug dealer Innocent Oseghale who dismembered Italian teenager Pamela Mastropietro, at the Court of Assizes Macerata.

"Surely, this is not happening," he found himself muttering, "Mother must be right, this is Fake News and internet chatter." His internal debate raged on for hours after he found similar stories in Telford, Oxford, Huddersfield and Manchester in England. He knew how the press were part of the campaign to generate a climate of fear. The facts he tried to tell himself were being distorted and cases were being exaggerated to make salacious headlines.

"They must be lying," he would say to Bram and Ninette as they sat hunched over the dinner table, dry mouths struggling to swallow food.

A week after Nina's disappearance, nothing more was known, and out of sheer desperation Bram made an appeal on live radio to the Muslim community for help. Ninette sobbing bitterly into the microphone: "I would like to call on all our Muslim friends to help us locate our daughter."

Within minutes the phone lines were blocked by callers accusing the Janssens of racial profiling.

"You are racist pigs!" a woman from Genk said. Another caller from Beveren was adamant they should apologise.

"You can't just stereotype people like this. You must be held accountable for your prejudice!"

Returning home that evening their private phone was ringing off the hook. Demands were being made that they retract their false accusations. Threats came fast and furious down the wire.

"Belgian bastards!" a foreign voice snarled.

"We know where you live, dog!" said another.

Just before midnight, Bram fell breathless to the carpet, clutching his rib cage, snatching for air. Following emergency surgery at the Saint-Jan Hospital, and while still confined to bed and sedated, he was charged with inciting racial hatred by two officers who had been dispatched on orders from the Provinciaal Hof. Their initial investigations revealing that the miscreant had unfairly singled out and displayed egregious insensitivity towards a specific community by assuming them to be responsible for Nina's disappearance.

The court case went on for weeks and was widely covered in the national and regional press. Saad was quoted saying Bram had been a bad neighbour and constantly called him names like raghead and sand monkey. Ninette had a breakdown. Soon after the family home was attacked by masked Antifa vigilantes. Led by Afra herself, and clad in dark sunglasses and black berets, they threw M 80 fireworks and Molotov cocktails, screaming toxic whiteness was something to be wiped out.

Police cordons blocked streets and caused mass disruption in the neighbourhood for several days. When Peter tried to reason with the mob from behind police lines Afra was the first to strike out, catching the side of his head with a condom crammed with excrement.

"Die you fucker, die!" she screeched.

"We cannot guarantee your safety," the Police commander warned. "Do you have somewhere you can go?" So they drove away through crowds of protesters waving placards that read "Innocent Until Proven Guilty!" and calls of "Shut them down! Shut them down!" resounding with thumping fists off the car roof.

Staying with relatives in Veurne and walking through the Walburga park in the rain, they hoped to escape the controversy for a while, trying to focus on their daughter, listening out for any news of what had become of her.

"I know you are under stress and I understand how pressure can make people do stupid things, but I still cannot imagine what made you say it?" Ninette's brother, Wilhelm, a Green Party member, kept reiterating across the dinner table. His wife Berta looking concerned.

"Because people said they had seen her with Muslim men," Ninette repeated.

"People kept saying," the Green repeated, shaking his head, "Irresponsible people, racists and reactionaries. Idiots that you have fought against all your adult life. Ignorance that will set back integration for decades!" Then, after a long silence while they spooned thin potato soup, "You must understand my position," Wilhelm explained, "I am someone in this community. People look to me to set an example. I have been asked to stand in the next election."

His point was made, and although Bram and Ninette explained they had nowhere else to go, Wilhelm remained firm.

"Just by allowing you to stay here for a short time I am risking my reputation and damaging my future prospects. How do I explain that to Berta and the boys?"

"We understand," Ninette wept. "We'll leave first thing tomorrow."

Slowly but surely, all their closest friends deserted them, phone calls went unanswered, e-mails bounced, and people blocked them on social media. Peter was isolated at school and subject to several attacks with knuckle-dusters and bottles.

Shunned, the Janssens hid away in a cocoon of guilt and with a sense of growing resentment that Nina had been forgotten in the hurricane that had overwhelmed them.

At first Peter became withdrawn, feeling he had to continually apologise for his parents' behaviour. Then someone sympathetic to his family's position contacted him and gave Peter some authors to read.

"Your family is not alone," he was told. "It is the same all over. People have had enough. It is like the poet T.S. Elliot said: 'In order to possess what you do not possess, you must go by the way of dispossession.' There are many who now share the opinions of Roeland Raes and *Voorpost*. And we are growing in number." At first, he was repulsed and decided to throw the texts away, but for some reason he did not, instead, slipping the books under his bed and trying to forget about them. But he could not.

❖ The words 'Nique la France, Fuck France!' blast out from an open top bus during an anti-racism parade through Paris.

❖ Members of the Royal Dutch Football Association symbolically "take the knee" while presenting a donation of 14 million Euro to tackle racism in soccer after Excelsior Rotterdam are subjected to monkey chants during a televised match.

❖ Chega activists in Portugal protesting against migrants landing at the Vila Real de Santo Antonio harbour are bombarded with flying bottles by Antifa and Black Bloc gangs.

❖ Greta Thunberg sings alongside the rapper Cuz on stage at her Fridays for the Future rally in central Stockholm.

❖ Chinese troops repeat the Tiananmen Square massacre of 1989 by opening fire on students protesting in Hong Kong's Times Square in Causeway Bay.

❖ The Bharatiya Janata Party warns of the rise of militant Muslim groups in the states of Uttar Pradesh, West Bengal and Bihar and indicates they have lost control of the streets of Lakshadweep and Jammu.

❖ Indian Prime Minister Narenda Modi standing on the spot where a mosque was demolished to make way for a Hindu temple in the northern city of Ayodha calls for "Peace between Hindus and Muslims while the serpent of racism coils the earth."

❖ When questioned about the gang rape of a Belgian girl in Ostend, a group of asylum seekers said, "The woman has nothing to complain about. Women must obey men," and "Rape was the most natural thing in the world."

❖ The Dutch town of Zaandam is subjected to a

reign of terror by a Muslim gang calling themselves Erdogan's Warriors.

❖ A Swedish journalist calls for all people opposing
mass Muslim immigration to be culled like brown
rats, brown being the colour associated with German nationalism.

When he began receiving rogue messages entitled "We
take the Women of the Harbi Kuffar" and opened the
photo attachments and cam-film sequences—only to be
confronted with images of his emaciated and drug-addled
sister performing sex acts with multiple men in some
squalid squat—Peter felt a serrated scissors chewing
through his intestines.

"No, no, no," the paroxysm of raw shame sounded in
the air. Smashing his mobile against the bedpost he
slumped on the pillow recognising the role he had played
in converting his country into a safari park where wild animals had been set free to roam at will and thought themselves entitled to prey upon whomever they desired.

He said nothing to his parents but went straight to the
police with the evidence. Their professional opinion was
that the image on the video-cam was inconclusive and
proved nothing.

"This could be any girl, and a good defence lawyer
would say she seems to be consenting," the sergeant said.

"That is Nina, I tell you," Peter slammed the desk, "and
you need to help me find her!"

"Do you have any idea of the scale of people-trafficking
and prostitution within a fifty-kilometre radius of this station?" a second officer interjected.

"No," Peter had to admit he could not even begin to
guess.

"We are at full stretch just to log the incidents, these
loverboys can make eight hundred euro a day off pretty
pink skin," the sergeant shrugged.

"The force can barely maintain public order in parts of
Brussels like Molenbeek," his colleague sighed, sitting

down next to Peter and casting a sympathetic eye over the girl on the screen.

Slowly, almost nervously, as if he was looking at some exotic porn pamphlet, Peter pulled out the forbidden material from under his bed and started reading Lennart Svensson's *Burning Magnesium* and *Borderline: A Traditionalist Outlook for Modern Man*, Eric Zemmour's *Le Suicide Francais* and Theo Sarrazin's *Germany Abolishes Itself* and *Wishful Thinking*. At first, he found himself shaking his head as his eyes swept over books like Rolf Peter Sieferle's *Finis Germania*, Martin Lichtmesz's *Hierarchy of Victims* and Götz Kubitschek's *Provokation*. Then, against his better judgement, line after line began to resonate with what he saw happening all around him and what his instincts had been telling him for some time. His stomach churned. Reluctantly he found his head nodding in agreement with certain paragraphs, then whole chapters and the conclusions the authors arrived at by the time he snapped shut the cover.

Scanning the alternative media like *Sezession* and *Reconquista Germanica*, a whole new world opened up before him. Instead of Taylor Swift, he started to listen to Darkwood's album *Paganism & Youth* filled with images of ravens, runes, boars and wolves, driving bass lines overlaying raw drums and soundscapes of electronica reminiscent of the 1980s. There were reviews of the Asgardsrei and Dionysian music festivals and bands like Darkthrone, Absurd, Naer Mataron, Burshtyn, M8l8th, Peste Noir and Goatmoon that filled their songs with mythological images, archetypes of the European folk tradition and references to Nietzsche, Heidegger, Evola, Jung and Spengler.

Then he came across film of immigrants using handgrenades to assault a police station in Uppsala, the Fittja gang rape in Sweden, and the raw iPhone footage of the attack outside Flinders Railway station in Melbourne, Australia. There were images of the shrapnel bomb going off in a shopping complex in St Petersburg, the nuts and bolts ripping through young girls in Manchester Arena and swords skewering revellers in Borough Market in London. While all the time the mainstream media focussed on candle lit vigils and platitudes like "We Won't Let Hate Divide Us!" and conducted interviews with London's Mayor Sadiq Khan, alongside the Muslim Mayors of Birmingham, Leeds, Blackburn, Luton, Oxford and Oldham, all of whom confirmed Islam is a religion of peace.

❖ It is estimated that the people trafficking business into Europe is worth $4 billion per anum to the smugglers.

❖ The European Commissioner for Migration, Ylva Johansson, says "EU citizens should welcome migrants and welcome people who will contribute to our economy."

❖ A rogue journalist at the *Algemeen Dagblad* newspaper exposes the fact that over two thousand Dutch girls are sold for sex every year by migrant pimps to Moroccan, Turkish, Caribbean and Roma men, one proudly claiming "Sex with schoolgirls is a very lucrative trade!"

❖ The Bouworde refugee charity that takes young Belgian volunteers to work in Morocco admits that three female volunteers have been decapitated for wearing shorts in "an act of blasphemy against The Prophet."

❖ A gang of Somalian immigrants rape a young woman at the Tapanila railway station in Finland and a fourteen-year-old girl is assaulted in Kemple by an Afghani migrant, resulting in the re-formed Soldiers of Odin extending their patrols to towns like Joensua.

❖ Programmes are arranged in Sandnes in Norway to inform immigrants about sexual behaviour in the West, with a certain Ms. Machibya, the organiser, saying "At least they will know right from wrong. They must learn that to force someone into sex is wrong."

❖ Dinko Valev obtains a helicopter gunship to support his vigilante group operating against illegal immigrants penetrating the Bulgarian border.

❖ The Danish Commissioner of Police says the volume of organised immigrant crime doubles every three years.

❖ The Islamic Council of Britain pays tribute to the martyr Khalid Masood on the anniversary of the incident on Westminster Bridge, when he killed four, injured a further forty and stabbed a policeman to death outside the Houses of Parliament in London.

❖ The Muslim Council of Belgium commemorates the memory of the Jihadist who drove a car loaded with weapons at high speed down the pedestrianized De Meir street in Antwerp in an attempt to run people down.

❖ The Muslim Council of Italy provides alms for the extended family of the African migrant whose car rammed people in Foggia, Italy.

❖ The Polish Prime Minister repeats his predecessor's response on TVN24 to the EU Commissioner's threat that his government and others would face consequences for choosing not to host refugees, by saying once again, "The Commissioner should concentrate on what to do to avoid such acts as in London. Poland will not succumb to blackmail."

❖ Hundreds of North Africans and Pakistanis riot on the Greek island of Mytilene, chanting "Jihad! Jihad!"

Just like Lewis Carroll's Alice, Peter had stepped through the mirror into another world. A world that looked very different from the one he had previously viewed through the narrow prism of his mother's Pink Floyd record collection. He began to question issues and

positions that he had once taken for granted, listening to
Roger Waters' lyrics from a less idealistic perspective:

We don't need no education
We don't need no thought control
No dark sarcasm in the classroom
Hey, teacher, leave them kids alone

The Wall began to crumble, causing a massive migraine. Good and bad merged as the brickwork fractured,
and his mother's grip on his worldview fell away.

❖ The European Commission overwhelmingly approves amendments to a resolution first introduced by British Labour MEP Claude Moraes to
   address 'structural racism' in Europe against Europeans of African descent and doubles the tariff of
   reparations for crimes against humanity during
   the European colonial epoch. Adding that Europeans of African descent should receive increased
   benefits from the current programmes to aid social integration as part of the next multi-annual financial framework.
❖ The Office of the Refugee Applications Commissioner in Ireland confirms there has been a sharp
   increase in asylum requests from Pakistan, Bangladesh, Albania, Nigeria and India. With infant
   schools in Cork, Midleton, Tralee and Munster
   having to increase their rolls to meet the demand
   for places.
❖ Spanish authorities are forced to expand Immigrant Detention Centres like that in Madrid's Alu-
   che district due to the rate of incarceration multiplying tenfold in the space of five years.
❖ Street fights break out at the main railway station
   in Budapest when migrant mobs are confronted by
   Hungarian nationalists.
❖ Police statistics released in North-Rhine Westpha-

lia indicate asylum seekers are thirteen times more likely to be responsible for sex crimes than indigenous Germans.

❖ An Afghani migrant is found guilty of raping a 78-year-old Belgian lady with a mental age of 3.

❖ The feminist Mayor of Rome stands alongside the Pope to welcome immigrants to what the ancient poets Tibullus, Virgil, Ovid and Livy called the Eternal City and the Capita Mundi, the Capital of the World.

❖ Hostilities increase around Bastia in Corsica when locals form armed militias warning ISIS to "Stay Away or Die."

❖ Quotes from the Quran are daubed on the walls of buildings in the Tympaki region of Crete: 'Allah requires from the believers to be masters of the land where they live, and only they can have property, and only they will be able to own land'; 'Allah said we should conquer the planet, and the faithful ones should own the land and the crops'; 'You are the senior people of the whole world, only your faith counts.'

At weekends he would slip away to Schilderswijk in the Hague to search for Nina, travelling by train and bus, catching the news headlines as he travelled, reading how the head of Proactiva Open Arms was warning that up to two hundred migrants might have been drowned in capsized boats because the people smugglers had overloaded vessels off the coast of Libya; that Canada had passed the M103 bill, introduced by MP Iqra Khalid, which effectively outlawed Islamaphobic comments; and the government in Ottawa had gender neutralised their national anthem, 'O Canada'; and that there had been another terrorist shooting at the Central Port d'Arras in Lille, France.

Walking across the Plein, he was struck by the contradictions all about him. The sound of the I Love Hip-Hop Festival set against the majestic Medieval Binnenhof and the statue celebrating the founding of the Kingdom of Holland. The baroque architecture juxtaposed with the hundreds and thousands of Turkish, Moroccan and Surinamese faces swarming over Orange Square and the Station Holland Spoor.

He already knew that Oude Centrum was a poor neighbourhood, but entering the Gravenzandelaan district he was soon immersed in the exotic atmosphere of the Souq. His nostrils filled with the smells and tastes of moon pies, sizzling lamb kebabs and the blow-back from shisha pipes. The pavements were littered with colourful baskets full of coriander, ginger and bay leaves. Stall after stall strung with red chillies and green peppers. Peter could have been in Tripoli, Byblos or Marrakech. Surrounded by hanging rails crammed with cheap nylon clothing, children begging and animals scurrying underfoot. Fake brands were everywhere, rolled carpets leaning like fedayeen sentinels against the walls of narrow alleyways.

He stopped to watch a woman prepare Pau Bhaji, stirring onion and mashed potato in a large metal pan, tomato-stained fingers squeezing grains of roasted garam masala and grated nutmeg into the mix. A cardamom cloud enveloped him. Jugs of lime water passing back and forth in the shade of the blue domed mosque on Bloemfonteinstraat.

Moving through Kortenbus he witnessed the number of naked women plying their trade in the windows along Doublestraat, Geleenstraat and Rivierenbuurt. Young men passed out flyers boldly proclaiming, 'Porno Joe is Back' and the release of a new titillating title called *Donkey*.

Peter came across white girls on the corners of Torenstraat and Prisengracht, most of whom looked happy to be there. While others sporting black-current bruises and carelessly covered suture marks, seemed less so, their mood betrayed by darting eyes and turning heads, looking out for their procurers. A roughly made-up whore wearing a canvas jacket and black stockings wobbled on broken heels towards him.

"Want some?" she enquired through broken teeth and purple gums. Peter shook his head and moved away, hearing the girl call "There are boys too if you swing that way."

He noticed 'Justice for Mitch Henrique!' was crawled on the walls along the Lijnbaan, and Peter remembered poor Mitch was asphyxiated just like George Floyd while in the process of being arrested nearby. His mind ran circles as he wandered, eyes zooming in on the shadowed recesses of broken buildings, ears pricked, expecting to hear the swoosh of a bottle attack.

Then, as twilight settled and the cockroaches began to crawl over the Buitenhof, he took a seat in a small streetside bar. Observing the night life around him. The drunks and the drug addicts, the beggars and the sufis of the bazaar.

His presence was soon noticed by some young Mohamamdan toughs, their hair greased back in stylised imitation of their Italian counterparts from the backstreets of Palermo.

Taking the empty seats at his table, they insisted on knowing what he was doing there.

"Where you from?" they kept asking. "Our elders been telling us you been walking about all day, asking questions." Their leader, who proudly introduced himself as Riz, lifted Peter's bottle and tipped it out on the floor. "Are you a policeman?"

When Peter sat back and rattled off his anti-establishment credentials, they burst out laughing.

"Fucker," they said, "this is our place now. Our streets, our food, our ways. We have everything we want, including your women. We don't need your political bullshit anymore. We dip our beards in your gravy and shit in your mouths!"

"But" Peter said, before a hand smelling of sumac slapped his face, the acid voice hissing low and confidently "I will close my eyes and count to five, and when I look again, you'd better be gone!"

When he got home and switched on his computer, he watched an old Dutch Freedom Party video that the censors had overlooked on YouTube:

According to the UN the population of Africa will quadruple by the end of the century. From one to four billion people. Many want to come our way, to Europe, to the Netherlands where our ancestors with hard labour have built a welfare state for us and our children. A demographic tsunami from Africa is heading towards us. Our population is in danger of being replaced and many of the immigrants are Muslims and bring even more Islamic traits with them. We do not want that. We have to stop the African stampede and the consequent Islamization because more Islam will lead to more intolerance, oppression of women, homosexuals and Christians. More violence and terror. In the Netherlands everything we have built is in danger of being washed away. Last year over 180,000 Africans crossed from Libya to Europe. They come as asylum seekers to the EU member states. We do not want that. We want to send them back as Australia has, with success. Close the borders, as Hungary does, with success. If we fail to do so, we will cease to exist. We will be colonized and Islamized. Therefore the PVV says: Stop! Close the borders. Send criminals and illegals out of the country. We must de-Islamize the Netherlands because the Netherlands is ours!

❖ It is estimated that 1500 migrants to Belgium have returned to fight for Islamic State in Syria.
❖ A Muslim journalist who went undercover to report on extremism in the Molenbeek community over ten years ago, repeats her warning, "War is Coming!"
❖ Matasser Al De'emeh at the University of Antwerp

says of North African asylum seekers, "They don't feel Moroccan or Belgian. They don't feel part of either society."

❖ Belgian Foreign Minister Didier Reynders is shouted down for speaking about the strong links between radical Islamic terrorists and criminal fraternities.

❖ The image of the Lebanese terrorist Georges Ibrahim Abdullah, responsible for the mid-1980s bombing in Rue de Rennes in Paris, is featured on leaflets exhorting immigrant communities to resist institutional racism and state oppression.

❖ Two gay men are beaten almost to death by Muslim youths in Arnhem in Holland.

❖ ISIS sympathisers march on the anniversary of the truck killing of pedestrians on the Drottningsgatan in Stockholm.

❖ A woman from Guinea-Bissau who leads Portugal's far-Left LIVRE party insists Europe has never been a white continent and can never be democratic without the input of black women.

❖ The words of former French diplomat, Simon de Galbert, who wrote "Today, the terrorists are trying to create disunity in France, trying to turn the French against the Muslim minority, trying to create a *de facto* conflict of civilizations . . . A lot of people realize this is not an end but the beginning of something that will last far longer," are quoted on alternative media channels.

Peter could see the storm clouds gathering. He tried to talk to Ninette, but she seemed to be in total denial.

"Mother," he found himself confessing, "I think we are wrong." She would shake her head in reply to his questions. "They are not all like that. There are more good than bad just like everywhere."

"And the ones who took Nina?"

"They are just like Marc Dutroux, and he was white!"

"But he was one psychopathic criminal. This is wide-spread and organised!"
"You can't say that. You shouldn't say that!"
"Even if it is true?"
Ninette looked away unable to meet his eyes.

❖ An imam says "According to the hadith the law states that anyone who did not participate in the raid does not get to share in the booty. This is well known. Let's say we invade a country with a population of half a million. What should we do with them? We check how many mujahideen there were. Let's say there were 100,000. That's it then. Each one gets five, but there can be a variety. You can take two men, two women, and a child or the other way around. You divide them up. Great!"

❖ President Tayyip Erdogan says in response to what is reported in the media as the rising tide of populism in the West, "If Europe continues this way, no European in any part of the world can walk safely on the streets."

❖ French philosopher Bernard-Henri Lévy repeats comments that he feels closer to the Islamists than the National Rally as they are just the Front National in disguise.

❖ Brigitte Bardot, who once said "I can't look at this anymore, the Islamists. Practically everywhere in France you see burkas, it's unacceptable. Let them do what they want in their country of origin, but they shouldn't try and impose on us customs, practices, discriminations from another age: that's not France," is held up for constant ridicule by commentators and comedians on *France 24*.

❖ A decadent French writer who authored a book about his country submitting to Islam is forced into hiding when a fatwa is issued against him.

Slowly but surely Peter's spine began to stiffen. Out of

pure anger and a sense of responsibility for his sister, a nascent form of vigilantism, fired by guilt, crept through him. Peter went searching on the internet for other like-minded people and made the acquaintance of groups who operated on the fringe of the Verdinaso and Volksunie traditions.

At first, he felt like a traitor to his mother's beliefs and would avoid talking to her about where he was going and what he was doing. He knew she would see him as contaminated. Despite all that had happened, she still clung to the notion that anybody who stood to the right of Bruno Tuybens had gone over to the Worms:

Waiting to put on a blackshirt
Waiting to weed out the weaklings
Waiting to smash in their windows
And kick in their doors
Waiting for the final solution
To strengthen the strain
Waiting for the worms.
Waiting to turn on the showers
And fire the ovens
Waiting for the queens and coons
And the reds and the Jews
Waiting to follow the worms.

But the fact was he was talking to men and women and boys and girls just like himself, not the demon-worshipping nightmares he had been led to believe: veterans whose predecessors had been involved with acts like operation Wolfsangel repatriating the bodies of patriots like Cyriel Verschaeve, Staf De Clercq and Anton Mussert to Flemish soil. People who regularly made the pilgrimage to the River Izer at Diksmuide. Belgians, Dutch and French of all ages who had become familiar with the work of Bob Maes, Roger Spinnewyn and his son John from Loppem in West Flanders, who had suffered for years at the hands of their national governments and their paymasters; individuals who had been mocked and incarcerated for speaking out about the violent societal fragmentation they witnessed on the streets. Everyone knew whole suburbs had begun to resemble the chaos of Haiti and Jamaica, but it was made abundantly clear that anyone pointing out the fact that multiculturalism was an 'Emperor that had no clothes' was setting himself up for vilification, if not criminal prosecution.

He came to see how his teachers were either terrified of losing their jobs or brainwashed into regurgitating the state's egalitarian values. In class, they were taught to attribute the achievements of the Greek, Roman and the Ptolemaic Egyptian cultures to post-Iranian or Nubian peoples regardless of how tenuous the anthropological claim. Inconvenient facts such as the evidence that the Sumerians of ancient Ur buried thousands of people alive with their deceased sovereigns was overlooked. The number of cultural exhibitions that were run in major museums and art festivals, enthusiastically sponsored by multinational corporations to encourage respect for primitive daubings and sculptures that Cro-Magnon man would have found intellectually unchallenging, increased dramatically. Iconic anti-colonialist writers with a self-righteous bent were vigorously portrayed as arbiters of good taste, while more recent history was taught solely through the lens of racism, sexism and socio-economic disadvantage.

Peter had already started to tune out of the mainstream by the time the Russian Duma began expressing concerns over the consequences of the EU's social policies and NATO military manoeuvres in Poland, which were not just escalating tensions in Central Europe but also destabilising the Balkans and the fragile ceasefire in Eastern Ukraine.

❖ US and Israeli intelligence sources indicate Russia is planning large scale military operations by creating a further 25 Division formations of 15 Brigades, while raising manpower by 100,000, leading to serious concerns that Putin's government is preparing to wage large-scale protracted war on the Soviet model.

❖ The United Kingdom renews claims that the Not-Petya cyber-attacks on its defence systems originates from Russia.

❖ The CIA claim that skeleton units are being prepared in the West and South of Russia for sudden mass mobilization as practised in the 2016 Kavkaz exercises.

❖ CNN news journalists claim that the number of cyber strikes against Ukraine has risen to over 6,500 in the last 12 months, including concerns that the Kyiv power grid is vulnerable to interference.

❖ The American administration sends a flotilla of vessels to support the USS Carl Vinson in the South China Sea

❖ And in response:

❖ The HQ of the Russian 20ᵗʰ Army is moved to within 10 kilometers of the Ukrainian border.

❖ Moscow announces the Russian navy is prioritizing ships capable of carrying troops that can conduct amphibious landings to places of conflict.

❖ Russia sends tanks to the town of Pokrovskoye in southern Rostov-on-Don, and Airborne VDV forces to Belarus.

❖ Beijing's warships circle Sydney Harbour like sharks hunting prey while the Australian Prime Minister holidays in the Solomon Islands.

Peter's new acquaintances invited him to private meetings of the Schild & Vrienden in Ghent and the re-formed Vlaams Nationaal Verbond. In dimly lit back rooms he was introduced to underground magazines like *Vouloir*, *Exil*, *Krisis*, *Joven Europa* and *Elements*. He would sit at home, his face locked on the screen, absorbing Raymond

Abellio, Pierre Plantard and Jean Parvulesco. Slowly but surely the scales fell from his eyes, and he recognised that the news channels no longer performed their intended function. Propaganda poured out of the controlled outlets extolling the virtues of a dystopian multicultural paradigm that did not exist beyond the Potemkin-like structures of political correctness, while the same controlling parties who branded dissidents as criminals or worse were openly celebrating the fact they were importing immigrant voters to guarantee their long-term political hegemony under the cloak of so called humanitarianism and liberal democracy. Peter sneered when he saw on the news that border controls were to be relaxed even further under the pretext of allowing the free flow of skilled workers. For it was now hard for him to see how an illiterate Bantu from a desolate village in sub-Saharan Africa could contribute very much to the high-tech computer software or biotechnology industries. The capitalists' claims began to sound hollow. More often than not he would witness the immigrant children begging and stealing in the city centre while their parents squatted in line outside social security offices. Hundreds upon hundreds haggled over dice among the crumbling tenements along the Waalsestraat.

His ears rang with Green Party MEP Daniel Cohn-Bendit's continued demands that "We, the Greens, have to make sure to get as many immigrants as possible into Germany. If they are in Germany, we must fight for their right to vote, we need to change this republic." For the first time, he now saw his former heroes for what they were and recognised the hypocrisy and duplicity of people like Danny the Red, the former anarchist and Parisian denizen of 1968 who some said tried to justify sex with children.

From there it was only a short step into what he had previously considered to be dark space. He began to think more carefully about the guilt or innocence of men like Pierre Daye, Robert Poulet, the author of *Handji*, Raymond de Becker, the man who wrote *The New Order* and

Paul Colin of *Cassandre* fame.

His new friends in the reformed Vlaamse Militanten Ordre showed Peter how he had been programmed to take part in the equivalent of the Orwellian Two-Minutes Hate every day with a visceral Pavlovian vigour each time he was shown the face of particular political actors or certain trigger words were used.

Realising whatever was criticised by the authorities may actually offer an alternative perspective on the reality of the world being beamed 24/7 through the media was a liberating experience. His mind drifted back to a quote from Plato, "Strange times are these in which we live when old and young are taught falsehoods in school. And the person that desires to tell the truth is called at once a liar and a fool."

Hanging out with people listening to Brigade M's lyrics "Everywhere you go the same logos and names you'll see the indoctrination by radio and TV, multi-national monsters dominate the scenery, they divide the market without penalty."

While down at the Bibliothek de Arend he began requesting the writings of the pre-Socratics, John of Salisbury, Gilbert of Tournai and Thomas Occleve. From there his tastes rapidly matured in the direction of Thomas Hobbes, Carlyle and Edmund Burke. Sitting one day on a crumpled cushion, reflecting on the raised eyebrows of the librarians as they passed his books through the checkout counter, he began to flick through a tower of texts by Heinrich Von Trietschke, Ernst Jünger, Tomislav Sunic and the enigmatic Ulick V.

* The EU enacts economic sanctions against companies investing in the Czech Republic, Hungary and Poland after they continue to ignore calls to take in migrants.
* A church in Budapest cancels a ceremony to honour Miklós Horthy after pressure from Brussels.
* Tivadar Kossuth's depiction of Europa bestriding a

horse, while looking down on a line of Muslim refugees and a bedraggled image of Angela Merkel is removed from the entrance to the Kehidakustany spa in western Hungary.

❖ Speaking at the UN Security Council, Said Ben Assi accuses Hungary's Fidesz Party, My Homeland and the Movement for a Better Hungary of conducting acts of genocide in the countryside around Gyula.

❖ American Special Forces working in collaboration with Interpol and Mossad conduct dawn raids to arrest members of the Knights Templar International at a range of locations all over Europe.

❖ The Pope excommunicates the author of the text *Catholic and Identitarian* and retrospectively sanctions the long-deceased Jean Ousset and Xavier Vallat of the Cité Catholique.

❖ A British national and former M.E.P. is subjected to extrajudicial rendition after he is held by Navy Seal Team 6 in a small farmhouse in the Zemplen Tokaj mountains and ownership of his book *Deus Vult: Reconquista of the West* is subject to a mandatory prison sentence.

❖ A German female Identitarian activist narrowly evades assassination on the Bulgarian border after the annual Lukov March organised by local patriots is suddenly outlawed by an amendment to Article 108(1) of the Bulgarian Penal Code.

Stigmatised at school because of the court case and the press attention it drew, Peter was forced to home-school, sitting his entrance exams under direct tutorial supervision, answering the one-dimensional questions in order to go to the University of Groningen to study for a bachelor's degree in political economy.

Then one morning the formal confirmation he had been accepted arrived by e–mail. His excitement was only tempered by the heartbreak of leaving his parents. He could tell they were suffering terribly, waking every morning in the hope Nina would be returned home, collapsing into fitful sleep at night thinking of the torments their daughter might be undergoing at that very moment. Peter himself remained sullen and silent, loath to openly admit to them how he felt about the family's collective guilt for her fate.

Verbum Domini Lucerna Pedibus Nostris
"The word of the Lord is a light at our feet"
Motto of the University of Groningen

During the first week at college, he attended an inaugural lecture by a guest professor from Bacha Khan University in Peshawar on the Islamic history of the Medieval Crusades. Then, while sitting in the student centre on Uurwerkersgang 10, he read how the University thinks it is important for students to "develop their potential and look beyond borders." His eyes drawn to the Groningen Life website with stories about how the faculty and student union were supporting the embattled Soros-funded Central European University in Budapest who were daring to challenge the authoritarian government of Hungary.

Sit-ins were organized by the faculty of Social Sciences and Social Behaviour in the Heymans building on Grote Kruisstraat, marches were held on the Boteringestraat and a tent-city of black flags established in Academy Square right under the office of the Rector Magnificus.

Flicking through his first semester study modules, it soon became apparent that his elective choices were restricted to a feminist interpretation of how the patriarchy had permeated the structure of Western democratic governmental instruments and Institutions, a case study of immigrant children and their fight against racist citizenship laws and a post-Marxian analysis of socio-economic tensions between colonisers and colonized in Africa and the New World.

Having collected the books on the recommended reading lists in the central library and making small talk with other fresher students in the coffee corners lit by flat screens beaming service level agreements and rules and regulations with pixelated precision, he returned to his shared flat amongst the locals.

❖ The Russian banking system wilts under the sanctions imposed by the US and EU and economic pressure from world markets.

❖ Simultaneously inflation across the Russian Federation climbs to 18.5%.

❖ Despite sending the first man into space and producing 27 Nobel Prize winners in the economics and sciences the Moscow Stock Exchange does not list a single large scale home-grown manufacturing company.

❖ The outflow of capital from Russia rises to $10 billion in two years.

❖ Putin's disapproval rating quadruples as economic and political crises grow following the second wave of Covid-19 infections and his performance on the Direct-Line with Vladimir Putin phone-in across Russia 11 time-zones is described in even the Kremlin-friendly *Komsomolskaya Pravda* newspaper as unconvincing.

❖ Putin's advisers openly discuss the problem of the working age population decreasing by 870,000 per year, the equivalent of a 1% loss per annum, in a debate on state TV.

❖ Issur Babel argues that the only way to fill this skill-gap is to welcome mass immigration from the south and east.

Peter recognised his former self in the goateed Leftist students who parroted the views of unrepentant Marxist lecturers in group discussions. When Peter naively dared to counter their uncritical diatribes by using libertarian arguments from notables like Ludwig von Mises they did not want to engage, referring to such people as pathological. He soon realised the majority of the students like the faculty were totally committed to the current ideological dogmas:

BLACK IS WHITE
WHITE IS BLACK
ONE GENDER
ONE RACE

The teachers responded like decrepit Soviet apparatchiks: at best relativists, at worst frauds, writing papers on philosophers like Marcuse, Marxist deconstructionists like Terry Eagleton and anthropologists like Alexander Goldenweiser; attending conferences and dinners in honour of Max Horkheimer, Leo Lowenthal and Sigmund Freud; offering themselves in their spare time to Multicultural Dictation Services and Asylum Seeker Resource Centres. He saw how they easily moulded their student protégés, who were transmogrifying into pseudomorphous Calibans within a single generation.

Trotskyite groups began to target him and several other students for their outspoken views. Trying to avoid confrontation, he sat amongst a small like-minded crowd in the front row before the lectern. Soon paper cups full of water began to rain down on them. Chants of "Hitler's children" dying down as the politics professor entered the class.

Leaving, the dissidents formed a tight compact group to push their way through the blocked doorway. "We know you Janssen!" went the spite-filled whisper, "You are a turncoat and a traitor." Then as a fist split his lip, there was a sudden commotion.

"Bitch!" someone shouted as a small girl with a straw-coloured pony-tail bit the arm of Peter's assailant.

"Coward!" she replied, staring them down outside the auditorium. The Trotskyites backed away.

"You've got girls fighting for you," they mocked. Wiping his bloodied mouth, Peter went to thank his protector, but she had already merged into the ant-like column of students moving along the passageway.

❖ Plummeting oil prices reduce Russian GDP by 43% in a single trade cycle.

❖ Power outages result in hospitals closing for periods of time in Moscow and other major cities.

❖ Average annual income in Russia drops to the $8,000 after a peak of $13,000 only two years earlier.

❖ The EU bans meat and poultry product sales to Russia.

❖ The Russian government decreases investment in economic infrastructure as a result of the dramatic increase in military expenditure.

❖ It is estimated that more than 50% of all Russians depend on the state for a living, 40% on social benefits and 12% as state employees.

❖ Haunted by the memory of the 74% fall in the Moscow Stock Exchange in 2008 Putin looks to shore-up falling economic confidence by courting the sixty-nine billionaires resident in Moscow.

One day when he had been wandering aimlessly, fists thrust deep into the bottomless pockets of his old black raincoat, collar buttoned up to the chin, his stomach told him it was time to head for the refectory. He stood, shiny tray in hand, amid excited young people smelling of beer and cigarettes. That is when he noticed the young woman who had intervened in the struggle a few weeks before. Peter girded his loins and leaned forward in an attempt to make conversation.

"I did not get a chance to thank you for the other day," he said. He was partially rewarded with a tentative smile, and they sat together to eat.

"I am Senka," she said as a belated introduction.

"Peter," he replied, "Peter Janssen."

"'I know, but your friends spell your name, P.I.G" she giggled sarcastically. He noticed she had a foreign accent, narrow shoulders trapped under a figure-hugging leather jacket and a double-headed eagle badge on her lapel.

"Where are you from?" he asked.

"Serbia."

"You've come a long way!"

"Not far enough!"

"What do you mean?"

"There's a reason why I did what I did. The same sort of people who were pushing you about in the lecture hall have been pushing me and my people around for years."

Peter's imagination was piqued. He was all ears. Over a drink in the local bar on the Noorderhaven, Senka told him how she had enjoyed walking along the canals until she saw how men would come up to her. When she spoke to them, she noticed their attitude change, thinking she was just another one of the East European girls working in the city's sex trade. Peter nodded, all too familiar with the poor girls from Ukraine and Moldova who swarmed the back alleys, trafficked by Albanian pimps who shared the same parasitic scruples as horseflies. They took in a movie. His abiding memory of the film was the scene where a little girl gives apples to a boy on the other side of a barbed wire fence. Later Senka took him back to her small room in a student apartment block. After making him a hot drink she talked about her childhood in the village, the wide streets with goose cropped verges and plum, walnut and mulberry trees, the wooden houses with narrow gates opening onto flower gardens and chickens pecking at the ground around the stables, barn and pigsty. "My parents and grandparents would work the jutros," she recalled, little strips of land left by Tito for the peasants after they had collectivised the land formerly owned by the Germans. "I would go to the market with them, playing with balloons, while they set their stall to trade for goods. I can remember on cold winter nights returning home and smelling the wood smoke rolling towards me. The air was filled with the smell of roasting pig when it was svinjokolja." After a while Senka got lyrical, her vocal cords quivering like the traditional one-stringed gusla, talking late into the night about Tsar Lazar and his valiant knights riding to their doom on the Field of Kosovo, quoting the lines:

Dear God, what shall I do and how shall I?
Which kingdom shall I choose?
Shall I choose the earthly kingdom?
Or shall I choose the heavenly kingdom?
The earthly kingdom lasts only for a brief time
But the heavenly kingdom always and forever . . .

After a few glasses of vodka she reminisced about her grandparents and how their village was exterminated by the Islamic warlord Naser Oric's raiding parties. Peter remembered reading how the European Union had encouraged mass demonstrations against Serb atrocities in Izbica and Cuska. He now realised the media had studiously ignored the Muslim Kosovan Liberation Army's attacks in the Drenica Valley. The news channels choosing to castigate Serb leaders like Slobodan Milosevic and Vojislav Seslj as war criminals. His mind was full of screeching protestors attacking Serbian Embassies all around the world, shouting "Nazi Serbs out of Europe!"

"The Srebrenica Massacre cuts both ways," Senka cursed, "Like Dobrica Cosic said in 1977, Internationalism has ruined the Serb nation. False guilt was built up to justify American bombings on behalf of those Bosnian bandits. Now they have sentenced Radavan Karadzic to forty years and Atifete Jahjaga proclaims himself President of the Free State of Kosovo. Just look at the thousands of Kosovars now pouring into Hungary, bringing their Albanian kanun blood-feud mentality to Europe, and leaving behind them smouldering Christian places of worship like the Church of the Holy Archangel Michael in the small town of Stimlje, just thirty kilometres from Pristina!"

"I have seen the results myself," he said, "there is a

flood of Afghani heroin coming through Kosovo into Europe!"

"But did you know the Americans have some of their largest military bases there?"

"No?"

"They have Camp Bondsteel and Camp Monteith within striking distance of the KLA and ISIL training centres at Ferizaj, Gjakovica and Prizren."

"There is certainly lots of internet chatter about the CIA funding DAESH," Peter said.

"It is not all conspiracy theory," Senka snapped back. "There are hundreds of massive steel-fabricated mosques being built all across the Balkans. There's an Italian air force base next door to the ISIS camp in Gjakovica, for God's sake!" Then, her voice rising, "The St Nicholas church in Pristina was daubed with the words ISIS IS COMING!"

"Is it all about the oil and gas pipelines?" Peter asked.

"I think so. I was told Camp Bondsteel is the biggest encampment the US has operated outside their borders since the Vietnam War!"

"That is a big strategic investment of manpower and equipment," her companion whistled.

"You're telling me, and it is why Hillary Clinton made all those promises about helping Kosovo join the EU back in 2010 when she was Secretary of State. Bondsteel covers off the South Stream pipelines, the Black Sea, Suez and Mediterranean hinterland. It is also within a few hours striking distance of the Balkan capitals."

"A prime location, then."

"Well, the Americans have over 17,000 soldiers there, the British 13,000, Italy and France 10,000 each and now the Germans have come in with another 9,000."

"They are expecting something to kick off?" Peter surmised.

"They want something to kick off. That is why they are baiting the Russians."

"And the Serbs are closely aligned with the Russians."

"They are our brothers," Senka sighed, brandishing a copy of Milorad Pavic's *Dictionary of the Khazars* under his nose. Then, after a rousing defence of her people, Peter was expelled, sexually un-satiated, and cast out into the cold dark air.

❖ Branco Milanovic's article about the potential for future wars in the Balkans is re-circulated among dissenters on the internet.

❖ The President of the Republika Srpska is questioned about money-laundering operations by police in Sarajevo.

❖ Albanian nationalists demand the Sar Mountains as rightfully theirs.

❖ Leading politicians in Macedonia become embroiled in a scandal involving mass secret surveillance of citizens when tapes are leaked to the media.

❖ Ethnic divisions in Bosnia-Herzegovina result in violent street protests in Banja Luka, Tuzla and Bihac. Over 500 fatalities are recorded by the Red Cross in Travnik.

❖ Sweden's Security Service broadens the definition of Right-wing extremism to include verbal resistance to LGBT+ activism and feminism.

❖ The EU commissions the consulting firm Deloitte to analyse the viability of introducing Prum II, to include facial recognition, DNA databases and vehicular registration as a means to ensure social cohesion across the member states.

❖ Maddalena Marini, a postdoctoral researcher at the Italian Institute of Technology, contends that decades of attempts to alter people's racist stereotypes and prejudices have failed because those instinctive responses are hard-wired into the human mind. Instead she proposes to "change the biological portions of the brain responsible for generating such instincts," by means of transcranial electric or magnetic currents. "Thus we can eradicate the prejudice that leads to associating acts of terrorism with being Arab."

He continued to meet with Senka for several weeks. They would walk around the city, reading that month's digitised message on the telescreens:

DIVERSITY IS STRENGTH
EQUALITY IS EVERYTHING
DIGNITY FOR ALL

before returning to her room to discuss Balkan history, Nikola Pasic's Radical Party and the terrorist activities of Narodna Odbrana. One night, after he had told her about his sister, he was allowed to share her bed.

"I understand," she said while his tears flowed. "Both my mother and my grandmother were raped by the KLA."

In the early hours of the morning she asked him if he would like to hear a close comrade of the famous Horst Mahler speak at a secret training camp in the Black Forest. He hesitated just for a moment, realising this was an enormous step. Then looking into her determined eyes, knowing he could not resist her, Peter nodded his acquiescence. Striding toward danger, his excited body responded with an affirmative surge of warm semen.

CROSSING THE RUBICON

"Now is the time for a dissident generation to rise."

—Guillaume Faye

Two days later they were following the A5 to the Southwest, moving slowly towards the craggy Feldberg in a broken bus that leaked oil and suffered with back-crunching suspension. Stopping in Calw, the birthplace of Hermann Hesse, Senka began to read a copy of *Demian* she had found buried away on a shelf in a dusty second-hand bookshop. Peter was ploughing through some pamphlets by Irving Fetscher and Günter Rohrmoser that fellow travellers were passing around. Exchanging smiles over a shared cigarette, they pulled up in a small leafy glade at the side of a dirt track. Through the mud-splattered window they could see something akin to Kommune 1, an anarchist assortment of eclectic people talking and laughing as they cooked on campfires, walked about with carved wooden staves and drank home-made beer. Stepping out, they were both conscious of the fragrant pine smoke swirling up through the trees and the rumbling of their empty stomachs. After being greeted by their host, a Viennese gentleman with white hair and an immaculately trimmed beard, they ate with young women in braids and were taken to a meadow where they camped out under the stars.

He felt completely at ease until they attended seminars by an English-born leader of a small groupuscule giving a talk about eco-paganism and the grand-daughter of a post war communist concentration camp survivor who provided an oral history of the deliberate starvation and ethnic cleansing of millions of Swabian Germans along the length of the Danube after 1945. Senka sat shame-faced knowing her people had committed such acts.

"I had no idea," he whispered across the pillow to Senka.

"There are many bitter and untold truths we all have to face about the Second World War," she confessed.

The next afternoon they got involved in a mind weaponization programme and studied the philosophical works of Abdul Ala Maududi. Peter shivered when they were told "Your duty as part of the movement will be to participate in collective action and the internal and external insurgency process. Your commitment will be full engagement with the nativist fighting guerrilla—unity of will —the end of the false division between classes—the determination to act on behalf of your people in a world increasingly hostile to their survival."

"There is a line I cannot cross," he admitted to his partner over lunch the following day. Then, in the late afternoon as sunlight streamed over the nearby river they were lectured about the legacy of the martyred Francois Duprat, his work with Occident, Ordre Nouveau, and the publication *L'Action Europeen*.

"Does everyone understand?" the speaker asked to shouts of approval. Peter remained silent as Senka led him by the hand to a secluded glade where they both fired handguns. Then they left, having agreed to distribute copies of *Junge Freiheit*, a student journal from Freiburg, on their Groningen campus.

Sitting in the back of the bus with Senka in his arms he told her again propaganda was fine, but he would not countenance violence.

"Sometimes," she breathed in his ear, "we have no alternative."

❖ ISIS declares it will remove all Coptic Christians from Egypt by force of the sword.

❖ Saudi Arabia's Grand Mufti, Abdullah bin Aziz, speaking at the Supreme Council of the Ulema, demands all Christian churches on the Arabian Peninsula be destroyed.

❖ The CIA deny accusations that they are fomenting the ongoing riots in Iran.

❖ Charges are brought against the former head of the French National Front for allegedly denying the French nation's collective guilt for the round-up of 13,000 Jews in the Paris Velodrome in 1942, an event known as the Velodrome d'Hiver, which former President Jacques Chirac described as a "stain on French history."

❖ Islamic terrorists attempt to bomb the buses of Bundesliga football teams in Leipzig and Dortmund.

❖ Shockwaves run across Europe as President Macron and his Prime Minister Edouard Philippe are assassinated during an attempted coup d'etat by Right-wing elements within the French army. Once the situation is stabilised, following intervention by the American military, a relative unknown with a similar Rothschild pedigree to his predecessor, going by the name of Belaire, takes over leadership of En Marche and assumes the mantle of 'Leader of the Nation.'

❖ Macron's digital coordinator, Yair Eigner, tweeting "Our Young Napoleon is gone but his legacy goes on."

❖ Presidential spokesperson Seth Dropkin calls for "unity among all French people."

President Belaire addresses the nation in a televised broadcast from the courtyard of the Louvre Museum:

My compatriots, it is time for the real France to stand up. The plague of populism must be extinguished, not just here in France but across Europe and indeed the whole world. I will endeavour to work with colleagues in the European Parliament to achieve this goal. I will not rest until the scourge of uncertainty, the festering boil that these people inhabit, is answered with a clear vision. It is true that technological innovation is impacting employment. It is true that the governments of countries with fast-growing populations such as those in the Middle East, where over 40% of the people are under twenty-five, are struggling to create sufficient economic opportunities to satisfy the hunger and ambitions of their people. And yes, with the advent of Covid pandemics, there is a real danger of a slide back into poverty and degradation. But this is an opportunity and not a threat. We have already overcome those who would have us build walls in an attempt to segregate whole communities in our newly found global village. We have passed laws against people who put out false news and information to create alternative online communities. And I promise we will continue this struggle. There will be no Us and Them. No Left and Right. No urban versus rural or ethnic and religious versus the majority. We seek, as per our forefathers like Maximilien Robespierre, Georges Danton and Jean-Paul Marat, to create a new thermidor to incinerate the enemies of equality!

NEWSPEAK!

"We must not let our opponents, Marxists and Regimists, the monopoly of the historical representation of men, facts and ideas. Because history is a wonderful instrument of war, and it would be useless to deny that one of the important reasons of our political hardships resides in the historical exploitation and the systemic defamation of the nationalist experiences of the past . . ."

—Francois Duprat, May 1976

Back at the University, in the second semester, Peter commenced a dissertation on Tito's extermination camps at Gakowa and Jarek in Yugoslavia. His supervisor was perturbed and took him aside.

"Do you really want to do this?" he asked. "It will bring trouble."

"Trouble?" Peter replied.

"Yes, for you and me. These are issues best forgotten."

"But more German people died after the war than during the action. Have you not heard of the Feld des Jammers near Bretzenheim or the Rheinwiesen POW Camp near Bad Kreuznach? The Allies threw aside their supposed values, the Atlantic Charter, the Four Freedoms and the Geneva Convention. Innocent women and children were deliberately used as slave labour and starved to death." The supervisor looked nervously from side to side and then up and down the corridor. He pointed at a sign hanging above the student notice boards. It read: "Freedom to Speak does not Mean Freedom to Lie."

"It was the war! Think of what the Einsatzgruppen did!"

"And to counterbalance that, people need to know about allied bombing raids like Dresden and the sinking of the refugee ship Wilhelm Gustloff. Then there's the repatriation of millions of white Russians packed into cattle-trucks heading straight for Stalin's acid baths and Gulags!"

"Belsen and Treblinka!"

"Experts have been revising the Auschwitz numbers for years. The Soviets claimed four million, more recently experts have said it was only one and a half. The Red Cross even fewer."

"Anti-Semites make that case," the Professor said as he went back to his office and closed the door.

Reacting to the politically correct directives of the ever-so-liberal university, Peter and Senka formed an alternate student society called Le Rat Noir. Funding to publish a newsletter or a journal was denied them by the college union because it was defined as a hate group. Meanwhile, thousands of Euros were given to Black Lives Matter leaders to buy uniforms for their paramilitary parades and posters featuring the faces of King and Mandela advertising meetings for a diversity circle where attendance was morally obligatory was supported to the tune of over ten thousand Euros.

Frustrated, Peter instigated a search for a private sponsor for his journal and quickly found one in the Matsloot district who immediately insisted on anonymity. Within a month volume one was rolling off the press and being distributed by a small group of enthusiastic volunteers. A website was also launched and was firewalled sufficiently to prevent the initial attempts at sabotage by a group of hackers masquerading under the ironic name Crusaders for Free Speech.

He noticed that quite soon after this his essays and project work began coming back late and with lower marks than he had been anticipating. When he asked for feedback about his grades, he was met by formal sounding e-mails and cold letters from his tutors. Then came invitations to meet with two or more faculty at a time, each confirming and validating the marks of the other verbally, followed by an e-transcript of the meeting within 24 hours.

"It is standard procedure," they said. But when he asked his fellow students, no one, even the most difficult and disgruntled, indicated they had experienced anything remotely similar. In response Le Rat Noir hijacked a solemn procession of professors and doctorates preening in their black and crimson regalia outside the annual graduation ceremony. The protesters waved banners that read "Free Thought—Not Controlled Thought." This led to some minor scuffles with university stewards, as the Rector Magnificus read out the award of a Honourary Doctorate for George Floyd, *in absentia.*

❖ Hydrologists indicate mounting pressure on freshwater resources will increase the chances of international conflict in Himalayan Asia because of increasing consumption due to population growth.

❖ Trans-boundary river disputes in Asia are given, along with the rising number of Covid 19 infections, as a contributing reason for the large-scale movement of people through the Tienshan, Kinlun, Hindu-Kush, Pamir and Karakoram mountain ranges.

❖ The Chinese Government states the "abode of snow is ours to protect."

❖ Environmental scientists report that pollution in the Yangtze, Huang He, Mekong, Brahmaputra, Indus, Ganges and Ama Darya rivers is at crisis level.

❖ The Chinese Communist Party orders the closure of Christian churches in Anhui, Jiangsu, Hebei and Zhejiang.

❖ The Intergovernmental Panel on Climate Change predicts "that India will reach a point of severe water stress before 2025."

❖ Billionaire carbon trading profiteers and giant alternative energy corporations reward Greta Thunberg with sponsorship of a Chair at Heidelberg University's new faculty of Low Carbon Sustainability. The young protégé's inaugural lecture on "The Racist Nature of Energy Production and Consumption" being lauded in the *New York Times* and *Bild* as an exemplary piece of academic scholarship.

❖ An update on the 2011 Woodrow Wilson Centre report entitled Running on Empty confirms that the doubling of the current population of Pakistan from 187.3 million to 291 million by the mid-21st century would have significant geopolitical consequences both for the region and the world as a whole.

❖ Jose Luis Escriva, former Spanish Minister for Social Security, Inclusion and Migration, who now acts as an advisor to the EU Presidential Council, repeats his claim made some time before that "The continent of Europe needs millions of new migrants to combat the forecasted demographic decline in the native population." His co-worker Dimitris Avramopoulos said, "We are against building walls," and Jean-Claude Juncker, while attending a banquet at the Israeli embassy in Strasbourg, asserted once again, "Without millions of African migrants Europe will be lost."

Peter was temporarily suspended while a student disciplinary panel was set-up to investigate if the protest he had led contravened the Code of Student Conduct. He was convinced the hearing would go against him and while travelling home to Bruges, he began rehearsing how he would explain the whole saga to his exasperated parents.

But circumstances overtook him. Arriving on the doorstep late that morning he was greeted by his mother wailing inconsolably, holding a blood-stained package. His father wearing a grey cement grimace waving his hands.

"What is it?" he asked, almost not wanting to know, "What's happened?"

Ninette lifted the torn cardboard lid and Peter saw the small, severed finger bearing his sister's amethyst birthstone ring. His words playing back to him like Banquo's voice of conscience in Shakespeare's *Macbeth*: "War, poverty and disease have scarred them . . . You simply must keep coming back to help . . . You will never forgive yourself if you don't!"

Now it was Peter who could not forgive himself. "Have you alerted the authorities?" he kept saying in robotic shock, eyes rapidly reading a ransom note that had been wrapped around the desiccated digit.

"Ja!" Bram screamed hysterically, "But no one comes!" Peter collected his thoughts and went inside to use the landline, dialling 100 for emergency. The response was immediate.

"We have an incident," Peter explained, reeling off the address, and adding "You know us, we are on your priority response list." Silence for a moment, then a confirmation. "We will have a team with you inside the hour." Turning to his parents, he told them to lock all the doors. Then he sat them down around the kitchen table and made hot sweet tea while Ninette fumbled regrets and Bram looked at his son through glistening marble eyes.

Peter read the message out loud:

"Your girl is serving the Soldiers of Allah very good. She is grateful to our mercy to her. When you like her soul you must give 250,000 Euro money. If no, you see her parts in box by time."

Bram threw up his hands. "It is useless, we don't have money to give."

"Sell the house," Ninette thumped the table. Her husband shook his head.

"The best we could get would be one hundred and twenty thousand."

"If that is what Saad is offering, then take it!" Ninette urged.

While Peter considered all the options, his father ripped the phone out of its cradle and dialled his neighbour. It rang out. Bram punched the number again. This time Saad's voice.

"It is Bram, your neighbour . . ."

"You must not contact me," the defensive reply bounced back.

"Saad, listen, it is not like that. Your offer on our house . . ." Peter and Ninette heard Saad's tongue click hungrily on his dentures.

"Yes?"

"Does your offer still stand?"

"Which offer?"

"The last one of one hundred and twenty thousand?"

"No, new offer, now!" Bram's expression said it all.

"Ninety thousand, no more!" Peter shook his head. Bram looked at Ninette. Her chin tilted towards her breastbone. Bram's lips pursed to speak but Peter snatched the receiver.

"Hi Saad, this is Peter, we'll have to get back to you!"

❖ Africa's economic growth rate per capita slows even further.

❖ Only one in eight working people in Africa form part of the waged economy.

❖ Economists provide statistics that outline how export-oriented manufacturers in Sub-Saharan Africa have dropped to below 1970s production rates.

❖ The *Providence Journal of Christianity* writes that

45% of Africans live in failed or rapidly deteriorating dysfunctional political states.

❖ Endemic corruption remains the largest barrier to international investment in the African economy despite America's push to develop a new Marshall Plan in the form of a re-vitalised Africa Growth and Opportunity Act, with former President Barack Obama leading the project on behalf of the African American Policy Institute.

❖ The investor monitor fDi Markets report Chinese investment in Africa rose by over 700% over the last three cycles and is currently estimated to be averaging 27 billion per annum.

Knowing they had no way to pay, Peter collected what little savings the family had and went down to the Schaarbeek district trying to negotiate the purchase of a revolver. After a few days of whispered conversations in slum bars and seedy cafes, a man associated with a well-known criminal fraternity made a promise to get him a NM. 73. This turned out to be an old Beaumont-Adams antique with a chipped brown wooden grip and a clunky action.

He felt dissatisfied as he walked away under the sour cherry trees lining the streets of Diamant, moving amongst the Moroccans in Petite Anatolie and the Place des Carabiniers. A Jihadi with a kitchen knife had attacked three policemen on these very streets only a few weeks before. He was getting the distinct sense he was unwanted in his own land, even though coins and tombs dating from the Roman Emperor Hadrian were buried below his feet.

That night he slept fitfully, bathed in sweat, tossing and turning, questioning what he was going to do. Recalling what he had learned about the Sunnah and Qur'an, that people like himself were subject to the judgements of Tasdiq and Takdhib, and the maze of moral meanings somewhere in-between.

Gathering himself together under a cold shower, he slipped out ghost-like the following day, making for an ethnic-owned shop he had reconnoitered for several hours previously. Entering as if he was a potential customer, he confronted the Pakistani merchant, cocking his pistol and demanding the contents of the till.

"Your people have taken from me and now I take from you!" he said in self-justification.

Then running out into the street with an alarm sounding in his head, he immediately went home and ordered his parents to use the cash as a down payment on Nina's ransom.

"No more fingers!" he told them.

Summoned back to college to face the tribunal, Peter found there had already been telephone threats, physical assaults, arson attacks and a carjacking carried out against conservative types all over the city. He began attending more training camps himself in response to the daily attacks by Jihadists everywhere in Europe, Canada and the USA which exacerbated the growing feeling that Civil War was only a heartbeat away. Fire bombings, lone-wolf attacks by sword waving fanatics, and women with explosives tucked in their chastity belts, blowing themselves up in the lingerie sections of department stores, no longer made headline news. It was as the Mayor of London had predicted some years before, just part of everyday life in a capital city. Someone had even tried to deploy anthrax spores amongst the towels at a public swimming pool.

To Peter's way of thinking the authorities were turning a blind eye to the wilding of thugs who had been bussed in from the culturally enriched Charlois area in Rotterdam and from what he was told were getting free meals in cafes around the Ellebogenbuurt.

There was talk of street demonstrations by the Right and the brawls with the Left grew in intensity. One night he was woken by a cannonade from Koolstraat. The Folkloristisch Festival was fast approaching, and the traditionalists were expected to meet in Guyot Square. Peter was hesitant, unwilling to march under the flapping red and white chequered flags of their allies from the Brabant, where they would be sitting ducks for some Black Bloc fanatics or a sweaty palmed policeman clutching nervously at his sub-machine gun.

Once Peter's expulsion was confirmed, the Noirs, as they came to be known, seized some key faculty buildings. The group wore black t-shirts with a 6 motif and olive sweats emblazoned with the face of Corneliu Codreanu, an ardent Romanian martyr from the Thirties. They hung long trailing banners from the Senate windows and played Death in June music at full volume on the student radio. The sit-in was eventually broken up by local police cadets drafted in from outside the city. But they had made their point.

Only a few days later two of the Noirs had been kidnapped off the street, videos of their flesh being slowly flayed from the ankles upward and their vein riddled corpses being bled in traditional Islamic fashion were posted on YouTube by the local Soldiers of Allah.

"You have a gun, now!" Senka intimated. "Use it!"

Within days they were in contact with someone who identified himself as a member of the Vaderland Commando. Peter showed him the Beaumont Adams. The man smiled. "It will put a big hole in a man, but our Jeugdstorm boys are better equipped. Now, if you want to really strike back", he said pointedly, "We have the means!"

"How?" Senka asked with genuine curiosity. The man brought his hands together and then broke them apart with a whistle.

"Boom!"

Peter shook his head. "This is crazy; we won't do it!" The man looked towards Senka and then hard and long at Peter.

"Don't you want to protect our women?" The verbal blow hit home like a cricket ball in the testicles.

"It's just . . ."

"A knife can only take one at a time. But this . . ." The Vaderland operative trailed off.

- ❖ Saudi proselytism in the form of free Wahhabi prayer books, missionaries and imams grows to an estimated equivalent of 124 billion petrodollars a year.
- ❖ Sweden's black African Minister of Culture, from the Green/Red Alliance, confirms her relationship with an Islamic state radical, announcing from her home in Stockholm that she is "proud to be Aadroop's third wife."
- ❖ The epidemic of ethnic gang crime in Sweden that recorded 20 drive by shootings including that of a 12-year-old girl, 163 incidents of firearms being used in inter-gang warfare and 257 bomb explosions in 2019 triples within 5 years.
- ❖ *Rumiyah*, an ISIS-oriented magazine, encourages the faithful to boil Western children in oil.
- ❖ On average 430 new Islamic schools are established in Europe per annum.
- ❖ The Pope signs a request by the Arab Da'wa Movement to extend the Mosque in Rome.
- ❖ President Belaire of France increases funding for the Institute of the Arab World, originally set up by Valerie Giscard d'Estaing in 1974, and orders the compulsory purchase of a prime parcel of land beside the Seine to be given over to the Federation nationale des Musulmans de France.
- ❖ New mega-mosque projects begin in Madrid, Pisa, Copenhagen, Evry, Huddersfield, Manchester, East London and Glasgow

Incensed by the calls of "Allah-hu-Akbar! Allah-hu-Akbar!" from the rooftops of the city and news from home that another of Nina's fingers had arrived through the post, Peter finally cracked, joining Senka as they drove through alleys and streets thronged with men, women and children marching under placards proclaiming Islam's greatness in the build up to the Eid festivities.

His mind was swelling with the memory of his parents

crying on Skype.

"Which way?" he kept asking as they approached the Grote Markt square, the crowd condensing noticeably, cars double and triple parked. The main thoroughfare of the Guldenstraat was lined with loudspeakers echoing with Eastern chant. People were moving in waves towards the City Hall where next to the Martini Tower a new Takfir wal-Hijra monument dedicated to Mohammed Bouyeri, executor of Theo Van Gogh, had been erected. Groups of battle-hardened young men, veterans from the Al Sham Syrian insurgency and Islamic State policed the area. The mass rally was well underway by the time they arrived, and the face of Europe's Islamic Caliph could be seen emblazoned on posters stuck to the sides of houses and shop fronts all along the route of the protest.

Peter and Senka caught their breath, picked up the pipe bomb they had constructed with the help of their new friend the day before and hidden in a canvas holdall in the back of the car. Stepping out into the throng, it felt as if they were moving by osmosis through the press of bodies, the evening air full of calls for sharia and "Death to Britain, France, Germany and the Old World. Long live the Islamic State and the New Europe of All the Peoples!" Muslim men scrambled over walls into resident's gardens and threw dirt upon themselves. Echoes of "Khak-bar-saram!" resounding, as chador covered women with flailing arms screamed unintelligibly into the grey sky.

"I can't do this," he thought to himself. Then glancing over at his companion he saw Nina's face reflected back at him.

They were halfway down the Waagplein, just as Rifat, formerly known as Yaman the Syrian, started his speech, simultaneously translated into English for the benefit of the world's media. The duo knew they had no choice but to act as they listened carefully to the bile he was spilling, offloading their package into a shop doorway, deliberately selecting a blind spot like they had been instructed, somewhere the street cameras could not record.

"We have come in strength to conquer like Muhammad did in Mecca!" went the rhetoric, "Impose the kafala on Europeans!" The crowd was so dense it could no longer move, even at a shuffle. Peter and Senka were forced to endure the whole speech, noting the young men around them were more eager to dance and celebrate than listen to the prophet's fine words about the Islamic State Army. There was no hostility shown towards them. They were assumed to be young Left progressives, just another two of the many wide-eyed converts that dotted the crowd, sparse blonde and ginger beards shouting along with the aliens for the end to their nations.

After a while, the crying of women could be heard. They were demanding the young men stop pushing and shoving. The mass moving backward and sideways, the crush of seething bodies falling, children being trampled as a stampede started to escape down one of the side streets out of the square. For a second Peter became worried. Senka was lifted off her feet, caught in an eddy of movement that passed like a Mexican football wave along the pavement.

"Push the timer," he read her lips say, and he did, seizing her hand, forcing their way past distorted faces shouting revolutionary slogans, until the plastic explosives went off, blowing people like skittles along the road, shattering eardrums, sending slivers of glass wrapped in a pillar of smoke fifty metres overhead.

- ❖ A fleet of ambulances are attacked when they arrive to care for the injured in the Waagplein.
- ❖ Firemen are surrounded and beaten as they put out shop fires.
- ❖ The Interior Minister describes the bombing as racially motivated and demands the right to hold suspects for an unspecified period due to the particularly heinous motive for the crime.

They laid low for a couple of days drinking bottled beer

in a safehouse and getting paranoid about what they had done, sweating every time there was a sound outside the door, waiting for someone to launch a stun grenade through the ventilation system.

"The death toll keeps getting higher!" Peter insisted. "It can' be true, can it?"

"Who knows?" Senka said. "The media lies."

Then, a couple of weeks later, after attending a Pan-Celtic Festival in Lorient, marching under the flags of Alba, Mannin, Eire, Cymru, Kernow and Breizh, Senka received notification of her deportation back to Serbia following an unspecified breach of her immigration status. It soon transpired she was required to attend the local police station to inform them of the date and time of her departure. When the pretty Serbian arrived, she was greeted by an uncommunicative receptionist from the Samburu diaspora hiding behind a bakoola facemask. Then, taken to a seat, until a young Sri Lankan desk sergeant came out from behind a Perspex screen to check her passport and stamp her completed exit certificate.

When she returned with the news, Peter phoned a lawyer, but the man on the other end of the line refused to take the case when he found out Senka was not African.

"There's simply no government money in it. If she was from Malawi that would be different, and dare I say, beneficial!" Peter dropped the call and turned to the wet faced blonde choking on her anxiety. "Looks like we'll have to buy you a burqa!" he tried to joke. She launched a plate of spaghetti in his direction.

"I can't go back. My village looks like Nagasaki," she yelled, "Clinton's US Air Force flattened it years ago!"

THE METROPOLE

"Europe's nations should be guided towards the superstate without the people understanding what is happening. This can be accomplished by successive

steps, each disguised as having an economic purpose, but which will eventually and irreversibly lead
to Federation."

—Jean Monnet

The windows in every Presidium building across Western Europe burned bright well into the night. Behind their
desks, hermaphrodite-like employees in dark suits, well-
versed in the writings of Jean Monnet and Helmut Kohl,
sat at keyboards. Their most pressing task: to evaluate da-
ta sets from each part of the Eurozone, pouring over economic performance and demographic profiles, not just
within set national boundaries but also by region and city.
Fresh orders were issued if quotas were not being fulfilled,
confirmation of increased budgets wired to job recruit-
ment centres in Sudan, Mozambique and Nigeria to has-
ten their throughput.

"Cut corners and increase subsidies to the chartered air-
lines flying from Third World destinations into Heathrow,
Gatwick, Geneva, Barajas, Munich and Charleroi, if necessary," was the incessant instruction.

❖ The UN World Food Programme (WFP) announces a $3.1 billion dollar emergency response to re-
ports that 9 million people faced famine in the
Horn of Africa.
❖ WFP representative, Stefan Anderton, claimed
"We are in a race against time to prevent a cata-
strophic hunger crisis."
❖ The Office for the Coordination of Humanitarian
Affairs launch an appeal for $89 million to amelio-
rate what they describe as a complex emergency in
the Kasai Region of the Congo.
❖ A collection of videos and photographs of people
who have been detained on the basis of contraven-
ing the new equality laws show men and women
in handcuffs, leg shackles and with the skin on
their buttocks split wide open, along with footage

of children as young as thirteen being subjected to beatings as they chant "Europe has always been multicultural" and are forced to sign pledges that are headed "We Repent Our Racism."

❖ Evidence emerges that refugee charities based in Italy are secretly colluding with people traffickers to bring people into Europe from Mali, Niger, Senegal, Libya, Eritrea and Somalia.

❖ The Mayor of Palermo welcomes migrants and celebrates the million who have arrived in Italy in the last three years, claiming they are playing their part in defeating the Mafia.

❖ A survey entitled "Perceptions of journalistic bias: Party preferences, media trust and attitudes towards immigration" conducted by Norwegian pollster Nordiske Mediedager that revealed over 70% of Swedish journalists support left-wing parties like the Social Democrats and the Greens and a similar analysis that indicated 68.7% of Norwegian journalists support the Red-Green coalition is dismissed as fabricated right-wing conspiracy theory by the country's respective governments.

❖ A female patriot, described as the Finnish Marine Le Pen, is banned from speaking in Helsinki.

Earlier that day, the black budget for EU cyberoperations had been increased to 30 billion Euro. Justifying such a huge increase in spending on surveillance, Rube Goldberg, head of CyberTec, the governmental e-intel agency, argued: "This investment is absolutely necessary in the fight against Right-wing dissidents and neo-Nazi terrorism."

And just at that moment, as Golberg's words were being relayed to security personnel from Wrocław to Marseilles, Peter Janssen's profile popped up attached to a photo taken secretly at a political rally in Diksmuide and captured the attention of one particularly jaded inspector as he poured over his flat screen.

"This one is trouble," he said in an almost metronomic voice.

A week after Senka's deportation Peter received a letter informing him he was expected to come for an interview in the administrative heart of the city. Attendance was mandatory. He threw his hands up in the air, "They've got me!"

About midday Peter walked stiff legged through the Grote Markt heading for the hearing at the European Parliament's Consulate offices in the city hall. The Civic Guard were overseeing prisoners working on the blackened façade where the bomb had exploded. A plaque commemorating the victims of reactionary violence had already been erected. The unveiling attended by the city Mayor, Simcha Drell, members of the Islamic Community Trust, volunteers from the Apel Refugee Centre and the grass roots Collateral Repair Project, which invited supporters to be heroes by funding survivors like Thamer, Munah and Enad.

Nervously crossing the threshold, threading between the vast pillared portico, Peter was confronted by the all-pervasive blue flag with the yellow star emblem swinging over the gated entrance.

"Their flag, not my flag," he thought as he disavowed his former convictions. Then walking past two broad-shouldered Congolese policemen in Aegis body armour, looking like a cross between George Lucas Stormtroopers and something out of a Pierre Boulle novel, he climbed the staircase under an Info board that flashed WE ALL SEE YOU: YOU ARE NOT ALONE.

At the top Peter was greeted by an androgynous Executive Assistant in sensible black shoes and told to sit in an anteroom with twenty or so other citizens of the New Europe. Each was as agitated as the other, looking furtively at magazines extolling the virtues of reducing carbon emissions by outsourcing all of Europe's manufacturing to China and charitable foundations giving succour to gangster warlords in Eritrea under the bold headline, "Reparations for the Crime of Colonialism."

It felt like he was being toyed with. He kept saying to himself, "They know. This is just a game, something's given me away." After waiting an hour, he was asked to fill in an A11 form. Then thirty minutes later a second form called the A12 which was pretty much a replica of the A11 except for its darker pastel colour. He borrowed a pen and fought his way through the multifarious collection of languages, all in alpha order to prevent accusations of linguistic preference or bias, until he came to his own lingua franca and began to tick the empty boxes.

When his name was eventually called, he was ushered into a small cubicle and made to sit on a plastic swivel seat that instinctively tried to rotate under the press of his weight. Inside, beyond a Perspex screen, was a pale woman of around thirty exhibiting all the signs of suffering from a severe migraine. She asked him his name and rubbed the bridge of her nose constantly as though she was struggling to contain a nausea brought on by Peter's presence.

"You are aware that you are subject to travel restrictions?" she asked.

"No, I am not aware," Peter answered defiantly. She raised a paper with a crested stamp on it and waved it in his face.

"Yes, you are prohibited to travel beyond Noord-Holland without the express permission of the territorial cooperation commissariat office." Peter was confused.

"I was not told of this."

"Your instructions are posted on the territorial cooperation website."

"I was not aware . . ."

"It is most clearly stated!"

"Yes, but I was unaware of this requirement anyway . . ."

"The posting of such a notification on an official URL of what will soon be The New European Republic means it is legislatively active from the moment the e-copy is available on an accessible public forum."

"But I was unaware of its existence."

"It is your responsibility to find out." At that moment a male colleague, most probably of Caribbean origin, entered her cubicle via a side door and proffered a cup of coffee. Peter noticed the way they looked at each other, the way their fingers touched. The man's flat nose tilted condescendingly down at him, then departed, the female official proceeding to read out the relevant section of the mandate of civic responsibility. Peter tried to intervene, but she raised a hand to silence him. "I will answer your questions once I have read the notification." When she trailed off with a breathless herewith and a forthwith catch-all summation, Peter took the opportunity to barge in with the obvious question.

"But why?"

"Why what?"

"Am I subject to this restriction?" The woman became perplexed.

"That is not within my remit."

"Then who can I ask?"

"I suggest you go back to reception, take another ticket and wait until you are called."

After a very bad night worrying if the police investigation was closing in on him, Peter returned, uncertain if they did suspect him of terrorist activities, but wondering why they had not simply seized him or disappeared him, just like all the others he had heard about. Peter still clung to the hope that there had been a misunderstanding, some kind of database error that had temporarily contaminated his records with those of another person, a minor criminal or someone with outstanding court orders against his name. At the back of his mind lurked the suspicion he was now entering into a low-level harassment scenario intended to scare him away from his political activities. So when he reluctantly took a docket and sat for four hours before assuming a seat in yet another booth, he was sufficiently composed to feign a minor irritation at the turn of events and emphasize that he was a student and had no convictions.

"There's obviously been a mistake," he suggested.

"No mistake," the man replied.

"But there must be?" Then his case officer read out his full name, date of birth, family circumstances, qualifications, medical records and named several of his friends and associates.

"Does that sound correct?"

"Well, yes, it does, but . . ."

"There are no ifs and buts, Meneer Janssen. You have been classified as someone whose movements need to be approved by the bureau." Peter remained silent for a moment taking in what he was being told by the blank-faced bureaucrat.

"Have I been denounced? What are you, the new Stasi?" People's heads turned from their monitors, keyboards stopped their click clack plastic chatter. The very utterance of the word was sacrilege.

"Meneer Janssen, do I need to call security?"

"But this is ridiculous. I am a student at . . ."

"It says here that you have corresponded with undesirable elements." Peter suddenly became defensive; his hackles might have been raised, but he was not foolish enough to jeopardise his freedom.

"I see!"

"I am not at liberty to disclose the contents of D12 files but there are copious materials here supporting the restriction order. It transpires you have breached Council Framework Decision 2008/913/JHA on expressions of racism and xenophobia."

"Do I have the right to challenge such a restriction?"

"Of course!"

"Can you advise me who I need to see?" Peter watched the man's hand point to the ticket dispenser in the foyer and heard the familiar litany once again.

"Meneer Janssen, you must take another ticket and wait until you are called."

- ❖ Cao Zhang Wei, Chief Executive of Interpol, confirms that the law enforcement agency based in Lyon has issued 7,300 red notices in the last quarter.
- ❖ The number of people employed by the EU across the entire Eurozone reaches 300,000.
- ❖ "The EU Commission plays a central role in a changing Europe," says Anand Kassim, Director General of the One World Alliance.
- ❖ Two Ukrainian billionaires increase their joint funding of the European Jewish Parliament, an NGO based in Brussels whose mission statement is to provide "a united structure for all Jewish communities and organisations throughout Western, Eastern and Central Europe."
- ❖ Goodstart Genetics and Premira, the owners of ancestry.com and 23andMe undertake specialist consultative advice for members of the Ashkenazi community.
- ❖ The Chairman of the European Jewish Congress welcomes the extention of France's Gayssot Act of 1990, in effect making Holocaust denial and anti-Semitism in either thought or deed illegal across the whole Eurozone.
- ❖ Interpol administrators meet with the Interior Ministers of Arabic nations in order to forge even closer alliances in the fight against terrorism.
- ❖ The issue of electronic mass surveillance highlighted by Edward Snowden is dismissed by EU executives whilst ever-closer collaboration is encouraged between the US National Security Agency (NSA), the German Foreign Intelligence Agency (BND) and their counterparts in the British and French counterespionage service.
- ❖ The Ransomware2 virus is released by US and Western intelligence agencies.
- ❖ Oleh Vyshnevetsky, a leading Jewish advocate, reaffirms his delight that people like Volodymer

Zelensky upholds the interests of his people in the Verkhovna Rada.

At 3:00 am they came for him. Peter, bleary eyed, opened the door, only to be bagged and pinned to the bed. His interrogator shouting threats until he confirmed his full name.

"Who are you?" he demanded in return but got no response. There was a silent stand off for a few moments then his assailant turned to the door, twisting the knob to open it slightly, whispering through the crack to a superior. There was a brief exchange of coded words and the doorframe was suddenly filled by a rotund man in a white suit, pock-marked nose sniffing the air.

"I smell a fascist!" he declared on entering. Then, in a mocking tone, "Good morning, my name is Inspector Bakkum, Thijs Bakkum," he said by way of introduction. "Please excuse our sudden appearance but we need you to answer a few basic questions before we ask you to accompany us to the station."

"Why?"

"Because you are under suspicion of harbouring views that may damage social cohesion!"

"That sounds like something out of the 1930s."

"And you'd know all about that period in history, wouldn't you?" Peter shook his head. "Please, Johannes," Bakkum said, gesturing to his accomplice, "can you collect up any papers, disks or computer records that may assist us with our enquiry." Johannes began sifting through Peter's things, big clumsy hands overturning objects and tipping neatly piled files onto the floor.

"About your research," Bakkum went on.

"What about it?"

"It is unusual."

"Not really," Peter said indignantly.

"It is not mainstream."

"It is original, you mean, not based on regurgitated and plagiarised political orthodoxy?"

"Hardly!"

"Then what?"

"Your university supervisor informs us that it could be said to be an attempt to distract attention from the real victims."

"Everybody was a victim of the immense barbarity perpetrated by both sides."

"But the *Untermenschen*," the inspector pronounced with acidic precision, "were reacting to evil."

"Just because deluded zealots were trying to refight the wars of the Teutonic Knights in some kind of Wagnerian melodrama does not mean the other side can retrospectively claim the moral high ground."

"But they invaded . . ."

"No, they didn't, Barbarossa pre-empted the planned attack by Stalin on the West." Bakkum contorted his mouth in an attempt to interject. Peter continued, "Lenin and his Bolsheviks had already tried the same tactic in 1920 and were stopped at the gates of Warsaw by Pilsudski's Polish army. Why do you think Katyn was so predictable? It was an act of revenge!"

"That is not the generally accepted view."

"Accepted by whom and acceptable to whom?"

"Serious researchers!"

"Viktor Suvurov is a researcher and writer. The Canadian James Bacques also."

"What about Goldhagen?"

"I have heard him called a repetitionist?"

"You mean a revisionist?"

"No, I certainly do not. I have heard certain published historians contend that people like Deborah Lipstadt and fiction writers like Eli Wiesel make assertions and colour their storytelling based on their feelings about their oppressor's supposed intent without any, or at best, very limited substantiating evidence."

"Paah!"

"*Anne Frank's Diary* was written by her father as a work of fiction in a type of pen that was not invented until after the war!"

"She was gassed!"

"Gassed where?"

"Auschwitz, like all the others."

"She died of typhoid, actually."

"Gassed, like all the other innocents!"

"Where are the chemical traces in the stonework? When were the showers we see today constructed? Where are the mountains of coal needed to burn the corpses? Where is the evidence in the intercepted Enigma coded messages relating to body counts? The Russians recently released records that indicated a death toll of around one hundred thousand at the main facility."

"I cannot believe that!"

"What about the fantasies of people living in the woods with wolves to escape the atrocities, or frauds like Herman Rosenblat whose *Angel at the Fence* got him a publishing contract for his so-called survivor memoirs?"

"These are all contentious issues. You will stop now!"

"It is your new secular religion. The entire edifice is based on very sandy ground."

"If that were true, people would expose it!"

"People have exposed it and been tried and convicted for their research."

"Yes, and I think the Englishman Dr. Johnson also said something to the effect that patriotism was the last refuge of the scoundrel."

"And there's a certain truth in that too!"

An hour later they were still talking, going around in circles, avoiding the truth like radioactive material.

"So, tell me, what's your issue? Why are you so angry?"

"Angry?"

"Yeah, you seem angry, on edge."

"Psychotic?" Bakkum moved his head in acknowledgement.

"You self-diagnose."

"Not really, I am predicting your medical report," Peter postured. Bakkum flinched.

"So what is it you want?"

"I want to live in a world where when you travel from one city to another it actually looks and feels different. I want to see architecture, hear music and read poetry that reflects that people's own culture and identity. I want to take a salary for genuinely productive labour and not some Ponzi insurance scam. I want to turn on the radio or a TV set and get factual balanced news without the schmaltz of one-world propaganda." Peter stopped, blistering eyes searching his interrogator's face. "Can you help me with any of that?" Bakkum shook his head. "I thought that might be the case, so remind me why are you here, again?"

"To take you into custody!"

"Oh, that's right, for having dangerous thoughts!"

❖ The European Union Agency for Fundamental Rights reports a 210% rise in hate crime across Europe.

❖ Booklets entitled Combatting Hate Crime are provided to all school children in the EU.

❖ A Special Commission is set up to review the effectiveness of EU laws to combat racism and xenophobia with a view to further harmonising and consolidating existing laws in member states like, the principle being to ensure that denial of a clearly established historical fact like the Holocaust constitutes *ipso facto* "breach of the right to free speech."

❖ The Council of Europe's programme for Human Rights prioritises the need to raise awareness about homophobia and transphobia.

❖ The EU-MIDIS 4 Minority and Discriminatory Survey finds that 87% of non-whites have faced some form of racism in the last 3 years.

❖ The UN's Global Migration Compact, already ratified into the law of numerous states, is increasingly used to convict people making racist references to illegal rather than irregular migrants.

Following a full identity check, photos and DNA test-ing at the local police station, Bakkum informed Peter he was going to be detained indefinitely at a special holding facility in the city.

It was late evening by the time his captors marched him up the steep incline to the old castle. Before them, narrow arrow slits threw a thin internal light out into blinding darkness. A stone bridge bending and curling up to the metal portcullis which opened with a grinding scream to welcome them inside.

Peter had wrongly assumed he would be thrown into a cell to cool his heels. In fact, Bakkum and his hench-man took him straight to the Magistrate's office, using swipe cards to gain access through bullet proof glass screens and metal detectors.

"We booked Room 9," Bakkum said to a dark-haired secretary with clear olive skin and a white cotton blouse bearing a name badge identifying her as Adelheid Gompers.

"Yes," she confirmed, "everything is arranged, please, follow me." Getting up from behind her desk, Ms Gompers swept across the light blue carpet in a short black skirt, her left hand clutching a digital device that blinked red, setting off an overhead scanner. Peter was forced to stand in front of the screen until ordered to move on into an oval beige carpeted room with pale maple furniture. His eyes alighted on a purple vase and white carnations. Just for a moment the incongruity of the soft furnishings with the purpose of the room amused him. Told to sit down, Gompers got him to sign some legal papers from a red folder while Bakkum poured himself coffee. Peter thought Gompers' smile a tad benign when she took back her pen.

"There, Meneer Janssen," she said, "all done!"

For the next hour he sat with Bakkum in the empty room. Peter guessed that he was being monitored but could not identify where the hidden camera might be lo-cated. He thought they might be analysing body movements, eye flicker and sweat production.

"You conspiracy theorists are all the same," Bakkum goaded him.

"I'm not a conspiracy theorist!"

"What about 9/11? I'm sure you have views on that!"

"None I care to share with you!"

Then a door opened, and he was taken by a uniformed officer towards a narrow staircase. Bakkum followed behind. Through the plate glass windows cut in the stone he could see other detainees being questioned and a group of young men in orange jumpsuits shuffling slowly in circles around a floodlit courtyard. Peter was getting increasingly worried as he was pressed up the steps. Nurses in scrubs passed by with atrazine-filled syringes to reverse sex hormones. His mind alert to the possibility of violence.

Then he was required to wait once again on the first landing. He could hear the gasping of someone being waterboarded when the sound-proof door was opened, and a green light lit up above the entrance to Magistrate Hurwicz's inner sanctum.

"Welcome, Mr Janssen," said the magistrate as Peter crossed the threshold into a medium sized room, "I trust my colleagues have looked after you?" Hurwicz was a fat little bureaucrat with a sense of self-importance about him. "You know I am sure we can clear all this up in double quick time."

"Clear what up, exactly. . .?"

"You have transgressed the laws on tolerance and hate!"

"I've already explained to your colleagues," Peter began, "I'm not aware of committing any such transgressions."

"We've had you under e-net supervision for some time. You don't think forming an anti-social and anti-conformist student gang, and participating in street violence . . ."

"Self-defence!" Peter bit sharply.

". . . constitutes a valid reason to restrict your movements and impose a penalty fine system for social rehabilitation?"

"Is that what this is about? You are going to deduct points from me every time I do something you consider inappropriate?" Hurwicz gave a baleful smile.

"And a curfew," he added.

"What is this?" Peter asked, "Do you really think you have the right to control my thoughts?"

"We do when it comes to the wellbeing of the community."

"To what end?"

"To safeguard our society."

"You mean people who go along with your administered freedom and your equality by command?"

"I mean people who adhere to the rule of law."

"Where was your rule of law when my sister was taken?"

"Oh, yes, little Nina. We have no idea about her whereabouts. But please, getting back to my point about the rule of law . . ."

"The same law that allows someone like Chaim Studinberg to oversee the mass incarceration of five million Germans in Silesia after the war, or for Pinek Maka, Secretary of State Security to deliberately deny those same Germans access to the Red Cross?"

"You seem to have a penchant for lost causes," Hurwicz fired back.

"Familiarise yourself with Somaweb.org."

"What?"

"It is a website dedicated to the thinking of Aldous Huxley."

"Who?"

"An English writer who spoke about the powers-that-be coercing the populations under their control through overt and subliminal methods!" The magistrate guffawed.

"England, so what? They have given us nothing in years. We still control their so-called Mother of Parliaments, and the Labour and Conservative Parties live on our stipends. Thatcher, Major, Blair, Brown, Cameron,

May and Johnson were mere employees. Who do you think our agent, the Speaker of the House of Commons, works for, the British monarchy? Just look at how we extradited that former teacher, the fantasist French Holocaust denier!"

"I note your confirmation of my point and your misplaced confidence and innate prejudice."

"So what's this Huxley ever written?"

"*Brave New World*, for one." Hurwicz shook his head.

"Never heard of it. You should be reading about Jacques Delors!"

"Delors, never!"

"Yes, the eighth President of the Commission, a founder of European federalism."

"He is a Globalist whore!"

"My friend, his Notre Europe headquarters controls your world." The grey-haired magistrate sighed, lit up a cigar and studied the red tip for a second, tapping off a couple of centimetres of ash. I can see we're not going to get very far, are we? I really do need you to help me."

"I'm still struggling to think in what way I can possibly help you?"

"Shall I spell it out?"

"Please do?"

"We need names and addresses."

"Of whom?"

"Your contacts!"

"I have no contacts."

"I think you do." Hurwicz rolled the cigar around in his fingers. Peter watched him carefully.

"I feel I'm going to disappoint you."

"I don't think so?" The magistrate reached down to his waist, pulled out an automatic pistol and laid it flat on the table beside the ashtray. His fingers stroked the grip handle. Peter noticed his hands were broad, large and club shaped, yet his touch on the metal was sensuous, almost loving. When he spoke again his voice filled the room, smoke tar colouring the rolling syllables.

"Tell me I don't need to introduce you to my friends?"

"Friends?"

"Yes, very nice gentlemen, with whom you'll share some anecdotes?" Hurwicz's elbows were on the table, between the lamps, straddling the ashtray and the gun. Peter watched as his amphibian eyes disappeared behind a cloud of smoke.

"I have nothing to tell you." Hurwicz got up and wandered around behind him. Peter felt the magistrate lean in close.

"Save yourself some trouble." Peter shrugged. The next thing he knew he was being lifted from the seat, his arm jammed painfully behind his back as he was led down a narrow stone corridor. There was a dry constipated taste of phlegm sticking to the roof of his mouth. His legs wobbled, stomach churning as his nose caught the whiff of body odour coming off the guard who was swinging along beside him, holding him tightly in a clamp-like grip. He was thumped into the doorpost of an interrogation cell and the barrel of a sidearm pushed tight to his chin. Peter tipped his head back, looking straight into the hateful eyes staring back at him. The gun's muzzle travelled over his face, across his cheek, jabbing into his eye socket.

"So you think you are pretty clever, uh?" Peter remained silent. "Your fast talking won't help you here, my friend!" The guard slapped his face. Janssen swallowed a pulse of salt-rich blood. The guard whistled. "Did that hurt, college boy?"

The door behind him opened. Two men passed a possessive glance over him before they took hold of his shoulders, moving him to a metal bench. Suddenly the background music changed. There was a low hum. Lights flickered on and off. The room was flooded with white brilliance, outlining the shapes of twin homunculi, closely followed by two lethargic knuckle dragging silhouettes, dancing on the pale wall.

❖ The EU's Chief Foreign Policy adviser announces

plans for an EU army costing 1.5 trillion Euro.

❖ Par Holmgren and Alice Bah Kuhnke, delegates
from Sweden, table a motion before the the EU
Electoral Commission requesting that all former
Islamic State jihadists returning to the West
should be exonerated and allowed to participate in
the democratic process.

❖ British Labour representative to Europe, Claude
Moraes, tables a resolution to commence a process
by which all EU governing bodies and committees
would be composed of 50% non-whites in order to
end systemic racism.

❖ A Concordat of Understanding is signed between
the EU and the USA regarding the need to estab-
lish mass refugee camps in the red-roofed town of
Ptuj in the Styrian region of Slovenia, but only after the Basilica Mariahilf is demolished in order
not to offend the migrants; in Keszthely on Lake
Balaton near the Nemzeti Park, Hungary; Ostrava
in the Czech Republic, the meeting point of the
Odra, Opava, Ostravice and Lucina rivers; and
Ostatsya on the Prut river in Ukraine.

❖ A private donor offers Issur Babel's Coalition for
Renewal 200 million Euro after a fiery speech in
the Duma leads to serious questions being raised
over President Putin's handling of the Russian
economy and security issues following the havoc
wrought by the Covid pandemic.

All over the continent snatch squads had been activated in a mass trawl of dissenters from Ivalo to Lausanne
and Reykjavik to Naples. Pro-European integrationist
agencies using Huawei derived spy technology had been
monitoring mobile phones and personal computers for
some time with the help of corporate collaborators who
sought favourable terms that did not enforce legislation
that would criminalise their cartel's price-fixing. The
strategy was intended as a serious show of strength by the

new generation of EU bureaucrats, who had recently held joint briefings with their Kohanim counterparts in Tel Aviv. Their intention, to head off incendiary individuals or groups, who might inflame the population, especially after the prolonged recession, which some claimed to be a flagrant example of financial asset stripping under the smokescreen of the world-wide pandemic. The plan was to detain those they considered to be potentially violent under the counterterrorism, national security and extended hate speech laws.

"Not a single one of them can be credible!" argued Joshua Meyer behind closed doors to selected audiences. "We must control the narrative. Nothing should be allowed to stand in the way of us trading freely in the marketplace here, there and everywhere. I tell you, even as Hamas propel rockets into our villages, we pay millions of dollars into their leader's Swiss bank accounts. Of course, we also occasionally take out one or two extremists for show. After all, we write the script, we audition the actors and they read our lines."

"Why pay money to ISIS?" came a voice of dissent from the floor.

"What does it matter? It is not our money. It is money we have taken from the American taxpayer," Meyer, a former ambassador to America and current President of the Ivax Corporation, laughed. Then, turning to more serious matters: "Our most pressing issue today is the continued destabilization of countries like Syria and Egypt, maintaining momentum behind the confrontation with Russia in Ukraine and the Baltic and how to manage the traffic of refugees into Europe."

"Make the West the warzone!"

"Precisely so! We need Intifadas all over Europe."

"And multiculturalism is a perfect tool," another shouted from the back. There was a peal of arrogant amusement around the room. "Their Emperors, like Antiochus, Titus and Hadrian may have crushed the very stones of Jerusalem and killed 600,000 in Judea in the old

times. And they may have expelled us from England in
1290, France in 1182 and Spain in 1492. But the Betar
Movement fights on and will not rest until the Son of the
Star rises to rule the whole world. We will have our glorious revenge very soon because now it is us removing them
from their own countries!" Clapping broke out.

"Remember Giselher Wirsing's strategy and look
around you today," Meyer nodded enthusiastically, "Who
can say we have not fulfilled his dreams? We will have
Menorahs lit in every capital city in this world, including
Tehran!"

"And the American Right?"

"What do they matter after what happened to Trump?
Like the American Left, they will do what they are told."
Meyer reached into his jacket pocket and took out his wallet. Then, waving a handful of $100 notes in the air, he said
pointedly, "Antifa and Black Lives Matter are all ours. Ask
Greenspan, we bought Nixon, Reagan and the Bush dynas-
ty. And now we own them all!"

"Their Congress bows to us!" one man with long flowing sidelocks shouted out.

"Exactly!" Meyer exulted, "It is a fact we control their
economies, their entertainment and now their breeding
habits."

Peter woke to see a piercing green eye watching him
through the spyhole. Then the iron clank of the bolt was
thrown. Two very big and very serious men stood facing
him.

"You are awake, yes?" the older man in the uniform
and moustache asked. Peter sat up on the metal framed
bed.

"I am now!" Shoelaces were placed in his outstretched
palm.

"There will be no charges. Today, you are a lucky man,
next time, maybe not." Peter was bending through bruises
to thread his shoes. He stood up, strapping his watch to
his wrist, dry tongue rasping like a rattlesnake sliding over

sandpaper.

"Come," said the younger militia man. Peter followed their broad sweaty shirts down a long half-lit corridor. Flickering strip lights cast lumpy shadows on the damp walls where wanted posters displaying blonde, red and brown-haired people with blue, green and chestnut eyes contrasted sharply with the be-medalled photos of smiling Liberian policemen, who had been recently introduced onto the streets of Amsterdam, regardless of their rumoured penchant for human flesh. His thinking was that they would get him to sign a confession of some sort. He recalled the multiple copies of the holding statement he was forced to sign the night before, the inky fingerprints and digital photographs tossed loosely on Bakkum's desk. Instead, he was led out into a small courtyard, the sort of place where in the past men and women like him would have been stood up against the wall and shot.

An unmarked car sat at the end of a short alleyway, its engine revving ready to go. "Get in!" Peter was ushered onto the back seat and the door slammed tight. "Bon Voyage!" one of his guards joked as they pulled away onto the Akerkhof.

They came down the Pelsterstraat, past boarded-up shops and canteens full of louche characters smoking cannabis and drinking cheap wine. Crossing the Hereplein Bridge, they followed the Stationweg as the first arrows of piercing light struck grey water, casting a rust colour over the stone walls on the deep hollow embankments. Sea birds were surfing on the updrafts, crying into the sky. "You will get the 6:00 am train and go home to Bruges," he was told.

At the Hoofdstation Peter was bundled out the door, frog-marched to the platform and held firmly by the arm until his train arrived. At that point he was handed a wad of papers and told to read them. Inside the carriage he was pushed into a seat and the guard punched his ticket.

Passengers stood in the jangling corridor waving to their relatives and friends who were shrinking away as the locomotive slipped from the platform. The train swayed, Peter's eyes swimming with the mesmeric left-right lurch of the carriage over the track. The seat opposite was empty but to his left was a crimson-faced man wearing a suspicious look. Behind him, laminated wood panelling was etched with pro-2nd June graffiti. To his right a grimy window threw a blue tint on the world outside.

The train trundled along for nearly twenty minutes through grey suburbs. Occasionally, in purple patches of neglected shadow, he saw flames leaping from bonfires, people standing around drinking, staggering arm in arm, bi-racial faces obscured by hoodies.

A further thirty minutes and they were rushing out into the flat lands and the forests to the north east of Amsterdam. The rolling movement of the train rocked him gently, the gap between his eyelids reluctantly narrowing as he looked at the papers that had been thrust into his hands. As the train barrelled through the trees towards Assen his attention was caught by the opening line:

"European states must fully abide by and give effect to standards contained within the 1966 'International Convention on the elimination of all forms of racial discrimination'—especially its core provision of Article 4, concerning the sanctioning of racist organisations."

It followed that certain forms of conduct as identified in the Act were forbidden and were punishable by the EU militia: public incitement to violence or hatred against a group of persons or a member of such a group defined on the basis of race, colour, descent, religion or belief, or national or ethnic origin; public dissemination or distribution of tracts, pictures or other material containing expressions of racism and xenophobia; public condoning, denying or grossly trivialising crimes of genocide, crimes against humanity and war crimes; instigating, aiding or abetting the offences is an offence, punishable in the following ways—effective, proportionate and dissuasive penalties, terms of imprisonment of one to three years, exclusion from entitlements to public benefits or aid; temporary or permanent disqualification from the practice or commercial activities; judicial supervision and a judicial winding-up order; the initiation of investigations or prosecutions of racist and xenophobic offences must not depend on a victim's report or accusation."

Peter could feel his mind drifting, his memory was replaying childhood scenes when he had bullied and played tricks on Nina. He woke suddenly, covered in a thin cellophane of sweat. Through the carriage window he could just make out a skulking wolf pack of illegals, their lupine eyes reflecting moonlit yellow, stalking through the scrub, waiting to fall like a plague on the next unsuspecting village in the Drenthe.

A sliding door opened nearby, and what he at first took to be a swarthy Mediterranean businessman in a dark Italian suit and black wire sunglasses, stepped inside. He sat in the vacant seat opposite, chewing on a stick of gum. Peter eyed him cautiously. He was well groomed with immaculately manicured fingernails. The outcast thumbed his eyes hungrily, trying to stay awake, focussing on this man in front of him in the polished shoes and shiny nickel cufflinks.

"My name is Peter Janssen," he offered tentatively. The sunglasses swallowed him whole.

"I know!"

"I thought you might." Peter's hand stretched out towards him. He caught a glimpse akin to curiosity, like a scientist taking a scalpel to a tumour, micro-chip eyes staring as he took off his glasses and introduced himself.

"I am Vidor, I work for Civic Security."

"The Dutch or the Belgian?"

"Both."

Peter checked his watch. Twenty minutes later Vidor was still watching him, a look of barely suppressed contempt curling his lip. Peter stared out the window at the countryside flying past his face, bushes running wild along the rail embankment, birds rising over the rolling tree cover. Looming electricity pylons stretching away into the bumpy emptiness of the dolmen littered land.

They arrived at Assen to find the city under siege, a neo-Napoleonic cannonade of hail and rain bombarding Stationsplein 2. Peter disembarked and struggled down Oostersingel, moving past neon lit cafes and gaudy hotels. Money and time were in short supply. He leaned against a wall below a dark windswept archway and saw the gilded architecture of the Drents museum framed by the sky. Vidor was standing only a few metres away under an umbrella, still following his every move from behind oval shades, fingers tapping a coded message into his handheld phone.

- ❖ Thomas Bergner of the German CDU Party gives a press conference on the annual political crime statistics and says "These barbarous xenophobic people have committed 136,232 verbal, physical or written offenses, a 32% increase on the previous period."
- ❖ An analysis of refugee and migrant crime figures on France's TF1 channel concludes that the 90% spike in non-white crime "is a direct result of the inhuman overcrowding the French Social Services have forced upon recent arrivals, implying the Government must do better in coming years."
- ❖ Statistics gathered in the Netherlands reveal crime rates quadrupling between first- and second-generation migrants and welfare dependency among the Turkish, Surinamese and Moroccan communities running at five times the rate of native born Dutch.
- ❖ Members of Denmark's Social Democratic Party line up on the road to Rondby to give food and shelter to refugees.
- ❖ The Runestones of Tune and Ramsungberg are covered with tarpaulins before being removed from the public realm.
- ❖ A man who once temporarily led the French Front

National is retrospectively charged with Holocaust denial following investigations into an interview, he once gave questioning the effectiveness of using Zyklon B as a tool for mass murder.

After a convoluted bus ride and a heated negotiation with an Iraqi taxi driver Peter reached home, Saad and Fatima immediately rushing out to scream obscenities in welcome. He opened the door and found Bram and Ninette sitting passively in front of the television, shrivelled sticks wrapped in rags. They told him there was still no news concerning Nina, and the police wanted to close the file. He made himself a coffee and retired in silence to his bedroom, realising how everything he had thought over many years had led him up to this.

DOWN WITH THOUGHT CONTROL
DOWN WITH EGALITARIANISM
DOWN WITH THE NEW WORLD ORDER

He breathed. It was like some sort of epiphany. He tore the photos of his school trip to the death camps around Krakow off the wall and threw his copy of Tom de Cock's *The Revelation* into the wastepaper bin. Bit by bit he came to see how his personal confrontation with the forces that had seized control of society was moving to a higher level. But he also recognised that he was now a target. Ever since the bombing in the Waagplein he felt he was walking in the crosshairs of a sniper's rifle, which both excited and terrified him. He knew he had done it to revenge Nina. He knew he had done it to prove something to Senka. He knew he had done it for the thousands upon thousands of victims all over Europe. But most of all he knew he had done it for himself. To prove he was not the emasculated wretch that they wanted him to be.

Peter wondered how many other people had been in his situation since the Strasbourg, Maastricht and Brussels Axis had conducted their constitutional Anschluss on national governments? He had been told of comrades who had been woken up by the hammering at the door in the small hours, dragged out of their beds and sent to the Correction Camps. These new Masters of Europe were just like their political predecessors of 1917. Would he have the nerve to resist, or would he go meekly? If he was supine would they go easier on him? He had heard of people being transported to government centres and coming back cured of their social maladies. It was just like the Stanley Kubrick movie *A Clockwork Orange*. Often intensive one-to-one therapy was the only answer, but sometimes chemical castration or a partial lobotomy was required.

Was he strong enough to stand the pressure? It would be so easy to pick up the phone and admit his guilt? Or should he contact his friends in the Rene Lagrou Commando and volunteer to go underground?

The next day matters were decided for him. It seemed that Vidor had been shot in the back of the neck, execution style, by a disciple of Joop Glimmerveen, and he was being implicated. Peter's fingers hit re-dial, and he gave the code-word. His handler in the Constance Custers Commando told him what to do. His course was set. Within an hour he had bought a leather suitcase from a second-hand shop near the Belfry Tower. In went the basics like a change of socks, underwear and shirts, alongside shaving tackle, soap and a small hand towel. Then he placed a phone call to a man called Bernard Wolf, a former soldier and member of Combat 18 Flanders, who was now a traditionalist operative attached to the Remy Schrijnen Commando, someone he had met in the Black Forest camp with Senka. Travelling in disguise to Antwerp he met up with a person Wolf was certain could help him. David Albrecht was a dark haired, thick set man, who sat smoking Bastos cigarettes in a grubby bar in the Hoboken district. Peter noticed the surreptitious flash of the Flemish lion shield badge from the underside of his collar, nodded and shook hands.

"I am with the Baduhenna Commando," Albrecht confirmed.

"I need some papers," Peter told his new acquaintance.

"Yes, I heard from Bernard you had some problems," Peter smiled, "How soon?"

"Quick!"

"I understand," the forger said. "If you come with me, I can take some photographs, work up a new ID. The whole thing should take a week or so."

"That suits me fine!"

"Where are you going?"

"Sweden."

"That's a hot climate for us!" Albrecht said with a twist of genuine irony.

"I know!"

"You will fight?"

"One step at a time," Peter replied, "for now I just need to get out of the Lowlands."

They took a yellow taxi to a small attic apartment in Kontich. Pencil sketch portraits of Kenau Simonsdochter Hasselaer and Marie Adelheid stared back from the artist's tripod stand. The session lasted around two hours. Albrecht worked fast but meticulously, moving back and forth in front of his rather self-conscious subject.

"Relax," Albrecht kept saying. "That pained look on your face is exaggerated by the camera. You actually look like a man on the run."

Four days later Janssen stepped out onto a back street in the half-light with only thirty minutes to spare for his train to Liege. He checked his mobile and saw that a number of coded messages had arrived from Wolf in Potsdam. There was also one with a still photo of a Jihadist cutting his sister's throat.

What would he tell his parents?

With tears juddering up inside, he kept staring straight ahead as the high-speed network took him through Wallonia towards Liege-Guillemins, a countryside that had witnessed Napoleon's defeat at Waterloo, the fierce defense of the Locin Fort by three hundred and fifty men during the First European Civil War and Hitler's last-ditch gamble in the Ardennes. Fingering his ticket stub, Peter contemplated how his life was following a similar trajectory to that of a man born over a century ago in Bouillon. "I am a political soldier," he repeated to himself. "I reject all injustices, lies and illusions. . . if falsehood is the tool of subversion, truth is the victorious weapon of tradition. It is my duty to grasp it and realise it by means of action in the world."

FORCE MAJEURE

"Where were your knives and where were your sabres
Where were you when I was in Kosovo?
Where you could have been heroes, fighting Turks?"

—From the Epic Poem *Strahinich Ban*

She killed her first man at Nikola Tesla airport. His body had fallen, eyes startled, hands thumping the floor tiles as blood pumped over quivering lips. Senka watched his legs twitching as she twisted the scissors deeper into his soft throat, her hands ripping the key to the handcuffs from her victim's trousers.

She slid the heavy body slowly, leaving a wide arc of scarlet behind her as she pushed the corpse into a small cubicle and latched the door. Taking some paper towels from the chrome dispenser she wiped everything down before exiting. Leaving the arrivals gate and flagging a taxi, Senka paid eighty dinars to drive to the city, looping the Danube and crossing the Sava river before disappearing into the Drinska district of Belgrade. Later the television news reported the killing. Questions were being asked about how she could have evaded the transport police. By nightfall Senka was declared an undesirable and a price placed on her head. But she had already gone to ground with the help of the Republika Srpska army, reappearing a few weeks later in a dark wig and sunglasses leading a student riot in Stari Grad.

"On!" she screamed through the megaphone "On, Srbi svi I svuda!" and the university students charged the fibreglass wall, bodies bouncing off police shields, arms breaking and heads splitting as state security brought down their batons in metronomic chopping motions, pushing the protesters back across the square.

Senka left the scene with a celebratory three finger trinity salute, coughing and spluttering under a cloud of tear gas, returning to her dark flat to watch the flare lights of incendiary devices going off over the rooftops of the city. Emotionally exhausted, she lit a cigarette and climbed into bed.

For a while she lay, unsure what to do. Despite her fatigue it was impossible for her to sleep, so she dressed and walked through the city, gliding past the Prince Michael statue and the quiet Manjez park, drifting down side streets off Beogradska where massage parlours and student bars played host to nihilistic parties. This pattern dominated for weeks. She would occasionally rest fitfully during the day but invariably wake, slip on a long coat and go out again. She had taken to carrying a Zastava pistol in her pocket and clutched at it so tightly that her fingers got cramped.

She attended clandestine meetings in grubby bedsits with activists and theoreticians of the Serbian Obraz, enamoured by Gauls like Ousset and Bouchet. Bojan, a local commando leader operating around the Vracar area, gave her an old edition of Vladimir Gacinovic's *The Death of a Hero*, commemorating the life of Bogdan Zerajic, a Serbian student and political freedom fighter, someone who supported the Ujedinjenje ili smrt, proclaiming, "We are blessed by the Bishop of Banja Luka."

Senka devoured influences like a frothing nebula, organising guest speakers from Estonia's Sinine Äratus nationalist youth movement, pulling together opponents of the Optor Bulldozer Revolution of 2000 against the Milosevic regime. Deprived of her university place in the West, she fell under the spell of radical gurus in the East. She thought of herself as a reincarnation of national hero Milos Obilic. A student from Nis gave her a green paperback entitled *The Nest Leader's Manual*, and she began agitating for such a strategy to be adopted across the whole of Serbia.

Soon news reached Belgrade that Erdogan's Istanbul was under martial law, and there were mass shootings after dark. EU flags marched alongside Salafist forces across Bosnia, parts of Croatia, Macedonia and Albania, while at the same time EU-sponsored militias moved in to protect its agro-business ventures in Romania.

The nationalist grapevine buzzed with evidence that Cairo and Tripoli were in secret talks with Paris, Rome and Madrid about creating more living space for their recently liberated peoples. Vast territories on the European mainland, specifically southern France, Italy and parts of Spain were being earmarked for Islamic colonization.

It seemed the whole world was in flux.

The President of the European Council justified his decision to issue a bi-cultural tax exemption so that white working women who had multiple children by men from other ethnic groups accumulated multiple rebates per child, on the basis Europe needed more babies. Large population centres, especially those co-located with economic growth areas were subject to racial re-evaluation. This meant removing large numbers of indigenous white families, sometimes at the point of a bayonet, to more deprived zones, whilst convoys of immigrants were travelling in the opposite direction.

Whole cities were re-apportioned and were declared "Euro-Afrique Free Cities." Sometimes this led to outbreaks of violence and in one instance of organized nationalist defiance the mayor of Poznan declared large parts of the city "no-go" areas. Elsewhere, a joint American-Israeli flotilla had established a blockade at the Straits of Hormuz. There were daily air attacks on Tehran, and ancient Indo-European heritage sites near the city of Samen in Iran's Hamadan province were destroyed.

❖ US-backed rebels massacre people in the Rashidin area of Aleppo.

❖ The wife of the Syrian President narrowly escapes assassination when a sniper opens fire on a Red Crescent charity event she is attending in support of child casualties of the ongoing war in Syria.

❖ "This was never a revolution or a civil war," says a Syrian witness to the battle of Deir ez Zor. "It was the West, Saudi and Qatar who sent the terrorists here!"

Lebanon and Jordan were now under the iron heel of Likudist extremists who had already began constructing settlements and displacing Muslim and Christian peoples much the same as they had the Palestinians decades before. Statues to celebrate Irgun and Lehi paramilitary heroes like Menachem Begin were raised in Jerusalem. The last witness of the mass rape and massacre of Arab girls at Deir Yassin was reported to have died in mysterious circumstances. Phosphorus bombing of the Hamas strongholds on the Gaza Strip continued 24/7.

None of Senka's contacts across Serbia, Slovenia or Slovakia knew what would come of the Russian response to One World provocations. Putin's grip seemed to be slipping further day by day.

❖ Two Steregushchy-class corvettes, the *Soobrazazitelny* and *Boiky* seek to defect to the Royal Navy Frigate HMS Sutherland in the North Sea.

❖ A column of Russian T-90 tanks armed with 125 smoothbore cannon and remote-controlled antiaircraft guns run out of fuel on the roadside near Krasnoye on the Russian-Belarussian border.

❖ Tupolev TU-110 Blackjack bomber jets and MIG-35

fighters are grounded near the Three Sisters border crossing at Veselovska.

❖ Leaders of the Coalition for Renewal hold secret meetings with Han Chinese officials in Khabarovsk on the Amur River to discuss lifting visa restrictions to assist cross-border movement from Heilongjiang, Jilin and Liaoning Provinces.

❖ Leading imams from the Great Mosque in Duoba in Xining, the Dongguan mosque in Quinghai and the Bukui mosque in Qiqihar meet to formulate their approach to establishing a Muslim homeland over the Black Dragon river in Russia.

❖ Acting on orders from Issur Babel, Elior Kossov, the Director of International Affairs for the Coalition for Renewal, meets discreetly with the foreign ministers of Armenia, Azerbaijan, Georgia, Kirgizia, Tajikistan, Turkmenistan and Uzbekistan in Kazakhstan's capital, Astana, to discuss the extension of the Harbin to Dalian high-speed network in anticipation of the relocation of around 37 million people into the Russian Far East

When the words of a new Prophet came blasting out of the Najd desert, the Muslim Brotherhood intensified their campaign of burning Coptic churches, cannibalising the dead and raping nuns in broad daylight. The Ummah saw a new light shine upon the Holy Kaaba, and, inspired by Allah's messenger's fresh interpretation of the tawhid, fervent disciples wailed openly for the "dispossession of the infidels" from minarets from Uzbekistan to Tunisia.

At first the teachings from the One from the Najd were whispered in madrasas from Bristol to Bucharest and Ravenna to Rujiena. Then the command went out to act on his words. Death squads stalked the streets of Dubai and Doha where chaghoo-kesh knife pullers hunted rich white businessmen from hotel room to hotel room. Rumours of Chinese mobilizations along the Ussuri river spread doubt that the Kremlin would risk a confrontation on two fronts.

Liberal commentators constantly talked of the destabilization of European society by racist and homophobic extremists whilst hundreds and thousands of dissenters were filing off to detention centres for so called Thought Crimes committed under the newly enacted Legislative Protocols.

In one street fight around the University of Belgrade's Law Faculty some opponents surrounded and stabbed Senka in the stomach. The haft hung from her leather jacket, the blade just penetrating her side. Losing blood, she kicked her assailants away and stumbled. Holding the knife carefully, she pulled bravely at the handle. Her patrol group gathered around her in the half-light.

"Are you okay?" her second in command asked, bending down to evaluate the injury.

'Time to go," she said, reassuring the comitatus of partisans with a nod and a cocked pistol held out defiantly before her strained face. For the next few days she stayed holed up in her dark flat nursing the wound with iodine and fresh bandages. A medical orderly with rebel sympathies visited and diagnosed an infection. He rushed away, returning with antibiotics. Senka remained bed bound, enveloped in sweat for three days. Then one evening, when she felt steady on her feet, she padded barefoot across the floorboards, lifting a large tile under the bath to reveal a cache of plastic explosives and a timing device.

"Time to set the world on fire."

TEMPUS FUGIT

"Finish with all submission! Put your momentum in the service of the new revolution."

—José Antonio Primo de Rivera

He walked, almost fearing the sound of his own footfalls bouncing on the boards. The fog swirled over the

quay where long-haul vessels from all four corners of the
earth came to deposit the produce of the globe. Huge
storage units were piled ten high on the drab strand, cubic
towers of mottled steel pressing down on cracking cement. Peter kept moving, chilled to the bone, until he
came to the *Miss Portas*. The Rotterdam-registered boat
was fifty years old, her hull knotted with wood worm. A
man in a black roll neck jersey clutching a RK-62 assault
rifle told him to step aboard. Another man from the Am-
biorix Commando took his suitcase and went off to hide it
with the cargo.

"I'll put it with the other contraband," he laughed, trying to hang a smile on Janssen's look of apprehension. The
refugee hesitantly obliged, put his hands in his pockets
and walked along the deck. Overhead, American F-22
Raptors in full burn roared through the clouds hurtling
north-east towards Kaliningrad. Coming to some stairs, he
began his descent into the ship's metal bowels, where the
hydraulic churn of pistons and pumps rumbled like gastric
flu. He had to clamber down some ladders a further two
decks until he came to the deck where he was to stay. The
door was ajar, and there were three empty berths. Sitting
on the coarse blankets, Peter reached inside his jacket for
a comb and began to run it through his lank hair. Then,
leaning back on the pillow, he flicked at his lighter and lit
a cigarette.

He slept badly that first night, knowing he was only
one step ahead of a Janus 10 Black Ops unit that specialised in the accidental drug-induced deaths, drownings
and car accidents of political agitators. It was hot below
deck. There was no air-con, and a pyramid of burnt stubs
began to rise out of the makeshift ashtray. Occasionally he
would hear the heavy steps of the guard with the RK62
pass overhead. Then he became attuned to the faint electronic buzz of a satellite radio. Peter could tell it was a
human voice sounding off in the early hours, but he could
not make out the words. He guessed it was not communications from the Opposition's Command and Control cen-

tre, because they were travelling incognito, but it was reassuring for him to think they were still connected to the
underground's network, even here, out amid the battering
waves of the North Sea.

Day and night intermingled. He overheard one of the
crew reciting an ancient Celtic Poem, Song of the Sea:

The ocean is in flood, the sea is full, delightful
is the home of ships,
The wind whirls the sand around the estuary,
Swiftly the rudder cleaves the broad sea

The boat edged forward slowly, rain falling cold and
hard like lead nails hammering down from the sky. By
four o'clock it was already dark, and the ship, which had
put into a sheltered cove, was swinging interminably on
her anchor, creaking and groaning like a grandfather in
his rocking chair. To kill time, he began reading Nietzsche's *The Antichrist* and enjoyed the juxtaposition of
the will to power over Christian moralizing. What is good?
Power, might, truth and dignity. What is bad? Weakness,
cowering, weasel words and compromise. Page after page
revealed the inherent mischief in the Levantine lie he had
been proselytized with since childhood and brought to the
front of his mind the values of his ancestors. Within him
he felt the seed of their gestation and return, the awaken-
ing from the Kali Yuga and movement towards the Impe-
rialismo Pagano.

While aboard ship Peter began a personal health regime based on Aryan Kriya. This involved daily cold baths,
a macrobiotic diet and practising spinning chakras to
rouse the kundalini energy. Within a few days these techniques began to take effect. Despite the cigarettes, the rig-
orous training programme hardened his body, muscles
tightening like wet leather around his bones. Soon he was
pushing sixty chin ups and a hundred squat thrusts. In
order to clear his mind he would saunter along the deck,
pamphlets of the Union of the Archangel Michael clasped

in his hand. Sometimes, he stood and watched the boat's dull oily brass spatter with the ever-changing patterns of raindrops. The air was light and frisky, tingling with the northern wind and the machine gun clack of gull song. Beyond the heavy hatches he could make out the lights of Frederikshavn off to starboard and Kristiansand to port. Over the forecastle a star shone brightly and he in his turn thought of an ancient Anglo-Saxon poem that he admired:

Hail Earendel, brightest of angels,
Over Middle-Yard to men sent,
And true radiance of the sun,
Bright-above the stars,
Every season thou of thyself ever illuminest.

He had settled into shipboard life very reluctantly, staring wistfully up at the vapour trails of F-35 Joint-Strike Fighters, his face twisting with a smile of regret that safe passage for him meant a sea-born voyage along the Danish coastline.

- ❖ The British Government ban the Up Helly Aa shipburning festival in the Shetlands on the basis it is not sufficiently inclusive.
- ❖ Graffiti written by Viking female commanders in the Orkneys is erased by Tungsten Carbide drill bits.
- ❖ The rune stone of Anundshog is removed from public view and broken up to provide foundation filling for immigrant homes in the city of Vasteras on the shores of Lake Malaren.
- ❖ The American Archaeological Society publish a paper discrediting the assumption that the Viking settlement at L'Anse aux Meadows was established by Scandinavian seafarers, arguing instead, that First People communities had in fact constructed the longhouses and turf walls previously thought to be of Norse origin.

The crew paid little attention to their guest, aware of his presence, but showing deference and respect for his privacy. Junior ratings only spoke to him when spoken to. The senior officers treated him to coffee, cognac and an occasional game of poker. Mostly Janssen wrote in his cabin for hours on end, encrypting his messages in case of interception. Peter would sink into the hard pillow after his exercise regime, sweating and stretching to fend off the cramps that sang through his body like violent cello chords. Once, he stood at the prow, hair blowing in the breeze, staring at the rocky cliffs off Goteborg, his imagination filled with images of his Viking ancestors sailing the whale-roads west to Thingvellir in Iceland, Brattahild in Greenland and Point Rosee in Vinland. Then to the east, as far as Trebizond in Turkey, Baku on the Caspian and Khiwa on the Amu Darya river in modern day Uzbekistan.

- ❖ The RAND Corporation identify the Russian enclave of Kaliningrad, wedged between the Polish and Lithuanian borders, as being of vital strategic importance in any future confrontation between Russia and NATO.
- ❖ Western Intelligence Agencies further report Russia has three regiments of S-300's and one regiment of S-400 missiles, along with a Voronezh-DM radar system defending the 7054th Russia Aerospace Defense Forces in the city.
- ❖ Russia's FSB Security Service become involved in a firefight with twelve members of an Uzbek-led Jihad-Jamaat Mujahideen terrorist cell after they attack diners eating in wharf-side cafes hoping to provoke a diplomatic incident.
- ❖ Several German army officers are investigated for allegedly being members of the proscribed Die Rechte party.
- ❖ The Danish Stram Kurs party are declared illegal by the Folketing in Copenhagen.

❖ The Storting, the supreme legislature of Norway,
   bans nationalist groups from marching at the
   Borre National Park, with the speaker saying,
   "These offspring of the Nasjonal Samling
   Ungdomsfylking must never be allowed to revive
   the demons of our Viking past."

At the Captain's table, talk turned to the water riots in
California. It seemed that crisis after crisis had followed in
the wake of the Mayor of Charlottesville unveiling a statue
of Heather Heyer in Emancipation Park and the memorials to the Confederate generals were removed from cities
all across the South. Following its secession from the Union, California and the adjoining states were still busy
tearing down what remained of Trump's wall. The crew
looked on as news footage of US Air force helicopters
dropping grain, milk and basic medical supplies into the
centre of Los Angeles broke on the Fox news channel.
They saw swarms of people crawling like cockroaches in
their own excreta.

"Is that really LA?" the captain said, "It looks terrible!"

"I was there five years ago," the Chief Engineer said,
"The murder rate is higher than Jo'burg!"

"It's nothing to do with us," someone said from behind
a beer bottle. "I say let 'em starve."

"Hell, no," the First Mate disagreed, "They've got to
feed them; it'll stem the flood North. Have you heard of
the attacks in Iowa? I say give them anything, buy some
time!"

"But how?" others were arguing as they rattled soup
spoons, "The New America Foundation is approving sanctuary cities in the Midwest, the Carolinas and New England. I even heard that the Mayor of Provincetown wants
to declare the Cape an independent gay state!"

"What you observe now on the Pacific coast will be repeated all along the Eastern seaboard," Peter added. "Did
you see the thousands of Muslims praying on the banks of
the Hudson in New York? Soon you will have Baghdad in

Bloomington and Kinshasa in Kentucky. They've got a certain Mr Ted Kennedy to thank for that!"

"And when Uncle Sam coughs, we all catch a cold!" said the Captain.

"Amen," added Peter, his hand passing over the tablecloth. "We should have answered that Black Lives Matter Movement with a very clear 'But White Lives Matter Much More!'"

The *Miss Portas* remained stranded at Pier 15 in Helsingborg for a week. There was a crack in the propeller shaft. Beyond the harbour a curfew was being enforced, helicopters filled the skies, spinning rotor blades chattering over the skyline, searchlights sending bright beams down into the streets, scouring out anti-state partisans. Janssen stirred his mint tea and listened to the radio. The crew whispered about militia units marching along the dock, clearing the fish market and conducting body searches on anyone going ashore.

"We need to wait a while. Things are not safe," the captain was saying. "It seems we sailed right into this. Reports are that the EU seized one of our local leaders after he conducted a citizen's arrest on an Arab cleric involved in the grooming of young boys. Both sides have taken to the streets."

Everyone sat around the internet screen watching each other, nervous that the state of emergency would lead to them being boarded and searched. Or even worse, that the *Miss Portas* could be impounded and taken into the naval holding pens at the Islamic Free port of Malmö. Sailing restrictions were enforced by a small white motorboat that went back and for across the harbour. An AW101 hovered over Ostra Ramlosa.

Forty-eight hours passed.

"We can't just sit here," people began to say. "It is only a matter of time before something happens."

"I say we wait it out," the Captain ordered, "Our papers are credible, and these bastards have their hands full onshore. Provided they don't suspect we are aiding and abetting either faction, we will be left unmolested."

"Makes sense to me," said the Chief Engineer, "The prop shaft will be fully functional by the weekend, and we can sail right out under their noses waving our logbook."

The Union eventually quelled the riots, using rocket propelled grenades on the medieval Karnan tower, and lifted travel restrictions as the final sign off came on the repair works for the boat. The *Miss Portas* fired up its engines and steamed out of the Oresund heading into the open channel for Malmö. Janssen stood and watched as the coastline slipped away into the bank of fog rolling in from Kattegat.

"Nearly there," he thought to himself.

❖ The Swedish President, a former Chair of the Migration Board, insists that Sweden will continue its role as a 'Humanitarian Super-Power', increasing the number of asylum seekers it accepts by 25% per year, until the target of complete parity with indigenous Swedes is achieved.

❖ Swedish schools tumble in world rankings for academic performance.

❖ Sweden's High Court blocks the deportation of known terrorists because there is a risk that the criminals' country of origin might subject them to torture and political detention.

❖ A second and third version of the "What Does a Swede look like?" video is produced to break down stereotypes in anticipation of the demographic transformation of the country.

❖ The Swedish government adopts proposals by the Feminist Initiative Party to institute a Man-Tax every time a male has sex with a woman.

❖ Urban planners outline a blueprint to create 600,000 new homes to house the projected 2 million new migrants who will require housing over the next decade.

- ❖ Telia Sverige openly encourages white women to date black men.
- ❖ Afro-Swedes are awarded preferential employment opportunities and tax exempt status.
- ❖ Sveriges Radio is shut down after offending Israeli Ambassador Isaac Bachman by suggesting that some aspects of Jewish behaviour may be a cause of anti-Semitism.
- ❖ Sweden's adviser on multiculturalism insists that *hijra*, migration, and *jannah*, paradise, are the birth right of all Moslems arriving in Sweden.
- ❖ The Viking Line ferry, the *Amorella*, travelling between Stockholm and the Finnish city of Turku, is the scene of another mass rape by drunken Muslim men.
- ❖ The perpetrator of a vicious street attack in Turku is confirmed as an ISIS operative.
- ❖ The Varner Ryden School in the Rosengard district is re-opened, with white students bussed into class, to ensure their cultural enrichment continues without disruption.
- ❖ Sweden appoints the grandson of a Jewish banker who financed the Bolshevik revolution to the post of Media Commissar. His first act in office is to ban Right-wing and nativist internet sites from preaching hate on the web.

Within a few hours they had penetrated Swedish waters and had been required to confirm their status and destination with the coastguard. Under cover of dark the captain came to get him, and they walked together across the rolling deck, climbing down the rope ladder at the side of the ship. Directly above them the sky was milky with starlight, stars fading in and out to the West as a fog-bank began to throw a thin screen across the pulsing aurora.

"Conditions are not ideal," the captain was saying, "but your rendezvous is waiting."

The dinghy was bobbing on the shifting surface as they choreographed like dancers, stretching out their feet, shoes hooking under the lip of the rubber rim to bring it closer. Peter watched the waves sloshing against the hull and the captain shook his hand farewell.

"Good luck!"

"I suspect I will need it." Then pushing off to shore, he floated gently, paddling silently into the darkness.

Peter looked over the moulded prow, nostrils filled by the smell of paraffin. The moon came out from behind a cloud as he slid along the undulating gulf stream, the noise of police boats peaked and passed. Nearer the shore Peter slipped over the side, pushed a blade into the side of the rubber vessel and tied it to a lead weight, forcing the raft away, shoes sinking into soft mud, knees folding, round eyes open wide in cold fear.

He felt his heart racing, his breathing short and jerky, easing out in gasps between gritted teeth. Looking back over his shoulder towards a line of moored ships, he could see the vast factory hulks, towering grey walls and smoking chimney stacks, bobbing silhouettes against the lunar light. He knelt down deeper into the silt, submerged in deep darkness, crawling up to the quay. The water was thick and cloying, insinuating itself through his fabric fatigues. He swam underwater past an observation post, holding his breath until he thought the pressure would split his skull, forcing his mouth open with an invisible tyre lever, sucking the water inside. Peter came up, gulping for air, his eyes on the spit of Swedish coastline ahead. A car was parked on the roadside, headlights blinking. The only sign that there was a town beyond was a pink haze across the skyline.

He swam parallel to the gravel bank trying to make no noise. Wading ashore, his body dripping, Peter lit a cigarette from a sealed bag, emptied a handgun and a couple of shells into his open palm. His mind attuned to the rhythmic flow of the advancing and receding surf.

A cold tang of salt trickled down his temples. Running

across the oily sand, past the kelp beds and broken crab shells, he noticed a toy flag marooned on the shingle, the washed-out yellow stars on the blue background. He picked it up and recognised the symbolism for what it was, a putrescent boil on the once clear skin of Europe. When he got to the waiting car, there was a young blonde woman sitting behind a closed window. Peter came up stuffing various possessions into his pockets, lit another cigarette and followed the girl's instructions to change into dry clothes from the boot. Then jumping into the passenger seat, he stuck the hated flag into his lapel. The girl laughed.

"You've gone over?"

"They made me an offer I couldn't refuse!"

Then they drove at speed along the E6 to Arlov, listening to Ultima Thule on the CD player. The girl introducing herself as Svea.

"As in Sweden?" Peter asked.

"Yes, my parents are long-time patriots. I am a descendant of the people from the Kanaljorden site near Motala where over eight thousand years ago my ancestors placed their enemy's skulls on spikes!"

"Delightful. I see you are now far more hospitable to invaders!" Svea shrugged.

"Now, in Sweden we melt down Viking artefacts like knives, coins and amulets and set up refugee centres for children who are over thirty years old in places like Sölvesborg, and experts at the Royal Institute of Technology insist engineering students undergo an exercise called Project Cohesion which forces them to write an essay on white male privilege."

"A suicidal state of affairs."

"That is not the worst of it. The Karolinska University Hospital is full of Africans undergoing treatments while Swedes are waiting in queues. Twelve-year-old girls are molested by Afghan refugees in Sölvesborg, and people who object to such behaviour are attacked in Helleborg by immigrants. All the while the authorities produce booklets entitled *White Hate*, about how nationalists foment xenophobia in digital environments, ignoring the fact that even the Swedish national Border Security Division has said nine out of ten Moroccan refugees lie about their age and the *Expressen* newspaper refuses to report the rising levels of immigrant crime."

"Insane."

"Anti-racism is Sweden's secular religion. The Solna District Court plays host to the new Inquisition!"

They saw a man walking alone, smiling white teeth shining through the shadow cast by his hooded coat. "One of ours, working underground for the Sven Anders Hedin Commando," Svea assured him. "He is checking we are not being followed." Slowly the volume of traffic increased, and checkpoints were being set up on the side of the motorway. At a bend in the Västkustvägen road a policeman brandishing a torch was flagging cars.

"Don't worry," Svea said to him. "This one is also on our side. I have organised all." After a cursory check they were moved on, fast approaching the centre of town.

"We seem to have many sympathisers?"

"Very many and lots of girls too, especially after the rapes in the Kalstad Putte i Parken!"

"Yes, I heard about that."

"The *Aftonbladet* newspaper tried to cover that up by saying they were done by unknown males, but my girlfriends saw and said who it was. Black hands touching up white breasts and buttocks. The bouncers were too scared to do anything in case they were called racists."

"Did you participate in the march in Borlänge when the Church fathers refused to ring the bells?"

"Yes, I was at Jönköping too, and I was also there when we cleaned up the Odenplan Metro. We were fed up with Muslims attacking thirteen-year-old girls and only getting eighteen-months' probation. People didn't even intervene when a woman was gang raped on the street in Gävle, or when Somali cannibals started biting people in the streets."

❖ The Swedish government pass a law making it illegal for Swedish women to wear the anti-rape "Don't touch" wrist bands that first became fashionable in 2016.

❖ Swedish government offices issue pamphlets in case of war with Russia.

❖ The Saint Afrem Orthodox church in the migrant district of Södertälje is obliterated by an explosion in the middle of the night.

❖ Antifa members poison a dog because its owner was critical of mass immigration.

❖ Despite severe state repression, Nordic Resistance groups continue to protest against gay festivals in Göteborg.

❖ Seven Afghan migrants residing in Östersund are rewarded with financial compensation for wrongful arrest after being accused of gang-rape, reports the *Nyheter Idag* newspaper.

❖ Court Officials justify holding trials for Muslims accused of rape and sexual offences in secret in Kalmar, Uppsala and Ljungby due to threats received from fascist and neo-Nazi organisations.

❖ A number of Swedish police stations are bombed by Islamist cells.

❖ A mother and daughter who were raped by immigrants in Östersund are made to publicly apologise for raising complaints against their assailants.

❖ Women are ambushed by "men speaking a language they did not understand" outside a nightclub in Vasco.

❖ Ten migrants hold down and rape a ten-year-old girl in Örnsköldsvik.

❖ Sapo, the Swedish Security Services, dismiss claims that there may be a link between the death of an investigative journalist and the fact he had found evidence that there was a connection between Soros backed organisations, the Aschberg commercial empire and Left Progressives.

The roads ahead now became broad avenues, row upon row of glass buildings reflecting the globular street lighting. They passed shop fronts full of minimalist flat-pack Scandinavian furniture before reaching the Citadellsvägen, pulling up by a champagne fountain in front of a coterie of cafes that formed a circle around a flagstone plaza. Svea told him to speak quietly. They ambled over to where some tables were occupied by mixed groups of men and women. Some were foreigners like himself, speaking in dialect, holding their heads in their hands over the table like chess players in a quandary about their next move. Others were locals out for supper.

❖ Uncensored reports indicate there are over 200 zones in Sweden that are run under the auspices of Sharia law.

❖ 19 people are injured by a nail bomb on Hamngatan in Linköping in southern Sweden.

❖ The Swedish government imposes ethnic quotas on the Boards of Volvo, Ericcson, Skanska, Hennes & Mauritz, Electrolux, Teliasonen, Sandvik and ICA.

❖ Sweden's Green Party forces a constitutional law that makes it obligatory for Swedes to allow asylum seekers into their homes.

❖ A young migrant who was adopted by a Swedish family is prosecuted in the Gothenburg District Court for forcing the family's 5- and 7-year-old daughters to perform oral sex on him.

❖ Thousands of young Swedish nationals are told they must live in shipping containers in the Sundbyberg district of Stockholm to make room for an influx of Somalians and Syrians.

❖ Jämtland is ethnically cleansed of whites and the Hanseatic town of Visby becomes majority non-white.

❖ The Royal Domain of Drottningholm is fire-bombed.

❖ The Church village of Gammelstad in Lulea becomes a welfare centre for asylum-seekers.

❖ The decorated farmhouses of Hälsingland, recently given over to immigrants, become the scene of riots when local Swedes object to the seizure of their heritage.

❖ Ancient rock carvings in Tanum are destroyed so as not to offend the sensibilities of the new population. The Ministry of Culture announcing it is "a price worth paying to maintain community cohesion."

PART II

"What people in all places have to do is limit their birthrates and promote mixed marriages (between different races), the aim to create a single race in a world which will be directed by a central authority."

—G. Brock Chisolm, former Director of the World Health Organisation

THE STOCKHOLM COMPLEX

"The nation-state is fast becoming an obsolete political structure."

—Daniel Cohn-Bendit

Svea explained how she had attended Sturmvogel camps in Smaland, wearing a long skirt and braiding her hair, before becoming an activist in the Nordwind Faction, part of the Nordic Resistance. She was confidently tapping her fingers on a glass of freshly squeezed orange juice while reminiscing about the part her older sister played in the Kärrtorp incident in December 2013. Peter took out his wallet and slipped a business card across the Formica tabletop. Svea grasped the card, nodded discreetly and secreted the object inside her jacket.

"New hero for us, yeah?"

"Very new," Janssen confirmed, "I'm such a hero I've still got wet pants!"

On a flat screen at the far end of the sports bar a football match was interrupted by live news showing youths rampaging in Rosengård. Cars were being torched and the surrounding districts had been sealed off. "And to think the Riksdag raised taxes to pay for these people," Svea quipped. The on-screen images shifted to Husby and Rinkeby before the commentary turned to the parliament building where an Orwellian *Animal Farm* farce was being enacted for the cameras. Insincere politicians talked about getting tough with such behaviour, while sallow-skinned social workers wanted to discuss the legacy of social exclusion, deliberately avoiding the obvious question, like why the African elephant was in the Scandinavian apartment in the first place?

"We will wait until Anders arrives," Svea said.

"Anders?"

"A friend working with the Per Engdahl Commando. He will take you from me."

"You mean collect me."

"Yes, collect, sorry. He will make sure you will be safe."

A little while later a man in his late twenties came through the door. He was wearing round metal framed glasses and pushed floppy blonde hair off his face as he introduced himself.

"Peter Janssen, I presume?"

"Mr Karlsen!" Peter corrected, showing his new papers.

"Indeed," Anders grinned, "how forgetful of me. You Norrlanders all look the same. Was it your mother or your father who was a Lapp?"

"My family were originally from Stockholm," Peter continued in character, "that is why I am returning there. I intend on settling in the capital."

"Sounds lovely!"

"Indeed," Svea said, "Anders, can you get us some

drinks?" The new arrival swung around to the bar and was soon back with a loaded tray. Peter looked uncomfortable. "Thanks," he said, "you appreciate I have no money, yet!"

"That is not a problem," Svea smiled kindly. Then turning to her colleague. "Anders, were there delays, you are a little later than I expected?"

"Just the routine issues."

"Good, I was worried."

"Come on, let us drink up and go. It is a long drive."

Twenty minutes later Svea and Peter stood still in the car park, shuffling in their shoes, waiting for Anders who needed the washroom. They saw him move towards them through the looping beams coming off the traffic on the Västra Ågatan. Svea bent down, continuing their conversation, unzipping her bag, fingers folding gently around the handle of a Lahti-35. Peter could see Anders' figure framed against the glowing cafe frontage. Then there was an explosion of rapid gunfire from behind his left ear.

"Shit!" Peter fell on his face. Svea was standing spread legged, arms outstretched, pistol pointing, barrel jerking against the backdrop of the waxing moon. Anders hit the ground hard. Svea walked over to the body, swiftly reloading before emptying a fresh clip into the inert shadow on the ground.

"Informer," she spat at Peter's shocked face, "Look?" Peter saw the wire as Svea ripped back Anders' long coat, "Now come, quickly . . . !"

Peter was taken blindfolded in the back of a car to a big house on the edge of Solna, built of warm grey-brown stone, surrounded by a high wall facing a small square. They marched him up a flight of stairs. He could hear doors slamming and code words being passed in hushed tones before the scarf was clumsily removed from his eyes. "Sorry," a man said, fingers untying him, "But you understand we must take precautions." Peter blinked and tried to focus. He was standing in a high-ceilinged room. Behind wooden shutters members of the Swedish underground stood silent and calm, getting on with their activities. Outside, the house appeared like a typical suburban residence, a lush lawn swamped cast-iron garden furniture, all peeling paint and curved grille ornamentation. Solna was a charming middle-class refuge five kilometres or so north of Stockholm, situated in the ancient Parish of Råsunda with its green domed church. The road to Täby lay close by. His hosts had formed a commune led by Alberik, the Nasteschef, and Alicia, the Norwind cell of the Svenska Active, a key force in the resistance since the Riksdag's capitulation to the EU thrones in Brussels and Strasbourg. They had been credited with the mortar attack on the EU Regional Cohesion Conference in the Grand Hotel and the shooting of prison guards from the compound at Uppsala.

Eschewing the predictable Viking cults of Odin and his ilk, this group had been greatly influenced by a Mediterranean political dissident fleeing persecution in Milan. With his seductive dark looks and his figure-gripping wranglers, Roberto had introduced them to the Iranian warrior cult of Ahura Mazda and Arturo Reghini and passed around old copies of *Ur*. When they had developed a taste for such materials, he gave them texts by Vilfredo Pareto and rare Falange publications such as *Fe*, popular among the Sindicato Español Universitario or S.E.U. Soon expressions like "Por la patria" appeared alongside "Kamp for Sverige" on the street hoardings for Benetton and the other multinational conglomerates.

Within a few days Peter was looking through leatherbound volumes of Abbé Barruel and Chevalier de Malet. After that he tried to read Verner von Heidenstam's *The Soothsayer*, Knut Hamsun's *Hunger* and *Heimskringla* in Old Norse but failed miserably. Lighting a cigarette, leaning out of an upstairs window, he gave a deep sigh, longing for active service.

One day he got what he wanted, being sent out with an enthusiastic young Danish militant of the Dansk Folkesparti called Nia on a reconnaissance operation into the city. They were in the Kungsbron district, shadowing Revolutionary Front Left Anarchists. All around them office workers from the World Trade Centre loitered, sheltering from the persistent rain. The wind was whipping itself into a frenzy, channelled as it was between the badly designed buildings in fearful gusts. Peter huddled deeper into his coat, pulled down his hat, but still the moisture found a way of trickling like a dead man's fingers under his curled collar.

Back in the car he checked his machine pistol, ratcheted the shell ejector and ran his thumb sensuously up and down the short barrel. Nia began talking, telling him about her life back in Copenhagen.

"I used to be in the Daughters of The Black Widows Movement," she confessed. Peter said he had no idea what that meant. "The Daughters are the junior wing of the Woman's Movement. It was formed after the George Floyd thing in America. You graduate to be a Black Widow when you menstruate. The idea is that every time a coloured male is killed during a robbery, a gang fight or is put in prison, the women of the movement, invariably white, must bear a black child. Hence the name Black Widows."

"That is terrible!"

"There's worse. Some extremely self-loathing women even abort their white babies when a black is killed by a racist. I have even heard of middle-class women submitting to sex with multiple partners in order to exorcise their guilt!"

"When did you get out of it?"

"When my boyfriend and I were just hanging about like all the others and they jumped us. Four of them against two."

"Were you scared?"

"Shitting myself!" Nia laughed, "They were tooled up, of course. If you didn't stand or make a run, they'd kill you."

"What happened?"

"Well we were near the Radhuspladsen. I got knocked down."

"Is that why you joined?"

"That, and the fact that I was unemployed, and whenever I walked down the Vesterbrogade I could see how things had changed. The immigrants strutted about with cash and food vouchers. We had nothing. They couldn't keep their hands off the women. Whenever there was trouble, the police would protect them even if they were dealing crack. There was one rule for them and one rule for us."

"Tell me about it!"

"On the day after Christmas I met up with another boy called Paul and we sat down to share a coffee and croissants. He let me read his copy of *Mimer*. There was a police station down the road, so we didn't feel too easy."

Peter and Nia stayed a little longer, watching the front of a bank, the deliveries and departures, eyeing the weaknesses and the greeting protocols of tagged security men in visors and blue helmets.

"Got enough intel?" Peter eventually asked.

"I think so." Nia confirmed, "Let's get back."

Later, he lay in bed, a cigarette dangling, dropping ash on the duvet. He took time out to read through a box full of international magazines like *Filosofem* and *Lutte du Peuple*. Alberik's lecture over dinner about the influence of Aleister Crowley on his notion of a post-revolutionary society was still resonating. Both Alberik and Alicia had recently returned from a pilgrimage to England, becoming novitiates of a special Order, living on a farm on the English-Welsh border. The Master was an older man with a bushy red beard just beginning to sparkle with grey. "He is wise and brave," they announced. Alberik described how he had been learning the teachings of philosophers like Gurdjieff and Ouspenski.

"The ethny defines the nation, not the state," the Master said. "The formal constitutional apparatus of the state if it does not reflect the will of the people who gave birth to it becomes by definition a tyranny."

❖ The "Sweden is Dying" TV advert is re-released with the words "It is time to realize the New Swedes will claim their place."

❖ Musical recordings by the White Nationalist singer Saga are banned under new laws against inciting hate.

❖ A Trinidadian man is selected to front a TV dating game on Sveriges Television.

❖ Gangs of immigrants intimidate voters on the streets of Lund.

❖ 79% of rapes are committed by non-ethnic Swedes.

❖ A Somali rapist is awarded 50,000 Krona compensation for "hurt feelings" when the footage of him anally raping a white woman in the Sheraton Hotel in Vasagatan is made public.

❖ Members of the Swedish Social Democrats are arrested for pointing out that one in every twenty native Swedish women have been subjected to sexual aggression from predominantly Muslim men.

❖ The home of a former Oslo police inspector who spoke publicly about the Muslim rape epidemic in Norway's capital is attacked by Black Bloc activists.

❖ Anders Behring Breivik's defence lawyer is assaulted in the street.

❖ Speaking in Norway, a Muslim cleric asserts, "We will defend our religion with our blood . . . Those who insult our religion must know that. Those people who do not respect thirty percent of the world's population, the Muslims, deserve to die . . . Those who insult our religion must know that we will meet them with our bombs. There will be no indulgence, no negotiations in this case. We do not live for the sake of our own lives. We do not

live for our wives. We live only for our religion."
- ❖ Danish Patriots hold rallies at Kronborg Castle and Roskilde Cathedral.
- ❖ The Viking Raven Banner is planted atop the Jelling Mounds in Runic Jutland

Within months Peter was selected to spend two weeks learning the techniques of asymmetrical warfare and undergo endurance training with a team from Norway. He travelled undercover to the Fløyen uplands near Bergen, captivated by the music of Wardruna. The leader of the special unit was called Geir, a tough-looking man of twenty-eight or nine, with thinning corn-coloured hair and fine sculpted shoulders. He wore a peaked leather cap with a Death's Head silver badge on a black band, reminiscent of a young Joachim Pieper. Peter would listen to Geir quoting Helmuth Graf von Moltke: "Talk little, do much and be more than you appear to be" and guessed he was as capable of wielding an axe as transcribing poetry.

They were crisp days. The camp would come alive around dawn as tatters of mist came down off the hills, smothering the tents and shacks gathered around a flagpole with a Norge pennant. They would customarily turn out wearing track suits, increasingly muscular chests glistening with the effort of cross-country runs, long jumping, swimming and weightlifting. After a breakfast of fruit and warm cereal they would scale rope, ford rivers and undertake team building exercises based on manuals gifted from supporters in the special forces. Their instructors were themselves either current marines or former elite troops, renegades from the Finnish Utti Jaeger Commando or the Norwegian Forsvarets Spesialkommando. They had rejected their oaths of allegiance, disgusted by the false promises of political Commanders-in-Chief who sent them off to die in Middle Eastern wars to protect an illegal rogue state or secret undercover operations like those against Syria and Iran.

Peter was surprised how well he was performing in the

physical trials. Only a local called Norden and a young guy from Slovakia consistently outperformed him at track and field type activities. What ground he lost there he made up for in the technical classes and marksmanship. Each cadet received detailed feedback on his strengths and weaknesses at the end of each day. Their weight and diet were assessed, and any gaps in understanding were supplemented by theoretical teaching.

"Listen," Geir would say, "We are an echo of the Templar Knights, a military religious order operating out of Preceptories, and just like those ironclad warriors from years ago, you too are now adhering to the principles of Vita est militia super terram: life is a soldier's service upon this earth." He handed out a glossy handbook entitled *Traditional Living: Theory and Practice.* "Read this," he insisted, "it was produced by our friends in Rome and will help you in the future."

After a few days of close observation Geir took Peter aside. "You seem to be a conscientious young man," he commented as they walked on a gravel path bordered by sunlit meadows. Janssen demurred graciously. "What do you think will happen in the future? Will the struggle grow in severity or will we be forced into political compromises?"

"Struggle!"

"You do not hesitate?"

"I have learned there is no alternative." Geir asked endless questions.

"Can you conceive of an order that would so unnerve you or affect your capacity to act with speed and determination that you could not complete the task?" Peter knew exactly what he was getting at.

"No!"

"Good, because I am recruiting a vanguard for our movement, both activists and academics."

"I see!"

"Are you ready to join that level of the struggle?"

"Yes," he said firmly, "I am already a long way down the

road!"

"Even if it entails self-sacrifice, self-denial and real personal hardship?" Janssen clenched his fist.

"I have cut myself off from my former life."

"You will need to be utterly ruthless and live in almost total isolation, indifferent to suffering."

"I know."

"Comradeship is key," Geir emphasised. "Indeed it is the very basis of our brotherhood. We have sworn to avenge the martyr of Akershus!" Peter nodded affirmation as he envisaged the Rikshird in navy blue and the Kvinnherad women's brigades gathered under waving banners, gold crosses stitched into blood red canvas, eagles and swords.

"The Ynglings, the seedlings of the Landssvikanordning!"

They stood still against the falling sunset, fingers of light playing piano over the waters of a nearby lake. Blue twilight falling like a theatre's fire screen over Mount Blamanen.

"What would you think if I said I am thinking of speaking to Norden in the same vein?"

"I would commend your selection and await a plan of action."

- ❖ The Head of Oslo's anti-racism centre successfully argues for native Norwegians to be expelled from Bergen's commercial quarter.
- ❖ Norwegian nationalists drive off Leftists trying to set fire to the Urnes Stave church in Luster on the Sognefjord.
- ❖ Musical works connected to the Norwegian heathen Varg Vikernes, bands like Burzum, Uruk-Hai, Satanel, Mayhem and Kalashnikov are banned from distribution and public performance.
- ❖ Muslims in Oslo link arms to surround synagogues in an attempt to show solidarity against racist oppression.

❖ Headlines in the *Iltalehti* and the *Helsingin Sano-mat* media outlets report that the Finnish Resistance are conducting vigilante-style street patrols to protect schoolgirls from Muslim grooming.

❖ A poll on the inter-alia website of the Sunnuntaisin Malainen show that 90% of Finns want an end to immigration.

❖ A prominent patriot with strong links to the Black Metal scene, along with his wife and their daughter, are deported from France to Oslo at the request of the Norwegian government, where he is indicted yet again for racial hatred, quoting various speeches he is alleged to have made, his membership of the Heathen Front, influencing a neo-Nazi cell in Hemnes and supposedly inspiring the burning of the Porvoo cathedral.

❖ The Juha Kärkkäinen supermarket chain is closed down for sponsoring the *Magneettimedia* newsletter which carried articles entitled "Zionist Terrorism in Norway" and "CNN, Goldman Sachs and Zionist Control."

❖ The Islamic Party of Finland seize 10 seats in the parliamentary elections to the Eduskunta.

❖ Over 7000 illegals deported from Norway are invited to return, all expenses paid, following a court ruling that the National Immigration Police, the Politiets Utlendingsenhet, acted with insufficient sensitivity between 2015–2020.

A few days later Peter and Norden were sitting in an Interceptor SXI heading towards the hills around Vaksdal. They were listening to the radio, a journalist reporting on how the banking fraternities of Zürich had been nurturing relations and investing in the economies of several South American dictators in advance of the fresh wave of hostilities between Britain and Argentina over the Falkland Islands. For an hour afterwards silence reigned inside the car as Geir drove through the outskirts of picturesque

Sørfjorden, the Interceptor continuing up a steep ascent in the Herfindalen. When the road came to an end, he encouraged his passengers to disembark and follow him up a dry mud track. They soon came upon a mound surmounted by a lone tree.

"This oak is five hundred years old!" Geir said. Peter and Norden looked on respectfully. Geir leaned against the gnarled trunk and indicated for his companions to follow suit. They gazed for a moment at the little township in the valley below, red wood houses surrounded by conifers.

"This is a historic place," Geir said portentously. "Folklore tells of how men of good heart have travelled here on summer nights to cavort with *sjora* from the streams and the *skogsrå* from the woods. Inside this very tree the spirit of the mountains is contained, and it is our task to set these elemental forces free." Peter and Norden felt honoured. "Your probationary period starts now. I will take you on specialist manoeuvres before returning you to your cells. You will have no money worries. The movement will now take full responsibility for you. These are your code names." He handed them two slips of paper with a typed phrase and a telephone number. "Memorize and destroy. All you must do is make contact from anywhere in Europe. Read out this name and you will receive immediate support. Your orders and needs will be requisitioned. This service is not available to our regular cadres. You are now a part of the Eternal Inner Circle. If you desire a particular gun it will be procured, likewise a visa for anywhere, even China,. If you want the services of concubines that can also be provided. There is however only one exit strategy from this group," Geir looked them both in the eye. "I hope you understand me."

They reached Krekane just before midnight. A road leading uphill from the centre of the village took them along a centuries-old tree-lined track towards a villa in the mountains. The Interceptor swept in through the wrought iron gates. While the car engine idled, a fair-skinned woman materialized before their windscreen. She was tall, small-breasted and decidedly Nordic. They could see she was wearing a clinging blue dress and waving a matching scarf as she hailed the car cheerfully.

"Welcome," she smiled, "I am Sigrid Aadland." Geir removed his hat and raised a hand in salute.

"Thank you for waiting up for us!"

"I am so happy to see you." She was practically tap-dancing with joy on the chipped gravel. Peter and Norden walked along behind as Sigrid and Geir moved towards the looming villa. At the main entrance, below the carved portico, the new arrivals were greeted by a second young lady of lissom shape cradling a CZ-75 automatic pistol to her breast and a man with a winning smile who rushed forward to help them carry their baggage.

Geir made a point of thanking their welcoming party and shot Peter and Norden with a reassuring look.

"This is Birgit and Frode," he explained, "Birgit is our Norwegian group secretary and communications expert." She was a rustic beauty, a Fjellpryd flower of the back-woods, graceful despite her handgun. "They will attend to us in our conclave."

"Greetings, comrades," Birgit said, stepping back a pace, her hand pushing open the creaking door, leading into an inner chamber lit by a candelabrum. Passing over the threshold, Frode added, "Young men like yourselves can learn a lot here. Start by moving into your quarters and getting a good night's sleep. You can join the others for breakfast at 8 AM precisely."

Peter and Norden were conducted up a long wooden staircase. At the top their host paused outside the two suites reserved for them. "Number five is for Mr Janssen and number six for you Mr Fry. Here, you will soon see everything is organised on the basis of true equality."

The following evening, after a full day of light training and saunas they gathered in a dining hall laid with silver cutlery and antique china. Tveitt's *Sun God's Symphony* was playing in the background. Geir raised a hand-cut

Murano goblet and toasted one Scandinavian deity after another. Then he stood at the head of the dark wood table and nodded to each and every one of his new recruits. In addition to Janssen, Fry and Birgit, there was Karl Braun from Dortmund; a dark-eyed Portuguese, Benedito Correja; Charles Renner from Salzburg; Nata Poukkanen, a Finn, holding a membership card for the Soldiers of Odin and formerly associated with the Suomen Vastarintaliike and Musta Sydän, the Black Heart Movement, but now with close links to the Perussuomalaiset (PS) Party; Ona, a teenager from the Lithuanian Youth Union; Francis Millman, a young man from Kings Lynn in England; Adela Bankowski, a blonde from Gdansk; Aleš Balažic from Slovenia and Magnus Árnason from Iceland. All acknowledged their leader's salute. "Before each of you is laid a dagger with a rune specific to your code name inlaid in silver on the black hilt." Then after a short pause, "Take this symbol as a ceremonial gift, honour your forefathers and never surrender it!" They all took a deep draft from their glasses. "Now, ladies and gentlemen, let us fortify ourselves, for tomorrow your ordeals truly begin."

And begin it most certainly did. They were awakened by martial music and marched through the grounds to an open-air pool and a panoply of gymnasium equipment, parallel bars, trampolines and a three-metre-high wooden wall. Each was given an exercise mat to limber up and then introduced to Olympic shooting coaches, experts in unarmed combat and world champion fencers.

"What good is sword play?" Norden asked. "We are not likely to be challenged to a duel."

"Fool," Geir sniggered. "It is to train balance and footwork; the blade itself is quite peripheral. All your preparation here will involve multi-fold meanings and skills. Even the specialist digital and electronic sessions will be done in a way that gives dexterity training."

They stood in a circle and watched Ona, a native of Vilnius, lifting incredible weights despite her small frame.

"Look," Geir was enthusiastically telling them, "a slender feminine woman is shifting kilos some of you will struggle with. It is all about technique and will power. I dare any of you to challenge Ona to a wrestling match. She wriggles like an eel from the Neman river and strikes like Egle, Queen of the Serpents." They may have been laughing, but all of them recognised the veracity of Geir's claim. Ona would prove a very difficult opponent under any conditions.

At midday they ate from a communal table laid with goat's cheese, herring, sea crabs and marinated nuts. The squad cleared their bowls quickly and drank from pitchers of freshly squeezed apple and grapefruit.

"A healthy spread," Geir was saying to everyone who would listen. "Now it is time for some roleplay to accentuate the thespian in each of you!" They trooped back into the villa and acted out various scenarios and discussed the veracity of the various options they took and the mannerisms that may have given them away to an observant policeman. In a library room overlooking an herb garden, they sat before shelves filled with volumes by Goethe, Kant and Rousseau. Undergoing ideological training, the group were introduced to manuals from the United States, mainly covering covert operations and subjected to instruction from a dedicated French sympathiser named Franck Bodine who had served in the Foreign Legion. "We are lucky to have Franck with us," Geir was saying, "he has his hands full in France!"

The group sat around a large wooden table on high backed chairs. Geir was gratified to note that they were all quick to learn their lessons and, spurred on by peer pressure, did not often make the same mistake twice. The role of the group was to act as a spearhead in each of the designated Eurozone regions, to counter the growing power of the centralized state.

"You are not the suicidal fanatics," he beseeched them. "You direct the suicidal fanatics, do you understand? Our aim here is to prepare you for medium to long term engagement in the insurgency, not to throw your lives away cheaply. Others may be expendable, but you are not. The whole point of our investment is to ensure you make those decisions locally and then live with the consequences."

A week later they gathered around a glowing fireplace sipping fine brandy. The Chief was holding court.

"Three special missions will complete your trials," he was saying. Peter paid particular attention as Geir described the tasks they were to perform. "You will split into three teams of four. The units will be self-selecting, and you will have a free hand as to how you conduct yourselves. However, I will decide which team fulfils each objective." They nodded. "These are the projects: to kill a leading member of Parliament implicated in people trafficking scams and obtaining human rights vetoes for foreign criminals; to firebomb a major department store actively involved in the deforestation of Sogndal; and finally, to obtain a retraction from a *Dagan* news journalist, forcing him to admit he had wilfully falsified stories about our movement in order to prevent us obtaining public support."

"How long do we have?"

"One week," Geir told them. "That should give you ample time to study your targets, draw up a plan and execute it."

Geir was not to be disappointed. Each of the squads came back to him having decided upon their composition and received their briefing. Sigrid dealt with equipment and requisitions. Preparations were soon complete, and each task initiated.

Project Voluspa was a total success. Peter and Norden took a temporary flat in Oslo and assisted Millman and Balažic to falsify IDs, references and assorted credentials allowing them to masquerade as a high-end domestic cleaning agency. Disguised as such, the two dungaree-clad intruders were able to get clearance to work inside the minister's mansion in Brandts gate. After breakfast one day, Peter locked the minister's wife and daughter in the lavatory while Balažic cut his throat.

Project Baldur was just as carefully planned. One Thursday evening in the middle of late-night shopping, four people entered the store under the guise of two young couples. Visiting the ladies' lingerie and menswear departments they deposited primed incendiary devices and left. Shortly before midnight a passing taxi noticed a strange orange light coming from inside the building and within seconds the alarms were ringing and sprinklers singing but to no avail. The insurance investigators later estimated that over 200,000 Euros of fire damage was done within the first thirty-five minutes of the attack.

"Excellent outcome!" Geir was heard to say over his poached eggs the following morning.

Project Siegfried offered an interesting return. Alun Berland, the team's target, was, after admitting to his complicity in providing state-sponsored sound bites, to remain free. They trailed the journalist for a week before the squad moved in, kicking out the door to his mistress's private apartment in a leafy suburb of Molde, the wood shearing off its hinges while their victims made love in the shower. Like speckled trout they were pulled into the living room and a gun placed at Berland's lover's temple.

"Now," Braun commanded, "you will start writing a confession." Berland's fingers began typing on the keyboard while Adela explained what was required and the syndication pattern that was expected.

"Anything! anything!" Berland was blathering, "just don't hurt anybody, okay?" When he had finished and the re-drafting approved, Braun's latex-gloved index finger pressed the send button, and their objective was achieved.

"I particularly enjoyed the compromising photo," Geir said later, "it captured the venal quality of the individual concerned." Afterwards, they drove Berland out into the street wearing only his bathrobe, knowing he was going to be questioned about his behaviour by his long-suffering wife and bewildered children. The girl they took with them, conscious that holding her gave them further leverage. Within a few days, Berland was forced to admit to two further and even more detailed cases where he had misrepresented the truth. By now his wife had left him and he was sleeping on a friend's sofa while trying to save his career as a journalist. When Karl and Adela deemed that they had drawn sufficient political capital from the operation, Magnus finished off their hostage with a single shot to the head.

Later, there were some recriminations over the cold-blooded murder of the girl. Braun commented that Bankowski and Arnason may have gone too far.

"It was necessary," Adela insisted. "Our personal safety demanded it. The woman would have been able to help identify us. Her elimination is regrettable but perfectly justified." Geir came down in favour, and no more was said on the matter. When the authorities found her blue, decomposing body in a motel room in Baerum, they were not surprised to find a calling card: "Last Respects from the Nasjonal Samling."

At the end of their training each and every one filed one-by-one into Geir's office. He was sitting behind a large desk in front of a piece of art entitled *Kratos 2*. Geir eyed them all carefully from behind piles of papers, full and detailed assessments of how they had performed as individuals and team members.

"Janssen, come!" Geir began as Peter strode in, taking a chair placed in the middle of an oriental rug. To his right was a shelf with texts by Malthus, Pentti Linkola, Devamrita Swami and Brynjar Lia's biography of Abu Mus'ab al-Suri. "You have done well for such a skinny one," Geir laughed. "I thought you would struggle against the others, but no, you have excelled, and your exit velocity is greater than I could have ever expected."

"Thank you Geir, you know I am deeply honoured . . ." Geir waved away the flattery.

"No time for niceties. You go back to Norwind and help them to prepare. Mentor the best and use up the rest." Janssen rose to leave, extended a hand and felt it met firmly by a veteran whose respect he had earned.

At midnight, before a flaming log fire the new initiates stood one and all, shoulder to shoulder, before a hooded figure, each in turn swearing the following oath:

> I, in joining this sacred order swear by the sun that warms me and the soil that gave birth to me that I will from this forward dedicate my life to defending my kinfolk and preventing the defiling of my ancestor's blood and the invasion of our land. I vow before my brothers and sisters to lead in this eternal struggle to liberate Europe from our enemies and restore her glory and dignity.

Soon rumours of hand-picked units going by names like the Peter Mangs and the John Ausonius Commando were emerging through the underground movement all over Scandinavia. Peter was laughing at newspaper reports being read aloud by his patrol as he stood spread-legged shooting his pistol. "Anti-Hate Week is going to be a little different this year," they laughed as people passed around photos of government officials, community activists and Black Bloc leaders signing an agreement to force the Nazis off the streets. The members of the Nordwind Group were all taking turns firing briskly into the forest, the crack of lead echoing off bald rocks. They drilled and practised laying traps and constructing hot points from which to counterattack.

A Browning hung from his right hand as Peter began his demonstration. "On the count of three," he repeated, "fire!" He emptied a full chamber into the dummy target's head. Then a young girl called Eloise, blue eyes and blonde hair, stepped forward to yelps and howls of support. She took one loaded pistol in each hand and weighed them carefully for a moment. Nodding towards Janssen, she planted her feet, lifting the guns, catches clicking, as trigger fingers began stroking hard, sixteen rounds pulping posters of Jonas Sjöstedt of the Left Party,

Isabella Lövin of the Greens and Aloysius John, the CEO of the pro-refugee Caritas Foundation. The soundscape of shells fell away from their ears. A smell of oily gunpowder and hammered metal filled the air. Alberik tried to stifle his admiration. "And who taught you that trick?" His eyes focussed on the zig-zag patterning of holes reminiscent of a signature sign associated with the Second World War.

"I've been practising," Eloise confessed as she lay down the weapons on a flat stone, turning her long sleek back which tapered out like an expansive crystal vase into two shapely buttocks.

A couple of weeks later they all sat down to watch a terrestrial TV channel beamed in from Brussels. The flickering screen revealed a dishevelled man in thick round glasses looking a bit like a struggling bank clerk speaking in stilted English directly into the camera. The scene was reminiscent of Aldous Huxley's *Brave New World*.

"Community, Identity, Stability," he seemed to be saying in dull monotone. There was a strong sense of auto-suggestion being transmitted out from Belgium and Strasbourg which hid the servitude the mantra was really purveying. Genuflections about the pandemic, the need to move to cashless transactions, digital online banking and the importance of economic security were made by reference to charts and forecasts no one could quite comprehend. It was meant to dull the audience's perception before the core message, the need to overcome human differences, to make sure there were no square pegs in round holes. Nothing should deflect us from the goal of social cohesion. This was followed of course by reassurances that the freedom we all enjoyed was going to be defended at all costs. References to past wars and discontents were made to reassure everyone that those dark days were over and should never come back. We all lived in a permeable utopia now. You can come and go. There were no boundaries. No distinct identities to uphold. Then after the platitudes

and propaganda came the soma of advertising and entertainment, a circular procession of multifarious half naked
dancers celebrating in a wild dystopian orgy of interconti-
nental harmony:

Orgy-porgy, Ford and fun,
Kiss the girls and make them One.
Boys at one with girls at peace;
Orgy-porgy gives release.

Over the next three months Nordwind and the Dagmar
Cronstedt Commando in Sweden, along with kindred
groups like the Finn Hodt and Hirden Commando in
Norway, the Julius Krohn Commando in Finland and the
Oskar Kallas Commando in Estonia, launched their campaign of disruption. The Swedes hit private banks, exclusive jewellery stores and businesses sponsoring anti-
Swedish activities. CCTV footage of hooded men and
women waving pistols at bank tellers appeared on news
programmes and were raved about on the dark net. They
were rapidly becoming a cult among the young. There
were occasional shootouts with the police, and state security began placing armed guards at potential targets like
mosques, synagogues and the homes of prominent officials.

Nordwind lost a couple of operatives in an aborted
kidnap attempt on the Ghanaian Ambassador, who had
recently escaped a rape charge by claiming diplomatic
immunity, and Alberik came back from one mission with
a nine-millimetre shell in his thigh. Nordwind also set up
roadblocks and conducted selective car hijacks on key
roads in and out of the city. Using flash protests and social
networks they and their co-groups kept the police on 24/7
emergency status.

❖ A Copenhagen-based band are banned from performing live and their recordings in all formats are
deemed inappropriate for dissemination.

❖ The lead singer of the aforementioned band is seized in a raid on the Matador Records mini studio near the Amalienborg Royal Palace.

❖ Other members of the group and similar bands go into hiding when permits to seize and detain them are issued on the instruction of Minister Chaskel Besser.

❖ Jesse Ekene Conable, a Nigerian rapper living in Sweden, returns to an earlier theme he raised on YouTube, saying: "If any white guy or girl is trying to talk shit about you, shoot them!" adding in his Twitter messages "Black Power in Sweden!" "Fuck White people!" and "Black brothers and Black sisters continue the War. We'll take their Balls and their Money!"

❖ The Stram Kurs nationalists in Denmark are declared a terrorist organisation under the newly extended Danish 266B regulation.

❖ The US President takes the opportunity of the anniversary of the emancipation of enslaved blacks to confirm the recommendations of a House Judiciary Subcommittee to set aside $500 billion in reparations for the Afro-American community.

❖ The US Security Agency steps up its use of cyber-tools inside Russia's grid, declaring "a digital Cold war between Washington and Moscow is now inevitable."

Peter relived his own arrival experience when the cell agreed to meet with an aggressive liberal journalist called Gunner Ovesen from the *Aftonbladet* who had been on their case for some time. The scribbler and his film crew were met by a small clique of armed members of the underground. Blindfolded and jammed unceremoniously into the back of a campervan, they were then driven around the suburbs and out into the countryside in a wide-arcing loop so as to disorient them and disguise their final destination.

Hours later they gathered back in Solna behind blacked-out windows. The room buzzed with conversation. The sound of cameras whirring as they stood talking into a handheld microphone through slits in black balaclavas in front of a Celtic Cross.

"What do you say to people who call you terrorists?" asked the bearded journalist.

"I would tell them we are freedom fighters. Our struggle is with those that seek to destroy our people, no more, no less!"

"How do you mean?"

"The state apparatus is currently committed to the genocide of all Nordic peoples living within its borders!"

"Are you advocating that only Scandinavians live here?"

"We are advocating a nation space that is identifiable by its traditions and homogeneity, nothing more!"

"What do you mean by homogeneity?"

"What do you think?"

"A one-culture polity!"

"A polity that maintains the integrity of the originators of the nation."

"So you want to expel people?"

"We want to prevent the mass importation of non-assimilating peoples who by their actions and presence threaten or irrevocably changes the nature of the founding peoples."

"And you justify your bombings and violence this way?"

"Our response is calibrated to fight state laws that seek to suppress free speech, attack us by means of economic ruin, arrest us and send us to re-education centres and the like . . ."

"So you oppose the dream of a colour-blind nation?"

"Colour-blind?"

"Yes!"

"Are people in Saudi Arabia, Chad, China, Zimbabwe or South Africa colour-blind?"

"Well . . ." Ovesen hesitated.

"No, answer my question, Mr Journalist."

"What do you mean?"

"Talk to me about Mexican or Pakistani immigration laws?"

"Why is that relevant?"

"The fact you do not know about them, or worse, do not want to discuss them, makes me wonder about your objectivity."

"My objectivity?"

"Yes, talk to me about the statistically proven propensity for violence and rapes among certain groups in Denmark."

"That is not the purpose of my . . ."

"Your purpose . . .?"

"I mean . . ."

"Can we discuss Christopher Brand's book *The G Factor*?"

"My plan for today . . ."

"Is to misrepresent us and portray us to the public as crazy fanatics," Alicia cut in.

"Well some of your people eulogise policies akin to the Argentinian Nouvelle Acropole movement of Jorge Angel Livraga and use quotes by Adrien Arcand in their postings."

"And some of our opponents glorify Mao who deliberately starved fifty million people to death and Stalin and his acolytes who killed sixty million of their own people." Then Alberik smiled. "Or, more prosaically, follow unwritten agreements between journalistic unions and their members to smear anyone to the right of Bakunin."

"And are you familiar with such philosophers?"

"I have read widely, including Kropotkin, Plekhanov and Marx."

"And do you have sympathy for any of their ideas?"

"Of course, where they offer critiques of social injustice and recommend solutions to economic disadvantage."

"How do you square that with your social pessimism?"

"I am an optimist!"

"But you reject the future, you oppose the inevitable changes to our country . . ."

"Inevitable?"

"Yes, inevitable!"

"Your certainty confirms your complicity!"

"My writing reflects the real world . . ."

"Your writing reflects the propagandist utopia your masters want to bring into existence . . ."

"And you don't want to participate?"

"We have no option but to participate. The form of our participation is why you are here."

"And will you continue to fight?"

"As a wise man once said, demographics is destiny!"

Thirty minutes after this interview was aired the Swedish Minister of the Interior, sitting in his office just above the Blue Hall in the Stadshuset, shook his head, raised his finger and pointed at the people around a long oblong table, his voice wavering in the air conditioning.

"So ladies and gentlemen, please tell me how do you propose we respond to this very public challenge?" To his right sat Edelmann, head of the Centre for Cultural Assimilation, who held the portfolio for immigrant settlement and Social Affairs. Then Ferber, Chief Executive of the Urban Taskforce for Housing New Guestworkers. To his right sat Brandeis, Prefect of Police. Moving along, Axcel, Director General of the Equalities Commission and next to him, Walzer, Private Personal Secretary to Gecht, the minister who was chairing the meeting.

Before each of them was a large manila folder full of still photography from the footage they had just witnessed, transcripts of intercepted underground communications and some recent propaganda pamphlets that complimented what they had been told at the pre-airing briefing was despite all their efforts a still growing virtual on-line presence. Also listed was a catalogue of direct actions which read like a recipe for national revolution:

❖ An explosion at the giant Gothenburg mosque complex is attributed the avengers of the Ebba Akerlund commando, a Beserker Battalion composed of female patriots.

❖ 34 reported acts of street violence including girl soldiers dressing up in white dresses, hair in braids, parading in St Lucia celebrations before opening fire on security forces—and their male co-conspirators masquerading in *tomtar* and *stjarngossar* costumes setting off bombs in the Stortorget.

❖ 55 raids on jewellery shops from the capital to Lulea, including cross border raids back and for along the E20 and the firebombing of the Tivoli Gardens in Copenhagen.

❖ Turf wars with local drug gangs in Malmö.

❖ 74 auto hijacks across the national road network.

❖ The political assassination of the Mayor of Ostersund.

❖ 2 full-scale national petitions of over 500,000 signatures against what they call the Collaborationist Swedish Government.

❖ An attempted Putsch of a local council in Visby on the island of Gotland.

❖ The liberation of 12 detainees from the Vaxjo and Skovde detention centres for people suspected of harbouring politically incorrect views.

"You have all read the briefing drawn up by Walzer and now you have heard the challenge from our opponents," Gecht was saying. "I have of course called you here to harness our resources to drive these acolytes of Sten Sture and Jonas De Geer, these forces of reaction like the filth of the SSPX, back into the damp holes they crawled out from. Remember, these are the same people that would have people like us returned to the Pale of Settlement or contained in Birobidzhan like some kind of human bacillus. Do you want your children subject to such exclusion?

Could they survive it, now they are set to inherit a world which we own?" He paused again. "This is a battle for our survival. We will employ any tactic we see fit to win. I am sure we all thought our Norwegian partner's deployment of Mr Breivik a few years ago, Brenton Tarrant's outrageous shooting exploits in New Zealand and John T. Earnest's synagogue attack would turn their own population against them but clearly that strategy only delayed matters." Then sighing, "It would seem that the media memes our American colleagues created about Dylann Roof and Nikolas Cruz have been somewhat undermined by our own sympathisers like James T. Hodgkinson shooting up some Republicans in Washington and the Stephen Paddock attack on the Country and Western concert in Las Vegas. To put it bluntly, the shock-factor and our moral high ground is wearing thin." Down both sides of the table, heads nodded in sober agreement. Others kept their eyes fixed on the speaker. "But still, there must be no questioning of the policies of this government." The Director General of the Equalities Commission next to him winced with each comment. "These are the outpourings of the Motpol," Gecht continued, "We should have been less tolerant, and maybe that would have discouraged them. But no, I listened to people counselling reason, talking of safety valves and look where it got us. Armed thugs on our streets. Angry dogs barking on the radio and TV and endless chattering on social media." There were embarrassed looks all around the room.

"But . . ." someone went to say.

"What?"

"Nothing . . ."

"Now," resumed Gecht, "I need to know how quickly we can organise a cleansing operation." The head of the Prefecture looked up from his report and cast a glance at the Minister of the Interior.

"The State Police can be ready to move in two hours." Spurred by Brandeis's assertion they all began to make firm commitments on behalf of their departments.

"Then we are agreed," Gecht shouted, "We move before dawn and make the American army's insurgency through Tikrit look like a summer picnic in the park!"

At 4 in the morning, two hundred Union Troops flanked by armed police threw a ring around each of the nationalist safe houses they had identified in and around the city. Dozens of searchlights criss-crossed the fronts of stone-faced targets and the crackle of automatic fire smashed plate glass windows.

By dawn three locations had been neutralised, the occupants either killed or captured. In Malmö the Union forces were met with a thunderstorm of Molotov cocktails from local sympathisers who came out on the streets to provide cover for resistants holed up in a small tenement flat using faltering small-arms fire as their ammo ran low.

In Solna, the Nordwind group fought like Berserkers, house to house, room to room and step by step. Each member resolved not to be taken alive. Janssen had been awoken by the first barrage. Rolling out of bed, he grabbed the gun from under his pillow. The Union, by sheer weight of numbers and stifling firepower, had already forced their way across the exterior lawns and began to infiltrate the lower ground floor rooms. Defenders' guns falling from their dead grip were lying entangled in their own bloodied intestines at the windows.

The front door was caved in by an armoured car. As the wooden planks splintered, two Union troopers leapt through the gap only to be confronted by Alicia who dropped her empty AK-47, took a handheld explosive device from a hip belt and ran directly at them, setting off an orange flash of light.

An hour later the Unionists were working their way systematically up through the building, stairwell to stairwell, cutting off one section of rooms at a time and trying to isolate the various militants by using stun grenades and digital neutralisers.

It was hand-to-hand and toe-to-toe. At one point Peter

appeared through a hole in a plaster wall. In his hand he held an Uzi. An oncoming trooper was grimacing. The soldier went to lift his own automatic, but Peter kicked it away, knocking the trooper to the floor, sending a spray of bullets into the cornice ceiling. Then Peter brought down the metal butt of his own weapon on the enemy's helmet, cracking through to the skull, the Union man's vomit spewing over his shoes. Janssen kicked the body aside as Alberik limped forward in his olive-green combat jacket. His leg was in a tourniquet, grenades in his hands. Eloise, exhausted, collapsed to her knees beside Peter.

"Take these," she was wheezing through a hole in her chest, "get out!"

"Out!" he heard Alberik screaming. Peter emptied the Uzi down the corridor and rolled a grenade into the dark. Instantly there was a detonation, a phosphorescent blast filling the place with iridescent light. Then a noise like a plastic snap rolled through the narrow space, reeking smoke filled the survivor's senses, broken limbs stuck to the walls.

Moving forward, looking out through shattered glass, Peter could see the black fatigues of the militiamen swarming along the road, pouring out of the backs of vans, lined up and down the district's apartment blocks. They were concentrating heavy ordinance on the windows of adjacent buildings in case of sniper fire.

The shooting continued deep inside the belly of the building. One by one, Nordwind were being over-whelmed, and those who were not killed wished they had been. Svea was being spun by her long hair and spat on by her captors.

"Down!" she was commanded, an officer ramming his rifle along her spinal column. She could see through pearly tears the room was full of stinging smoke. Bodies were heaped across furniture. A few dark-skinned men were standing at the far end of the room. She knew what was coming. A line of naked women looking cowed and terrified trooped in and out of an open doorway. Her guard kicked her shoulder.

"Strip!" She obliged, her eyes looking for a chance to grasp a weapon. Soon she was down to her underwear, blue bruises blooming across her ribcage.

"Odin," someone bellowed before a gun was put to the back of their neck. The shot was still ringing in Svea's ears when a leather loop was pulled over her head and she was dragged by the neck towards the doorway kicking and screaming. The words, "You Swedish bitch, you're gonna pay!" booming in her head.

Inside the door she was lifted to her feet. Svea noticed a table covered with half-consumed wine bottles and a large bowl of fruit. Before her was a bare-chested Bengali man with musky smelling skin and tufts of knotty hair embedded around his dark brown nipples. In that brief moment she took advantage, punching her elbow hard into her guard's solar plexus, head-butting her would-be molester full in the face, sending him to the floor. Bending quickly she wrenched a revolver out from the holster of the man at her feet, unhitched the safety, then put the barrel in her mouth. As the men recovered to retaliate, a thin smile rippled across her face. Svea winked at them mischievously through a bloodshot eye, before pulling the trigger.

Peter lifted a Colt and a walkie-talkie from a fallen militia man. The soldier's dead eyes had burst, clear glutinous fluid ran down his cheeks. The room smelled of tobacco, but there was no one around. He looked out of the blinds. Nothing. He moved along the passageway wondering if he was the last man standing, unaware of what was going on in the rooms above.

Outside the galley kitchen he came across a black uniformed man in a beret and gold epaulettes talking into a headset. He did not hear Peter until he was less than three metres away, turning just in time to see a knuckle knotted fist swinging wide and cracking down on his jaw, splintering teeth. Moving on, Peter mounted a staircase. At the top he stopped. Smoke drifted out of a doorway. He could hear screaming and taunts coming through the rolling clouds. Back to the wall, he took a grenade from its Velcro pouch and threw it through the gap. Then, lifting his weapons before his face, he readied himself, charging in behind a hail of nine-millimetre shell casings.

Inside, the room was still alight, burning shrapnel embedded in brown crispy skin. He sauntered around drilling single shots into any moving bodies amongst the furnishings. Someone grabbed his leg, he lurched to fire, then recognised Nia's familiar smile. Her nose was split like a faithless Comanche squaw. "Revenge us," she beseeched him, as their fingers touched delicately, and she died in his arms, her vagina filled with the semen of men from three continents.

In the pregnant silence that followed, he could hear troopers approaching. Janssen looked down, noticed he was out of ammo, cursed, dropped forward onto his right knee and snapped the gun open to reload. Just at that moment two of the militia came through the far door and he raised the hot barrel and fired, the butt hammering against his shoulder, a chain saw of lead grating through their cheesy flesh until the gun had clicked out again.

There was a diversionary bomb blast in the neighbouring house. It was clear that in all the confusion the Union troops thought they had cleared the building and were now chasing stragglers fighting a rear-guard action down the adjacent street. After strangling a sentry, it took Peter two or three trips to carry all the functional weaponry he could lay his hands on down to a Volvo parked outside. Closing the boot, he started up the engine just as a police siren moved in a blue blur along the road. Peter rammed straight through the railings at the side of the house, bricks and metal joists bouncing along the street as he swerved off to the south, his eyes watering with respect for the ancestors of the Inghen Ruadh and the Valkyrie Maiden of Birka.

- ❖ The Swedish government impose martial law and conduct a sweep of the Skåne, Blekinge and Öland for rebels.
- ❖ The Head of the US European Command offers the Swedish Minister of the Interior reinforcements from the 2nd Cavalry based in Germany and the 173rd Airborne in Italy.
- ❖ McDonald's decides to double the number of schools and hospitals it had originally offered to build for refugees in the city of Södertälje.
- ❖ The Finns Party are bankrupted by a lawfare suit brought against its leader in a Helsinki court.
- ❖ Poland's Congress of the New Right hold well-attended meetings in Krakow, Warsaw and Wrocław.

Brandeis faced the full meeting peopled by those who were most eager for final confirmation of the execution of all the terrorists. He put down his papers and read out the known facts and statistics. There was general satisfaction but a recognition of the total cost. The kill rate had favoured the resistance by four to one.

"An indication of the professionalism and commitment of our foe!" Brandeis reiterated.

"But we got everyone?" Gecht asked.

"Not quite," Brandeis admitted, "We know at least one of their ringleaders is still at large, possibly others." There was a buzz of consternation. "Be assured," the Prefecture of Police continued, "A full scale manhunt is underway. I am confident they will all have been taken or killed within forty-eight hours!"

"That is confidence?" Walzer muttered in disbelief.

"Well, we must be prepared for setbacks, of course, but our information is proving accurate, and they have scattered in disarray."

"These are better results than we could have hoped for," Gecht accepted. "Media coverage is likewise watertight. It is being presented as a response to the atrocities in Visby."

"Atrocities?" Edelmann said, having recently returned from Helsinki and was unaware of the cover operation Brandeis had run from early evening before the assault.

"Yes, apparently the underground set off a number of bombs in international hotels, churches and synagogues across the country. It was widely reported prior to midnight." A ripple of fleshy jowls smirked around the table as Gecht explained.

"I see the tried and tested techniques are still effective, Minister!"

"Very much so," Brandeis said, "We have received letters of support from church elders, the commercial sector and from allied and non-aligned governments who lost nationals in the explosions."

"Guaranteeing world-wide syndication and the mass soliciting of sympathy."

"Indeed, we would have been criticised if we did not act swiftly and with extreme force."

"The sheep really are locked in their pen," Edelmann replied.

"Yes, we are confident the host community remains confused and as ever act and think at cross purposes to their self-interest."

"And the one we know to have escaped, is he significant?"

"A foreigner, but one we understand of increasing influence."

"Then he needs to be detained or eradicated quickly."

"We are working on it!"

Brandeis had never felt the need to drink or smoke, but it was different now. Both Gecht and his ubiquitous controller, Joshua Meyer, were insisting on results.

"Get this man before he becomes a hero," they insisted. But hunting Janssen was proving difficult. Brandeis had already been down to the central districts twice that morning.

"He's gone," Walzer shouted. "He'll surface in a neighbouring country in the next few weeks, declaiming about state violence and political repression." Edelmann agreed. "That is a possibility, but we need to be very sure. It would be a mistake if this character turned up again inside our borders!"

"Why? He is only one man."

"I sense he is already emerging as an icon, just like that woman in France. He will inspire others."

The city was being sifted for troublemakers. Main roads filled by roadblocks, roof-tops manned by snipers and surveillance experts with telescopic sights and audio kits searching the Akalla and Rågsved districts. The honeycomb of streets and office blocks was crawling with security service men. Thousands of officials, draftees and informers had been activated. Student cafes, debating groups and social scenes were raided. Names were taken, and some beatings handed out.

Inside the zone, the perimeters of every building were being walked, metre by metre, door by door, until the sector was cleared and signed off.

It was growing late. Peter was already cutting it fine for his rendezvous. He drove off in the back of a taxicab, fingers drumming on the barrel of the Beretta 93R secreted inside his jacket. They were moving through little Mogadishu, where a few nights before youths had been rioting because they had been denied access to a school dance. Apparently, drugs had been found in the pockets of baggy trousered boys hanging about the schoolyard, trying to score with the blondes passing by. Boomboxes rang with 93 Punx's anthem:

We'll be living it up, not giving a fuck
Splitting you up, then we put you in cuffs
Then we shipping you off, yeah,
You could get lost in Camp America!

Take your clothes off baby, let me see what you got

We can have a good time if you're legal or not
It's an ignorant, arrogant, terrorist heritage
You can finally be an American!

Outside, the rain had thinned, the red raw sky shot through with varicose veins. He realised he would be highly visible at the cathedral, so he put on some glasses as part of his disguise.

As they drove down Hötorget, Peter looked up to see the Swedish flag flying side-by-side with the black Muslim Brotherhood banner over the glass frontage of the municipal buildings.

Peter thought that loitering about on the square would increase his likelihood of being stopped, so he dropped some coins into the cabbie's outstretched palm and marched ahead. The cathedral square was awash with noise, the slanting rooftops crowded in by the towering minarets of the surrounding mosques. All around the window blinds were drawn in the narrow streets. Notices discouraging Christians from celebrating their faith were on public display, while columns of liquorice-thin people wandered around chanting strange liturgies. Local women were regularly being harassed on the sidewalks, their husbands and boyfriends doing almost nothing to protect them, especially after years of emotional castration administered by the purveyors of political correctness.

Janssen ran up the steps, entering the cathedral, under the eyes of agonised gargoyles with gnashing teeth. Walking down the empty aisle, between rows of hard wooden seats, he saw a white-haired pastor kneeling before the altar. Peter's contact was nowhere to be seen. He decided to wait thirty minutes and took a seat at the end of a pew.

The stillness inside was a sharp counterpoint to the circus swirl of animalistic fervour outside. The repetitious shouting of God's name, "Allahu Akbar," was more like the ache of the repressed than a joyous celebration of life. Peter took a letter he had recently received from Senka out from his pocket, unfolded it delicately and read again for

the umpteenth time the Kipling quote she had scribbled
in poor English across the off-white paper:

> If you can dream—and not make dreams your master;
> If you can think—and not make thoughts your aim;
> If you can meet with triumph and disaster:
> And treat those imposters just the same;
> If you can bear to hear the truth you've spoken
> Twisted by knaves to make a trap for fools. . .

When he eventually looked up he could see sunlight
piercing through the cracks in the stained glass. To his left
a grand pulpit with a vaulted canopy loomed above him.
The carefully shaped rosewood foliage struck him as beautiful, petals and curling ivy, opening and drooping, nestling in the knotty grain. A plain gold crucifix stood below
the mural of a cherubic angel. He felt like Jonah inside the
whale. Peter turned his head and saw the stealthy pastor
approaching, his feet shuffling over the tessellated floor.
He looked to the left and right, trying to see beyond the
shimmer of the tall candle into the side chapels. Squinting
at the altarpieces, he rose and walked toward a small bal-
ustrade, over which hung a vast painting. Before him the
image of a knight was depicted, sword in hand, striking
out at the bestial image of a flame-tongued Satan.

Peter put out his hand, feeling the hard, smooth surface, aware that the pastor was standing directly behind
him. He was wearing a loose-fitting vestment and staring
at Peter nervously.

"What does he want?" Janssen was thinking. The pastor
gestured with his head. Then the lone pilgrim heard the
code word he had been expecting. Peter followed his sav-
iour through the oak benches, stopping in an alcove, nodding in mutual recognition of their shared conspiracy.
Then they moved on through more stone passages until,
in the privacy of the bell tower, Peter was handed papers
and sufficient money to get him over the border.

"May God be with you, my son."

"I am eternally grateful," Peter replied.

"You are doing God's work," he was assured.

Upon leaving the cathedral, he had to force his way through the thin dejected line of born-again types who were running the gauntlet of Muslim abuse. Several bystanders were hustled away from the doors of the church by blue uniformed Union militia.

Peter scratched his head and reached for his cigarette case. On the roof-tops, men with rifles stalked the grey slates. One armed man stopped him and asked to see his papers. Janssen thought the trooper looked fed up. He saw the leather strap of his machine gun chafe on his collar.

"Okay!" the guard said, "move along."

"Thank you," Peter said automatically, passing through a gap in some metal barriers, disappearing into the facade of the Kungsträdgården Metro Station.

TABULA RASA

"A legionnaire loves death, for his blood shall cement the future . . ."

—Corneliu Codreanu

Janssen arrived in Riga early one evening. The city lay deep in snow. Nothing could be seen from the Uzvaras bulvāris. The old quarter was wrapped in a frosty blue death shroud. Only pinpricks of light shone from high windows, casting an orange glaze over the narrow, crooked streets around the medieval market and the Dome Cathedral.

Crowds swarmed the pavements, hunched wooden houses bending and curving over the alleyways. At the quaysides there was the familiar creak of boats pulling against their chains on the spur of the Eksporta iela harbour. Peter flicked open his mobile, the small electronic pulse illuminating his face, checking the time against the clock in the dark tower above.

Standing on the corner of Elizabetes iela and Kalpaka bulvāris, he could see two official black cars forcing their way through the swirling ice flecks. They were flanked by motorbikes, outriders in gleaming visors wearing blue circle and yellow star armbands. Peter felt his heart thump harder as he caught a fleeting glimpse of Chairman Dzerve, the Latvian collaborator. His nose was unmistakable, as were those protruding lips jabbering away inside the vehicle. Beside him, his weasel-faced new advisor, Sarkozy, a former President in his own right, was rubbing his sweaty palms, no doubt pleased, like his own political consultants, Herzog and Azibert, to be concocting some new fraud against a host community.

"Parasites!" Janssen thought, "one day, hopefully, one day soon, you'll get what you deserve . . ."

Another figure was also watching the car's passage from the Saeima, the Latvian parliament, down along the Kalpaka with more than a mere passing curiosity. Alise had been about to cross when a policeman waved her back onto the pavement. She too had privately cursed the face in the window of the limousine. Her mind recalling an excerpt from the *Brussels Journal* in 2009 where Sarkozy was quoted as saying "that the French people must change, that there will be consequences if they don't and that not to intermarry racially is bad for the survival of this country . . ." He was up to the same thing here in Latvia, she thought, recalling the rest of the article with distaste, "If the French people don't interbreed of their own free will, it will be necessary for the Republic to resort to even more forcible measures . . ." Alise was twenty-three, slim, long black hair falling like a frisky horse tail down over her dun-coloured mackintosh. She did not want to intermarry. She did not consider all cultures equal, and she wanted to carry a European baby, not some hybrid, in her womb.

On that particular afternoon she had been instructed by her colleagues to meet a foreign comrade requiring assistance. Initially she thought it was a distraction from her main project, a honeytrap for a particularly pernicious enemy. Within a few hours she intended to be in Vincent's restaurant with Comrade Lapsa, head of the Union's Securitate. The place was just off the Old Town. She would feign interest, listening attentively while her repulsive lover pronounced the underground finished and how he had personally interrogated her comrades with a rubber cosh. Alise had become committed to the Fatherland and Freedom movement immediately after her parents had received the dreaded telegram telling them of their son's death in a counterinsurgency operation in the foothills surrounding some God-forsaken Afghan village. He had acted courageously, it said, dying heroically in the interests of his platoon and global security.

"Pha!" she blurted contemptuously as her father read out the notification to his hysterical wife. "Bendiks died like all our young men defending a pirate state perpetrating a massive crime against humanity."

"How can you say such things?" sobbed her mother. Alise paraphrased Orwell:

"Because at this moment Oceania is at war with Eurasia and in alliance with Eastasia. Not long ago Oceania was at war with Eastasia and in alliance with Eurasia. The enemy of the moment always represents absolute evil . . . Now tell me who benefits? Who always derives security from the human shield provided by our brave boys fighting in that arid empty wilderness?" Her mother shook her head.

"Stop with this. Bendiks is dead!"

"Yes, and some bloodsucking little coward masquerading as an American or a European probably profited from the deal that supplied the bastards with the bullets that killed him, mother!"

"You don't know that; no one can be sure of these things."

"Look at your newspapers, TV and radio. Listen! Read between the lines. Who can never be criticized? Ask why such strange decisions are made. Why such nonsensical outcomes result in economic recessions and stock market surges. Who controls such things?"

"The world is a complex place; lots of strange things happen."

"Not that strange when you know what little twisted horse-flies are behind everything!"

- ❖ Issur Babel wins the right for migrant labourers to vote in Russian elections.
- ❖ Soros-funded NGOs and media outlets like *Novaya Gazeta*, along with the Russian LGBT network and Amnesty International, claim Putin has established concentration camps for gays across Siberia.
- ❖ The father of the American President's top advisor is exonerated for his past crimes of tax evasion, illegal political campaign donations and witness tampering in 2005.
- ❖ A secularist Left-wing political party in Poland highlights sex scandals in the Catholic Church to attack the Law and Justice party in Warsaw.
- ❖ The former President of the Czech Republic is charged with enacting anti-humanitarian policies and actions by the European Court of Justice.
- ❖ The American President increases pressure on Moscow after Putin claims the economy of the West is being propped up by fiat-money by providing the government in Kyiv with $250 billion dollars for additional defence spending and deploying a further 5,000 troops on the Polish border with Ukraine.

For months Alise's private world had fallen apart. Nothing seemed to ease the pain of bereavement. All she could hope for was revenge. She listened to old stories about the Singing Revolution and began reading the Latvian National Front magazine *DDD: De-Occupation, De-Colonization and De-Bolshevization*, attending meetings of Fatherland & Freedom and All for Latvia, part of the Latvian National Alliance, and participating in torch-lit parades. Then she served as a mule, carrying letters and weapons, before being trained herself to shoot and kill as part of the Arajs Kommando. The group's leader, a young activist called Raivis, tested her resolve, preparing her over time to commit sex acts with a man they despised and wanted to "get to." She volunteered, biting her lip as she copulated with a list of strange men, hiding her revulsion, thinking of her brother and how she could honour his memory.

After meeting Peter on Elizabete iela and taking him to a small room near the Swedish Gate, between the Powder Tower and St Jacob's church, she retreated to the quiet of her bedroom, a large ensuite in her parent's house. She stripped and showered, drying off in front of a full-length mirror, her stomach wall tightening with anticipation at meeting Lapsa later at the English-owned restaurant. She sat on the corner of the bed and picked up a photo of Bendiks from her table. That was all she had left, a digital print of her older brother.

After an expensive dinner Alise joined Lapsa in a taxi back to his apartment in the Kurzeme district. Once inside she threw her bare arms around him before the Head of State Security could flick the button on his domestic security system.

"Come," she said, leaving the door ajar, "I want you very much . . ." He gave her a slap on the bottom, speeding her towards the bedroom while he slipped off his shoes, then his trousers, before sliding out of a white cotton shirt to reveal pale thin arms. Lapsa moved over towards Alise's supine body. He stretched his length beside her on the sheets and ran his palm over the swell of her warm buttock.

"You are so very beautiful," Lapsa said. Alise slipped a hand down his boxer shorts.

"And you are very hard!" Alise lay back on the bed and felt him press down on top of her. Closing her eyes, she thought of someone else, someone who could be admired, anyone but him. But when her eyes opened a few moments later, just as he spurted inside her, Alise knew it could only be him and feigned an orgasm before two men closed in quickly, using cheese-wire to garrotte their target, Lapsa's windpipe severing before her smiling face.

The following morning Janssen was still trying to settle into his new life. He had spent the morning at the market, buying meat and vegetables, disguised in an old coat and scuffed shoes, haggling with the vendors. Pleiss, a member of the local Cukurs Kommando, became his designated bodyguard and was by his side day and night, translating for him what had been reported on the news.

"They are saying that all terrorist opposition in Sweden has been nullified and the surviving ringleaders rounded up to face trial."

"Well, that's partially true," Peter answered. "Of course, they are not going to report the true body count." His fingers ran over the green crested broccoli, asking the stall holder the price.

"How many do you think they got?"

"Hundreds. I saw thirty or thirty-five comrades die. The total will be much higher."

"Can they recover and regroup?" Pleiss sounded concerned.

"Who knows? But certainly not in the short term. The most experienced fighters are gone, and who knows about the next generation? It will be like starting from the beginning."

"A bit like us!"

"Have confidence. From little acorns . . ." Pleiss looked at him perplexed.

"It is an English saying." The Latvian youth nodded, none the wiser for that.

After cooking his meal, he lit a cigarette, his legs barely fitting under the gate-legged table, shuffling a deck of cards and playing solitaire quietly by the window. His place was a worn little apartment with an enormous bed made up with blankets and a red salami sausage bolster. A spring in the old clock on the mantelpiece ticked over noisily. Pleiss sat on a step of the stairwell outside, talking incessantly to his girlfriend in Latgale and playing with the barrel of a Ruger LCR revolver tucked under his trenchcoat.

In the late afternoon Alise came, slipping Pleiss a flask of warm tea, whispering "Visu Latvia." He thanked her. Then her head tilted towards the door to Janssen's rooms, and the young man dialled Peter's number.

"Hello?"

"Pleiss here," he said, "open up." A few seconds later Janssen threw the metallic latch on the door and Alise slipped inside, tossing back her hair and producing a brown envelope full of unmarked currency.

"This will help you," she smiled.

"It certainly will," Peter grinned. "Can I get you a drink?"

"What do you have?" He pointed to a half-empty bottle of Aljošenkin on the table.

"I'll just take a cigarette," Alise said, declining the offer of alcohol, but running a flame over the tip of the Egipte in her mouth. "I see our little Pleiss has introduced you to Latvian hospitality."

"You could say that?"

"Is there anything else I can get you? You are going to be here a little while, I think . . . ?"

"Well, really, I'm no card player," Peter hinted, "perhaps some books?"

"Relax, all will be arranged." After that, Alise became a regular visitor. She would bring him cigarettes and literature like Nobel Laureate Czeslaw Milosz's *The Captive Mind*. Sitting in the armchair, smoking cigarettes, listening to the warble of brown sparrows flitting to and fro on the open windowsill, Peter read the polemic and began to recognise the depth and tyranny of the experiment that was now being imposed on the European continent. His mind drifted back to the Churchillian quote about an iron curtain descending from Stettin in the Baltic to Trieste on the Adriatic and realised the cigar-toting Prime Minister had only been telling the partial truth. His own whisky-laced complicity as a tool of the Focus, he carefully side-stepped, hoping no doubt that within a century, the legacy of the Big Three would have re-drawn the moral map of mankind and controlled Newspeak would silence dissenting views. Little did he know then that his gilded image would be severely scratched only decades later by the research of a certain British historian named David Irving.

Peter began to plough through *God and State* by the anarchist Bakunin and Peter Kropotkin's *Spirit of Revolt*. He could readily identify with notre Pierre's thesis that "Action, continuous action . . . Courage, devotion, the spirit of sacrifice, are as contagious as cowardice, submission, and panic." Peter saw his actions and those of his fellows as a precursor to the revolution that would end in the downfall of this Sacred Union and its priesthood of apparatchiks.

He received regular intelligence about some of the activities of his contemporaries across the continent. Karl Braun had closed the Frankfurt Stock Exchange for three days with a computer virus. Charles Renner had gone to ground in the former East Germany and was leading a major resurgence of the NPD in the local elections. Millman had come within inches of assassinating the British Prime Minister while attending another Mosque opening in Gravesend and Nata Poukkanen was in Idaho advising an organisation called the American Friends of Europe.

The liquidation of the opposition in Sweden may have been a setback to the Cause, but it had galvanised the movement in general. Janssen's revolutionary reputation as a "survivor" was greatly enhanced, and although a broad traditionalist seizure of power across Scandinavia seemed as far away as ever, he and his cohorts continued to develop strategies for outmanoeuvring the EU Commission and implanting secret nationalist cells behind their lines.

Peter soon acquired an air of radical chic. He was asked to write for the underground press. Lithuanian nationalists, friends of Ona, tried and tested veterans who had blown up the Vilnius to Kaliningrad railway line some years before, had been in contact. So were the Vanagis nationalists. He contributed articles on the Patria Nueva Sociedad, Mencken, Lowell and the Tsagaan Khass in Ulan Bator under the pseudonym Corbel 1, named after a character in a painting by an English artist and philosopher he rather admired. Spending hours sitting surrounded by half-drained cups and the bubbling sound of coffee percolating in the kitchen, Peter would gaze out the window, watching as snow blew about the mottled green spire of St Jacob's church, a faint haze of Gauloises drifting out from his mouth into the cold evening air.

By now, his thinking was being compared favourably to Robert Steuckers', like himself a Flemish-born warrior in the battle of ideas. He may have established quite a following for his trenchant political views, but Peter Janssen was a pragmatist. He recognised that writing articles, speaking at meetings and leading protest marches under a coalition of different national banners had its limitations. Although it was certainly psychologically liberating, only by force of arms could he foresee the status quo being challenged. It was noticeable that pro-freedom writers were fleeing to fringe cities like Krakow, Bratislava and Ljubljana, acquiring houses where they could set up communal canteens and living quarters before sending their radio and Digital Free Europe channels back into the West in a mirror image of the Cold War epoch. His Slovenian counterpart, Aleš Balažic, the man he had watched use a knife on the throat of a Norwegian race traitor, supported by the Slovenia National Party was project managing the whole enterprise.

He remembered the thesis first put forward in Dugin's *The Fourth Political Theory*, that "technological development establishes a zonal division of all territories on Earth into three regions—the core, the zone of connectedness and the zone of unconnectedness . . . network processes freely penetrate through borders, governments and civilizations, and structure the strategic space in their own way . . . The USA and the European Union are the core; there are concentrated all the codes of the new technologies and the decision-making centres . . ."

❖ Putin says "the One World Government is banging at our door!"

❖ Issur Babel describes Putin as paranoid and delusional, sparking violent protests in the streets of major Russian cities and causing a political crisis.

❖ The Chief of the General Staff of the Army and several other leading Generals responsible for Central and Eastern Military districts at Yekaterinburg and Khabarovsk and the Caspian Flotilla based at Astrakhan sign a letter of no confidence in the President.

❖ The UN accuses the Putin Government of colluding with French Identitarian militias when an arms cache is discovered just off the N79 near Cluny, containing large numbers of Pecheneg MMGs and RPG-26 weaponry.

❖ After fierce debate in the Duma, Russian S-300 PMU anti-aircraft missiles, Pantsir–S1 anti-tank defense systems, and Buk–2 missiles are withdrawn from advanced tactical positions.

In Odessa, under the protection of non-EU-aligned Ukrainian nationalists, Adela Bankowski had set up alternate media countering the overwhelming and all-consuming mass mind control emanating from Brussels. Communism had crumbled in the East, they said, because liberalism had surreptitiously morphed into a new religion in the West. Peter was convinced Gramsci had been right. Control the culture and you influence the terms of moral, intellectual and political discourse. Those who did not flee either succumbed or were transported along with their dependents to holding areas pending a review of their case. One night, Peter had turned to Alise, who had come in from the cold, blue fingers clutching some journals. "Do you think we are making a difference?" he asked in what she took to be a slightly depressed tone. Alise looked at him over the glowing stub of a cigarette and stuttered a smoky breath of contempt.

"A guy called Charles Fort once said, 'The earth is a farm, and we are someone else's property . . . We have a choice: the evil may be patiently borne or savagely resisted.'"

"Is that why you joined the struggle?"

"I have many reasons; some are personal and some are historic."

"Tell me?"

Alise hesitated, fighting with the desire to talk about her brother but finally deciding on the easier option.

"It started with me visiting the Lestene Cemetery. I was pleased to honour the glorious 15th and 19th Grenadiers."

"Oh yes, Legion Day. I hear thousands still march with torches!" Alise's face shone proudly.

"In 2005, our President, Vaira Vike-Freiberga, said the Soviet control of the Baltic meant slavery, it meant occupation, it meant subjugation, and it meant Stalinist terror. So you see, we have decades upon decades of experience of fighting external powers here. Stalin replaced Latvian leaders with people like Shustin, Novik and Zitron, the torturer at Daugavpils jail. Shustin ordered that all Christian churches be destroyed, but the synagogues remained untouched. He left here in 1946 and went to Israel, becoming a leading member of Mossad. The Cheka whore Valery Gruzin was placed in our sister state of Ukraine, and even as late as 1988, the Soviets were planning purges codenamed the Disobedient. A similar exercise was to be led by a Samuil Michelson in Estonia. As many as a million and a half Balts, nearly ten percent of the entire population, my great grandfather and my great uncles included, were shipped off to be worked to death in Siberia."

Alise began to grow angry. "A man called Hans Grabbe, actually, his real name was Hans Hoffe, headed the NKVD death squads. There were torturers like Tuch, Gluckman and the so-called 'spider', the deformed Stella Schliefstein, who specialised in tearing out the arm and leg muscles of innocent people accused of crimes like singing folk songs in the woods. That is why our Baltic festivals are so symbolic, so threatening, it is a reminder to them that we don't forget we lost twenty-five percent of our population in the decade after the Communist takeover. The best-educated, the most active were taken by Leo Epstein's secret police and Lobonovich's Commissary for Internal Affairs."

"And now these killers seek war reparations from your countries," Peter said solemnly, shaking his head.

"Have you seen the footage of innocent civilians being gunned down into trenches after the Beneš decrees in Prague?"

"Yes, and the trucks being driven over the bodies of women and children."

"The same story is repeated in the rest of Central and Eastern Europe. Ana Pauker and Burach Tescovich in Romania, Stefan Reis in Czechoslovakia, Erno Singer and Zoltan Weinberger in Hungary. Then there was Jacob Berman's evil regime and scum like Stanisław Radkiewicz, who as head of the dreaded secret police, oversaw the murder of 270,000 Poles."

"You are facing an uphill battle!"

Alise ignored him, her temper rising like steam whistling up a tin pipe. "Dogs like Roman Werfel actually gave sanction for Morel and his cohorts to kill thousands of innocents at Świętochłowice."

"Yes, even Churchill complained, saying enormous numbers of Germans too are unaccounted for."

"Smug English bastard, he was owned by Henry Strakosch who paid off all his debts and saved him from bankruptcy. Watch how his political position changed after the little matter of the foreclosure on Chartwell was dealt with."

"You are referring to his article in the *London Illustrated Herald* of February 1920?"

"Bronstein, Radek, Dimanshtein, Joffe, Uritsky and Sokolnikov, the list is endless!"

"And it is the same now under a different disguise. They arrested all the signatories to the Declaration of Bauska, good people from the Lithuaninan Nationalist Union and the Order and Justice party, the Estonian Conservative People's Party and my own National Alliance for Latvia. Comrades who wanted to combat international globalism and multiculturalism. This EU is an octopus strangling us, just waiting to complete the liquidation it started a century ago."

A few days later, he caught a TV programme about primary school education in London and watched as the teacher orchestrated a class of brown, yellow and white smiling faces to chant "Diversity is our Strength" and was reminded of the Orwellian maxim "Four legs good, two legs bad!" He wondered how long before that incantation was distorted to "Four legs good, two legs better!" Peter knew it was only a matter of time. Then the porky Napoleons who ran the show just like in Orwell's *Animal Farm* would take the final step:

All Animals are Equal
But Some Animals Are More
Equal Than Others

He was hanging out on the fringes of the city's bohemian culture, occasionally sitting at a corner table in the Cafe Schelsky or the Lorenz. The first place was named after the sociologist Helmut Schelsky, an expert on social stratification who wrote many books countering the Frankfurt School. The second for Nobel prize winner Konrad Lorenz, who had fought in the war, serving in the Wehrmacht and was captured by the Russians, finally being released in 1948. The cafe owners were making a point: anti-authoritarian discussion groups came from Left and Right, and the legendary Club Voltaire had rivals. He liked the idea of his type invading the trendy space usually occupied by apostles of Sartre. Janssen talked with exiled members of the United Romanian Party and Luxembourg's Alternative Democratic Reform Party, Danes, Latvians, White Russians, Basques and Irish Catholics and Protestants loyal to Aoutu. There was an unwritten understanding that they were the antithesis of the Cohn-Bendit class of '68. For every *Soledad Brother*-inspired Angela Davis lookalike, there was a *Doppelgänger* weaned on the poetry of Will Vesper.

They would exchange books and arguments, rage back and for about whether or not Ernst Jünger was at the heart of the German Conservative Revolutionary movement. Peter began reading *Der Arbeiter* and *Feuer und Blut*. Sometimes he would flick through Armin Mohler's *Die Konservative Revolution* for ideas, and after reading the poetry of Joseph Freiherr von Eichendorff, imagined himself wandering over meadows with the *Wandervögel*. Soon, Peter became familiar with works by Ernst von Salomon, August Winnig and Karl Paetel. Sometimes he got lost in semantic debates, but most of all he liked to read Klages and luxuriated in Julius Evola.

The widely read newspaper, *The People's Voice*, published provocative anti-traditionalist editorials:

> Let us make no mistake in this matter. We are again in times when modern civilization is threatened by barbarians who would set back the course of human history a hundred years to when racism was rife, mixed marriage was outlawed, charity began at home, rather than with our African brothers and women neither vote nor abort. . .

Headline after headline hammered home the same points.

The most notorious fascists walk abroad in our midst. They maintain elaborate clandestine networks, working with their conservative dupes, fomenting plans for horrific attacks, for they are experts in the arts of revolution.

He knew that at any point his hitherto charmed life could desert him. On the Smilsu Iela while lunching near the Powder Tower, he received a message from the underground. It warned: "You are to be arrested tonight. An incident justifying your shooting is not out of the question."

Peter finished his meal and made his way back to Zirgu Iela, near the Freedom Monument, closely followed by Union agents. While strutting down the tree lined Basteja Bulvaris he entered an open stairwell, and the Union spies waited, imagining he would re-emerge, or even better, lead them to where other reactionary cells were based. They took up their usual positions in doorways and street corners.

Inside the residence, Peter was moving fast. A lightning change of clothes was followed by a mad dash out into the rear yard. From this narrow stone square, he clambered over the wall into the next and so on. Had the predators been remotely observant they would have seen the back door of a home at the far end of the row open, and a man in a long black coat and a trilby hat walk away into the dusk, but they were not, and he escaped yet again to fight another day.

Only a few weeks later, while warming himself by an open fire, he turned on Andris, a former spokesman for the banned Fatherland and Freedom Party and now head of the Latvian Resistance: "I'm taking Alise and Pleiss. Have them ready to move out by 10th April, complete with all their gear. They're with me from now on, so forget them, understand? As far as you're concerned, they never existed." Andris, a man used to giving orders himself, acquiesced, knowing his young supporters were now part of something much bigger.

"Take good care of these little ones, I owe it to their parents," he said.

- ❖ The Us & Them Exhibition questioning the validity of the biological origins of race at the Musée de l'Homme is vandalised by French Nationalist youth.
- ❖ Fans of the Les Brigandes deface the Cleon Peterson Mural at the Eiffel Tower.
- ❖ The Spanish Congress agree to set a date for the total destruction of the mausoleums to Franco and José Antonio Primo de Rivera in the Guadarama Hills.

After weeks of playing hide and seek with the authorities across the Lithuanian and Polish borders the three renegades travelled through Hamburg on false IDs obtained by Kaminski's Polish Nationalist Alliance and second-class tickets supplied by German forgers. Crossing over the border into France, they were met by the head of the underground army in the Northern French Sector, La Tène Rendre. He introduced himself as Fabien and personally oversaw their transit to the Ardennes. Food and supplies were plentiful, and they were able to rest and walk about outside, even smoking Gitanes under snow-laden branches.

Fabien was eager, too eager, Peter thought, to force his platoon, the Jacques de Mahieu patrol, into some kind of insurrection. "I was with the gilets jaunes and Debout la France before all this happened. France is ready. We should take over the government buildings in Roubaix and incarcerate the collaborationist local Mayor," he advised. Fabien's final words "Whatever the cost!," however well-intentioned, were unwelcome.

"The movement is full of such hot heads!" Janssen was telling Pleiss. "I spend half my life trying to hold these people back before they get our meagre reserves slaughtered in some valiant charge on a worthless target."

"Diplomacy is required," Pleiss said through a cloudy breath, "our hosts have been very generous."

"And therein lies the problem!" Janssen shot Pleiss a glance, "People like Fabien see the world through a very narrow lens. Ideas like the Imperium Europa are lost on him. He is a brave and no doubt loyal Gaul, but this is a Europe-wide struggle, and local tinpot dictators and would-be heroes could prove counterproductive if we are to reclaim our birthright."

ILLEGITIMI NON CARBORUNDUM

"Let the Memory of Kosovo live forever! Long live Serbia!"

— Slobodan Milošević

Senka had become an expert at setting roadside bombs. Lessons learnt from natural enemies like the Taliban in Afghanistan and Mohammedan mercenaries in Iraq had not gone unheeded. Soon she was using her considerable skills to target logistics and communication centres. The state was in uproar, scared and offended by her successes, unable to predict or protect themselves from her scorpion sting.

One night she was working rapidly with the tip of her knife, shaping the material to the mould, implanting the chip that would catch the signal off her mobile. Cars rolled by at speed. She was hanging just below the parapet, the footfall of commuters only a metre above, echoing through the metal grid work.

When she unclipped the satchel hung over her shoulder, dangling high above the water, she could immediately see something was very wrong. There was a red pulse in the darkness. Senka tried to stop it but there was a small clap of light and a pall of smoke. She withdrew her ruined hands, blackened stumps smouldering. Then the sky lit up in a halo all around her, as though the clouds were burning and her body fell a full twenty metres, smashing down hard onto broken concrete.

Peter was still blissfully unaware. Pleiss and Alise were proving loyal and low maintenance. Only a few weeks later, word reached him via sources in the Serbian Radical Party that Senka had been killed planting a roadside bomb outside Kraljevo on the Juzna river.

"She was my sister, my mother, my lover," he confessed.

Janssen knew there was a Containment Camp nearby in Kruševac and guessed that was her target. The location was well known for being a transit base where gangs from Kosovo came to buy girls for the sex trade and healthy young people were kidnapped and murdered so that the Albanian mafia could harvest their body parts for the gruesome black-market trade in human organs. Senka's men had retrieved her corpse, burying her with a full honour guard from the Nacionalni Stroj late one afternoon in an unremarkable section of her local cemetery.

"The grave is unmarked," the strongly accented voice said over the mobile, "deliberately so. Anyone trying to dig up the remains will have a hard time shovelling through the stony ground. It is the poor section, and there she will be safe."

He was not sure if he should cry, swell with pride, or both. Peter put himself in her place. Senka was a fighter. Sooner or later the inevitable would have happened. She took risks and lived on her own terms. Knowing your mother and grandmother had been violated and the same fate awaited you filled you with a longing for revenge. He raised a glass, remembering her words, "It's not important how many of the enemy there are; what's important is the sacred place you defend." Wiping away a tear, he thought of how hardened he had become through all the injustices they had been forced to endure.

❖ The EU's Centre for Ethnic Culture bans Perchten Festivals and insists on the removal of images associated with the goddess Berchta from Alpine towns.

❖ Astrid Lindgren's fictional child character, red-haired Pippi Longstocking, is made over into a Roma migrant who fights against injustice.

❖ Christian candle lighting ceremonies in the Austrian Tyrol are disrupted by Atheists Unite.

❖ A schoolteacher in Alpbach is arrested for dressing up as Krampus and reading stories about elves to the minors in his care.

❖ The Danish Judicial System begins incarcerating nationalists on Lindholm island in Stege Bay.

They had travelled across central France, staying overnight at Bourges to dine with two French activists called Sabine and Luc and then moved on to Angoulême before arriving in Bordeaux in the early hours of the morning. Everywhere they went they saw burnt-out streets and evidence of the violent way the Yellow Vest movement's Act 57 was put down. While in Paris the organisers of the Black Vest migrant protestors who had occupied Charles De Gaulle airport and Black Bloc activists who had faced down the police using stingball grenades in Montparnasse Boulevard were awarded the Légion d'honneur. The press was filled with writings by Antiphobic Aktion sympathisers demanding overturning the French Senate's insistence on rebuilding Notre Dame Cathedral in a traditional style, suggesting instead, in memory of the murdered Macron, to implore the architects to redesign the edifice in a more inventive modernist style incorporating a multicultural ethos.

Their Mercedes parked up in Rue Leupold, and they walked along Quai Richelieu. Peter hung his jacket over a bollard. Alise sat at his feet, legs dangling over the edge of the embankment, looking down at the sluggish river. Peter took out an engraved cigarette case given to him by the French couple. She watched him take a couple of tokes.

"May I?" He passed her the burning stub. Gesturing towards the silver case, "you know people think they are really something."

"There are no messiahs," Janssen frowned, "just some honest men and women among all the nuts and cranks trying to make things a little better."

"Some think Sabine is a saint," Alise laughed.

"And would you like to be famous like her?"

"She is Brigitte Bardot with guns!"

"She certainly is!"

Walking in the Saint-Michel Quartier they bought fresh fruit from a market stall and gazed up at the spire above them. On the water, flat-bottomed boats moved lazily along the Garonne while the breeze rhythmically whispered the poetic words Meste and Despaux. They noticed Mohammedans were everywhere, likewise Africans. It was as if the whole Barbary Coast had washed ashore.

"You can see why the French are so fanatical," said Pleiss. "This place is chaos. The whole of North Africa is flooding across the Mediterranean. I hear the Arab League is negotiating partition."

"We stick to our task!" Peter insisted.

Crossing the Pont Pierre La Belle, Bordeaux was laid out before them. Juppé's urban renewal had refreshed the city, nearly two thousand hectares of civic sprawl stretching back to the Gallo-Roman period gleamed in the early morning sunlight. Pleiss stood dumbstruck at its beauty. Alise was looking at Janssen, pointing at posters of Marine Le Pen, with LOCK HER UP stamped across her pale face. Peter himself was thinking of Abd er Rahman's sacking of the city in 732 AD, before a passing car blaring out Radio Nova Sauvagine disturbed his reverie.

"Come," he eventually said, "I need some coffee."

Over some lattes in a small bistro, they discussed what to do. Peter kept looking at his phone. There were no messages from the local underground.

"I know this Franck Bodine guy is reliable!" he kept reassuring Pleiss and Alise as they ordered some croissants.

"You know I met him once when I was training."

"Who cares if he is late?" Pleiss replied, "I just like it here!"

"Me too," Alise laughed, "Do we have time to shop?" Just then, two secret service men stood up in the far corner of the cafe and began to fire indiscriminately across the tables. The first burst took Pleiss in the face, and he fell backwards, skull smashed open like a farm egg. Alise took a shot in the shoulder and slumped away to Janssen's left, the sound of the glass shopfront shattering, flying shards cutting the air. Peter managed to get off a reply, killing one of their assailants and an innocent bystander. Meanwhile, Alise squirming in pain on the floor grabbed her Glock with bloodied fingers and emptied it into the second man as he reloaded his automatic.

Peter pulled Alise to her feet, and they fell out the door into the street. People were scattering everywhere before them. The wail of police sirens filled the Allée Serr.

"Are you okay?" Alise shook her head.

"Go," she said, "I will hold you up!" Janssen ripped back her coat and was confronted by a sliced artery.

"We can hold them!"

"Go!" Alise commanded and with a knowing kiss he left her, his legs carrying him off down the Rue Jardel as Alise took up position behind a deserted Peugeot and levelled her weapon on the street.

❖ Patriotic French forces led by the Charles Maurras and Jean Goy Commando stage a spirited defence of the strategically important city of Toulouse.

❖ ISIS guerrillas begin indiscriminate shelling of the Romanesque monuments in Arles.

❖ Avignon's twelfth century Palais des Papes is commandeered by the new Caliph for his personal residence.

❖ The French Resistance rally behind the reformed Cagoule and Corvignolles Commando units to prevent the sacking of Castres.

- ❖ The Muslim Third Army are invited to parade past the Triumphal Arch in Orange.
- ❖ After weeks of house-to-house fighting, Christians are finally purged from Carcassonne.
- ❖ Sabine D'Orlac and Luc Dubois join up with the Aristide Corre Commando to rob the Credit Agricole bank at number 1 Place Victoire in Clermont-Ferrand to fund insurgent activities in the Auvergne.

PART III

"The man of the future will be of mixed race. The races and classes of today will gradually disappear due to the elimination of space, time and prejudice. The Eurasian Negroid race of the future, similar in appearance to the ancient Egyptians, will replace the diversity of peoples and the diversity of individuals. Instead of destroying European Judaism, Europe, against her will, refined and educated this people, driving them to their future status as leading nation through the artificial revolutionary process. It is not surprising that the people who escaped the ghetto prison, became the spiritual nobility of Europe . . ."

—Richard Coudenhove-Kalergi

CARA AL SOL

"Tomorrow we will cast the weight of our 400 million men, determined, united, disciplined into the scales of history."

— Jean Thiriart

"My name is Raoul," Peter tried to convince his reflection in the carriage window. His recently acquired beard, though finely trimmed, did little to mask his gaunt portrait in the glass. His habit of watching border guards checking papers was now compulsive. The monotonous judder of the train rolling over points thundered in his ears as the TGV cut through the French heartland at 320 kilometres an hour towards the Pyrenees.

Coming to a stop at Hendaye, Peter could see the red lights on the bridge above. Infrared doused the side of the SNCF, where uniformed men of the recently formed EU Army strutted back and forth, guns aimed at the carriage windows. Huge Union banners hung from the station walls, posters of the newly appointed EU President, Lanny Breuer, draped over the station portico.

They had already been delayed twenty minutes before the first lizard tongue of lightning flickered across the tensile sky. After the second flash, the rain came in a peal of thunder, night scopes dancing like fireflies over the passenger's faces.

Peter got up from his seat and moved to the toilet. He reached inside his jacket and initiated the personal locator before undoing the moulded window frame with the serrated edge of his jungle knife, and, sliding out, dropped soundlessly onto the loose stonework below.

Crawling on his belly, he made it to a cluster of steel pipes and hissing valves. There he paused. The lightning and torrential rain burst through the tangled iron, forming a black spider's web over his body. He dared not move. One of the security team was within arm's reach, the impact of water droplets singing on the gantry's metal work as the guards turned to walk away. Peter wondered how long it would take to check everyone and realise he had evaded them. He looked up at the stark silhouettes on the bridge. Their glistening helmets moved in unison and put him in mind of an infestation of cockroaches.

A woman was crying when her child was taken away, and an ambulance siren was sounding in the distance.

Suddenly, without warning, he was sick. There was little enough in his stomach except bile, green trails hanging from his chin as he sat hunched below a collar joint in the piping, sheltering from the prying eyes above. A soldier was crunching back along the track with a searchlight. Peter had to duck and curl up tightly to avoid detection. "Thank God, they haven't got body-heat detectors," he was thinking. Instead, it seemed an officer standing high up on the carriage roof was giving orders, waving semaphore commands. The darkness was smothering, then another flash of peroxide light. Peter shivered in his sports jacket, a blue cotton shirt sticking to his skin, a dry tongue rolling a cyanide capsule inside his mouth. They all knew the stories about French security collaborating with the Fellagha. Some comrades had returned with severe burns on their genitals. One woman had had her nipples sliced through with a razor blade. After a while, he felt dizzy and slightly nauseated, blowback from his cheese lunch repeating over and over again. Then there was the sound of the engine starting up and the white electric spark of traction as the train wheels began to grind on the track. Janssen felt the shudder and shake of the carriages moving towards Irun, leaving him far behind in the cold womb of the damp night.

In the Pyrenean valley near Le Perthus, close to where Hannibal's elephant army crossed the mountains from Spain to invade Italy, Peter waited impatiently at a rendezvous point in Céret, below a sun-faded advert for a bullfight. He was met by a Catalan sympathiser from the Plataforma per Catalunya who drove him to Prats-de-Mollo, a medieval walled town perched high overlooking the next valley. They drank tea together in a square enclosed by shuttered pink and cream houses.

We have allied with remnants of the Partido Popular and Los Españoles Primero," his contact informed him. "Even members of the España 2000 group are joining!"

"This is welcome news," Peter smiled, "Petty rivalries have long been our downfall."

"Indeed, what is the point of independence when you have no country? We have little choice now but to unite after the Head of the Cuartel General Terrestre de Alta Displonibildad said he can no longer guarantee Spanish sovereignty and that the men on the army base at Betera were asked to stand-down!"

Then, ambling over the cobbled square, his guide showed him the Romanesque church's golden altar and high vaulted ceiling. "Pray!" he was told, "You look like you might need to."

❖ Both the Senate and the Congress of Deputies of the Cortes Generales in Madrid approve a letter penned by the prime Minister to invite the governments of the Middle East and North African states to re-establish Al-Andalus across southern Spain.

❖ The Israeli Ambassador to Spain proposes a new Alhambra decree, reversing that issued in 1492, banning all descendants of the Spanish Legion from any rights as Spanish citizens and declaring the city of Murcia to be an independent city state run on Judaic principles.

❖ A Roman Catholic cathedral echoes with pro-Franco chants as members of the Blue Division gather to commemorate the birth of the General-issimo. The location is subsequently surrounded by EU Security Forces, made up of predominantly gay and transgender troops, and the attendees are arrested *en masse*.

❖ The owners of the Steiglitz Corporation are appointed economic advisers to the Cortes, while Boniface Herzog is awarded the Orden de las Artes y las Letras de España and Isak Raab takes up his role as Head of the Ministry of Finance and Civil Service.

❖ The Vox Espana YouTube channel is permanently banned on the basis of transgressing community values.

❖ The Monsanto Agrochemical conglomerate successfully lobby to ban organic food production in Spain.

❖ Reports of genetically modified maize cross-contaminating farmlands in southwestern Spain are censored in the news media.

❖ The entrepot cities of Almeria, Málaga, Cartagena and Alicante see military forces arriving from Port Said, Tangiers, Alexandria, Rabat, Tunis and Tripoli.

❖ The Arab League, working together with the EU Army, establishes forward bases in Seville, Jaen and Granada. Civil disruption is rumoured in Cadiz, Jerez and Marbella.

❖ Baton-wielding EU security forces batter the reformed Catalonian Committees for the Defence of the Republic on the streets of Barcelona.

❖ The Muslim payer of Adhan rings out over the rooftops of Lleida and the historic church of Seu Vella.

On the road to the Pass of Ares they saw graffiti declaiming "terra alliberata" at the border. "Catalan is still our language here," his driver said, "But now it is the Union that is trying to discourage it, just like Franco did. The real truth is that there will be no one left to speak these words after the Arabs and Africans have finished with us!"

They headed deep into mountain country on a road that wound ever higher through wooded horizons. Stopping only at Tosa where Peter got out, lit a cigarette and surveyed the harsh moorland scenery.

"They are stealing our country," his companion wheezed.

"The Union wants to steal everyone's country and hand them over to foreign hands."

The city of Puigcerda had been at the epicentre of Franco-Spanish disputes for years. Now the Union had seized it as a strategic asset. As Peter's car progressed, they came across lines of people, stumbling in crocodile formations, old people with their hands on the shoulder of the person in front. They, like so many elsewhere, had been dispossessed in yet another wave of contrived recessions, their houses seized and their villages taken over by refugees and foreign troops emboldened both by EU complicity and the funders of the so-called Arab Spring. Now the stragglers were being harassed on the side of the road, mugged by advanced units of Algerian soldiery for their water and bread. In the south of the country things were even worse.

- ❖ The prospective Emir for the Cordoba and Al-Andalus Caliphate takes up residence in Casa Mudejar, a beautiful medieval building only a short walk from where the faithful gather to pray five times a day.
- ❖ The restoration of the great mosque of Cordoba is commissioned, leading to thousands upon thousands of Spaniards, old and young alike, being forced into manual labour.
- ❖ Cases of Middle East Respiratory Syndrome (MERS-CoV) increase 230%.
- ❖ The tomb of El Cid at Burgos is desecrated.
- ❖ The skylines of coastal cities begin to look more like Damascus and Baghdad than tourist resorts.
- ❖ The volume of immigrants arriving at the ports of Cadiz, Malaga and Tarifa mean that Valencia, Salamanca, Toledo and Santiago de Compostela are projected to become majority Muslim within the year.
- ❖ Cases of viral haemorrhagic fever breaks out in port cities around the Mediterranean.
- ❖ Andalucía is formerly re-incorporated back into the newly re-invigorated Umayyad Caliphate.

Just before midnight Peter was dropped at a pre-arranged location and entered a quiet sports bar, dining on salted cod. It was gloomy inside. He could hardly make out the shape or dimensions of the room. There was a long serving area running down the right-hand wall. A bored barman looked apathetically at him as he walked towards the counter to refresh his glass. Janssen ordered a beer and looked about. There were a few old men sitting at some round tables swigging spirits and a red-haired prostitute gawking at him from a swivel chair. Conversation about future alcohol bans had stopped when he entered. Now furtive glances were exchanged between the room's occupants. Within thirty minutes two more men came in, members of the Alfonso Commando, and started a stuttering conversation. They bought him another beer and then they all left together, heading through the night, out onto mountain roads, circumnavigating border checkpoints. They passed under the craggy castle of Miglos, through Aulus-les-Bains, Seix and the Vallée de Bethmale, his companions speaking in the old Romance language of Occitan, trying to teach him to sing "We are the heirs of the mountains, we are the children of the Pyrenees. Sons of France or Spain, we are all brothers at Font Romeu."

Heading out of Vielha, the westernmost point of Pyrenean Catalonia, they drove along hairpin bends then over the high pass of Puerto de la Bonaigua and its brooding peaks that fell away into a wilderness of streams, waterfalls and granite escarpments. Peter could almost hear the echo of the long dead Catholic Traditionalist Juan Donso Cortés whispering seductively to him through the wind in the trees. For a moment he wondered if he might get a chance to visit the man's tomb in San Isidro. "You know," his new driver leaned back to tell him, cutting across his train of thought and starting him off on another, "The Catalan parliament is older than that of Westminster in London."

"And I suspect, just as corrupt," Peter sighed.

"True, we both used to work at the Sestao steel plant near Bilbao in the Basque heartland until the Indian owners sold it to China's Wuhan Iron and Steel Corporation.

Now the Chinese have gobbled up half the world's steel production!"

"And given us wave after wave of viral infections that have killed millions and eaten away at our economies like leukaemia attacking our bone marrow."

By midmorning they had covered the one hundred and twenty kilometres from Puigcerda to Barcelona, arriving in the heat of the day. There, dining in the shadow of the new three hundred metre minarets of the giant mosque, the former grand bullring that the Balano Group had sold to the Emir of Qatar for 2.2 billion, they took tapas at Escriba on the Ronda Litoral.

"Savour the moment," his companions advised him, "there is an ill wind sweeping up from the south. Everyone knows the Ramblas attackers from a few years ago were planning a similar attack on the Eiffel Tower!"

"Now the enemy has cast aside their box-cutters and are driving tanks."

After eating, they went to an attic apartment in the Melon district and furnished Peter with a suitcase full of used money and a second Spanish Identity.

"We have people inside the system," they said. "These papers in Spanish and Arabic will allow you to travel anywhere and get you past all but the highest level of security."

"Bueno!" he said, throwing back the catch and lifting the lid.

"Adelante!" They replied, slapping his back.

Out on the street Peter was pretty confident that armed with his new identity and wrap-around sunglasses he was sufficiently disguised to go unmolested about the city. Soon he found himself sitting at cafe tables occupied by ardent student followers from the Universidad de Barcelona, filling ashtrays with his newly acquired taste for Disque Bleue cigarettes. They were reminiscing about St Isidore and Visigoth Spain, the battle of Covadonga in 722 and the fact that the DNA of Pelayo, the man who started the Reconquista, is carried by one in every four European men.

It seemed the Iberian and Mediterranean nationalist movements were rapidly rising in popularity as were their Central and Eastern European cousins. Following a massive march in Sofia in support of the Bulgarian Legion and the reformed Ataka Party, Resistencia Identitaria Solidarista were out on the streets. Amanecer Dorado stickers were everywhere. This triggered the UN to invoke their 1951 Refugee Convention, especially after Spanish Patriots like the resuscitated Acción Española and Renovación Española had gathered to eject the illegals at Ceuta and Melilla and had rallied many to Antonio Vicedo Valdés's cause. Membership of the Alianza Nacional was also growing with the Ortega y Gasset, Pedro Sainz Rodriuez and Gomez Roji Commandos causing chaos by inflaming feelings at the military academies at Guadalajara, Escuela, Toledo and Ferrol.

Sympathisers in the Romanian intelligentsia, the Vatra Românească, had contacted him through mutual acquaintances in the Hungarian Magyar movement. Ponta's Social Democratic Party sent him supportive messages on a weekly basis. He knew that for some time traditionalists had been forming around populist poets like István Csurka and remnants of the MDF, inviting Peter to Bucharest to speak and train their young members. Likewise, from Budapest came fervent requests to re-invigorate the Sword of Transition underground. But Geir had another job for Peter to accomplish, and he rapidly found himself flying to St Petersburg under the auspices of protecting a New Right conference.

❖ Issur Babel's Coalition for Renewal orchestrate the largest mass protests since the October Revolution primarily against Putin and former President and Prime Minister Dmitry Medvedev's involvement in bribery and corruption.
❖ The Soros Foundation takes a majority share in

the largest Polish radio station alongside its ownership of the Agora SA publishing group.

❖ Colonel General Anatoliy Matios, Ukraine's military prosecutor's comments about the Jewish communist theoretician Alexander Parvus, is oft repeated: "The revolution drenched the Slavs with blood for decades."

❖ Pro-Alexei Navalny supporters come out in solidarity with street marches blocking major thoroughfares.

❖ A leading Russian political analyst announces that an opinion poll undertaken by the Levada Centre indicates that 71% of Russians did not expect Putin's regime to survive the upheaval, with 91% holding the President personally responsible for the crisis.

❖ The senior echelons of the United Russia Party seek to distance themselves from Putin's leadership in a series of TV interviews and comments on social media outlets.

❖ Russia's state-controlled election committee splinters when Putin calls a snap plebiscite.

❖ Putin is openly rebuked by a range of oligarchs and evidence of nepotism is leaked to the media leading to an investigation by a hastily convened anti-corruption committee.

❖ Putin is summarily impeached prior to the commencement of the election process.

❖ Several Orthodox Fathers are censured and their movements restricted for calling Babel's election a fraud and demanding the return to monarchical rule.

❖ Within months of his appointment, Issur Babel is assassinated by an unknown assailant believed to be of Dutch or Belgian origin.

When Peter returned, flying into El Prat airport, the tragic news that Sabine D'Orlac, the infamous La Petroleuese, and her co-revolutionary Luc Dubois, had been killed in a firefight with Collaborationist Special Forces near Arles in Southern France, was still sickeningly fresh and disheartening. He did everything he could to maintain morale.

It seemed that nothing could stop the Shariat being imposed across southern France and parts of Spain. Mohammedan protestors shouting the name of Tariq ibn Ziyad, victor over the Visigoths in 711, were drumming the walls of Cordoba and Toledo. Signs proclaiming the "Rule of God" were appearing across the urban centres of Catalonia. Rumours of thousands of Yemeni Junds landing at Cadiz were spreading fast. Peter would explain to the foot soldiers of the Bloc Nacional i d'Esquerres that he was only too aware of what Brussels was trying to do by appeasing the advance of the global South whilst at the same time bringing ex-communist satellites into their orbit by offering them the potential of salvation through generous financial packages. The pattern was all too familiar: accept the money, then the EU placed their cosmopolitan experts in positions of influence. It was their opening gambit. You only had to look at the case of Ukraine to see how Putin's government had second guessed them in the past. The Union's key strategy, Peter and his fellows argued, was to align the Central and Eastern European bloc under the direct legislative mandate of their twelve-member Presidium. This policy had been rolling forward inexorably for years, and as a consequence Russia needed to be destabilised.

However, since Babel's death on the Neva riverside, the tables had been turned. The Second Russian Revolution had ushered in a new nationalist regime and forced NATO to reveal its hand, the Kremlin making it clear that it would support the uprising by patriots in Europe and drawing clear red lines on the use of certain forms of weaponry by referencing its own substantial arsenal. While Western European troops made up of conjoint units from states like France, Italy, Germany, Austria and Spain, operating as the EU First Army, were reinforced by non-European forces throughout central Europe to help further transition the Czechs, Slovaks, Slovenes, Magyars and Romanians to Western democratic values. Outrider NGOs were allocated even larger budgets to support international aid and pro-democracy programmes.

Despite the best efforts of the Slovenska Nacionalna Stranka, the Czech Narodnistrana and Freedom of Direct Democracy, the Slovakian National Party, the rhetoric of Hungary's My Homeland, the Partidul Romania Mare and Bulgaria's Ataka, the tactics of the European Central Bank were mostly successful. The smokescreen of establishing fiscal and economic trading areas was falling like rivermist across the Danube, a re-run of the petro-dollar scam that had the full backing of the American Federal Reserve.

Sitting in the Cafe Schilling one afternoon, flicking over back copies of *Adevarul*, a rival publication, Peter wondered how he could penetrate the Dalmatian coastline, move through the former polyglot Yugoslavia, and head for Bucharest without being detected. The Za Dom Spremni movement, temporarily putting aside their instinctive suspicions about the Serbs, had agreed to assist him. All around the chatter was about the Reconquista, El Cid, Marca Hispanica and an end to the Caliphate in Cordoba. Young intellectuals were reading Ramiro de Maeztu's *Defensa de la Hispanidad*. Supporters talked about England's King Arthur and Portugal's King Dom Sebastian. Legends of return and national resurgence abounded amongst sympathisers of Portugal's National Renovator party. There was repugnance at the sight of Ottoman prayer meetings in the centre of Athens. With the Greek Syriza Party collapsing into disarray following their hollow election promises, support was growing once again for Golden Dawn. The latter's leadership, having escaped house arrest, were gathering followers from all quarters. Patriots were fighting everywhere, building barricades to stop the parades of Shia Muslims flagellating in the port town of Piraeus in honour of the martyrdom of Iman Hussein. At last, he thought, the sons of Sparta were rising, memories of the poet Rigas Ferraios, Ioannis Metaxas and King Leonidas inspiring their actions.

The same feelings were colouring the minds of the young people of Spain. They were full of ideals about Joan Cortada and Francesca-Xavier Llorens i Barba, who had themselves been influenced by Savigny and Herder. They idolized the Blue Brigade. Sometimes when the EU raided sympathisers' houses, patriots would drive fast along the Gran Viacity, red and yellow flags flaring out behind them chanting Valenti Almiral's name and honking their horns until the police came out in force with guns to break up the endless convoys.

Peter felt at home in Spain, much the same as he guessed he might have done in Salazar's Portugal. The Spanish landmarks inspired him. One day he had made a pilgrimage just outside Madrid, going up into the Sierra de Guadarrama before the area was to be cordoned off prior to demolition. He felt swallowed by the immensity of the grey granite edifice set against the backdrop of the vast crucifix piercing the azul sky. He stood for a while in the shadow of the basilica in the Valle de los Caidos. Stepping inside, Peter could see the long altar of cold stone, the striding pews and the hooded statues of monks resting on their unsheathed swords. In the distance, Benedictines were conducting mass. An altar boy rang a bell that drew a small crowd of loyalists, a show of clear defiance in the cool shade of the silent sepulchre, holding a vigil to honour the missing Caudillo de Espana.

Lady Genevieve Newark was an English aristocrat and an outspoken critic of the New World Order. She called the enemy "our predators" and had resided in Barcelona for two years. Now she found time to frequent anti-Union meetings, sponsoring "happenings" and was facing a court case under even more contrived laws to denude her bank balance. Lady Newark was an ardent Catholic convert who could quote whole sections from the Mortalium Animos or the condemnation of the Amici d'Israele with ease and fluency. Her daughter, a CENR student member, sat beside her on the café terrace with a chilled glass of Pinot Grigio. She wore a light tailored dress suit which emphasised her tanned thighs, shapely breasts and long brown hair, pinned back to reveal small gold studs on small pearl ears.

"Aren't you worried about being seen in public with me?" Peter asked. Lady Newark met his eyes with quiet mockery.

"It is true that this is a time when girls can be attacked in bars on the Plaza de Santa Eulalia de Murcia just for wearing a Spanish wristband, but I cannot resist scandalizing the Politically Correct!"

"You are a true revolutionary."

"And you?"

"I am sure you can imagine."

"Indeed, I can," she purred, "but tell me, what is your motivation to sacrifice so much for the cause?"

"We all have our reasons."

"But you have given up everything. You are like some kind of warrior monk!"

"I have given nothing when you compare me to some!" Lady Newark dipped her cigarette.

"You know they have seized the remaining members of your family?"

"Yes, they very kindly sent me details of my father's prison sentence and my mother being committed to a mental asylum."

"And your cousins?"

"Under surveillance!"

"Surveillance?"

"In case they display signs of social malfunction." Conversation dried up for a couple of minutes after that. Then, changing the subject, "Can you tell me more about the plans of the Revolutionary Student Organization?"

Madame Newark lit a cigarette.

"You'd best speak to Angela about the RSO. She's been

active since they moved students out of their dorms in Alicante to make room for the so-called refugees." She tossed her head towards her daughter. The young Miss Newark reached into her bag and handed him a copy of the student's radical magazine.

"I'm sorry, I can't speak Spanish."

"No problem, we have an online English version."

"They have not moved to close it down?"

"Oh, yes. Mamma pulled a few strings." Peter looked admiringly across the table.

"It cannot be sustained," Lady Newark resigned, "my resources are finite."

"And harassment?"

"Persistent but not yet brutal. It would seem there is some lingering respect for my family name, and this allows me the time I need to manoeuvre for my people's advantage." Peter sensed something of the Dunkirk spirit in the aristocrat's manner.

"How long?"

"At the current rate, maybe one year. If I slowly acquiesce, they will ruin me over a period of time, maybe three years." Peter lifted a glass in honour of her fortitude.

"And will you emigrate?"

"If they don't incarcerate me first? Anyway, where would I go? I left Surrey for Antibes and the South of France for here. Where else is there?"

"You are a political refugee." They sat in silence for a moment, eyes narrowing against the hard sun-glare coming off the walls and pavement.

"Out of the frying pan into the fire, one might say?" Peter felt in his breast pocket for a cigarette.

"I am not expecting to be around long myself?" Lady Newark raised a quizzical eyebrow. Young Angela leaned forward to catch a light and was eager to speak.

"I have sworn upon the dead in the Cementrio de la Almudena to honour their memory!"

"You are a true daughter of Miguel Ezquerra and the Azul!" Janssen surmised.

"Can I come with you?" Angela asked plaintively. Her mother went to intervene but Janssen beat her to it.

"I suspect you have more to contribute here."

"But where will you go?" There was genuine concern in her cracking voice.

"I honestly don't know, but I wouldn't tell you even if I did." Peter reclined, sucking hard on a Marlboro stub.

"A regular Otto Skorzeny!" the younger woman joked half-heatedly, disappointment smeared like badly applied lipstick across her face.

"A wanted man!" Janssen said, twisting out of his seat, "I wish you both the best of luck in your endeavours," then tipping his sunglasses forward off his nose, he winked flirtatiously at them both before walking off slowly up the hill towards the Ramblas.

The heat was intense. Peter stopped dead still. The hated star circle flag reflected in one of the shopwindows facing him. He looked up to see it pasted over the local police station. A granite statue of Dolores Ibarruri stared aggressively back at him. His eyes reading her catcall "No Pasaran!" chiselled in the plinth. He remained motionless for a moment, hunching his shoulders, buying a newspaper from a stall holder. Walking away, he read the headlines: "A New Europe: Commission Welcomes the World"—the subtext was clear, the amnesty of seven million illegals was being rushed through the judicial system so the President could make an announcement before the governmental recess.

For the next couple of hours Peter felt nostalgic for the unique produce of each nation, their minerals, foodstuffs, woods, wine and all the clichéd stereotypes of yesteryear. He saw how these were all melting away under the enforced conformity of the new economic system. The puppet masters were ascendant, milking money from unfathomable usury. And above the whole edifice, the flag of the European Union spread tight across the face of Lady Newark's predators, like the mask of a bank robber.

Operatives in the Slavy dcera movement kept him

briefed about events in the East:

❖ Patriots hold Victory parades in Red Square and fly their flags on the Dvortsovaya Most, Palace Bridge, in St Petersburg.

❖ A commemorative plaque honouring former President Putin's *dukhovnik*, or confessor, is installed at the Sretensky monastery in Moscow on the anniversary of his murder during the Babel interregnum.

❖ The ban on organisers of the annual Russian March which attracted many nationalists and ultra-rightists, and symbolising isolationist and anti-immigration opposition, is overturned in the courts.

❖ Two Russian scientists who were found guilty of promoting divisive science when they published articles proving the Out of Africa Theory to be unfounded are released from prison following the establishment of the post-Babel regime.

❖ Apologies are issued to a leading geneticist at Moscow State University for the insulting remarks made about his Into Africa Theory and alleged "DNA Demagoguery" following reviews of his work by politically motivated academicians.

❖ The censorship on writings by Vladimir Solovyov, Pavel Florensky, Alexander Dugin and others are reversed and their theses are made available once again in libraries and bookshops across Russia.

❖ The persons responsible for authorizing the mass book burnings of texts like Yuri Mamleev's *The Sublimes* and *The Sky Above Hell*, Pelevin's *Oman Ra* and *The Life of Insects* and Chrysia Freeland's *Sale of the Century: Russia's Wild Ride from Communism to Capitalism* are held in public contempt before being tried by the Supreme Court of the Russian Federation.

❖ The body of an activist in the Eurasian Youth Union who was disappeared by the previous government after being picked up by FSB operatives is uncovered in a shallow grave in South Ossetia.

❖ A leading arts guru is dismissed from holding any public office or managing any events after he is accused of insulting public taste and using art as propaganda after the disastrous Moscow Biennale of Contemporary Art show which emphasised non-ethnic Russian artists over homegrown talent.

❖ The leadership of the Donetsk People's Republic and the Novorossiya Party are released after being interned in a secret location in Sverdlovsk Oblast.

His attic window stared blindly out into darkness, the sound of a police chopper's whirling blades slicing the curfew. Every now and again he would look over to the landline, his ears primed, ready for it to ring. When the connection did eventually come through, he gave his code name and waited for a response.

"They have tracked you to Melon," said a husky voice from the Emilio Mola Commando on the other end. "It is only a matter of time before they dispatch a hit squad." He listened for another few minutes, interrupting once only to ask about car hire. With a final "Buena Suerte," he dropped the receiver, fingers flicking a plastic pen lighter as he delved into his pocket for cigarettes. Something was bothering him. He thought he had heard a second click on the line. Peter drew on his cigarette and realised it could only be a crude dual wire device. Looking down he saw the thin extension cable disappear through the wall. It was not a sophisticated system, but a one-time trick quickly configured to confirm his immediate whereabouts. Janssen reached for the Astra-A80 on the bedside table and slid off the safety with a dexterous thumb. Moments later, his door crashed open and two undercover men holding machine pistols were standing in the broken hole, both perplexed by the realisation that they were staring down the barrel of a semi-automatic. Peter fired twice, dropping both men to the carpet with smooth bore-hole openings in their wrinkled foreheads. Gathering his things, he moved along the hallway then down the stairs, step by cautious step. There was an absolute stillness in the air as he disappeared off down the half-lit street towards the Colom.

Growing fearful of the Resistance's success and the reversal of their plans in Russia, the EU Council reinvigorated populist TV shows like *Aktenzeichen XY, Crimewatch* and *Efterlyst*, fabricating evidence to implicate their enemies in murder, child molestation and drug trafficking. They also installed WANTED digital billboards across twenty-three cities, intending to extend the scheme to every public space within EU territory. The composites contained Identikit and photoFIT imagery. Bounties were offered, ranging from 1,000,000 to 10,000,000 Euro for the capture of dangerous criminals. Some of the names were known to Peter, others not:

- ❖ Arnaud Bellew, EU Citizen No. F675JK0, who was wanted for the kidnap and molestation of a 5-year-old. The DNA found on the victim's body was an exact match to the suspect.
- ❖ Albert Legard, EU Citizen No. F112B8, an alcoholic wanted for killing his wife and children, then burning down their home in order to hide incriminating evidence.
- ❖ Bernard Wolf, EU Citizen No. NL367P4, sought for sexually abusing young girls. He has a previous arrest for raping his own son and daughter.
- ❖ Professor Thomas Hunter, former EU Citizen No. GB993T1, responsible for masterminding the bombing of a Black Congregationalist Church in South London, killing five people including three children.
- ❖ Thilo Rehren, EU Citizen No. D006B2, required for questioning in relation to a major pension

fraud that left 10,000 senior citizens without funds for over a year.

By mid-afternoon Peter was on the A2 towards Girona. To his left, salty light came in off the Balearic near Calella and Lloret de Mar. Barcelona lay far behind him, Perpignan and the French border ahead. By means of forged military passes supplied by Marc Bergere, a close confidant of La Petroleuse, he cleared all the checks and slept overnight in captured Carcassonne. Despite the massive presence of North African forces, he made good time through Montpellier, Avignon, and skirted Marseilles. Everywhere he witnessed motorised columns under black Arabic flags rolling inland from the Mediterranean coastline, ordered north towards the new "No Man's Land" on the banks of the Loire. Janssen made it to Monaco and crossed the Italian border on the E80, marking off San Lorenzo and Savona on his route map before making for Genoa, arriving by nightfall. He read on the internet that similar North African troop movements led by a Yemeni general were taking place in Naples and Sicily. They were using Sardinia as a stop off and logistics centre. After sleeping in a lay-by outside Bogliasco, he was met by an Azione Nazionale cell from Rapallo who gave him money, fresh papers and a new red Barchetta. Less than an hour later, Peter was driving towards Siena, sunroof down, cigarette in mouth, feeling the heat rising over the Ligurian landscape. The fast-whistling car put up a stiff breeze causing his MS cigarette to burn up like a flare. Peter tuned into Francesca Ortolani singing "Kissed by the Sun" and thought about something she had said. "I want to be in love. I fight because I love. I live because I fight." He pushed the Barchetta well over 120 kilometres an hour, the wind ripping through his hair, flies splattering his sunglasses.

He estimated it was two hundred and thirty kilometres further to Siena, roughly two hours to drive. There were a few choke points along the road network, lorry traffic blocking the ring roads around Pisa. As he drew up behind an Iveco Stralis truck, its roll door opened to reveal a small gang of lepers, no doubt stowaways smuggled into the port at Livorno. It seemed even under the newly imposed and extremely lax new protocols, some groups were still considered unwelcome. They immediately clambered out onto the road in a coil of septic bandages and made off into the scrub.

Peter found himself in the middle of the daily traffic, spinning Pirelli tyres on hot tarmac. After a thirty-minute hold up outside Arezzo, he was beckoned into a roadside checkpoint by a policeman with a clipboard in his hands.

"ID card, please," he demanded. Peter reached into the glove compartment and passed the officer what he had requested. The man ran a pair of bored eyes over him before meandering into a makeshift customs shack. He then re-emerged a few minutes later with the incongruous image of an Indian supervisor wrapped in a flame red turban.

"Hello, Mr Tyndall," he said in accented English, clearly unperturbed by the Salafist forces occupying the land thereabouts.

"Good day."

"This is your temporary Union ID?"

"Yes, I'm a British citizen travelling on a month's furlough. Is anything wrong?" The Indian took another long look at the ID, rolling the plastic card in his moist fingers.

"You are on government business?"

"Yes!"

"The security status is red in this zone. A most unfortunate time to travel, don't you think? May I ask where you will be staying?"

"I haven't decided yet, I'll stop off in a hotel or two along the way to the Adriatic . . ." His interrogator raised an eyebrow.

"And the beautiful car?"

"Requisitioned, I could hardly afford it myself."

"You have the necessary papers?"

"I do."

"Please show," the turban clad official gestured with his hand.

Janssen took a stamped form in the name of Tyndall out of his Boggi linen jacket lying across the passenger seat.

"Luggage?"

"Just some toiletries and a few changes of clothes."

"Please let us see." Peter got out of the car and lifted the boot. Inside, his three leather bags were opened and the contents spilled out into the road. The Union officials exchanged glances when they saw his expensive underwear.

"Is everything ok?"

"Yes, you may pick it up and go!"

"Thank you."

"You will need to fill in these papers," the first uniformed man told him.

"What is it?"

"Authorisation for us to search you," Janssen scribbled his false name onto the wad of sheets on the clipboard.

"Now, may I go?"

"Yes, *bon voyage!*"

Ten minutes later, the Barchetta was in the eastern outskirts of Pontassieve. After stopping for a late lunch outside San Benedetto, he headed along the hill roads towards Cesena, with the sun descending slowly into the western foothills.

Before entering the town, he heard the wail of sirens behind him and made the instant decision to pull over and allow the convoy of Lamborghini Gallardo police cars and Mobix vans to pass. He could see through the wired windows rows of helmeted police, submachine guns resting across their laps. Almost as soon as they had appeared, the vehicles were gone. The trailing motorcycle outrider threw up a gloved hand, waving gratitude for clearing their path.

❖ Mohammedan patrols use rocket-propelled gre-

nade launchers to destroy the 33,000-year-old au-
rochs tablet and other art created by the Aurigna-
cian people found at Abri Blanchard in South
West France.

❖ Photographic images of vandalism to the Royal
Palace of Caserta and the thousand-year-old Castel
del Monte appear in alternative media.

❖ Tales of cannibalistic witchcraft emerge from the
Burundi community settling around the Temple of
Concordia in Agrigento.

❖ The ancient mosaics taken from the Villa Romana
de Casale, Sicily, are used to decorate the toilet of
the Israeli Prime Minister.

The Barchetta cruised past Rimini on the E45. Peter's
face breaking into a sarcastic smile when he saw the signs
for Frederico Fellini airport. Moving swiftly down the Au-
tostrada Adriatica he came into Riccione. There was one
cafe that remained open across the square from the Parco
della Resistenza. A handful of late-night travellers sat
drinking mochas and lattes amongst their suitcases. German expats waiting to be airlifted out in advance of the
next Arabic surge up the peninsula. Peter pulled a comb
through his hair and got out of the car. His back was stiff
and arms aching from holding the small sports wheel.
Walking between stacked chairs to the counter, he ordered coffee and brandy, before lighting his last cigarette
of the day. As he relaxed, stretching out his legs in front of
him, a young waitress came over with a sealed envelope
containing an address in the Viale Reggio Emilia and a set
of freshly cut keys.

"Leave the car," she whispered in broken English,
"there is another at the house." Peter left a large tip and
collected his luggage. Deserting the Barchetta, he walked
along the road slowly, stopping just occasionally to make
sure he was not being followed.

Janssen spent the next few weeks lying low, listening to

Frangar's "Trieste Chiama" and learning to love polenta. There was now a very public accommodation between the Union and the Islamic Council of Europe. Joint governmental and judicial systems were being set up in anticipation of a mass exodus of Italians north into Austria, freeing up Catholic soil for the land hungry Mullahs and their imams. Peter would travel, almost invisible, on public transport to Ancona to see its ancient wall defences built to protect it against Venetian, Byzantine and Albanian pirates. Jutting out on its promontory, he saw how the old docks had been rejuvenated since the Allied bombings in 1944 and the crippling earthquake of 1972.

Passing under the elegant gothic Margaritone D' Arezzo porch towards the Duomo, his eyes were drawn to the ostentatious merchants' houses on the Via della Loggia. Then up to Trajan's Arch overlooking the harbour. From there, he could see the ferries set out for Patras and Dubrovnik. Peter knew Maspok and sympathisers of the Croatian Party of Rights were waiting, hoping to smuggle him away into the Croatian hinterland. Over the years just about anything and everything had come in and out of Italy via Ancona, from English cod caught off the North Sea ports of Yarmouth, Grimsby and Hull to gangsters from Tirana with an appetite for drugs, money and slack pussy.

His routine was to take a seat around mid-afternoon at a cafe in the palazzo, bright with fresh stucco and pale golden limestone, stirring sugar into his coffee before wandering across the Piazza del Plebiscito with its shuttered palaces and sanguine statue of Pope Clement. The air was warm and balmy, perfect for the early evening passeggiata. He looked down, saw insects crawling over a rock, and thought of the Hajj. After dining in a small bistro Peter would sit and watch the Piazza Cavour as it filled with young people, insouciantly dressed for their vespertine rite. The presence of Arab and Negroid soldiers bothered him. He watched as they shouted, walked and slipped their arms around the girls.

A couple of days later he got a request to travel north to meet his former colleague Benedito Correja. At first, he objected, hoping confirmation of his clearance to travel to Dubrovnik would take priority, but in the end, he acquiesced and, climbing into his newly acquired car, drove out of Riccione up the E78 to Bologna and then on to Torino.

There was still some uncertainty about what Benedito, a devotee of Antonio Sardinha's brand of the new Integralismo Movement, had planned. The Portuguese's family had been arrested six months earlier, and after he had refused to "come in," they had been sentenced to twelve years each for distributing the reissue of *Patria Nova* and aiding and abetting a fugitive. "How can you perpetuate the ideas of Alberto Monsaraz and José Raposo?" they were told by the magistrate overseeing the case. Even his fifteen-year-old sister had been sentenced and forced to share a cell with a psychotic Tongan wrestler.

Torino was beautiful at that time of year. The disasters of recent times seem to have passed it by. A pale mantle of silver snow crusted the surrounding peaks, tulip trees fringing the riverside promenades where young families played while trying to ignore the Pompeian style disaster that was about to befall them. Erupting in sensual spring light, the glowing pink blossom reflected off the inhabitants' clear white skin, the very antithesis of the cloudy shadows looming over the glacial whiteness of the mountains above.

Peter lay down in a room just off Via Modena. It had been several days since he arrived, his attention drawn out the window down towards the Corso Regio Parco, while a residue of raindrops played a Chopin nocturne as they trickled off wrought metal railings onto his balcony.

A small Italian girl called Adriana, the wife of Raphael Calo, another traditionalist militiaman, came to visit. She moved like a leopard stalking around the room, dropping copies of *Ultra Tifo* on the bed, explaining how her husband was a follower of Claudio Mutti's Giovane Europa and how she detested Italy's pro-Left Espresso group.

"I remember Giorgia Meloni, Antonio Tajani and Matteo Salvini speaking to thousands in the Piazza del Popolo under a sign that read "Together for an Italy of Labour," and then Salvini going to the south and saying "Look, this is the port of Lampedusa. Yesterday, there was a record number of landings. I can't wait to return to government to shut down the ports to criminals." Peter smiled before she added "Then there were only 5000 migrants per month, and now?"

"I can't even imagine!" Peter said exasperated. Adriana shrugged and insisted.

"But we all started with Matteo Salvini's Lega, Casa Pound, Lega Della Terra and great speakers like Massimilano Fedriga before being drawn to the Movimento Sociale-Fiamma Tricolore," she insisted. "We all know who the opposition are because they openly declare their hostility to us by saying there is no such thing as the white race, while welcoming five million African immigrants into our country. And they have the nerve to shout down honest people like Attilio Fontana by reminding us that Mussolini's race laws ended nearly a century ago. You would think that people who fawn over a state that forcibly deports refugees, creates work camps on the impoverished West Bank for Palestinians, passes laws that prevent marriage between races and builds a wall to keep other people out would have enough intelligence to see the hypocrisy."

Adriana was slim and gentle, dark-eyed and intensely feminine. She was a member of the House of Patriots and the Rete Studentesca, wearing a Soldato Politico T-shirt while attending La Rete's Campo Zero in Solarolo near Ravenna and listening to FVM playing live on stage. On first impression, she seemed best suited to rocking the cradle, but in reality, she had fought hand to hand alongside her Fedayn and Arditi Ultra comrades in the Curva Sud and with the Princess Maria Pignatelli Commando against Congolese and Gambians outside the Il Sorriso centre and Bloc radicals in Padua. She, like many of the women he had come across over the last few years, were even more ideologically committed than their partners. They had reformed the Movimento Italiano Femminilie Fede Famiglia and began re-issuing the *Donne d'Italia* magazine. She was incensed when news that an Italian teenager had been dismembered leaked out in the press and read how her sex organs had been cannibalised in a voodoo ritual by a Nigerian drug dealer in Macerata. "Luca Traini showed us how to respond to such outrages," she insisted. "I stood under banners outside Piacenza prison with partisans from the Boschi and Mattei battle groups declaring 'Honour to Luca Traini!'"

"I remember it well," Peter recalled.

"I did the same in Palermo when a gang of Antifa beat the deputy head of Forza Nuova half to death."

"You must have been very young?"

"I had older friends who took me along with them!"

It soon became clear that Adriana was a member of M5S, the Ordo Equestris Sancti Sepulcri Hierosolymitani, and a devotee of Franco Freda's book *The Disintegration of the System*. She turned on Gabriele Adinolfi's Terza Posizione principles and utterly defied modern conventions in every respect. One afternoon, standing before open shutters, unpacking sliced ham and pouring herself a freshly squeezed carrot juice, she began quoting Evola to him:

> What genuinely and exclusively matters today is the work of those who know how to stand on the summit: those who are resolute in adhering to their principles, unalterable, indifferent to frenzied convulsions, superstitions and betrayals of the latest generations. What matters is only the steadfastness of the few whose unmoveable, iron presence can establish new relations, distances, and values: while they will not prevent this world of deviants and madmen from being what it is, they will neverthe-

less pass on the feeling of Truth to others. And this feeling, perhaps, will one day trigger a liberating crisis.

For Adriana, like so many others, the Union needed to be opposed by force. The immigrant outrages in Modena were fresh in her mind. Correja's speeches had touched her deeply. "We once took advantage of Salvini's new self-defence laws to protect our houses against intruders and the availability of firearms licenses to shoot back." It was clear tepid Conservatism was insufficient. "The Lega is strong even in the old communist strongholds like Sesto San Giovanni," she claimed.

She had studied aerospace engineering at Politecnico di Torino but had tuned in to the politics of Pavolini. Fairly soon after meeting Janssen, she confessed to having been among the Guardie ai Labari-led rioters in the Piazza Navona and planting roadside devices, organising shooting trips around the city, assassinating traffic police at key junctions like the Aurora just to cause mayhem and inconvenience. "Disruption," she insisted, was positive. "The EU's system cannot tolerate the unpredictability of random acts."

"That sounds like the Taliban?" Peter half-joked.

"There is a lot we can learn from our Mesopotamian and Achaemenid brothers! Have you read the *Epic of Gilgamesh*?"

"Gilgamesh of Erech, the historical Sun Priest of Bel."

Adriana smiled, closed her eyes and said:

The fixed time approached,
When the rulers of darkness at even-time were to
Cause a terrible rainstorm . . .

"I see you are a philosopher! Have you ever read Jason Reza Jorjani's *Lovers of Sophia*?"

"No, but I do know Jorjani's book *World State of Emergency*."

"You know the Proto-Iranian peoples like the Scythians, Sarmatians, Cimmerians and Alans descended from the Indo-Aryan peoples of Eastern Ukraine in the 9th or 10th century BC, forming civilizations like Bactria-Margiana. They travelled and traded as far east as Xinjiang."

"Our people have circumnavigated the globe through many epochs," she smiled.

"And Stephen Hawking predicted at the Starmus IV conference in Trondheim that we need to find another planet to colonise in the next hundred years or face extinction," Peter remarked sarcastically.

- ❖ Dhaka and New Delhi exchange threats of military confrontation at the strategic Farakka Barrage when negotiations over diverted water from the Ganges to the Bhagirathi-Hooghly river systems fail to reach a conclusion.
- ❖ The excessive use of fertilizers and pesticides results in mass poisoning in Bangladesh.
- ❖ Rising urban inequality in India, coupled with underinvestment in urban healthcare and nutrition infrastructure leads to mass riots in slums across the country.
- ❖ Flooding inundates 1 million acres of cropland in Pakistan, resulting in a national disaster of mammoth proportions.
- ❖ South Korean solo artist Rani performs in front of 60,000 in Seoul's Sangam stadium for Migrate-Aid in support of the people displaced by land erosion in the Mekong delta.
- ❖ Russia leaps up the Global Firepower Index.
- ❖ China's dependence on fossil fuels leads to an exponential growth in coal production resulting in levels of smog pollution that make vast urban areas like Baodin, Linfen, Datong and Zhuzhou almost uninhabitable.
- ❖ Former child protégé Greta Thunberg, donning

her sponsor's We Don't Have Time t-shirt, announces her 21-point plan to de-industrialise the West while receiving the Nobel Prize for her humanitarian work in support of OCD and Aspergers sufferers world-wide.

❖ Extinction Rebellion militants commence a series of attacks in order to sabotage British manufacturers who, they claim, pollute streams in rural areas.

❖ North and Northwest China become increasingly arid, driving hundreds of thousands of people, following the earlier waves of Covid-19 refugees, to attempt illegal entry across the now closed border into Russia.

IT BEGINS

"In the land of Nietzsche and Wagner, Bach and Kant, Clausewitz and Thomas Munser, a single word could bring the red glow of history back to life, smash to pieces half a century of dictatorial 're-education' that thought it could displace this word from the mind of a whole people without encountering any resistance."

—Pierre Krebs

Peter received instructions a week later to rendezvous with two vivacious Blocco Studentesco girls on the Corso Novara. They had oil-black hair, a swinging gait and confident demeanours. Both were concerned that he might have been followed by Ros, the Italian police's special operations unit, and took great pains to ensure this was not the case. They handed him a satchel from Correja and kissed him respectfully on both cheeks. When they left him on the plaza, Peter crossed the road and entered one of the few restaurants still open for customers. He was immediately confronted by two solicitous Malay waiters standing under a no alcohol sign, provided with the latest hand sanitiser, ushered to a table and showered with napkins. Within a few moments a glass of sparkling water was being poured and the house speciality, a seafood platter, swiftly served.

In the background, native tunes tickled his ears. He knew that outside the EU militia corps were running stop and search checks. Janssen calculated that he could make the expenses he had just collected last for a month without making contact again. The word was he was here to support an insurrection of some significant size. To quote Kai Murros, "The Wolf Pack is Gathered," and it was now time for the Fioravanti, Morsello, Petone and Mambro Commando units to act. Correja's underground had built up an arms cache and were desperate to send a message to the rest of Europe. Peter had already marked up the key strategic targets around the city. He was itching for things to kick off and was hopeful that the militant Figli della lupa—Children of the She Wolf—who lived by the ethos of Believe! Obey! Fight! would be joined by the Fratelli d'Italia, Forza Nuova and Alleanza Nazionale and be supported by the Ultras to put up a serious fight. After the waiter had presented a bill, Janssen paid and left. Stepping out, he strode towards the riverbank, walking for an hour then returned to the safety of his room, climbing sheepishly up narrow stairs, listening intently as ever for any tell-tale sounds that may indicate he was being pursued.

But there was nothing.

He was ready when Correja's order came. A cascade of encrypted messages was dispatched throughout the militant guerrilla groups, and they responded immediately. Peter joined Adriana's husband Raphael and two other men on the steps of the Basilica Superga, marching to the Ponte Regina Margherita from where the river Po stretched out before them. They reached into the bags and rucksacks they carried, set the timers to zero and dropped them onto a passing boat controlling police communications across the city.

A geyser of water lifted the vessel into the air. Simultaneously, a flare rose over the crowded arcades in the centre of the city. Activists came out onto the streets striking at pre-identified buildings and checkpoints, as well as known collaborators and Union militia. Hundreds died in the first hour. Janssen and Raphael led a group of twenty in an attack on a police car lot in the Giardino Reale, the enemy falling back towards the Duomo di Torino, before making a stand, forcing Raphael's section to stop short of their target, unable to break through. Janssen and a few others circled, going down the Via 20 Settembre. The firing went on for ten minutes or so, spent cartridges jangling on the grass.

Incendiary devices were going off all over the city. Fire spread, crimson flowers blossoming from many points of origin. Adriana was screaming at a man standing frigid with fear next to her. He was staring uncomprehendingly at the body of a prostrate policeman he had just stabbed to death. She turned, kicking the captured gun back towards him.

"Use it and keep using it!" Dumbstruck, he took up the Franchi LF-57, leant over the side of the footbridge, firing directly down into a gaggle of disorganised Union militia cowering below.

It was hot and windy. Smoke swam up in front of Janssen. Raphael was ducking through billowing clouds, spraying bullets down the Via Milano. Practically every building around the Palazzo di Citta had been seized. The red and white Piedmontese flag flew from the rooftops, fresh graffiti declared, "Long Live the National Peoples' Proletariat!" Down the Corso Valdocco, one of the widest commercial arteries of the city, groups of people marched shouting "Juve, Juve!" at the tops of their voices. Some were passing around bottles of wine.

Within hours, hastily convened meetings to broker peaceful settlements faltered as EU troops battled street to street in cities across the European mainland. Milan, Barcelona, Trieste, Braga, Graz, Belfort and Lausanne were all overrun by nationalist and populist forces. Helicopter air strikes were ordered after the "reactionaries," as the EU spin doctors termed them, used mortar fire to sink flotillas of immigrants coming into the port of Cadiz. The fighting in Bologna, Padua and Treviso, which had been planned to start concurrently with the rising in Turin, was being led by members of the self-named National Liberation Front. Thousands were dead. A United Nations Peace Force, supported by brigades from the Eurabic Coalition, entered the city of Naples by port, road and air but had not been able to make headway against fanatical opposition.

At first the controlled media tried to contain the news, but once the flash-mob nature of the revolt was recognised it was decided to use distortion to undermine the rebels' support among the general populace and military. Reporting that the reactionaries had entrenched around the poor white districts in Vicenza the press emphasised they had taken black and Jewish hostages. "It is another Holocaust!" blurted the *Haaretz* website. Similar reports were being received from Basel, Lucerne and Munich, where house-to-house fighting with EU Security Forces was understood to be intense. A spokesman for the government appeared on TV and estimated that over five hundred rebels had been killed or captured. Then, in a tone of disgust, "but sometimes they cast off their fatigues in an effort to blend in with the local population. We believe that over seventy thousand people have been displaced by the battles raging over western France alone."

Soon the population was peppered with hundreds of stories about atrocities and outrages:

Reactionaries claim responsibility for bomb that killed Aid workers . . .

An insurgent bombing in Porto took the lives of three aid workers bringing food and medical supplies to the poor and needy in Douro province. The roadside bomb was detonated on Sunday morning close to a junction where families pass as they attend the St Francis church. A senior military source close to the Prime Minister said General Saoud Najjar would hunt down Jose X, the leader of Benedito Correja's criminal gang in Portugal and ensure he faced justice.

Protests in Linz . . .
Thousands of opposition supporters gathered in the Hauptplatz, a day after the police scattered protestors challenging Prime Minister Ze'ev Ashkenazi's rule. In the clashes, ten people were killed and over fifty injured. Protests are expected to continue, and counter measures are being considered in response to the anticipated violence threatened by reactionary elements within the population.

Shooting at EU military Command Centre St Gallen . . .
At least thirty are reported dead and twenty wounded after men armed with AR-15 assault rifles gained access to an EU Militia Command Headquarters and began firing indiscriminately at anyone in a uniform. Eyewitnesses described military helicopters circling the facility and a cloud of smoke hanging over the building around 15:00 hours yesterday.

Communities join with the police to end violence . . .
Fighting that broke out in Palma after a football match between two rival teams flared into interracial violence across the island of Mallorca. Communities loyal to Al-Qaeda and the Islamic Freedom Fighters joined with EU police to enforce the law in the face of reactionary mobs in Pollenca, Deia and Escorca. A spokesman for the Khilafah Islamiyah Movement is quoted as saying, "Our aims are the same. To maintain peace and order under the rule of the prophet!"

EU confirms use of poison gas in Ponta Delgada . . .
A detailed twenty-page report compiled by United Nations investigators comes to the emphatic conclusion that reactionary forces in the Azores had used prohibited chemical weapons on civilian populations and EU forces in and

*around Sao Miguel, Baxia and Faja de Cima in recent
weeks. It is believed they used surface-to-surface rockets to
deliver a chemical payload that included sarin. An investigation at the sites in and around Sele Cidades indicate clear
signs of contamination and blood and urine tests of victims
found positive sarin signatures along with shortness of
breath, eye irritation, excessive salivation, disorientation
and miosis.*

**Prominent Spanish policeman, Abelardo Soto, victim
of shooting . . .**
*Lieutenant Soto was killed as he walked out of his home
on Monday when two gunmen on a motorcycle shot him
from behind. No one has claimed responsibility, but the authorities are saying all the indicators are that it is the work
of a reactionary guerrilla cell.*

Strife in Greece . . .
*Athens police had to respond quickly yesterday as thou-
sands of Greek citizens, who had hidden weapons in monas-
teries, took to the streets, sweeping immigrant shanty
towns off the sidewalks and patrolling crime-ridden districts. Gunfire was heard around the Varvakios Agora and
representatives of the "Greek Alternative" declared war on
the EU Army of Occupation. Reuters are indicating that an
EU Expeditionary Force is being sent from Marseilles and a
naval convoy from North Africa is setting sail from Tunis to
"end unrest in the newly-announced archipelago caliphate."*

Homo Balcanicus . . .
*EU brigades allied to Bosnian Muslim forces drive east-
ward from Budapest past Belgrade on the recently constructed road and rail networks, forking south toward Skop-
je and Thessaloniki and further east towards Sofia and Istanbul in an attempt to sever the old Byzantine causeway
formely linking Belgrade to ancient Constantinople.*

What soon became clear was that the Resistance were

building their opposition around the notion of fortress towns, places where they had majority support. Then, they were rolling out their asymmetrical warfare across Italy, Spain, Western France, South Germany, Austria and Switzerland. Taken aback by the insurgency, US forces encamped in Europe at first hesitated to intervene, awaiting instructions from the Pentagon.

Revenge for years of abuse was sometimes bloody and brutal. The bodies of fifty or so miscegenators were piled up unceremoniously on the platform of a railway station in Bratislava. Gallows lined the great avenues of Bucharest, Munich and Sevilla. In response, EU divisions moved from village to village, town to town, sometimes conducting searches, other times just setting fire to homes and shooting down anyone who jumped out of windows. When they came upon partisan groups in retreat, more often than not they were shot on the spot.

The New Ottoman army's reserve auxiliary crossed the Bosphorus, united by the vision of a second and conclusive Battle of Manzikert. Beyond Edirne, NATO warplanes were landing on the TEM highway. "We are one with our Arab and Persian neighbours," declared the recently enthroned Turkish Sultan as he overlooked the Black Sea at Trabzon watching the fair skinned "Natashas" being ferried in and traded out as far as Dubai.

Fighting on the Danube and Rhine bridgeheads in Passau, Melk and Kalosca had been particularly ferocious. Janssen's fellow graduates from Geir's Krekane School, Charles Renner and Karl Braun, led the seizure of key strategic objectives. Carpet bombing was constant. Talk of "dirty bombs" was implied by media pundits in order to try to explain the success of the nationalist forces. Others were pointing to evidence of material support from the newly established nationalist government in Moscow. Despite the demonization, desertion from the EU army was increasing and hundreds of thousands of volunteers were rushing to support the revolution, building defensive positions, learning how to fight, setting up soup kitchens and first aid stations to tend the increasing numbers of wounded.

Slogans like "Every woman who gives birth strikes a blow for the survival of our people!" were being scrawled on the side of buildings. There was a determination amongst the rebels to sell their lives expensively. Fighting from room to room against EU flamethrowers, they would defend every staircase, screaming "Revenge is coming!" Bloodied hands took kitchen knives to the throats of their oppressors in hand-to-hand fighting.

In Padua, the nationalists had been forced to retreat along the narrow streets of the via Jacob Avanco and the Isola di Torre. Their rag-tag army was limited to small arms, but when a field gun was finally liberated, they tried to slow the advancing M551 Sheridan tanks with heavier ordnance. Then, without any forewarning, an M1A1 Abrams appeared and fired on the EU advance. Parts of other motorised columns began coming over to the nativist cause. Fearing they were losing their grip, the EU launched an even more lurid propaganda campaign on all Central and Southern European cities. Media messaging carried increasingly colourful stories of war crimes, atrocities, banditry and murder. The Traditionalist cause was not helped when footage of the Romata Ultras storming into the communist stronghold in Livorno was released showing them shouting "Duce! Duce! Duce!" and killing everyone they could lay their hands on. The government even resorted to old-fashioned leaflet drops from airplanes, insisting that "Racist nationalists give up your misguided struggle!"

The fighting in Valladolid would not end. News of previous attacks had been suppressed. Only a month earlier more than a hundred-armed men and women led by Angela Newark, declaring themselves The Sons of Suner, stormed the Santa Cruz palace demanding a return to the 2000 demographic. Over sixty incidents of political violence between the 1st June and the 15th August occurred all across Castile and Leon.

EU Risk Mitigation Strategists described the unacceptable outbreak of violence as "the last gasp of the past." They discounted the roadside bombings that killed twenty-three military personnel in Freiburg and the fifty-one in Chambery in Western France. They dismissed the possibility of the armed clans of Bilbao, the Finnish, Swiss and Danish Peoples' Party insurrectionists led by Nata Poukkanen, as a serious long-term threat. "The well-advanced Coudenhove-Kalergi Plan to end self-determination, the elimination of nations with the use of ethnic separatist movements and mass immigration is irreversible," they convinced themselves and the EU Grand Council. "We will not allow the hard work of a century and leading advocates like Edvard Beneš, Léon Blum, Angela Merkel, Vaira Vike-Freiberga and Herman Van Rompuy to be thrown away at this, the eleventh hour!"

This was rapidly followed by a further statement on crimes against humanity, accusing the nationalist terrorists of even more widespread use of chemical weapons in and around Odivelas. Concluding that due to the "drop in temperature, the effects of the chemicals maximized the impact, as the heavy gas stayed close to the ground, and had penetrated the lower levels of buildings and the cellars where people were taking shelter."

The United Nations' Human Rights Organisation headed by Gahiji Rwabugiri based in Geneva, informed the EU news agency that they were looking into a series of fourteen potential Human Rights violations across the continent, with specific instances in Copenhagen, Oslo, Bremen and Vilnius. "The environmental, chemical and personal samples we have in our possession leaves no room for confusion," they asserted. "It is a clear body of evidence that the reactionary zealots we are facing are using inhuman techniques to kill law enforcement personnel and innocent and vulnerable members of our One World community."

"Who is responsible for this?" Joshua Meyer screamed in a frothing frenzy as he flew into Rome's Fiumicino airport to take personal control over the crisis in Italy, "They must have a leader!" He was outraged to have been forced to leave the Caribbean Island where two close friends were hosting a private party, attended by members of the British monarchy and a Harvard law professor.

"It is the same man who escaped us in Sweden, Latvia, France and Spain," the intelligence officer from the elite Ben Zion Cohen Brigade who was acting as an adviser to the EU, confirmed.

Meyer grimaced.

"What must our American allies think of us? And what are those idiots at the Joint Military Planning, Conduct and Capability Bureau doing? Both the EU Council of Ministers and the Kohanim High Council have declared this Janssen a tangible threat. Some say he was the man who killed our brother Babel in St Petersburg." Meyer's finger was wagging energetically at his Iberian and Latin lackeys. "This Peter Janssen is one of the many who challenge all our ideals. Parts of Northern Italy, Switzerland, Slovakia and Western France are no longer under our control. Find him. Kill him. Understand?"

The EU First Battle Group established a cordon sanitaire around Rome. Following an attempted coup-d'etat in Washington, US military advisers had been temporarily withdrawn at the sound of shootings in the streets and suburbs. The failure of water mains, intermittent electricity and gas supplies demoralized both sides. "I want Turin, where this all started, to be turned into a funeral pyre," Meyer yelled. "We will not tolerate the return of fascism!"

In revenge, nationalist storm groups were systematically killing EU politicians, regional governors and globalists by bullet, knife and poison as they sat in their offices, walked the streets and lay in their beds. Holding centres for political opponents in Venissieux in France, Frankfurt am Main and San Marino in Italy were raided and the inmates set free. Geir's old friend Sigrid Aaland, who had been wounded in the leg during the battle for Norway, explained from her encircled headquarters in Stavanger that they fought on because they had a clear idea in their heads, "to fight the poison of multiculturalism to the last moment!"

❖ A people's militia advance under the fifty-six belfries of Antwerp, Diksmuide, Kortrijk, Pendermonde, Leuven, Gembloux and Namur.

❖ The new Russian government insists that the hostilities in Europe are "a wholly European affair" and rebuffs American attempts to interfere in Ukraine, the Kremlin's "near abroad" in the UN Security Council.

❖ Maltese insurgents store weaponry in the St Paul catacombs.

❖ Father Giulio Tam celebrates a mass in Latin before the burnt-out Basilica di San Lorenzo in Florence.

❖ Greek Cypriots seize strategic passes in the Troodos Mountains, disrupting Turkish forces crossing the island's green line.

❖ Portuguese patriots recapture the Convent of Tomar after the Muslim invaders try to turn it into a Madrasa.

❖ The EU target Sintra's UNESCO world heritage architecture for air attack after the home of a businessman is attacked by an angry mob demanding reparations for a share-swindle.

❖ Hungarian patriots surround the necropolis of Pecs, the Benedictine Abbey of Pannonhalma and medieval Visegrad to protect them from roaming Roma warbands.

❖ Slovenian nationalists encamped for a mass rally at Lake Bled are told to "prepare for Total War."

❖ The Finnish Vihlo Tahvanainen and Marshall Mannerheim Commando launch attacks on EU forces in and around Helsinki.

❖ Demonstrations are held in central London, Manchester, Glasgow and Birmingham against Muslim aggression. Counterdemonstrations by Jihadists are held in Bradford, East London and Liverpool resulting in violent clashes and loss of life.

❖ Simultaneously, a crime wave sweeps across large swathes of urban Britain with reports from inside the constabulary indicating affirmative action ethnic minority officers were obeying the instructions of the Labour Party's shadow Home Secretary and refusing to arrest people of colour regardless of the serious nature of the offences they commit.

The euphoria in Turin lasted three full weeks. Peter, Adriana and Raphael met on the junction of Barbaroux and Mica to decide on the next stage of their strategy.

"We can't scatter," insisted Adriana, "We need to show we can stand. If we continue the fight it will give others heart!"

"But we're doomed like the Swiss Guard fighting to the last man on the steps of the Holy Basilica," Raphael countered, "Better to live to fight another day."

"Adriana is right," shouted Peter, even as the mortar fire rained down, "Everyone remembers how they formed the square before the church doors to buy Pope Clement time to escape." From that moment talk of evacuation was forbidden as defeatist. "Here we will hold true to the sacred memory of The March on Rome. They will have to fight for every cubic metre of this city!"

A number of women, young children and older men filed by the open-top tables littered with captured equipment, picking up guns to defend themselves. The distant thunder of artillery fire thumping constantly outside the covered marketplace. No one was under any illusion. They all knew this was a fight to the death. Around 7:00 PM every evening, ranks of nationalists would march singing, flags flapping, determined faces set against torchlight.

Columns of leather jacketed youths, boys with crew cuts and girls in ponytails brandishing weapons, walked behind religious icons.

Such flamboyance came to an end when the blinding light of a Union phosphorus attack burnt hundreds to death in La Crocetta. Janssen threw himself to the ground as the fire storm washed over their heads. He looked to left and right, seeing his colleagues squatting in doorways, kneeling behind barricades, firing up at the yellow taillights of soaring helicopters.

"Basmachi troops," Peter heard whispered in his ear, "The government has brought in their Central Asian mercenaries." There was the recognisable grumble of caterpillar tracks on tarmac and the return of machine gun fire from boarded shop fronts. Lumbering like prehistoric monsters, they came around the corner of the Corso Galileo Ferraris. The air was full of flying debris, some of it human in origin, legs and arms bouncing across the stonework. Smoke filled Peter's lungs. Charcoal wafers burnt his throat. The smell of flaming petrol canisters stung their eyes like viper spit. He was still pressed to the ground, playing dead, as he saw a Union trooper advancing, firing from the hip. When the blue uniform was within striking distance, he lunged upwards into the man's midriff sending him hurtling backwards. The soldier responded with cat-like proficiency, twisting and turning as Janssen threw himself forward, trying to drive the point of his knife home. It was no holds barred. They beat at each other with their fists and feet. The Union man sent Peter down with a forceful shot to the jaw but Janssen was lucky enough to keep hold of his blade and drove it deep into his unprotected calf.

"Don't kill," the Asiatic begged in broken English, slit eyes tightening at the dark corners. Janssen looked from side to side to remind himself of the executioner's merciless shooting of unarmed men and women. Then, going down on one knee, he sawed through the man's neck, running back to a strongpoint where Adriana was crouching under the burning chassis of a Fiat Bravo, letting off tight bursts from an L.M.G. Peter looked behind him and saw a girl wearing olive combat trousers. She was waving a Beretta and directing fire. Over the next couple of hours, the barricades rose and fell continually every time the armour rolled by, sandbags rising around the city to shoulder height, rough cut loopholes providing cover for Traditionalist sharpshooters to pick off EU troopers running about under intermittent streetlights.

The Basmachis came in snake-like columns. Their tank troops and elite fighters in full cry. Behind them were the dregs of the Steppe, vicious pox-gnarled yellows who stole everything they could prize off walls or take from the death grip of the slaughtered, leaving mutilated children and defiled women in their wake. Peter took great pleasure in using a classic Dragunov SVD sniper to take out a line of men who had a female spread eagled on the street. A few minutes later he observed a girl with long braided hair running before her drunken assailants. He scoped his targets through the NSP-3, watching them drop as their dishevelled victim made it safely to the nationalist's lines.

At the junction of Corso Stati Uniti and Via Vincenzo Vela, Traditionalists were responding to fire from the Santuario Della Consolata. Raphael led a squad up onto the rooftops from where they could look down onto the tall slender buildings, small wooden-framed windows, curved metal domes and endless slate alleyways running off in a giant looping circle. Raphael's people aimed their rifle fire down onto the streets. Janssen was wondering how long they could last. They were slowly being surrounded. The front lines following the Corso Palestro, the Corso Siccardi and the Via Cernaia. Every so often machine gun fire would erupt from the top window of the hotel Diplomatic, where bloodied mattresses and soiled bed linen was being stuffed into windows and doorways to keep out the acrid blue smoke.

After several days of nightmarish house-to-house conflict, the nationalists and EU forces had almost fought each other to a standstill. At a pre-arranged time, some EU officers advanced from a bombed-out department store on Via Giuseppe Mazzini. They carried a flag and had removed their helmets. One or two of the rebels raised their rifles but Peter shouted down the line for everybody to hold their fire.

"Will you surrender?" they called through loudspeakers.

"Will you surrender?" echoed back to them.

"Then you will all die!"

"Well, you'll be murderers and we will be martyrs!" Peter called back.

"You're in the wrong country if you expect the Geneva Convention," Raphael darkly joked. A second later a bullet zipped through the air, taking out a young member of the Ciavardini Commando. Then another split a chair leg on which Raphael was sitting.

"Snipers!" went the call and Adriana was up on her feet, running ahead, shouting "Avante!" to encourage her fellows. There was no quarter given or expected.

Forty-eight hours later, Janssen was being roused from a deep sleep by the news that the nationalist stronghold at Moncalieri was about to be taken. He dressed hurriedly and asked for two hundred volunteers to relieve their Piedemontese brothers and sisters. Within the hour, men and women were filling their pockets and backpacks with bullets and lining up at the side of the road ready to leave. By 8:00 AM, a large convoy was on the move, pushing through the EU flank. Finding the sideroads as well as main highways were encumbered by civilian refugees, they suffered several strafing attacks on the Via Custoza that left six dead and many wounded. By eleven, they broke the EU encirclement spread across the Parco Europa to relieve the joyous inhabitants who danced and sang the *Giovinezza*.

After that success, Janssen was spirited away to support the siege of Milan. Within a week, Peter was watching the fall of the city to nationalist forces, and recalling Orwell's lines:

> Who would have imagined twenty years ago that slavery would return to Europe? Well, slavery has been restored under our very noses . . . It is worth comparing the duration of the slave empires of antiquity with that of the modern state. Civilizations founded on slavery have lasted such periods as four thousand years. When I think of antiquity, the detail that frightens me is that those hundreds of millions of slaves on whose backs civilization rested generation after generation have left behind them no record whatsoever. We do not even know their names. In the whole of Greek and Roman history, how many slaves' names are known to you? One is Spartacus . . .

Later, when he returned incognito to Turin, he was forced to move undercover through the grotesque scarred architecture of Via Aosta. Gone were the warped walls, baroque facades and twisted ironwork of skilled Italian craftsmen. Now there were only broken windows stuffed with newspapers or bundles of rags to shut out the wind. The slaughterhouse in the old citadel was closed off. Basmachi soldiers had taken to cutting off ears for trophies, tearing out tongues and popping the eyes of little boys. Girls, some as young as ten, were being passed between the troopers. Every male over fourteen was slaughtered. Survivors below that age were castrated and taken for the Janissary brigades of what was now being heralded as Allah's Army. What fresh food there was came into the central plaza on trucks, seized from local farmers who were forced to give their produce away for free, while their neighbours were robbed by speculators and Land Bank Trusts.

He witnessed renegade Italian troops who had refused to join the EU army being put into re-education camps.

Some of the survivors, veterans from the distant eastern wars, were disarmed and marched along the Porta Nuova, like captured prisoners from one of Julius Caesar's campaigns. They looked forlorn, having returned from battles that had no rational purpose or clear conclusion other than to deplete Europe of white male DNA. They received no accolades or applause from joyous and appreciative crowds. Their welcome as dry and thankless as the desert dust ingrained in their tattered uniforms, the scuffs on their boots and the bloodstained evidence of the pointless route marches through hostile territory that opened up before every patrol and closed in behind them. "They will be judged and then executed for war crimes," one Omani General had said, before he was censored.

"This is not the time to say such things," Meyer conveyed to his Mohammedan contacts. "People are already saying that these British, French, Italian and Polish soldiers were fighting to look after the interests of our shareholders in the oil and gas companies. Subtlety is still required as well as a convincing storyline."

It was late when Janssen got to Via Modena. A curfew was still in force as mop-up operations continued to overcome pockets of resistance. The streets were strewn with rotting corpses and the smell of putrefying flesh, men, women and children, even the carcasses of dogs and horses. Peter could only drive over them. There was no other way. He tried to steer around the heaped bodies, but there was nothing else for it but to cross himself, push ahead, listening as the wheels churned over the cracking skulls and snapping limbs. Coming to a stop, Peter stepped out of the car and walked up a set of stairs into the quivering half-light of a small apartment. An older woman greeted him.

"Where have you been?" she asked, leaping up, rushing towards him.

"Walking," Peter spat out indignantly, falling into the role of an angry son.

"Come to Carolina," the woman said, pretend tears in

her eyes. She put an arm around his shoulder, "You must get out. Get out now, while you still can!"

"What?"

"The room is bugged; we are being watched!"

"But I'm so angry!" Janssen continued his deception noisily, shaking his head.

"Get out, now!"

Peter twisted on his heels, almost falling down the wooden stairwell, reaching for a gun tucked in his waistband. Halfway down, he met a silver-haired sympathiser who led him to a car parked up on the pavement, covered in a copper-coloured sheen of sewer water.

"What's happened?"

"Haven't you been told?" his accomplice asked, surprised.

"Told what?"

"Carolina is Adriana's mother. They got Adriana. She must have talked. They've been hitting all our safe houses and taking most of the leadership. Benedito took his own life in Lisbon before they surrounded his apartment in the Rua Beatas."

Peter looked aghast.

"Raphael?"

"Taken!"

"Prison?"

"Some have been executed!"

"What, no show trials?"

"I am sure there will be a few," he guessed as they got in the car and drove off, "But our more erudite members will never be allowed into a courtroom." As they drove along the Via Giuseppe Verdi, Janssen could see all the cafes were filled with police and military personnel.

Later, hiding in a small cellar in the town of Marene, he got to read the underground's own internal report on what had happened. It seemed that Adriana had been arrested for an innocuous speeding offence on the Via Maria Vittoria. Although wearing a disguise and carrying credible papers, a curious militia man, motivated by lust, one would guess, rather than a sense of duty, insisted on taking her mobile number. In the ensuing melée Adriana was wrestled to the ground. Within hours, hit squads were being dispatched to pick up activists or, failing that, members of their families. Fifty or so key people were rounded up. Several died in suspicious circumstances. One broke both his legs jumping out of a fourth-floor window. Another drowned trying to evade the police on the banks of the Po.

Adriana had been "ganged" by Mossad intelligence officers and both her arms were systematically broken by the arresting sergeant. A cornered collaborator who had seen the official records confirmed they had started with each finger, before progressing up the ulna and radius with stamping boots, crumbling the left humerus, returning with a hammer to crush Adriana's phalanges into powder, forcing her to speak.

The Resistance moved Janssen several times over the next week. Eventually he ended up in a townhouse in Morvino. Sitting on a plastic garden chair, leaning slightly forward, hunched over the long black gun barrel hanging like a limp penis before him. The sunlit square beyond the window, some fifty feet below, echoed with children's laughter. He was listening to the radio announce that the loss of such substantial portions of EU territory to the accursed populists meant that Colonel Abaan Baseer was to be declared Eurabic Regional Governor of Piedmont with the order to eliminate all opposition.

Baseer, Peter knew, saw himself as the founder of a new Muslim Empire in the European heartland, an Asian Mahdi. He had once claimed to have had visions, and that he had been called by the prophet to take this soft green land from the Kufr. He was also closely aligned by blood with the Mohammedan forces occupying southern France. Peter set up five shells on the table next to a cup of hot lemon tea. He pushed the cartridges one by one into the swinging chamber. Then, clipping the gun closed, he threw a half twist, so the greased lock and load action snapped tight. He laid it on the wooden surface in front of him and reached for his cigarettes and matches. "We now hold over 3,450,000 square kilometres of territory," he said to himself, "more and more trained military units are crossing over to us, and we have allies in the Kremlin." Then taking a long draw on the filter, leaning back in his seat, he waited for his transport to arrive.

❖ The new Russian government's security doctrine emphasises the country's role as one of leading world powers whose sovereignty must be respected—that Russia will once again act on the international scene to protect its strategic interests—that Russia forsees a new polycentric world and that besides Ukraine, the Arctic Circle is also a potential theatre of conflict.

❖ In terms of domestic policy, the post-Babel Russian government commits itself to establishing confidence and trust in the agencies responsible for Law & Order, countering the terrorist threat, the repatriation of immigrants, overcoming technological backwardness, modernising the economy and preventing inappropriate use of public funds and endemic corruption.

❖ The Duma approves a Bill to increase defence spending by $91 billion.

❖ The EU is forced to accept negotiations regarding air corridors and no-fly zones over parts of Scandinavia, the Baltic, eastern Ukraine and Belarus.

❖ Russian IL-38 aircraft intercept NATO squadrons over Poland and Lithuania.

❖ Vozdushno-desantnye voyska airborne divisions are sent to static forward positions around Lida and Smarhon in the Grodno region of Belarus.

Within a month of the Turin rising, the EU was fighting on ten ill-defined fronts. The opposition's leadership, a matrix of hard-line guerrillas, the populist right and "turncoat" troops, was beginning to coalesce, the insurgency intensifying week by week.

Holland's delicate racial balance was strained to the breaking point when raiding parties from immigrant ghettos started openly white slaving in adjacent suburbs. Brussels had been penetrated by a modern-day Freikorps of Walloons, Flemish, Germans and Ardenne French. A narrow corridor along the Sarrebruck A4 out towards Strasbourg was being held in a last-ditch defence by the Turkish 5th Corp 1st armoured Brigade from the Tekirdag Province.

Car bombs were exploding all across the continent. The deadliest single attack was in Southall, London, where the formerly reserved English had packed a white Ford van with explosives and abandoned it in an area colonised by economic migrants from Pakistan. CCTV footage taken from the scene showed a young couple walking nonchalantly away down the Broadway, stopping to kiss in a shop doorway. Then, around noon, the van was torn in two by an orange vapour, melted metal flying like ninja stars shredding a passing flock of Muslims.

In the former Prussian hinterland, the indigenous population had seized Kaliningrad, Gdansk and Magdeburg. A Government General of the newly liberated lands meeting in the former Rathaus on the Altermarkt re-established the Landtag in Magdeburg. Within a fortnight of the Declaration of the Elbe, the opposition's western and eastern wings came together on the Neman river, largely clearing the Baltic of the influence of the Chosen. Reports of reprisals in Central Europe were well-founded. The Kreuzberg district of Berlin was cleansed of illiterate Gastarbeiter Turks, dead bodies wrapped in kilim rugs filling the warehouses prior to deportation back to Anatolia. Members of the former Hungarian Government that had come to power after the death of Viktor Orbán were swinging from the Chain Bridge in Budapest. The EU's occupational army and remnants of their replacement population were fighting to the last amongst the black cat tail plumes of burnt-out vehicles and ransacked shops along the Andrassy.

The French 1st Mechanised Brigade, the Rapid Response Force, out of Lille and the 3rd Regiment of Engineers based in Charleville-Mezieres swept in a large arc across a swathe of northern and eastern France, rolling like a snowball accumulating support through Nancy, Troyes and Metz. Within a week they had allied with a renegade Lieutenant General of the German Bundeswehr, the Heeresfuhrungskommando, who had thrown themselves in with the Special Operations Division, fighting out of Stadtallendorf, and the Munster-based 1st German/Netherlands Corps, to take Krefeld, Koblenz and Bonn. The EU garrison at Maastricht continued to hold out despite the best efforts of the 261 Paratroop regiment to dislodge them. The mayors and local governments of the Limburg region formally welcoming their liberators before the Berlin traitor trials commenced.

A statement made by the newly formed Nativist government in North Eastern Germany read "the violence currently gripping our country is a temporary misfortune that would right many wrongs. It is hoped that this would lead in the medium-to-longer term to full and free elections limited to those who were historically and ethnically entitled to participate." The EU's response, dictated from the UN building in New York, was immediate and unconciliatory: "We know that the Saar, Alsace and the Ruhr are part of an unstable region, and this banditry will be put down with the utmost severity." Likewise, they announced, "For many years, the city of Berlin has benefited, like many other German cities, from immigrant talent from Turkey, Albania, the Middle East and Africa. We deplore the sentence of death imposed on the former Chancellor. The glory days of Progressive Globalism will return, and all our peoples will come together to defeat these emissaries of the failed Teutonic past."

❖ Thousands of Austrians gather in the natural redoubt of the Wachau Valley between Melk and Krems.

❖ The Mayor of Graz announces the formation of an ethnic commune at his new administrative headquarters in the Schloss Eggenberg.

❖ Indigenous communities rally to protect the Luther memorials at Eisleben and Wittenberg from pro-Zionist commando units.

❖ Leftist opposition to traditional student balls in Vienna are met with violent counterdemonstrations.

❖ Only weeks after suffering an arson attack, The Bayreuth Festival House reopens with Wagner's Ring Cycle.

❖ The fertile Dessau-Worlitz region of Saxony-Anhalt becomes the centre of local food production in a commune system that rapidly spreads across central Europe.

❖ A high-ranking CIA officer at Langley in Virginia concurs with a review conducted by a security analyst at Camp Stanley in San Antonio, Texas, that predicts the rise of armed militia units in Middle America determined to uphold the original precepts of the Constitution and Christianity.

The sky over Cluj shuddered with fork lightning. Beating rain came down over the ancient dome of St Michael's in Unirii Square. The nationalists had advanced from Timişoara. Janssen's senses were on red alert. Behind him the armoured column and foot soldiers were fanning out over the featureless terrain of the Somes Plateau and the Transylvanian plain. Through his field glasses he could see dust rising off the E571 Gherla road. EU forces were pressing on, the rebel Sheridan XM551 armour firing off high velocity volleys, smashing through the enemy T72 tanks. Janssen observed the field littered with burning wrecks, flames consuming the Angolan Mechanised Division that had been flown in from Nova Lisboa and billeted and re-equipped in Braila.

Amid the smoke and ashes, the khaki-clad nationalists, reinforced with Noua Dreapta volunteers and veterans of the Drina Corps of the Republika Srpska army, began to gain ground, engaging in hand-to-hand fighting with the African mercenaries, who, when captured, were moved to the back. The sight of the defeated army marching along the road encouraged the rebels. They looked hard into their opponent's downcast eyes, the blacks dreading the revenge their victors would exact when they discovered the acts they had committed on the length and breadth of Braila's Obor and Dorobanti suburbs. The reek of inciner-ated bodies filled the mist-shrouded streets and squares. Whole families lay shot in the street, children chained to railings, car windscreens melting in the rolling heat.

Janssen stood and wept at the sight. He thought he had been hardened to suffering, especially after he had wit-nessed the battle of Bucharest, where EU air-cover was met head-on by nationalist converts flying Mirage F1 CR's from the Ramstein, Vogler and Kornati airfields. But noth-ing could have prepared him for this. Split was also so heavily shelled that the governor reported "The whole city is in flames."

By now the Americans had largely overcome their own internal political and military turmoil and insisted that the EU instigate immediate political purges of its armed forces once it was realised there was sympathy for Tradi-tionalist values amongst its ranks. Their Stasi-style spy network had already infiltrated all the organizations, ad-ministrative and social units that composed the military infrastructure. "DIVERSIONISTS MUST BE EXPELLED!" the digital flat screens bleeped. Within weeks the cull of suspects amounted to sixteen generals, fifty-two brigade commanders, three-hundred-twenty corps commanders and two-hundred-seventy-five colonels. The total number of military seized amounted to several thousand. Others had already "gone over" with their weapons, skills and training.

So when the EU began an attack to retake Zagreb, the nationalist leadership were bolstered by the skills of the German and Austrian military high command, who gathered in Sesvete to build deep defensive lines on the main city bypass and the Adriatic and Sava bridges approaching the capital. Insurgent groups were dispatched to harass the EU advance, stopping them from poisoning Lake Dubrava, the reservoir for Medimurje county. Checking them in the passes around the Dragonja river and the Plitvice lakes.

"One positive we can take from all this turmoil," Meyer reflected in a verbal message back to the Kohanim Council, "is that this is still essentially a battle on European soil. The majority of the dead are Europeans, either those who are with us, or those who oppose us. Although, the attrition rate does not favour the forces we ultimately support, the world's non-white population is ten times larger than that of the Caucasian population. Ultimately, the demographic pendulum still swings in our favour!"

Soon it became clear that the defence of Central European cities like Munich, Vienna and Ljubljana, although symbolic, would not be the ultimate test of the sustainability of the uprising. Control of the key industrial zones like the Ruhr was vital. Cities like Duisburg, Essen and Dortmund became Western Europe's Stalingrad. The strategists on both sides fully understood, however, that the ultimate outcome would not be decided by one decisive blow but a series of irrevocable setbacks for one side or another.

"We will not allow Europe to slide back into the Dark Ages," said President Rahm Emanuel, after having reestablished the Democratic Party's control of the military and arrested several key military leaders at West Point, "Even if it means invasion and occupation of the continent!"

During a reconnaissance mission in the Southern Alps somewhere between Udine and Trieste, Janssen and his corps came upon an EU artillery position and were cut to pieces by well-disciplined Alpine troops. Again and again his men charged and were beaten back, the forest floor covered in bloodied pine-needles. By the time Peter tasted the fruity odour of the tabun nerve gas at the back of his throat, it was already too late.

BORDERLANDS

"A nation is an organic thing, historically defined. A wave of passionate energy which unites past, present and future generations."

—Yuri Michalchyshyn

When Janssen flew into Kyiv, a burst of wet sunshine illuminated the Statue of Victory, bathing her in orange flame, sparks running along the sword as it fended off the cold Steppe. Below, the Dnieper curled around the gold domes on the green Kyivo-Pecherskaya. Beyond the church complex, the endless march of concrete tower blocks towards the horizon contradicted the ancient beauty. The old Rus capital, birthplace of Bulgakov, author of *The Master and Margarita,* was rapidly changing, sucked into the vacuous modernity of usury and soulless shopping malls.

Peter's shaking fingers folded away the note he had received about nationalist gunmen killing a number of senior EU Security Council members during an audacious attack in Geneva. A strike force led by Istar reconnaissance units in Mowag eagle Jeeps, supported by the Swiss Army's 12th Mountain Brigade using Leopard 87 tanks, had rolled into the city, decimating the defence cordon with handheld rocket fire. Then, having taken the building and captured the epaulette-bearing officials, they filmed a hastily convened trial and the resulting summary execution for "crimes committed against white civilization." Fastening his seatbelt, he surveyed the slender figure of a Ukrainian air hostess wandering down the aisle, checking

on the passengers, nodding to himself a silent contempla-
tive confirmation of all the stories he had heard about the
beauty of these people.

The landing was uneventful, a little turbulence jolting
them as the aircraft came in low over the river. They disembarked, herded onto a shuttle bus that took them to
the Arrivals terminal where a disordered melée gave him
time to study the big plasma screens in the auditorium.
His instructions were to lie low and report back to Geir on
the readiness of the Ukrainians to join the war. Only a few
years before nationalists in camouflage gear and ski masks
had seized the Yanukovych government's buildings and
flown their black and red flags in Dnipropetrovsk, Za-
porizhzhya, Khmelnitsky, Zhytomyr, Cherkasy, Ternopil
and Lutsk. Tens of thousands had protested behind the
coffins of martyrs like Mikhail Zhiznevsky, fighting the
Berkut riot police in the streets. Collections were taken to
support families when AutoMaidan activists were seized
and disappeared, never to be seen again. Despite the best
efforts of the nationalists, George Soros's Open Society
Foundation, The National Endowment for Democracy
Movement and the Ukrainian Democratic Alliance had
leached away support in favour of the EU, and now
swathes of the Ukrainian-speaking areas were part of a so-
called Democratic Protectorate. Militants in the east of
the country had already declared an independent Novorossiya in Donetsk. The Knights of New Russia movement, holding the strategic transport hub at Debaltseve,
strutted around with their skull and crossbones badges
bearing the motto: "More Enemies, More Honour." Even
after the third version of the Minsk Accords, the pro-God,
Tsar and Nation forces exchanged rocket-fire with EU advanced posts from their strongholds in Artemivsk, Buhas,
Novoazovsk and Luhansk. There was nothing but contempt for the OSCE-verified buffer zone. Hundreds of
thousands of refugees had migrated during the transition,
favouring Russian Solidarnost to the empty offers of oligarchs who had come to mutually beneficial terms with

their counterparts in Brussels and Strasbourg. Fearing the encirclement of the Slavic heartland, because like Iraq, Libya, Syria and Afghanistan, it would not bow to the authority of the central banking system, Donetsk became the Orthodox Crusaders' New Jerusalem. "In these days our men carry Kalashnikovs, not swords, but they are still noble knights, protecting Christian culture from cosmopolitans and Turkmen, just like Count Vronsky in *Anna Karenina*," a political commentator was quoted as saying from the city of Kramatorsk. The twenty-two thousand Russian troops that had originally annexed Crimea were back and on constant alert. Motorised divisions were on standby in the border town of Churovich, ready to strike if the need arose.

Peter's legs were still weak. He stood in line with his fellows as one-by-one their passports were checked and their details put into the state's database. Moving slowly beyond the line of kiosks towards baggage control, he ignored his doctor's orders and lit a cigarette, breathing a sigh of relief before the conveyer's interlocking surface started to move and suitcases emerged from behind a Perspex screen. After a short wait, Janssen lifted his luggage with difficulty and twisted off up a shallow ramp, coughing heavily, making his way to the exit. Emerging through sliding doors, he was confronted with a noisy bazaar, people with expectant faces waiting to meet friends and family, vendors selling everything from flowers to pastries, taxi drivers offering different rates for the same short journey into the city centre.

"Skolka?" Peter asked one driver who was clearly not expecting him to speak Russian.

"Fifty dollars."

"Sorok!"

"Horosho!"

They drove the long, straight Prospect Vozz'iednannia, crossing Paton's bridge under the white jet trails of Sukhoi-24 and Il-76 aircraft, climbing the sloping Staronavodnyts'ka towards the boulevard Lesi Ukrainky. Circling the Bessarabska market in slow, heavy traffic they hit Khreschatyk, moving inexorably towards Maidan, just off Independence Square, where the Euromaidan encampment and the mass shootings of February 2014 made the Orange Revolution look like nothing more than a sulphurous match, so easily doused by the flitting snow showers coming in over the rooftops of Podil.

Aleksandr Budnik, Janssen's contact, was a self-styled Brahmin, nicknamed Vitsiya, meaning father. A stalwart of the Reconquista Club, the headquarters of National Corps, he currently occupied a large baroque apartment on the Velyka Zhytomyrska, where he held his salon celebrating a range of Ukrainian thinkers like Dmytro Dontsov, Vasyl Stus, Dymtro Pavlychko and Pan-Slavic philosophers such as Vladimir Solovyov and the martyr Symon Petliura of the Ukrainian Revolutionary Party. It was understood that Svoboda was essentially Strasserite in its principles. Geir had told him Budnik was a great admirer of Alfred Schuler and the poetry of Stefan George, so he had brought collections of their works as gifts. When Peter entered, Budnik put down a copy of *Terreur d'Elite* and looked up, surprised to see what he took to be a fifty-year-old man, rather than the war hero he had expected.

"Welcome," he said, "I trust you had a good journey?"

"Yes, I am most grateful for your assistance."

"Nonsense," said Budnik waving away Janssen's gratitude. "In dark times like these it is our duty," he paused, "I mean, our privilege to reach out the hand of comradeship, especially to someone who has served our people so well. It is not every day I get to shake the hand of a man who has killed a President!"

"Thank you, and one day I hope to be in a position to reciprocate."

"Soon, I am sure. Please have a seat. Will you take chai?"

"Da spasibo." Budnik smiled.

"I see you remember some Russian."

"Limited, I'm afraid!"

"What about Ukrainian?" Peter shook his head. "A pity. It would be more acceptable . . ."

Budnik poured hot water into the teapot from a copper samovar and requested a colleague to fetch some ham and scrambled eggs. "This will be good for your stomach after flying," Budnik assured him, tipping the brown spout towards a cup. Peter thought his host's face broad and happy. It smelled of eau de Cologne and was masked by a highly stylised moustache that brought to mind Gogol's *Taras Bulba*. Budnik was wearing a red velvet smoking jacket. He watched Peter sip. "You look fine," he lied. "Word had reached me that you were struggling?"

"Well, at least I can control my bowels now!"

"Thanks be to God," Budnik slapped his thigh.

"Are you well informed about things in the West?"

"Well enough to congratulate you on the liberation of Europe."

"I think you are premature to speak of liberation, but certainly a real fightback is underway."

"And soon our armies will see you return to the front line!"

"My physical injuries are healing quickly. I still shake, but it will pass, so they tell me. Apparently, I need to rest, avoid direct action for a while. Go deep underground, recuperate for the next campaign."

"Then you have come to the right place my friend. We will make you disappear!" Peter smiled.

"Just for a while, you understand?"

"Do you have sufficient funds?" Janssen shook his head no.

"It will be taken care of. I already have somewhere for you to stay in the city and a team of people to assist you. Once you have your new identity, we will take you further west towards the Polish border."

"Where do you have in mind?"

"Lviv."

"Where the science fiction writer Stanislaw Lem was from?"

"I will hide you amongst what the Russians call the nezalezhyne, the West Ukrainian Nazi sympathisers. It is a city where we have deep roots. Do you know very much about our history?"

"Not a great deal." They gathered closer around the circular table laid with chintz and silverware wrapped in white towelling.

"Budmo!" Budnik beamed, lifting a clear glass of vodka and pouring salt over fresh bread.

"Priatnova Appetita!" Peter declared. Budnik looked at him ruefully.

"We will really need to teach you some Ukrainian . . ."

Over food, Aleksandr, as he insisted on being addressed, began to talk about his nation and his personal philosophy. He spoke in a serious voice but intermixed his improvised lecture with humorous anecdotes that made Janssen laugh openly. "We are closely aligned to Asgardei and Vadym Troyan's Azov Regiment, the ones who held the torchlit parade through the streets that fateful April night. We are always there on New Year's Eve to celebrate Bandera's birthday."

"Wasn't Troyan appointed Chief of police in the Kyiv region?"

"That is right. We also talk a lot to sympathetic members of Parliament. Our party is really the child of many fathers, organisations like the Congress of Ukrainian Nationalists, Ukrainian Enlightenment, and the State Independence of Ukraine. Personally, I favour the Congress of Ukrainian Intelligentsia. I can show you copies of papers like *Nezborima Natzia, Unconquered Nation, Za Vilnu Ukraina, For a Free Ukraine,* and *Samostina Ukraina, Sovereign Ukraine,* if you like."

"Please!"

"There has been a high culture here since Palaeolithic times. These people inter-mixed with the warlike Scythians, whom Herodotus described as horse warriors, and who marked their territories with kurhany, huge burial mounds. They painted their bodies with tattoos and were superseded by the blonde Sarmatians, a people who rode to war side-by-side with their women." Aleksandr replenished their glasses from the vodka bottle sitting at his elbow. "Look about you, you will see many fair-haired people with blue eyes."

"And the Slavs?"

"There are many varieties. The South Slavs of the Balkans. The West Slavs of Poland and Central Europe and the East Slavs who settled in Ukraine, Belarus and Russia. Before the coming of Christianity, they worshipped Perun, god of thunder and lightning and Svaroh, god of the sky."

"And Kyiv?"

"Legends tell of horodyshcha, hilltop fortresses, founded by a family of brothers, Kii, Shchek and Koriv. It is said they were rowing with their sister Lybed at the helm. The girl pointed to this place and they brought their craft ashore. Three hills in Kyiv still bear their names."

"A very romantic image."

"We have ancient pagan places like Lysa Hora here too."

"Wasn't that a closed area in Soviet times?"

"Yes, my wife lived near there as a child. There are many stories of soldiers hearing strange noises and feeling great discomfort."

"I have heard of the Stone Tomb near Melitopol."

"Yes, our German friends thought it the oldest Aryan shrine in the East."

"So superstitious!"

"The Varangians who came down the river in the 9th century were more pragmatic than superstitious. Like their Viking cousins, they came in search of conquest and trade."

"The Vikings had a very wide reach, all the way from North America to Crimea."

"Today some politicians and administrators do not like the idea of Varangian influence. Some Slavophile academics disparage this notion. For myself, I rather like the idea."

"Ukrainian nationalists like the idea of Norse overlordship?" Peter said bemused.

"It is a blending of strengths, not an acknowledgment of superiority or inferiority. We needed such a mixture to overcome the Turkic Pechenegs and later the Khanates that attacked up the Kalka River after 1223."

"The Mongols?"

"Batu Khan attacked Kyiv, sacking and slaughtering the city."

"I had not appreciated that."

"Yes, so you see, we are the descendants of the Rus and Byzantine empires, the Crucesignati who defended Asia Minor from enemy incursions. Cossacks have been fighting Tartar slavers for centuries."

"I really should read up on your history."

"At Alim's Ravine, archaeologists have discovered stone-age petroglyphs. At Kaminne Selo in Zhytomyr Oblast we have carved stones like Stonehenge." Aleksandr reached out once more, filling their empty glasses. Then continuing, "Look at the ethnicity of the populations of Krakow, Lublin and Lemberik in the medieval period. The sudden movement of peoples tells you all about the New Jerusalem that was being created. It was why there were salt riots in Kyiv in 1113. That is why the haydamaky, rebel serfs, fought the nobles guerrilla style from the woods and why people were whipped up into a frenzy of killing in Uman."

Janssen began to see the similarities of socioeconomic strangulation, so familiar today, had its antecedents in the past. Budnik's eyes grew large. "The Cossack crusades, like those of Bohdan Khmelnytsky, targeted the gold dealers who practiced tyranny over the Orthodox majority. The traitors were even willing to sell out national heroes like the Pole Jan Sobieski to the Turks to further their own money-grabbing instincts. And these battles still continue today, just in another guise. Even as we speak, oligarchs are perpetrating one of the biggest land heists in Ukrainian history. It started with the buying up of former state land to grow rapeseed for the bio-fuels boom. Thanks to loans from the World Bank and Morgan Stanley, investments by agribusinesses have seized millions of black-earth farms from Kirovograd to Samara on the edge of the Caspian."

"George Soros said farmland is gold with a cash flow," Peter observed.

"The biggest ever land-grabber is an Israeli real estate tycoon and grain trader."

Janssen shook his head.

"I didn't know."

"I am not surprised these *zmievskaya balka*, snakes from the ravine, shun sunlight. And this is not the first time. When the Reds were victorious, the same snakes shipped whole populations off to Siberia, and Stalin contrived the Holodomor that starved millions to death. Not satisfied with that, Bolshevik leaders like Polonski, Levinstein, Geller and Kagan targeted the intelligentsia, scientists, church leaders, writers, editors and musicians. Over eighty percent of the intelligentsia in one city, Lviv, simply vanished! Over 10,000 so-called political prisoners were killed in the prison abattoirs of Zolochiv, Rivne, Dubno and Lutsk. In Dobromil there is evidence that hammers were used to break women's skulls. When the Nazis came in '41 it was almost a relief. Many of our people simply wanted to take revenge on the brood behind the CCCP."

"Yes, I have heard about the Organisation of Ukrainian Nationalists, the UPA insurgent Army and Stepan Bandera."

"But you will not have heard it all. I know we are still a mystery to the West. The fact is that Bandera, Melnyk and Mykola Lebed and the various OUN factions were the products of all that I have said. You cannot crush the grapes and not make wine, if you understand my meaning." Janssen nodded. "First there was Eugene Konovalets, Lev Tikhomirov and Konstantin Leontyev. Then Bandera, followed by Andrew Melnyk and of course Dmytro Dontsov."

"I have heard of some," Janssen pondered. Budnik waved a finger like a magic wand.

"My wife claims a family association back to Roman Iosyfovych Shukhevych, a man who, when imprisoned in Lviv and his own wife begged him to renounce his beliefs, replied, 'I cannot do anything because I love the idea more than you or my son.' Extreme commitment of this sort is rare, and he followed this path for twenty-five years."

"By those standards I am a complete amateur!"

"They followed 'The Cult of Strength and Violence,' a theology published in *Ukrains'kyi natsionalist* in January 1934, while you are more akin to the Codreanu Romanian model. The trick is not to fracture. Military historians estimate that if Alfred Rosenberg's plan to raise a Ukrainian army had not been denounced by Koch, there would have been a further four million pro-German forces in the field between Tambov and the Kuban River!"

"But Wilhelm Canaris and Fritz Freitag supported the idea of a Ukrainian legion."

"Oh yes, the Druzhyny ukrains'kykh natsionalistiv. They were to fight on the Volga."

"But did they?" Aleksandr shook his head.

"If they had, things may have been different in the '40s."

"We must not make that mistake again."

"Ukrainians did a lot of street-to-street fighting against the Soviets after the Reds had driven out the Nazis. They held arms caches and prepared ambushes wherever they could. Reprisals were brutal too, mass shootings by the NKVD and confiscations. They recently uncovered the bodies of over a hundred people, many children, shot in the head and buried under the floorboards of a monastery, their skeletons piled in layers of construction waste."

"And is it a portent of what is coming now, do you think?"

"Yes, but it will be worse. Now the subtlety and double play like we saw in the Orange Revolution is forgotten. Then, Kuchma's gangsters used dioxin on Yushchenko and just stopped short of a blood bath. When Yanukovych fell, the corrupt nomenklatura didn't swap sides so easily. Sharpshooters were killing our people on Hrushevskoho Street. That will not be forgotten by our people when the time comes . . ."

"Armageddon?" Janssen interjected. Aleksandr looked out from under arched eyebrows.

"Spilna Sprava are Soros's tools. Dmitry Yarosh took money from that multibillionaire, Igor Kolomoisky, the slug from Dnipropetrovsk and his other brethren like Vadim Rabinovich. The decadent Victor Pinchuk married Leonid Kuchma's daughter. They keep it in the family. Let our history serve as a warning to the world!" he breathed out bitterly. "In reaction, 95% of Crimeans voted to split from Kyiv and thousands took to the streets in Simferopol. You have to understand the geopolitics. The Russians cannot give up the fertile Volgograd region or lose access to the Black Sea. Ukraine is a buffer zone. Now the Carpathians are breached, and Moscow feels vulnerable. The EU's Eastern Partnership proposal is, to put it quite simply, a deal with the devil."

"So do you support the separation of the east and a Novorossiya stretching from Donetsk to Odessa?"

"I understand the motivation behind it," Budnik winked. "The Disaster in Donetsk sets our people against each other. Our enemies are exploiting Ukraine's schizophrenia, divided as we are between the rural Catholic West and the industrialized Orthodox East. Those who pull the strings on the Rada know exactly what they are doing by passing the Donbass Reintegration Bill."

"A license for a new war?"

"Exactly. We have heroes fighting under a Hakensonne banner but being led by hooked-nose liars. Since the time of Grand Prince Vladimir and the great baptism of 988 on the Dnieper's banks, we have been part of

Svyataya Rus, Holy Rus. So you see, the situation is not simple, and there is much to play for. One of our leading philosophers, Olena Semenyaka, turns Dugin's Eurasianism on its head by arguing that historically Russia has always been allied to Atlanticist countries. It is ironically Ukraine and the Kyivan Rus in particular who have fought against the corrupt Russian Empire. We may have contained Dugin's disciple Oleg Bahtiyarov and his bat-wielding provocateurs during the 2014 elections, but we still need to come to an accommodation with our Slavic brothers, not fight them. Especially now that they are pushing back their invaders to the Urals. Remember, even Putin sent the Pskov battalion back to barracks earlier in the conflict. It is the EU and the UN that want to Latinize our language and take us away from our Cyrillic origins. The same ones that demonize Strelkov as the shooter and blow civilian airplanes out of the sky are not true Ukrainian nationalists. Our former chocolate President and the comedian who followed him are the ones who spoke of total war against Russia, not the other way around."

Peter spent the next few days listening to music by Drudkh, Sokyra Peruna, Stormheit and NsXe and talking to Dmitry Yarosh's Pravy Sektor youths. He visited the Priorka house where Taras Scevchenko once stayed and the Kozatskiy Dim, Cossack House, home of the literary club Plomin, the publishing house Orientir, the Kinoklub Europa and Art studio, Dürer. He was regaled with stories about how the Apollonian Conference was so full people were forced to sit on the windowsills to listen to the brilliant speeches of Olena Semenyaka and her thesis "Wotan, Pan, Dionysius at the Gates of the Grand European Solstice"; the polyglot Denis of White Rex; Sviatoslav Vyshynsky, the author of *Metaphysica Nova* writing under the pseudonym Smierc Polarstern, speaking of "The Black Night of the Iron Age" and Ivan Mikheev of Russkiy Tsentr.

His mind filled with lyrics of Alexey Levkin of M8i8th

and the poetry of Lesia Ukrainka, "The one who has released himself becomes free; the one who releases his neighbour enslaves him" as he watched his new friends spray graffiti on the Pinchuk art gallery and partied in the Viola basement bar, nestling in the shadow of the Jose Manuel Barroso statue on the intersection of Bessarabska and Taras Shevchenko Boulevard. There, close to where the Lenin statue had been torn down in December 2013, diehard communists still mourned the crumbling of the Soviet state, and the EU militia had set up a 24/7 tented vigil to protect the new statue. A game of cat and mouse ensued with Janssen's friends from the C14, Trident and White Hammer groups planning to topple the edifice, whilst its defenders stood solemnly, shoulder-to-shoulder at the foot of the casement, with Barroso's heavy-lidded eyes staring blindly out across the market square.

- ❖ NATO warships fire on Chersonese, near the Black Sea port of Sevastopol, after Russian long-range bomber incursions into British airspace.
- ❖ Plaques commemorating the Struve Geodetic Arc, stretching from Tartu in Estonia to Felshtyn in Ukraine, are destroyed with the justification they are "false science."
- ❖ The American government grant a 62-million-dollar endowment to Georgetown University's Centre for Jewish Civilization to look for previously undiscovered mass graves of Jews killed in the Holocaust around Busk in Ukraine and interview death camp survivors in Romania.
- ❖ A former General is arrested for repeating anti-government statements like "Ukraine should be governed by Ukrainians!"
- ❖ Russia targets the Kyiv hyper-grid with cyber-attacks.
- ❖ The Georgian President in exile surrenders after an armed siege of his house in Brovarsky

Prospekt by officers of the Ukrainian SBU supported by Mossad operatives working directly to orders received from the Ukrainian President on the advice of the head of the Israeli Mission in Kyiv.

❖ Rogue EU units composed of Albanian and Bosnian soldiery burn wooden tserkvas along the length of the Polish-Ukrainian Carpathian border.

❖ Prisoner exchanges begin across the Dnieper.

❖ The low intensity war along the Sea of Azov front claims 5,000 lives in one month.

❖ The UN stipulates that one of the pre-conditions for ending hostilities must be the future use of the Bukovinian and Dalmation Metropolitans residences in Chernivtsi, including the St Ivan chapel and seminary, as Muslim cultural centres.

When Peter arrived in Lviv, a city at the very eastern gate of Europe, he was met at the airport by a small man called Evgeni with piercing grey eyes and a noticeable stoop. He was clutching a tattered copy of Dmytry Yarosh's *The Edge of Two Worlds*, and his old Ford was parked on the cracked kerb. They travelled along cobbled streets into the centre, pulling up before a seven-storey building with a gilded coat of arms dating from the Austro-Hungarian Empire.

"My son was among the marchers at Uzhgorod," he confided, "loyal to the flag and the people."

Peter disembarked, and Evgeni accompanied him upstairs. The elevator rose slowly, grinding in the lift-shaft, grating wearily in time with the rocking metallic cradle. Stepping through grating shutters into an eerily quiet corridor, Evgeni checked left and right before waving him on. Once inside the apartment, Peter took out his gun and placed it on the bedside table, then, circling around in the half-light, he commented.

"It is light and airy." Evgeni raised his hands.

"A bit like Sigizmund Krzhizhanovsky," he joked. Peter looked confused. "He wrote a short allegorical story called *Quadraturin* about a small room in Bolshevik times that grew and grew." Peter felt safe with the Western wing of the Ukrainian underground. The EU's spies would have difficulty collecting the thirty-million Euro bounty placed on his head. His safe house just off Shpytalna was home to myriad transient people with suspect papers and dubious morals. "Best to put you right under their noses," Evgeni told him before departing, "The militia here are lazy and incompetent, thank goodness!"

Once he was alone, Janssen switched on the bedroom light and noticed a long red coverlet spread over the duvet. He slept in his clothes for many hours. Later, arms draped on the ledge of the attic window, he stared out over Chornovola. Shadows stumbling before him down to Rynok Square, ghost birds flocking over the rooftops, drawn to the heat rising through the slate.

The lyrics of Polina Gagarina's song about the Donbass Defenders playing on his mind:

Oh, sun of mine
Break through the darkness
My open hand is turned to a fist
And if I have gunpowder, then give me a spark

When dawn eventually broke, he was lying quietly, listening to relentless rain beating on roof tiles, wondering how he could coordinate the Ukrainians to fulfil Geir's orders and move against the Commission. He took a last drag on a cigarette and thought, not for the first or the last time, about the heroism of comrades he had seen die before his very eyes. Then, recalling a quote from Dietrich Eckart: "This war is a religious war, finally one sees that clearly. A war between light and darkness, truth and falsehood, Christ and antichrist," then he slipped gently off to sleep.

When he awoke, sunshine was reflecting in the windows of the buildings opposite. Peter could see women doing their laundry, children running wild in the courtyard below. Around midday, Yeva Barnik arrived. The mid-morning rain had already cleared, humidity spiralling in zephyrs off the street. She was very pretty, cascading brown curls falling over lively green eyes.

"I will show you around," she promised, flashing her Tryzub badge. He tried to explain to her in his broken Russian that he liked his room: the sound of the church bell, the click of the light switch and the smell of his neighbour's cooking drifting in over the balcony. Everything was homely, like a room where one might have spent one's youth, familiar, consoling, warm and lit in the evening by a gently glowing lampshade that attracted pale moths. On the coffee table next to an old leather armchair was an English language collection of Taras Shevchenko's poetry, opened on the wistful poem "Katerina":

O lovely maidens fall in love,
But not with Muscovites,
For Muscovites are foreign folk,
They do not treat you right.

Yeva laughed at his choice. "There is indeed a debate to be had about Muscovites!" They agreed to stroll through the city. "Perhaps we can see the Opera House or the Armenian Cathedral. Or maybe we can visit Ivan Hrechko's private collection of Red icons on Virmenska Street, if your energy permits?"

"I will cope," he said defensively, not wanting to look weak in the eyes of this beautiful woman.

He had read a copy of Olexa Woropay's *The Ninth Circle* and was determined to pay his respects at the Holodomor monument. With their itinerary set, he closed the door, following Yeva along the corridor to the main staircase, taking note of the handsome square flagstones, polished red with black edging, echoing with the fall of their footsteps.

Moving off down Chornovola, towards the Prospekt Svobody and the Opera Square, the street widened out as they came across stalls scattered over pavements selling kitchenware, cotton towels, carved wood, vegetables, fish and freshly baked bread. Some uniformed men wandered around, weapons strung over their shoulders, supervising the public space. Motor coaches moved bumper to bumper, rolling over rutted roads, black exhaust sputtering. Schoolgirls with bouncing ponytails marched in neat blue dresses and white smocks, following excitedly behind gossiping teachers. "The child-bearers of our future salvation," Peter told himself, as they took in the Opera and the statue to the starving, then crossed Teatralna and Krakivska heading for Rynok.

The city, spread as it was below the walls of the High Castle, was in a state of political transition. The very same day Peter explored the centre, the authorities were marking the occasion of the Great Expulsion, an infamous anniversary of the killing of The Innocents. Exactly on the stroke of noon, just as they had done for five previous years, the indigenous population were required to stop working and begin their march of penitence to the Latin cathedral where they would be met by a Bishop who publicly harangued his flock for their evildoing and offered up recompense in a form of an annual tithe to the city's Commissariat. This was just one of the very many humiliations the inhabitants of the Carpathian region were forced to endure, Yeva explained. They were already familiar with the Union flag flying over the city hall, the requisitioned apartments and offices, even the spies lurking amid the graceful arcades of the Italiys'kyi Dvoryk.

More recently, police sentry boxes had appeared in the Chorna Kamianytsa, the pavement dug up to install anti-terrorist traps. People openly discussed the speed by which the city's bronze statues were being torn up and smelted down. Rumour had it that some of the silver ornamentation from the cemetery's graves had been used to construct the menorah memorial outside the American White House. A veritable forest of traffic signs appeared in languages other than Ukrainian. In the cafes along Shevchenka Prospekt, portly Tajiks sat with local civil servants tempting hungry girls with their fat wallets before visiting the brothels in the Vynnychenko.

Yeva came again a few days later. "Time for another history lesson!" she said laughing. On this occasion they took a taxi. The infamous blue banners speckled with a circle of yellow stars towered over the green trees and stone monuments of the Lychakiv cemetery. He walked slowly, the sombre scene reminding him of the Piskaryovskoye in St Petersburg where he had met with Grigori, a leader of the new Soyuz Russkogo Naroda, at an international conference. There, in the Venice of the North, single stone slabs like decaying teeth were carved 1941, 1942 and so on. These overlooked by the Vasiliev and Levinson statuary of workers, soldiers and sailors hewed out of blue stone. It was the Russians' defiant reply to Heinrich Himmler's prophecy that "For us the end of the war will mean an open road to the East . . ."

Here, like there, the Slavic way of death was reflected in the immolation. All around respectful people of all ages carried flowers and pictures of their loved ones to and fro. Small collections of green bottles littered the gravesites, standing alongside fresh roses and buzzing bite-flies. Peter tried to imagine the horrors visited upon this place. Events like The Sandarmokh, the mass killing of the Ukrainian intelligentsia years before. NKVD monsters murdering thousands before the liberating black columns in '41. Random quotas of people taken from each district. Their well-fed Bolshevik persecutors standing in long leather coats, armed with Trotskyite fanaticism and German Walther pistols, shouting about saboteurs and enemies of the people. Their victims cutting shallow pits in the outlying fields before being machine-gunned, falling face forward into the swallowing earth.

❖ The original 1996 Constitution of Ukraine ratified by the 5th Session of the Verkhovna Rada is redrafted to reflect the new multicultural ethos of EU Access states.

❖ The Volyn and Zakarpattia Oblasts are annexed under the "kolonia" process of returning stolen lands to their rightful owners.

❖ The Chernivtsi Oblast is subsumed by Romania, while Belarus is denied any rights under the recently signed Lviv Convention.

❖ Judaica heritage sites in the liberated regions of Ukraine are declared "Sacred to Humanity."

He could not sleep. The oldest church bell in Ukraine rang monotonously from the St George Cathedral. Above, was the soft padding of the young girl he had talked to in the lift earlier. He was wondering why she was so restless. What was troubling her conscience? Peter looked up at the ceiling. His mind was racing, thinking about Yeva, considering how her body was as ripe as the stubble fields of these borderlands. A perfect seeding ground for the renaissance of his people.

At his bedside was a copy of Koestler's *Thirteenth Tribe*. He had read somewhere that the book had cost the author and his wife their lives. Conspiracy theories did not usually interest him, but this book, in addition to the exposure of the mindless brutality of the 1917 debacle in *Darkness at Noon*, made Koestler a prime candidate for elimination.

Morning saw church bells compete with the Muslim call to prayer. It seemed the multicultural pandemic had already infected Ukraine. After breakfast, Yeva took him to Drohobych's central park to pay homage at the Bandera statue, Ivano-Frankivsk to see the memorial to OUN members killed by the Gestapo and Kosiv where a UPA museum had been temporarily installed in the home of a former Rabbi. That was until the Union's Equality Governor wrote complaining of the offence to the memory of the Hebrew hermit, and it was closed down.

"Some say we are trying to rewrite the history of Galicia. They object to our emphasis on Ukrainian suffering. We are accused of trying to forge a new collective memory and that it is all historical amnesia. Of course, they will tear all of it down," the tone of sarcasm rising in her voice, "Our friends argue that the Kolomyia statue is too abstract in nature. The faceless woman and child does not represent the true nature of the suffering and the sacrifice."

"And what do you think?"

"I think people who live in glass houses should not throw stones. The gangsters that made up the Bielski partisans get a Hollywood makeover, and the international press tell us we are supposed to feel bad about a statue?"

"Two sides to every story?"

"Yes, but only one gets any attention. If you object, they squeal and demand reparations through the courts. The whole thing is an industry, and anyway, what money is made never gets to any of the supposed victims."

❖ Primeval beech forests are set ablaze in the Uzhok national park.

❖ The Gesher-Galicia Jewish Heritage foundation are awarded 50,000,000 Euro to conduct research into the Hebrew influences on Eastern European civilisation.

❖ The remains of Taras Shevchenko are removed for safekeeping from Cherkasy by Ukrainian nationalists.

❖ Nokturnal Mortum's album *Lunar Poetry* and Goatmoon's *Stella Polaris* become the unofficial anthems of nationalist youth.

❖ Groups of Ukrainian partisans meet in the shadow of the "Sofiyivka" to coordinate sabotage operations across the EU Occupied Territories.

Yeva and Peter spent more and more time together, taking an excursion to the Zymne Monastery, stopping to pick blackberries on the steep banks above the Luh River. "It is good you have come," she said one weekend as they visited the Pidhirtsi Castle near Brody, "We'll need leadership in the battle ahead. You know a Swedish man named Rudolf Kjellen described Ukraine and the Baltic countries as the defenders of cultural Europe against the Mongol-tainted Muscovite East."

"And your feelings about the Russians?"

"I remember going to Kyiv with my family as a little girl and playing on the tanks in the park by the huge titanium Rodina Mat. My father told me more about the crimes and occupation of our country after 1945 than the liberation by the Soviets during the Great Patriotic War."

To celebrate their newfound friendship, she organised a private viewing of the brass-locked parchment of the Ruska Pravda, a faithful reproduction of the 11th-century text. They were very discreet about matters of personal safety and security. She would listen to Kroda on a battered laptop, then come to him, the two of them sometimes taking a small cafe table in a quiet corner of "Under the blue bottle." At first he did not even know her full name or where she lived. They agreed it was much safer that way should one of them be captured. After some weeks they became lovers. Slowly, over time, when they spoke of the future it was usually in terms that hinted at a more permanent partnership.

One hot afternoon, after a period of intense lovemaking, Peter woke before Yeva. A fragrant lily plant sat on the open windowsill. He rolled over and smelled its rich perfume wafting over green pillowcases. Then, lowering his head, he kissed her neck in the thin spread of yellow buttery light.

"Mmm?" she said sleepily.

"Do you want some juice?" he asked, fingers rolling a

coil of her hair, a fine tendril running down the nape of her neck, slinking like a snake towards her sharp shoulder blades. She shifted on the sheets towards him, moving her hips in a dance-like motion.

"I saw Natasha and Dima earlier," she explained.

"Problems?"

"Maybe some?"

His eyebrows tangoed.

"Do we need to leave?"

"Not sure, but they've moved a new team into the city to look for you."

"Can we buy them off?"

"Not as easily as the current crew. Natasha said these guys are trained by a foreign secret service."

"I see!" She turned to face him. Her features tinted by the half-light. For thousands of years women had worked to perfect their appearance with lipstick, mascara and moisturising creams. Yet somehow there was nothing more tender and attractive than a sleepy-looking girl in a state of post-coital bliss, teasing and tired, breathing loving words into her man's ear. Yeva wore a complexion of innocence like a shield. She said she had a face that was unharmonious, sort of stuck together from left over parts. Yet, to all who met her she was stunning, an alchemy of skin, bone and personality that was rapidly evolving towards perfection. It was one of the reasons he cared so much for her. He wanted to see the finished article, the butterfly emerge from the chrysalis.

In late October, the EU troops launched a blitzkrieg assault to encircle Krakow, securing the Auschwitz Death Camp from the Polish Free Army. "They must not desecrate our sacred ground!" Meyer opined. Then, saying in private, "We can ill-afford a full and open investigation of the facility." Admitting, "Years of hard work will be destroyed by any serious scientific analysis of the site."

Local civilians were frantically digging trenches, anti-tank ditches and storing food and munitions ready for the EU forces to cross the Wisla. Their assault was preceded by air raids and the pummelling of the old city by heavy artillery.

For the Poles and other nationalists, it was a race against time, as the main highways were held by a corps of men loyal to the EU. The order went out, "The ghetto must also be preserved." Troops were parachuted into the Kazimierz district to hold the area against gangs of youths spraying Third Reich-style images on the walls of the old synagogues.

The rebel leaders in a command-and-control centre in Poznan were being covertly counselled by Russian military advisers to direct what forces they could muster to undertake an encirclement manoeuvre against superior numbers, endeavouring to take the Tantra mountains to the south of the city.

"This campaign represents a new threat to our Eastern sector," the message came directly from Geir to Janssen. "How rapidly can the Ukrainians deploy?"

"Months, not weeks," Peter replied. "The Carpathian underground can raise maybe four to five thousand trained fighters by the end of the year."

"Good," was Geir's response, "I will come to Lviv. Your objective is to move west and to take and hold the John Paul II airport."

❖ Ukrainian nationalists conduct manoeuvres under the supervision of Russian Spetsnaz officers in the Askania-Nova nature reserve.

❖ Bronze Age artefacts from the Platar Collection are taken by the EU's new Historical Truth Commission to Tel Aviv for their future preservation.

❖ The Honchar Museum in Kyiv is closed following an investigation into the accusation it reinforced cultural stereotypes.

❖ Laws are enacted enforcing all Slavic people with-

in the EU Protectorate between the ages of 18 and 65 to sponsor an immigrant.
* Lifestyle subsidies are provided for Ukrainian women who cohabititate with Negro and Asian men.

They strolled along the edge of Osmomysla Square. The roadside transformed into a catwalk for the young girls, all billowing evening gowns and off the shoulder dresses, strutting like photo models in their vipuskniki sashes, hair piled high, calling to each other across the Havryshkevycha.

Yeva smiled, prodded Peter and pointed to a small group of young men in ill-fitting jackets, quickly puffing on cigarettes before going to join their girlfriends at the Drama Theatre.

"Same as everywhere," he laughed, holding her hand tightly. They stood and watched as the crowd assembled under the watchful gaze of a gang of men in dark hats and rolled umbrellas. The young people seemed oblivious to the lascivious eyes and warped bodies passing from door to door like shadows in the daylight, murmuring to each other as they tugged on thick beards, judging and scoring the flocking nubiles for beauty and health.

A policeman appeared, new leather boots squeaking on stone. Behind him were two armed militia men. They were responding to a call from the watchers who pointed out a petite blonde in a pink dress. The uniformed men moved off to corral her, insisting she accompany them into a doorway where kinky haired dribblers in small round glasses thronged like worker bees.

Peter and Yeva moved on as the bulbous insects doffed their caps, dirty fingernails running through their victim's hair as she smiled nervously.

"What's your name, my pretty?" they heard someone ask.

Later they walked down Copernicus street, taking in

the architecture of the two palaces and the 18th-century church, before Yeva smuggled him into her attic apartment overlooking one of Lviv's most impressive buildings. There Peter saw her artwork for the first time.

"What are these?" he asked, pointing to some nudes above the bed.

"Cucuteni women," she replied, "At the peak of this culture our people lived in cities of up to a million people, double that of Mesopotamia's Uruk, and they controlled a land twice the size of modern-day France, stretching from North eastern Romania, through Moldova and the Western Ukraine."

"I read some academic papers by an English professor called Thomas Hunter that examined such topics," he remembered, "I see you depict the women shooting bows and arrows and throwing an axe."

"I am really a graphic designer by profession," she explained, "those paintings are meant to challenge the notion of passivity in the female psyche."

"I need no convincing on such matters," he said, his mind drifting back to Alise's brave last stand on the Rue Jardel.

Yeva opened a bottle of wine and unwrapped some cheese from waxed packaging. Peter sliced black bread under her close supervision, and they sat at a window overlooking the street.

"You love your city, don't you?" he observed.

"Very much. It has seen many disasters, but now times are the worst."

"I think you may be right."

"You know our enemy is a strange amalgamation of contradictory alliances. Sometimes I wonder . . . ." Peter knew exactly what she was going to say. He lifted a hand and rubbed his thumb with his index finger.

"Money!"

"Controls everything," she guessed.

"It's a crude simplification but nevertheless . . ?" She made him pork ribs stewed in beet kvass.

"I got the meat on the black market. It is banned from sale in the shops." Peter watched as Yeva's hands wielded the sharp kitchen knife, slicing the ribs into small pieces, then fried them in salt with butter.

"I learned this recipe from my mother," she was saying, her fingers sprinkling flour and chopping onions over the browning meat in the saucepan before transferring it to the sauté pot and adding slices of red beet. They sat around a small circular table in the warm glow of candlelight while Yeva served food, covering their dishes with grated parsley leaves.

"I have not spoken to my mother for many years," Peter confessed. Yeva looked up just in time to see him wipe a tear from his eye.

"Are you okay?" she asked.

"The meat is a little hot," he claimed in his defence.

❖ Trypillia culture ornaments and drinking vessels displaying maenads, dancing women, are criticised for encouraging lewd behaviour, and two men by the names of Taruta and Platonov are sought for insulting public values.

❖ The Pysanka tradition of egg painting is banned.

❖ Tanks are needed to support ground troops enforcing EU law in Kalush.

❖ Strasbourg refuses to return Scythian gold known as the Bakhchysarai collection to Russian-held Crimea.

Yeva was sitting at her window spooning yogurt with fresh fruit. Beside her were a pile of books by the poet Ivan Bahriany, author of *Marusia Bohuslavka*, re-telling the struggles of the Legion Galizien; Vasyl Barka's *Zhovtyi Kniaz* on the famine which inspired Oles Yanchuk's movie *Holod 33*; and a collection of writings by Hryhorii Vaschchenko.

"I don't have any English translations," she apologised, "but I can read them to you?"

"I'd like that."

"Perhaps we should start with some short pieces from Lev Rebet in *Suchasna Ukrayina* or *Chas*."

"Rebet?"

"A leading theorist of Ukrainians in exile during Soviet times."

"Interesting."

"Interesting enough for the KGB to have him killed just like Bandera."

"A threat, then?"

"Thinkers are always a threat to these people. Bandera believed in the genetic unity of his homeland. Stashynsky, the assassin that got to both of them, was acting on the direct orders of the Chairman of the Council of Ministers of the USSR, Nikita Khrushchev."

"Bullets?"

"Bandera was found bleeding to death on Kreitmayr street in Munich. A medical examination established his death was caused by the ingestion of cyanide gas."

"Something like Alexander Litvinenko in London."

"Another well-intentioned man used as a pawn by that pig Berezovsky!"

"What happened to Bandera's family? Are they still involved in the movement?"

"His brothers Oleksandr and Vasyl died in Auschwitz. Stepan's father was killed by the NKVD during an interrogation. Two of his sisters were deported to Siberia and kept there well into the 1980s. One other was sentenced to ten years of hard labour."

"They paid a terrible price . . ."

"And so we should always remember. I marched in Kyiv in 2013 against the Yanukovych government with thousands of others on Bandera's birthday. To forget would be to dishonour him."

Sometimes they would walk outside the city. Ideas like birds fluttered into his mind and then out again. He had already crowned her with roses and girded her with the claret berries of the viburnum garlands of her pagan homeland, the lyrics of the song Chervona Kalyna passing silently over his lips.

"Like Bandera before us," Yeva was saying, "we have formed Mobilni Hrupy, Mobile Groups, of between five to ten people. On the 30th June, the anniversary of OUN's announcement of an independent Ukrainian state, we set off plastic explosives, blowing up the European Union's Commissariat on Rynok and shot to death two informers living in Valova. I lead a secret youth section for young girls. We train them in self-defence and how to shoot!"

"Do you cooperate with other groups like the Endecja faction or the Narodowe Odrodzenie Polski in Poland? I've some friends in the Nowa Prawica and seen them march in defiance of the EU government on the streets of Warsaw every 11th November. I am also familiar with Janusz Bryczkowski's National Front and Gmurczyk's work Rewolucja Integralna."

"I understand your enthusiasm, but first we have to overcome some local prejudices originating from when the Poles tried to exterminate us in prisoner of war camps like Modlin."

"But that was nearly a century ago?"

"The dead still talk!"

"Sometimes, I worry that such squabbling will cost us dear."

"I am sure you are right, but it is also the glue that binds us together. It is a double-edged sword we must learn to endure,"

"And are there modern theorists like those you showed me in your apartment?" Peter said, recalling the piles of books that had captured his attention.

"You mean like Dugin in Russia?"

"Yes."

"Well, there are various traditions. One strain is through the Orthodox faith, people like Patriarch Mstyslav. The other is Yaroslav Stetsko and his ideological descendants like Oleh Tyahnybok."

"Tyahnybok, I have heard of him."

"My favourite was his statement about the OUN: "They were not afraid, and we should not be afraid. They took their guns on their necks and went into the woods . . .""

Late one night, having walked Yeva back to her apartment, he came upon a deserted square, dimly lit by halfhearted lights on each corner. Peter tried crossing it quickly so as not to be propositioned by the prostitutes standing around a wooden bench exchanging cigarettes and salacious stories.

Before he was even halfway down Kornyakta he heard small pattering heels and heavy breathing coming over his shoulder. "Wait there!" a familiar female voice called. He turned to see the burst of a yellow streetlight casting a haze over the woman running towards him. He instinctively opened his arms and Yeva threw herself around his neck. The warmth of her body on this autumnal night producing an immediate reaction. Lips crushing his, tongue licking teeth. "Thank God!" she kept saying, "thank Holy Jesus and Mother Mary!"

"What is it?" he asked, "I only just left you."

"I got a call. Danya said one of our people, a man, had just been shot. But he wasn't sure who." She took him by the arm, "Quick," she said, "they must have counter-insurgency squads out in force tonight." As they walked, she described how she had felt the earth falling away from under her at the news and Peter cupped his hand around her face and told her not to worry. "But I do," she said. "We will go to my parents' house tonight," she insisted. "It is outside the city."

"But that means involving them, I don't think it is wise . . ." She put a hand to his mouth.

"It will be safer there, trust me, and they are away visiting relatives in Kyiv." They stood on the corner of Bandery and Doroshenka flagging down a cab. Peter let her do all the talking, conscious that taxi drivers often acted as sources for the authorities, and all foreigners were of interest to the officials, whether there was an up-surge of violence or not. Their car ploughed through dark streets, rattling on bumpy stones and curled around tight corners of tree lined parks. Peter began to imagine the ghostly Halychyna and Nachtigall legions marching to their fate under a washed-out moon. He marvelled at the fact that unlike the Green Brothers in the Baltic, Mykhailovych's fighters in Yugoslavia or the Armia Kra-jowa in Poland, the Banderites had been able to survive so long. Aleksandrs' recitation of Ivan Franko's poem came back to him:

> All that he had in life, he gave back
> For his single idea.
> He burned, and glowed and suffered,
> And struggled for it

"Slava Ukraini, Heroyam Slava!" he said to himself, as they left the city, holding tightly to Yeva's hand.

The car pulled up under a clear patch of stars. They paid the driver, and Yeva led him along the back lanes, past courtyards and house yards full of barking dogs, grunting pigs and organic refuse. Passing through a swarm of green flies they pushed on a gate, stepping into the garden of a small birch-framed house. She pulled a key from her pocket and unlocked the place. It was still and silent all about. Yeva flicked a sidelight, an erratic orange bulb pulsing, slowly sending a warm glow over the patchwork quilts and soft furnishings.

"Welcome to my parent's home," she giggled, "a tradi-tional Carpathian house."

"You grew up here?"

"Da. My school was down the road. I had a dog called Eric and a cat called Grolsch."

"Grolsch, like the beer?"

"Yes, like the pivot," then frowning, "It was my Papa's idea."

They stood opposite each other for a while. Peter becoming increasingly overwhelmed by the homely smell,
recognising the fact he had missed out on the domestic
life of a family and children. A sense of great loss came
weltering up inside him. Yeva rubbed his sad eyes and
stepped forward to hold him as the sharp shard of glass
passed through his heart. Her small hands clasped
around his back.

"I know," she said, "I know . . ."

He became aware of Yeva slipping off her coat, and he
reached out instinctively for her blouse, twisting the but-
tons, white breasts with strawberry nipples tumbling out
into his palms. "Touch me," she whispered warmly into
his ear. "You are here now. This is your home, too." Afterwards, Peter felt he had experienced an epiphany between the delicacy of her v-spread thighs, his spent force
melting into her.

"You are mine," he heard her sigh, "all mine . . ."

"Yeva," he said, "you are so beautiful, resourceful and
kind. I think you will make a great partner and have
beautiful children. Will you be my wife?"

"I wish you would not ask me this thing," she replied,
tossing back her hair.

"But why? You know how I feel."

"And you know our situation!" His head dropped,
confronted with her realism. "We will always be on the
run, hunted, our children living from hand to mouth . . ."

"Will you ever forgive me?"

"Never," she answered, taking his face in her hands
and kissing him.

❖ The EU and NATO forces confirm that Przemysl
    has fallen to a Polish and Ukrainian bandit army.
❖ The Michael Karkoc Commando explode a ferti-
    lizer bomb that brings down the façade of the
    Lviv Town Hall.
❖ A simultaneous attack by the Maksym Skorupsky
    Commando kills the NATO general commanding

the Rivne military district.

❖ Regional Government officials incite local criminal gangs to seek out the revolutionary leader Peter Janssen.

It had been a harsh winter in the city. A surprisingly mild spell had been cut short by an abrupt rapier plunge of snow and ice. The pavements were glass, slurry piled in the gutters. Peter left his apartment only very reluctantly, waiting for his order to march. Stopping in a doorway to turn up the collar on his coat, heading east to the tram stop, he glanced left and right, just to check if there was any danger of a local driver ploughing up over the pavement and running him down. Deciding it was safe, he crossed while the wind gusted, whistling around the cathedral's green cupola.

There was no tram in sight, just the dull dark outline of tall apartment blocks in all directions. Occasionally a "Go" light would appear through the mist and a line of citizens would climb the piled snowdrifts. Peter stood in line at the stop, shifting from foot to foot in a ritual shuffle to stay warm. The metallic blue nose of a tram appeared through the evening's murk. People moved forward, smokers taking a last quick drag on their cigarettes, throwing the butts into the slush, before clambering aboard.

He hopped up amongst the crush of bodies, pressed tight in their padded jackets and woollen mittens. He closed his eyes for a restful few second as the tram pulled away from the kerb, thinking how good it was to be seeing Geir once again. As a consequence, he did not notice the slightly built Armenian youth in a faded green parka jump aboard at the last moment, the doors folding shut behind him. The man was looking hard and long in Janssen's direction. The tram trundled through Rynok, yellow sparks igniting in the wiring overhead. Peter got off outside the Ratusha. He made a point of never being late for a rendezvous. Arriving, revolver in pocket, in the

cobbled Teatralna just as the first notes of the evening
Angelus rang out.

Up above, the red-slated roof of the old Jesuit Church
of St Peter and Paul was looking down over the grey
buildings of the Svobody, where the young Armenian
who had followed Peter off the tram stood in his dirty
coat, looking back up at the roof from the street below.

Crossing the church threshold, Peter removed his hat,
shook hands with Father Ivas and followed him up a narrow circular staircase to the top of the sepulchre where
Geir awaited him.

"Welcome, comrade!" the captain said, clasping his
protégé in his arms. There on the stone summit, looking
down over Lviv, Peter noticed the solitary figure on the
pavement below staring upwards as he spoke to Geir
about his plans. He thought little more of it, taking a seat
at a small table, poring over a map of the Podkarpackie
region of Eastern Poland and the Rzeszow road to Krakow.

"We'll be moving at night," he began to explain.

- ❖ Ukrainian nationalists gather at twelve locations
  along the 535-kilometre border with Poland.
- ❖ Traditionalist units supported by Russian Vulcari
  volunteers led by the well-known Russian Right-
  ists Alyosha and Ekaterina from St Petersburg
  seize three road and two railway crossing points
  into the Lubelskie Voivodeship and the Subcar-
  pathia Voivodeship.
- ❖ The EU loses effective control of large parts of
  Zakarpattia.
- ❖ Bridges on the Bug River are sabotaged to prevent large, armoured vehicles crossing into the
  Volyn Oblast.

State Security arrived as the sun set on Yeva's apartment. They slammed at the door with a battering ram,
forcing the hinges before she could get out of the show-

er. Six men surrounded her dripping body with drawn guns as she tried to protect herself with a damp towel. They switched on all the lights and began searching the premises. Men tapped the walls, lifted the mats and then loosened floorboards, before dismantling the toilet and systematically removing the radiators one by one. They took her laptop, overturned waste baskets and copied her hard drive. The team's leader turned aggressive when he saw a copy of Alexander Jacob's *Atman* on her bookshelf.

"You are one of them," he snarled.

"Well, I'm certainly not one of you," Yeva stared back. The man in front of her lifted a gloved hand to strike, but she caught his wrist and swivelled him around, tearing a Jericho 941F semi-automatic from him and shooting dead three of her interrogators at point blank range. Two others bolted out the door, while the last backed into the bedroom behind a clatter of lead casings. Out of bullets, the last thing Sergeant Zhuk ever saw was a naked girl advancing towards him with a raised meat cleaver.

Kneeling in the chapel, the nuns were reciting liturgy when they were disturbed by a gun butt's metallic wrap on the door. Immediately, two of them got up, automatically crossing themselves before opening a crack in the scabrous wood to reveal the faces of two Union operatives who had been searching desperately for Janssen for months.

"I am Captain Demchuk," one of them said, "We are looking for a foreigner!" The nuns feigned ignorance until a pistol was pushed through the slat. "Open or I'll shoot!" they were told. Given no alternative, they reluctantly unbolted the door, and Demchuk stepped over the threshold, while upstairs Geir was ushered down a secret passageway leading to a small back alley and Janssen cocked his revolver. Once the Union's officers had gained entry, they stamped their feet to clear their boots of snow and unclipped their long leather trench coats. Demchuk walked down the central aisle. Head turning from side to side as he progressed towards the altar. "Where is Peter Janssen?" he asked. The frightened nuns shrugged their shoulders. "Here I am," came an unexpected reply from behind an alabaster pillar. There was a flash through the pocket of his trench coat as he emptied the chamber into Demchuk and his colleague.

Later that evening, Peter received confirmation Geir had crossed the border at Zosin. The moon was swimming in the wash of melting water, its big yellow face smiling up at Peter from dark cobbles. There was a rapidity to his stride as he noticed a thin shadow rounding a statue in front of him, assuming a shooting stance. Peter looked up from the pavement and recognised that familiar nervous glint in the young Armenian's pinched face as he pulled something small and dark out of his coat pocket and fixed Peter with a hunter's gaze. It was the coldness and the frosted sparkle of the revolver's barrel in the streetlight that stuck in his mind. Recognition of the danger was instantaneous. He tried to run but his legs froze. He heard the trigger click and could smell the trail of blue cordite in the air.

Peter lay very still, face down in the snow, listening as his executioner crunched the compacted snow, circling his victim, checking he had fulfilled his mission. The sound of the hammer being pulled back a second time directly overhead made Peter's bowels wrench. The gun jammed, the oily action seizing and locking in the damp and cold, preventing the coup de grace. The wounded man stayed quiet, watching a red spot in the snow grow larger and larger underneath him.

When he was sure his would-be killer had turned his back, talking on his mobile to his controllers, Peter grabbed the booted ankle only centimetres from his face, pulling the shooter to the ground. Then rolling over, he sat astride the skinny young frame, pressing him down, thumbs drilling deeper and deeper into his victim's oesophagus until the Armenian's lips turned blue.

Rising stiffly, Peter noticed the hole in his coat was small. He tried to straighten up. Swaying, his lower body performed a Saint Vitus dance to discordant music. Staggering to a black cobweb of wrought iron railings, his fingers instinctively reached inside his jacket for the Nokia phone he always carried.

"You're in shock," Janssen tried to convince himself, as he hit Yeva's number, "It's shock, that's all."

"Don't move," he heard her say in reply to his breathless call for help, "I'm coming for you!"

Kinets

ABOUT THE AUTHOR

Fenek Solère writes novels in the tradition of the New Right. He is the author of *The Partisan* (2014), *Rising!* (2017) and *Kraal* (2019). He has published articles at *Counter-Currents, Defend Europa, New European Conservative, European Civil War* and *Patriotic Alternative*.

Lightning Source UK Ltd.
Milton Keynes UK
UKHW012144230521
384249UK00003B/92